Naiad

The Narun – Book Two

G. M. Worboys

Published by G. M. Worboys
Website: gmworboys.com

Print Edition 1.0 (January-2014)
First published Jan-2014

ISBN 978-0-9874583-2-2

Cover image and design by G. M. Worboys

For Sue. For being here, for spoiling me, for helping me past the doubts. For making this possible.

Contents

What Has Gone Before *1*

Prologue 5

Searching *9*

1. Home 11

2. Plans 25

3. Journey 41

4. Samgha 68

5. Search 85

6. Separate 110

7. Lies 145

Finding *181*

8. North 183

9. Ice 210

10. Water 246

11. Zarana 283

12. Healer 318

13. Shadow 355

14. Waiting 380

Appendix *405*

Glossary 407

What Has Gone Before

(From *Dryad*, The Narun – Book One)

John Caldor, grief stricken by the loss of his wife and daughter, believes that the beautiful woman he sees emerge from the forest must be his daughter's imaginary friend, reinvented by his own broken mind. The woman, Asha, tries to explain that she is real, a being made of prana, the stuff of life.

Humans cannot normally see her kind – the narun – they have no material, flesh-and-blood body. They can only be seen by those with vedana, the sense of life, a sense that has woken in John through the agonies of his grief. Asha's people are the aaranya, forest dwellers, dryads. There are other narun peoples: naiads, nereids and others.

While he is with Asha, John can only believe her, and believe in her, but when she is gone his doubts assail him – she cannot be real. One night it comes to a head and Asha leaves in tears.

John finds it is not so easy to ignore his heart. Despite his words to Asha, he is not willing to let her go. He takes time off work to search for her in the forest, and there he finds another of her kind, Andrei. This cheeky young man agrees to lead John to the Glade, the home of the aaranya.

Asha had returned to John's house while he was at work but she is captured by two humans, Ian O'Dwyer and Darren Davies, with equipment that lets them detect and disable the narun. The humans are aided by a strange narun, Sando, who remains hidden within his protective silver suit. Asha is taken to the city and imprisoned in a laboratory beneath a large facility called the Forest Conservation Research Centre. In this laboratory she meets Dr Henry Karlin, a human that can see her. Karlin, always accompanied by Sando, performs experiments on Asha, as he has others of her kind, in an attempt to discover the secrets of prana and the narun.

At the Glade, John hears some of the history of Asha's people and learns that they fear she has been abducted by narun working with humans – a repeat of an ancient war that had devastated the narun.

An epiphany on the journey home, the discovery that narun speech is a limited form of telepathy, finally convinces John that Asha and her people are real. John is accompanied by aaranya from the Glade: Andrei, Barma, Tilvy, Darnu and Garjae. He is also given a small creature from the Glade, a brevi named Casseta.

John and his aaranya friends overpower Ian, who was waiting for them at John's house, and they drive to the city. Ian escapes from them and they are forced to try and hide in the unfamiliar city.

Asha meets other narun prisoners. She is eventually shown some strange, small and distorted narun beings that, at first, she cannot identify. She opens her senses to one of the beings and discovers it is Ellie, John's daughter. The being is the life from Ellie's human body that had been pushed violently from the flesh, becoming what the narun call a preta – a hungry ghost. The young girl's mind is lost or hiding behind the insatiable hunger of the tiny being. Asha discovers that she has an unsuspected talent for healing, and the doctor hopes that Asha may eventually be able to heal the preta.

Waldron Stephenson, a human, and another narun called Jaimee, visit the laboratory briefly. Stephenson, Jaimee and Sando appear to be the ones truly behind what has been happening. These are aided by the dhumraka, a strange narun people with a dull grey skin.

John and the others are shown around the city by Senna, a young aaranya woman of the city that has taken a fancy to Andrei. They meet Senna's father, Taiza, an aaranya with unusual interests for a narun, and Guyen (Uncle), an old aaranya man that shows them how to hide from the detectors used to find the narun.

During an attempt to rescue Asha and the other prisoners, Darnu, Garjae, Barma and Tilvy are captured and taken hostage.

Guyen, Taiza and some other city aaranya come to John and offer their help. John is befriended by a young human woman, Tracey, and she is present in the confusion after John receives a call from Karlin saying that John must come to the Research Centre or the hostages will die. John introduces Tracey to the aaranya.

John presents himself at the Research Centre where Karlin tries to convince him that he should help their efforts to study the narun. While they are distracted, Tracey and the aaranya begin to rescue the prisoners, mostly aaranya but there are also two jalaja – naiads.

When Sando discovers what is happening he reveals himself to be a different sort of narun, neither dhumraka nor aaranya. He also reveals the ability to influence minds. John frees himself of Sando's influence by punching him, and some dhumraka try to take Sando to safety. On the way out Sando recovers enough to command three of the dhumraka to make certain that everyone else is trapped. Using his control over their minds, he insists that "all must burn".

Guyen is killed protecting Tracey from the dhumraka, but the fire is started and many remain trapped. Sando is injured by Barma but escapes. Karlin and most of the preta are killed in the fire, but Ellie is saved. John breaks through a wall to release the rest of his friends from the fire. They make it out of the Research Centre and return to a refuge in a distant park. Asha has to heal Barma after he was seriously injured when hit by a car.

Asha and John acknowledge their love for each other. It may or may not work out between an aaranya and a human but, if it didn't, there would be time to be unhappy later.

4

Prologue

Brothers

The limousine moved off smoothly as Sando settled himself on the rear seat.

"Good to see you, brother," Jaimee spoke to him.

Unlike the dhumraka, the grey companions that Sando had just left behind, Sando and his brother, Jaimee, were narun more closely resembling the aaranya – and humans – but of porcelain paleness. Pale skin, short, white-blond hair, and pale, almost colourless eyes. Everyone except their mother claimed that the brothers were identical. When their moods were in tune even Sando often felt that he was looking in a mirror. But not today.

When Sando didn't respond to his greeting, Jaimee asked, "Where are the others off to?" He indicated the dhumraka walking down the footpath.

"I told them we'd pick them up in a few days," Sando said in even tones. Then anger grew in his voice as he said, "You took your time getting here."

Jaimee shrugged, a distinctive gesture, familiar since childhood. "Peren told you why."

"Yes, flight schedules. Where is Helix anyway? Since it was picking her up that gave you so much delay."

"She's back at the hotel, directing another operation via the Internet."

"Fuck that! What about here? Some of those arrogant bastards escaped the fire, one of the dhumraka saw them coming out. They *owe* us and I mean to collect. And that fucking human, Caldor, it

5

was him driving them out. He bloody well hit me!"

"You've been here too long, brother, I think that awful Australian accent has been rubbing off on you. Anyway, I thought Peren said the human had punched you. That's a nasty wound for a punch." Jaimee pointed to the still healing gash on the back of Sando's neck, near the base of his head.

"That wasn't from the human. Someone, one of the aaranya, came up behind me with a stick. Damn near killed me." Sando leaned forward to show the full extent of the wound. It was ugly and deep, only by feeding deeply and often had Sando managed to heal as well as he had in the last five days.

"Ouch. You were lucky. If I'd known it was that serious I'd have come sooner, we could have got Helix later."

"No, it was better this way. I want to catch up with these aaranya. I want to find their Glade and burn it to the ground!"

Jaimee gave his brother a sympathetic look, but said, "I don't think we should be too rash. We still want to get hold of Asha again, Karlin's pretty little dryad. It was lucky for us that she escaped the flames too."

Sando opened his mouth to let go another tirade, to release days of pent-up frustration, but Jaimee stopped him with a look.

Sando closed his mouth again and nodded. Jaimee was right, revenge could come later.

"What do you suggest?" Sando asked.

"After going through the newspaper reports, I had Stephenson here make some enquiries for us," Jaimee said.

Sando looked across at the seat behind the driver. Facing them, sitting quietly and watching the two brothers talk, was Jaimee's pet human, Waldron Stephenson. He was a big man with sparse red hair, well dressed, and outwardly confident and brusque in manner. He was also extraordinarily rare: an adult human that could see and speak with the narun, he had been able to all his life. But whatever the outward appearances, Stephenson was Jaimee's servant.

Jaimee continued, "Darren Davies survived too."

"Was he badly injured?" asked Sando in surprise. He had assumed Davies must have died in the flames with Karlin.

"Not at all," Jaimee told him. "Apparently he got out early enough that he even managed to get past the authorities, like your friend

Caldor. He's back at his nest, and no one else seems any the wiser." Jaimee gave Sando a curious look and added, "That woman you spoke of, she must have survived too. There were no human female remains in the ashes."

Sando glared out the window at the passing humanity. "Didn't anyone bloody well die in that fire?"

"We know Karlin and the preta did – and too many dhumraka."

Sando looked back at his brother. "I only sacrificed them because I thought we were getting rid of the others. There's no way that Caldor should have escaped."

Jaimee shrugged.

"Fuck!" Sando said in frustration and looked out the window again.

"It seems to me that this Davies could be an asset for us," Jaimee ventured.

"But he can't see the aaranya, what use is he going to be?"

Jaimee explained what he had in mind.

"So you think we should pay him a visit?" Sando asked as his mind started to catch up with his brother's thoughts.

"Stephenson here can remind him that there are still people that know his past," said Jaimee.

"And so if he'd like to stay out of trouble," said Sando.

"He'd be well advised to work for us," finished Jaimee with a grin.

With their mood and thoughts now in tune again, Sando felt more content than he had since the events of the previous Friday. "What about O'Dwyer?" he asked. "We know he got out."

"Someone, we assume it was Ian, emptied his flat, but no one has seen him."

"It was Davies that found him the first time, he'll know where to look."

Jaimee nodded.

Sando matched his brother's smile, it was good to be back where he belonged.

Searching

1. Home

John put his hand forward to touch his daughter. He was nervous, of course he was, but he was not going to back out now that Asha had finally relented.

The being, no longer human, was held gently but firmly in Asha's arms. Asha told him that it was his daughter, Ellie, and he had to believe her. But he couldn't see it. He had to touch it. Her. In touch he hoped to find the evidence that his eyes couldn't see.

They were standing at the edge of the forest outside his home. The huge trees rose pale and tall, reaching in immense straight lines for the sky far above. It was late afternoon. The sinking sun reached through the trees, across the cleared area behind the house, and cast contrasting patches of light and shadow that flickered as a breeze brushed the distant leaves.

John closed his eyes, concentrated, and reached out with his vedana, his recently acquired sense of life. He could feel the strong presence of each tree, their living essence reaching up with their trunks and down deep into the soil with their roots. Asha's presence stood out from the glow of the trees like a strong beacon, an intense spotlight that almost overwhelmed his concentration. Her presence was something more to him now than simply a sense of her prana, her life. He could feel the other narun standing back near the house. He could also sense the life in his own hand reaching out to Asha and his daughter. Finally, he pushed his senses toward Ellie.

Grey. Her impact on his vedana was similar to her impact on his sight. Her presence was a pale grey as if the batteries that drove her light were running down. Barely the size of a two year old human child, her build was emaciated in the extreme and her skin was stretched like that of an ancient. Ellie had once had beautiful bright blue eyes, but this being had pale, milky and apparently unseeing globes deeply sunken in her too apparent skull.

Ellie would have been – was – more than six and a half years old now. He had thought she was dead. He had buried her material, human, body. Surely he should be thankful, ecstatic, at finding her alive; that, as a praanin, a being made only of the stuff of life, prana, she still lived. She was now effectively a narun, like Asha and the others, but she was weak and fading. The narun called her a preta, a hungry ghost. Ellie's effervescent personality was cut off behind the physical and psychological torments that had distorted her praanin body into this alien being.

The process that had made Ellie a preta, the violent expulsion of her praanin body from her material body, was usually fatal. Ellie had survived this long only through the special healing talents of Asha, but even so she was almost certainly dying. She had barely enough intensity to retain her spirit, her self. He should be grateful that she was still alive, but he couldn't help wondering if life was a good thing if it had to be spent like this.

He opened his eyes and looked at Asha and nodded. He watched as she reached out one hand to touch the tree next to her, still holding Ellie firmly in her other arm. Her hand merged with the tree. The bark of the tree appeared to reach out and embrace her hand, the pattern of the bark extended part of the way up her forearm. Sensing that flow of life, Ellie rested back against Asha, and John took that moment to gently hold one of her tiny hands in his.

He couldn't help it, despite his preparations, a gasp escaped his lips and he jerked his hand back. Asha looked at him with alarm, but he shook his head, he couldn't stop now. He turned his right hand up and looked at his palm. It felt as if it had been dragged over burning sandpaper, but its appearance was unchanged.

"This doesn't hurt her?" he asked quietly.

"No," Asha answered. "Her need, her hunger, tears at the prana of your body. It is not a conscious action, I am not sure she has any conscious actions now. Your body's prana doesn't have the strong prana skin of a narun, you cannot prevent her from tearing at your essence and so you are damaged. Let's stop this, John."

12

"No! Not yet. As long as she is not hurt, I want to try again."

The pain in his right hand was easing, but given a choice he decided he'd rather sacrifice his left. He kept himself from laughing, he didn't think Asha would appreciate his humour. Yes, this was important enough, he truly would sacrifice a hand, an entire arm, to make some real contact with his daughter.

John braced himself, reached out and took Ellie's hand in his. Ellie turned to face him, her white, sightless eyes seemed to question him. Even though he was ready for it, it still took everything he had to keep from pulling away again. He clamped his mouth closed and breathed heavily through his nose to cut off any audible indication of the pain.

He closed his eyes and pushed his senses past the burning in his hand. He ran his hand up her tiny, fragile arm to her shoulder and neck, and around the back of her head. Even beyond the fire where their skin touched, he could feel the desperate need of the being. It – she! – wasn't trying to hurt him, she was simply driven by an intense but completely blind hunger.

John stood, lost in concentration, for some minutes. He ignored the pain slowly tearing further and further up his arm. Tears poured from his eyes, not from the pain of the contact, but from the thought that this strange, desperate being was his daughter. Try as he might he could not reach any further. He could not sense any deeper. He had failed. But he understood now, nothing could surmount that much torment. If she was there – and he trusted Asha completely, Ellie must be in there somewhere – she was beyond his strength to find.

"John?" Asha called tentatively.

The familiar compassion of her voice pulled him from his trance. Feeling the sensation of hot daggers entering his arm above his elbow, he let out a gasp and pulled back. He stared at the being in Asha's arms in horror. "Ellie!" he called. Not in recognition, but in anguish that he could not help his child when she so obviously and desperately needed it. He turned from Asha and Ellie and stumbled deeper into the forest, holding his injured left arm protectively in front of him.

Behind him, Asha called Senna over and handed Ellie to her, then she rushed after John. She caught up with him quickly and stood in front of him to make him stop. "Show me," she demanded when he started to turn from her.

John held out his left arm for her inspection. "I'll be fine," he said bitterly.

Asha studied his arm, touching it gently. To John it felt as if parts of his arm were moving of their own volition, nerves and muscles twitched and felt as if they were realigning. The pain calmed and became a dull ache.

"You don't need to do that!" he snapped. "Don't waste your efforts on me." He tried half-heartedly to pull away from her touch.

Asha tightened her grip, but she had already withdrawn her senses, she had done as much as she could, time would achieve the rest. "You will be fine," she responded, "and I'll *waste* my efforts wherever I want."

Her angry tone reminded John of one of their first meetings, when he thought she had a very short temper for a figment of his imagination. This thought drained his despondency and he smiled.

"What?" she said, her tone still angry.

John laughed, and that didn't help. "I'm sorry," he said, "but you are beautiful when you're angry."

Asha hesitated, and then laughed and hit him. Her temper was as quick to go as it was to rise.

"Thank you," said John, holding up his left arm, "it feels much better."

"The damage is real. You need to take it seriously, John. Too much damage like that and you could even lose your arm. Your material body and the prana that gives it life work together, when you hurt one you hurt the other."

John looked surprised, and then returned to his earlier thoughts. "I couldn't find her. I was sure I would feel what you feel." He shook his head. "I'm her father!" he finished, as if that explained everything – he supposed it did.

Asha tried to reassure him, "Even the others can't feel it. None of them can reach deep enough, it's uncomfortable even for them. They believe me, they've seen what I can do now, but to them Ellie is the same grey and hungry preta that you see."

"How come you can see her?"

"I don't know. Darnu says that I must be a healer. I've heard the

14

stories, but it was nothing I was ever able to do before. I don't know what happened with Karlin in that awful prison, but whatever it was has released something within me."

"I could have told you, you were special," said John, reaching for her.

Asha smiled and stepped into his arms.

Holding her, John found the strength to ask the question that had been hovering on the edge of his thoughts since he first understood that the being was Ellie. "Is she doomed?" he asked. Asha stiffened in his arms. John caressed her hair and continued, "I've done more than see her now. I know she is every bit as weak as she looks, and I've felt the torment of her hunger. You've been trying to help her for weeks, but she is still not far from death. ... Is she dying?"

Asha pushed away and John let her step back. "I'm not giving up!" she said, angry again.

"I'm not asking you to. I don't want you to," said John. "I will do anything, give anything, to save her ... but I'd rather know now if there is no hope."

Asha moved back into his arms. "I'm sorry," she spoke against his chest.

Misunderstanding, John said, "No hope at all?"

"Not that," she said, shaking her head against him. "I'm sorry for getting angry. There is hope, there has to be. Don't you humans have a saying: where there's life there's hope? Ellie is alive. She is stronger than she looks. We will get her to the Glade and perhaps the life that is so prolific there can help her."

"Oh," John started. He had almost forgotten the intense life of the Glade, so much had happened since he had seen it. "Will Ellie be able to go into the Glade?"

"Yes."

"Do you think that may make a difference?"

"It will make a difference." As if feeling a change in John's bearing, Asha pushed back again and looked up at him. "I can't be certain it will be enough, I'm not offering guarantees. Just ... just *don't* give up. With the Glade, and what the elders know, there is still hope."

* * *

Sitting in the local pub, the tavern as it liked to be called, Jason looked across their drinks at John. "I get the distinct impression you left a lot out of this morning's recital," he said.

"I didn't think either of you would want all the gory details," said John. It was his first day back at work. The morning had been spent speaking with Stan, his boss, trying to explain his extended absence from work. John had asked Jason to sit in too, to save having to repeat his mix of half-truths and outright lies. Once he'd alluded to having some obscure problem with his brain, and was now seeking help – he hadn't explained what sort of help – his boss had been all sympathy and concern. He had offered to do what he could to help, it was enough to make John feel guilty.

"No, I guess not. It just doesn't seem quite like you, that's all."

"You've seen one of my little episodes, Jason. I'm not sure I was completely myself when I ran off. But I'm a lot better now." By reminding Jason of the night he saw John talking to someone that wasn't there, John hoped to persuade Jason to drop the subject.

Jason nodded slowly before responding, "You do seem more like yourself now than you've been since, ... you know, since Samantha and Ellie."

"As painful as some of it was," agreed John, "there was an element of catharsis, even an epiphany of sorts. Samantha and I had leaned on each other, depended on each other, more than either of us ever admitted. Without her I was lost. But I've found my feet now. Things are still far from perfect, but I'm not lost any more." It astonished John to discover how much truth he could tell, and still give so little away.

They both paused and took some mouthfuls from their drinks.

"So with this brain thing," said Jason, "are you likely to have more episodes, like that other night?"

John shrugged. "It can't be ruled out apparently." John thought he should cover himself, just in case Jason heard him talking with his friends again. "They don't think it's serious. I'm not about to flip my lid or anything." He grinned at Jason, trying to lighten the mood.

Jason looked up from his drink. "I just remembered. There was a guy looking for you, from Samantha's university. A little guy. I don't remember much about him to be honest. Hang on, he left me his card." Jason dug around in his wallet and handed over a plain white

16

card with a name and mobile telephone number on it.

John took the card and nodded at the name. "Yes, I know Ian all right. I'll call him some time." John wondered if Ian was still running. He put the card in his pocket.

"How's pregnancy treating you?" John asked, hoping to redirect the conversation.

It worked. Jason launched enthusiastically into describing everything that had been happening with Liz. His wife was apparently revelling in the experience, and Jason was every bit as excited.

So this is what it feels like, John thought to himself, to crack open the door back to his normal life, the one he had abandoned in his search for Asha. He wondered at the pressure he could feel still pressing on the door, trying to push it closed again. Was it his own reluctance, or were there other forces at work?

* * *

John returned his hire car, the station-wagon, and a week later traded in his sedan for a station-wagon of his own. He kept all the coverings he'd bought for the hire car and used them to transform his new car into something more comfortable for his friends.

He exchanged several telephone calls with Tracey. Her life had returned so quickly to its usual routine that she felt disoriented, as if that Friday had been a dream, some sort of psychedelic trip. She clung to John's calls as her only link to the events of that day. He promised that they would see her again just as soon as his friends were ready to visit the city.

Weeks passed with no word from his friends.

The brevi, Casseta, had stayed with John when the others had returned to the Glade. The tiny creature was like a small sugar glider, but with glossy, deep ginger fur, and darker ginger and white stripes running along her back to the thick tail. He was grateful for her company. He had grown accustomed to her warm presence when she was merged with his body, was comforted by it, but more than that, she was a constant reminder that it had all been real, and that the others, that Asha, would return.

He would call Casseta out of an evening and she'd run over his arms and body, and around the room as he worked – there was little better to do with his nights than work. He was finally able to return to working in the spare bedroom that he and Samantha had used as a shared office. He removed the fly-screens from the windows of this second-storey room so that when he opened the window Casseta could easily go out into the trees when she wanted. Most nights she would scamper off for an hour or so, leaving John feeling more desolate than ever. Each time she came back he would greet her with great relief.

It was a Thursday. He'd started the day strangely flat, and his mood deteriorated as the morning progressed. By lunchtime he was feeling surly and angry with the world. Jason kept quiet over lunch. It wasn't until after lunch that John looked at the calendar on his desk and consciously recognised the date. Today was the first anniversary of his wife's death. Twelve months ago today her car had run off the road, killing Samantha instantly and eventually leading to the loss of Ellie's human existence. Realising that he was going to get no work done now, he decided to go home and see if his sorrows had kept up their swimming skills.

There was a habit that he'd not lost since first meeting Asha. Every time he came home he would walk around to the back of the house, and then stop and stare into the forest looking for her. Only after watching for some minutes would he relent and enter the house. The habit was so ingrained that, even in his depression this afternoon, he found himself walking around to the back. To his complete surprise he found Barma and Tilvy sitting at the garden setting. He ran to them, his sour mood dissolved and a great smile spread across his face. Tilvy stood up quickly and he gave her an enthusiastic hug.

"Careful," she said, laughing. "Don't forget you're stronger than us."

"I'm sorry," he said, releasing her quickly. "It's just so good to see you both." He gave Barma a more sedate embrace.

John looked around. "Is Asha here? Andrei?"

"Andrei, Senna, Milla and Darnu went out into the forest for a while, we didn't expect you home so soon. Asha is still back at the Glade," said Barma.

"Is she ... is Ellie ... ?"

Barma started to reply but Tilvy interrupted, "It's probably better if Milla explains, John." Seeing the concern on his face she added, "She's okay. They're both okay."

"That's a relief," came Andrei's voice from the edge of the forest, "I thought you may have decided we were all imaginary again."

John turned around and grinned back at him. "No, Andrei. I decided that no one was masochistic enough to have you as an imaginary friend, so you must be real." They embraced and John murmured, "I am very pleased to see you again, my friend."

As he pulled back, Andrei asked, "You missed me?"

From behind him Senna said, "Yeah, like a sore thumb." She gave John a hug.

John saw Milla and Darnu coming out of the forest. "So you've come to take advantage of my Internet connection, Milla?" he asked.

"As a matter of fact I have," came Milla's deep and husky reply. "Also Andrei keeps pestering me to teach him to read and write, and that would be easier here if it is okay with you."

"We want to learn too," put in Tilvy, her arm around Barma.

"That's fine. Everyone come in and I'll show you around." Welcoming their distraction from his grief and plans to get drunk, John continued to babble, "You're welcome to use whatever you want, make yourselves at home. I'll show you how to use the computer, it's pretty simple. Obviously you can let yourselves in and out this back door any time, so you don't even need me here." As they entered the house, John asked Darnu, "Garjae's not with you?"

"No. He wanted to keep an eye on things back at the Glade."

John nodded. Obviously Garjae hadn't given up on Asha, still hoping she'd come to her senses and stop paying attention to this stupid human.

John showed Milla how to turn on the computer and access the Internet. How to search for things, and not to be too surprised at the things they found. "You're all adults I guess, so there's nothing here you won't understand, well, as much as anyone.

"Keep in mind that the Internet is pretty much open slather. Any idiot with a computer and some spare time can put up whatever they like. Most of it's pretty harmless but there are exceptions. The trick is learning to identify those parts that can be considered mostly reliable from those parts that are just people offering their own, often misguided, opinion, or passing on something they heard from the guy down the pub. Ask almost any question and you will find people expounding with great conviction on almost every possible answer."

Milla picked it up very quickly and began to get involved in reading what he'd found, so John left him to it. Most of the others ended up following John back downstairs.

John started to show Andrei how to use the television and remote control, but Senna interrupted, "This one I know already."

While his guests flicked around the channels, John went into the kitchen to fix himself dinner. Sitting alone in the kitchen he felt his bad mood returning so he finished up quickly, poured himself an ample drink, and went back into the lounge room to see what they were watching. Tilvy and Andrei were arguing over the remote control.

"That always happens," observed John.

They both looked up. Tilvy hit the mute button.

"My father once claimed that remote controls had caused more arguments than religion and politics combined. He told me it was better when someone had to get up to change channels."

Seeing that he still had their attention, John continued, "I did have an idea while I was eating. While you're learning to write, or at least type on the computer, how about writing emails to Tracey. I'm sure she'd appreciate hearing from you."

"That's a good idea," agreed Tilvy, "someone useful and fun to practise with."

Milla came into the room with Darnu. "We heard the TV go quiet, it seemed like a good time to come down," he said. "Come for a walk with me, John?"

John put his drink down and followed Milla out, the others stayed in the lounge. John could hear the television start up again, the sound flickering as someone started searching through the channels.

Milla led John outside and into the night, stopping at the edge of the forest. Milla was about to start talking when John interrupted.

"Before you start, Milla, and before I accidentally-on-purpose forget ..." John murmured to his arm and Casseta slid out, twitching her tail back and forth to pull it free. "Thank you, Cassey," he murmured sadly to the tiny creature. "I've loved having you with me. I will miss you." He touched his lips to the brevi's soft fur. "There's Milla, you can go home now. Tell him ... tell him, thank you

20

very much." He held out his arm toward Milla, who reached forward to complete the bridge. As their hands touched, Casseta scuttled rapidly across and up Milla's arm. She rushed to his face and appeared to whisper into his ear.

Milla's eyes raised and looked back at John, they glistened at the joy of meeting with his companion again. While the two communed, John turned and walked a short way to study the trunk of a tree. After a minute or so he turned back and saw Casseta's glowing body disappearing up a tree deeper in the forest.

"You better keep your window open tonight," said Milla, closing the distance between them.

"You think she might visit me?"

"She has been happy with you for this long, I think there is a good chance she may choose to stay with you."

"Did you know this might happen?"

Milla shrugged. "At the time it seemed necessary. I will miss her, but if she chooses to stay with you then who am I to complain?"

John wasn't sure what to say. He felt guilty at the hope he was holding out that she would choose to come back to him.

"It's okay, John, there's nothing to feel bad about. The brevi are not pets, and they are more than companions. They are part of our Glade and we respect their choices."

John nodded his understanding. "Thank you," he said quietly.

For some moments more they stood there silently, looking into the forest where Casseta had disappeared.

Milla said, "Asha asked me to apologise to you. She wanted to come with us, but she needs to keep trying with Ellie."

John nodded.

"Ellie is stronger than when you saw her last, and she continues to improve, but very slowly." Milla turned to look at John. The night was dark, there was no moon yet, and they'd left the outside lights off, but vedana allowed John to see Milla clearly. "Despite that greater strength, Ellie remains obviously a preta, and her mind remains cut off. It seems unlikely that even the power of the Glade will be enough to bring her back, but we haven't given up. Part of what I hope to do here, with the resources of your Internet, and if necessary books that you can get for me, is to see what human knowledge can help us."

John turned back to the massive tree he had been studying, and laid his hand on the trunk. He could feel the life gently pulsing beneath the bark. Still staring at the tree, he asked, "Do you know what today is, Milla?" He didn't wait for Milla to answer. "Today is the first anniversary of my wife's death. In a few weeks it will be the second birthday that she's missed since dying. I missed *celebrating* the first birthday because I was busy mourning our daughter. Samantha would have been twenty-nine this year."

He turned to look at Milla. "Do your people do that?"

Milla raised his eyebrows in question.

"Humans have rituals with time and events. You can sort of understand it with happy events, birthdays and weddings and such. Any excuse for celebrating and having a good time has got to be a good thing." Turning back to the tree, John rested his hand on it again. "But humans do it for tragic events too. The first anniversary of this tragedy, the tenth anniversary of that one. And, as you've just heard, personal tragedy turns old celebrations into new commiserations: the first Christmas since, the second birthday since ... and *she would have been* – past tense has never been so pitiful," he finished bitterly.

From behind him Milla responded, "We are not so time conscious as humans, but the passing years still affect us. We have some annual celebrations, and personal tragedy still sits heavily on us in many of the same ways. We are not so different."

"I would like to see our daughter again, Milla. Can she leave the Glade?"

"No, I don't think so," said Milla cautiously, he was having difficulty keeping up with John's mood. The conversation felt disjointed. "Her body is unable to retain its essence for very long. However much Asha keeps giving to her, the prana is quickly lost. Only inside the Glade is the environment strong enough, is life concentrated enough, that her body can retain its strength. If you come to the Glade you may be able to see her briefly outside, but she certainly can't make the journey back here."

John nodded absently. For reasons he couldn't explain, this felt like something he already knew or expected. "I was wondering if you could help me to find a shorter way to the Glade. I was thinking that there must be roads or tracks that we can find that would let me drive closer, and perhaps that might reduce the time it takes for me to get there." He looked back at Milla.

"We can try," Milla agreed, "it may take some time to work out, but we can try."

Later that night Casseta did return through the open window. She nuzzled at John's face, curious about the tears that wet his cheeks. "Hello Cassey," he whispered, "I am very pleased to see you. I hope you'll stay." After a few minutes the brevi nuzzled at his arm and merged into his body. Despite the brevi's comforting presence, John continued to stare silently into the dark room, and tears continued to stream down his face. So much had happened in the last twelve months, but nothing could remove the sorrow he felt. He missed Samantha, he supposed he always would.

* * *

The next few months were a very hectic time around John's home, and it helped to keep him distracted from bouts of melancholy.

The reading and writing lessons advanced quickly. Senna learned fastest of all. Growing up in the city meant she already had a good start, and her progress inspired some heated competition amongst the others. A close pen-pal friendship between Tilvy and Tracey progressed quickly. John purchased Tilvy a small mobile telephone and showed her how to text with it so the two could chat even when Tracey was at work.

For a time Andrei seemed obsessed with the television, he would stay up watching for most of the night. The aaranya were familiar with television from the excursions of their youth, but Andrei revelled in the freedom to choose his own programs and to flick and pause on a whim. Others would come to watch but quickly got bored, or frustrated with Andrei's constant channel changing. Reruns of old movies and comedy series were his favourites, but everything from the news to the most patronising of children's shows appeared to be worthy of some attention.

"Ay, caramba!" Andrei exclaimed to John one morning as he came downstairs, still rumpled from sleep.

It was a reasonable imitation of Bart Simpson, so John responded, "Don't have a cow man."

Apparently satisfied, Andrei grinned and wandered back to the television.

"Na-nu, na-nu," Andrei greeted John on another morning.

John just stared back at him.

"Fly, be free!" Andrei said.

John thought he should recognise the voice but that was all.

"Mork from Ork?" Andrei asked in his usual voice. "Mork and Mindy?"

"Oh yeah," said John. "I've heard of that. Not sure if I was born then."

Andrei shook his head and turned back to the lounge. "Shazbot!"

Eventually Senna lost patience and threatened to break something. Andrei looked up at her in surprise, as if he had no idea how much time he had spent staring at the box. The television went off and no one saw either of them for a few days.

John purchased a second computer so that Milla could continue his research without interruption. Every few weeks Milla would be forced to return to the Glade; as an elder he was bound to the Glade in ways that the others weren't, but the others, too, would generally return at irregular intervals.

On some weekends John would take some of his friends to visit Tracey, or to meet with some of the city aaranya. On other weekends Tracey would come to John's home. John had trouble imagining what it must be like for her to be surrounded by people she couldn't see. He doubted if he would be as comfortable and relaxed about it as Tracey appeared to be. He asked her about it during one of her visits.

"It is strange," she admitted, "but as they've become more familiar it's like I can feel them around me. I don't think I'd like to be put to the test, to be told to point to each person in the room, but I'm rarely surprised now when Tilvy does anything near me."

John nodded, he could understand that. When Asha was near he always knew it, he could feel her in a way that was more intense than with the others. Did that mean that even Tracey had some vedana, some sense of life? Or was there something more, some sense beyond even vedana?

2. *Plans*

Déjà vu.

John stood in the dark hallway. Outside the rain fell in a heavy roar, drowning out almost all other sound. He was alone in the house. Andrei and Senna had gone to the city with Tracey, the others had all returned to the Glade. He had been walking from the lounge to the kitchen for a drink when the power went out, leaving him standing there in the dark.

The familiarity of the situation was so strong he could feel the ghost of that pain taking hold. The crack in his head twisted and made his head hurt, reminding him of the change that had happened that night. He leaned against the wall, breathing heavily. He lost track of time as he stood there in the dark, remembering that night, its causes and its consequences.

He was woken from his reverie by a light knocking on the back door, only faintly heard past the roar of the rain. If he hadn't been standing in the hall he would probably have missed it. The crack in his head relaxed as a warm and familiar breeze wafted against it. Asha!

He pushed himself away from the wall and rushed to the door. He pulled it open and saw her standing there looking forlorn and bedraggled in the dark rain. Her expression was both hopeful and uncertain. "Asha!" He stepped out and picked her up in his arms, spinning around, oblivious to the cold downpour.

Asha laughed and kissed him. "Stop it, John. You're getting saturated."

"I don't care," he replied, and spun further out into the dark. "It's just so good to feel you again." He put her down and ran his hands over her cheeks and back through her hair. "You're here," he sighed, barely able to believe it.

They stood there in the dark and the rain, and kissed. They touched each other as if to prove that neither had changed, to prove that this was not just a dream.

But it was winter and the rain was cold, eventually John began to shiver. "Time we went inside, John, before you catch pneumonia or something," Asha spoke into his ear.

The power was still out. Asha simply let the water run off her at the doorstep, John had to disappear upstairs and work his way around in the dark for a towel and some dry clothes. Back downstairs, John sat on the sofa and Asha sat next to him, leaning in under his arm.

"Ellie?" he asked when they had both settled.

"I've left her with my grandmother," said Asha.

"Grandmother?"

"You met her – Kaia. She's not exactly my grandmother, there's a few greats involved but she doesn't like anyone to use them, she says that the *grand* is bad enough."

"I did wonder when I met her, you have the same eyes."

Asha nodded against his chest, and then John felt her body tense before she spoke. "I've done all I can for Ellie ... but it's not been enough." She paused, giving John a chance to interrupt, but he stayed silent. "Her mind is still cut off. I think that may explain the way she looks. Without an active mind there is no will, nothing to give her a sense of who and what she is. There are no praanin plants outside the Glade, and this may be the reason why."

When John remained silent, she pushed herself back to look into his face. "Say something."

"Milla tells me that she can't leave the Glade," he said quietly.

"No, or not for very long."

"How long will she live?"

Asha leaned back against his chest again. "I don't know. If she stays in the Glade she might have another year, perhaps a little more. It's really hard to tell."

John mused quietly, "I wonder if I could find Sando and Stephenson again. I wonder if they will eventually find a cure for what they've caused – they must have had some reason for doing it."

"And Jaimee," said Asha with a shiver. She still hadn't forgotten the way he seemed to see right into her.

"Have you spoken to others about them?"

Asha nodded. "After what we told him, Milla is convinced that Sando and Jaimee are twins, like me and Sarva."

John looked down at her with surprise. "Huh?"

"You know I'm a twin," she explained, "that Sarva, my twin brother, wandered off north some years ago." John nodded gently against the top of her head. "Well twins are really rare among our people. When Sarva and I were born our arrival was met with great excitement. Apparently, if any of our people are going to have powers, like my ability to heal, it happens most often and most dramatically in twins. It disappointed a lot of people when there was nothing special about us by the time we became adults."

"I could have told them differently," he murmured into her hair.

"Milla thinks that Sando and Jaimee are probably talented twins, and that may explain Sando's ability to influence minds, and whatever it is that Jaimee can do – I'm sure there's more that we haven't seen."

"And Sarva could be wandering around somewhere with his own special talents too?"

"I guess. It may not have shown up yet. I don't know what it was with Karlin that made me find my talent."

"Need, would be my guess," said John.

"Maybe," Asha agreed, "if so, then Sarva may not have needed his talent yet."

"Or he may have. I wonder what it is," whispered John.

"I wonder *where* he is," said Asha.

Unable to find a more delicate way to put it, John asked bluntly, "So is that it? Is there nothing more we can do for Ellie?"

Asha sat up straighter and pulled away from John. She turned and sat cross legged on the sofa to watch his face. "Milla has spoken of one possibility."

John waited for Asha to continue.

"Actually there are a few possibilities, but they're all related. Ours is an old stand. We have one of the oldest Glades on the Australian mainland, but further south, in Tasmania, are forests much older than here. There, there is a stand and Glade older than any other we

27

know. They are an isolated people, and like it that way, but Milla thinks we could probably talk to them. Being such an old Glade it is possible that they may know more than we do here."

"Is there something in particular that he expects them to know?"

Asha shrugged. "Not really, but given their age he thought they might be worth asking. The alternatives are so much further away." Seeing that John was waiting for more, she continued, "Some elders remember tales of a powerful healer, a long, long way to the north. The details are vague. If she still lives, she's on the continent to the north – perhaps Myanmar, maybe China."

"China doesn't exactly narrow things down. Where's Myanmar?"

"You might know it as Burma. You humans can't seem to make up your minds what to call places. Anyway, that's why he thought we could try Tasmania first, it's closer and smaller – we're less likely to get lost."

"But they've no specific reason to think we'll find answers there?"

"Not really, no."

"You keep saying *we*," said John. "You and I?"

"Getting anywhere on my own would take a long time, months or possibly years to make my way north."

"I was thinking that you'd need to stay here to look after Ellie," said John.

"As long as Ellie stays in the Glade there's not much more I can do for her," explained Asha. "I need to go because I'm probably the only one that has a hope of being taught how to heal her properly. We just have to hope it is something I can learn because we can't afford to take Ellie out of the Glade."

John closed his eyes in thought. This was going to take some planning and lots of money. "Just you and I?" he asked eventually.

"Milla thought it would be better if there were more of us. He thinks the same group may want to stick together – since you did so well in rescuing me." Asha had been watching John speculatively, he was obviously deep in thought. As she finished speaking she leaned in and kissed him on the lips.

John's eyes opened in surprise and then he reached forward and drew her closer. They rearranged their bodies carefully, never breaking the kiss, until they were stretched out on the sofa. Asha's body was light but oh-so warm against his. The urgency of their embrace increased and John felt his body responding as Asha's body stirred against him.

The power to the house chose that moment to come back on, and the light flickered on in the room. Several thoughts ran through his mind at once, none of them seemed very appropriate. Before he realised what was happening, John found himself laughing. He tried unsuccessfully to choke it off.

The kiss broke off and Asha sat back to one side while John sat up and tried to pull himself back together. Seeing the puzzled and hurt look on Asha's face, John hastened to explain. "Oh. No, Asha. No. I'm sorry. It's me. My head. It can't be trusted." He tried to reach for her, but she sat back.

"Explain," she demanded.

John wondered where to start. "There's a few things really. Remember when I thought you were a figment of my imagination?" Asha nodded. "Back then I had thought to myself that falling in love with you must be like kissing a mirror."

"What do you mean, kissing a mirror?"

"It's a joke, a taunt usually, I doubt if anyone really does it. But kids tease each other, when they're learning about, well, sex, that they must practice kissing by kissing a mirror. Various connotations follow about how much you must think of yourself to do it. Of course, it probably helps if you can see yourself in it," he added.

Asha nodded and smiled, "Keep going."

"Okay. Since then, obviously, I know you're real, but I also know that no one else can see you. That led me to thinking about what I must have looked like lying there kissing you, and what it would have looked like – you know – to someone else, had it gone much further. And ... and that image struck me as funny."

Asha tried to look at him seriously, but couldn't hold it and burst into laughter. "Okay, you're right. It is funny. It was also incredibly bad timing and in poor taste, but I forgive you." She finished with a grin, and moved forward into his arms. As John stroked her hair, she continued, "You said there were a few things. What else?"

"I guess the next thing is that I really need to spend some more time out in that cold rain before we do much more of this."

Asha was quiet for a few moments before she replied, "The rain's stopped."

John felt himself blush. "You know what I mean. You must have felt me. I don't mean to impose ... I don't ... It's not something I can control."

"Don't you want me?" Asha's voice came to him quietly.

"Oh God, yes! Asha, isn't it obvious, but—"

Asha laughed. She sat up and grinned at him. "That was my turn."

Relieved, John laughed.

"Was there more?" she wanted to know.

John hesitated, if he thought the last part was difficult, this was much worse.

Asha sat back. "This must be bad."

John looked down. "Even supposing you wanted to ... you know. I have no idea whether we can, whether it's possible."

A smile lit up Asha's face. "Is that all?"

John nodded without lifting his head.

"I don't know either."

John looked at her, his expression slightly pained.

Asha moved closer, touched his face and grinned. "But it could be fun finding out." She touched his lips with her fingers. "As for whether I wanted to." She kissed his lips. "I thought I'd made that abundantly clear." She kissed him again, harder. "I do look human, even under these clothes," she assured him, and kissed him again. "Do you want to see?"

He did.

* * *

The next day it was a very happy, almost smug, John that drove into the city. Asha sat in the passenger seat watching the traffic. Every now and then they'd turn and look at each other and burst into uncontrollable smiles and laughter. They would reach out to hold hands until John next needed both his hands on the wheel. The night had been an education for both of them. Asha was right yet again, it was fun finding out.

The lounge room in Tracey's house was a sparsely but comfortably furnished room. It was only dimly lit because the vertical blinds had been turned enough to make sure the neighbours couldn't see in. Tracey, Andrei and Senna were sitting around a small coffee table in the centre of the room, scraps of paper all around them. Conversation had been going well.

"Sorry about all the paper," Tracey apologised. "I try to get it all cleared away before Mum gets home, but even so she thinks I'm writing a novel or something."

"Maybe you should," said Andrei and then, grinning at John, continued, "The Adventures of John and his Amazing Imaginary Friends."

"I'm not passing that one on, Andrei," he said.

Andrei grinned back and then looked down and started madly scribbling on his pad. While he was doing that, Senna came over and hugged John and Asha. "It's good to see you two together at last."

Tracey laughed as she read Andrei's suggestions. "Oh, I do like this one," she said, "*The Mystery of the Drawn Drapes*. I have been wondering what my neighbours are thinking."

"I'm not invisible," said John, "I'm not going to get you into trouble or something am I?"

"No. If Mum asks, I'll just tell her that you're my publisher."

John groaned. "Speaking of your mother, have we got a while before she comes home?"

"Yeah, heaps. She's out with her new boyfriend, she won't be back till late tonight."

John settled on the sofa with Asha and they explained about wanting to look for help from other Glades. John said, "I think we should skip Tassie and just head north. It's going to take some money to do all this and I don't have enough to throw it around. North is where the rumours lead so let's just jump straight to it."

Tracey looked at him doubtfully. "Are you including me in this?"

"To be honest I was hoping you might agree to help from here. A human to visit my house occasionally and see if Milla needs anything. Someone I can phone or email and ask to do stuff. Not exactly exciting, but it could be really useful."

Tracey nodded. "It sounds like you could end up slashing your way through jungles and mosquito infested swamps and things," she mused. "That's not really my scene."

"Not mine either," said John, "but that could be where we're headed."

"Are Tilvy and Barma going?"

"I am hoping they will agree to help you out at this end."

"Well we're coming with you!" said Andrei.

John looked across at Andrei and Senna. "I must admit that I sort of assumed you would. I'm sorry, Senna. Is that asking too much?"

Senna smiled and shook her head. She put her arms around Andrei. "Andrei's bound to find trouble wherever he is, and it's less embarrassing in front of strangers." She paused as a thought occurred to her. "I'll want to tell Dad before we go."

John nodded. "We can't go straight away. I've got to work out how to get everyone to where we want to be – and I'll probably have to make some sort of preparations with work. It's really hard to know how long we'll be away."

"Can't we just fly?" asked Andrei.

"Maybe we can charter a plane to Darwin or Cape York or something," John said, "it's only money after all. Or we could drive. It'd take longer but I imagine it would cost less. But actually getting you all out of this country, and into one of the ones we want, that's a problem I don't know how to tackle just yet."

- - -

Tracey stared at the movie disc covers in front of her, barely registering the titles. Andrei and Senna had gone back with John and Asha yesterday, and her mother had gone out with her new boyfriend again, so tonight was a night alone. Maybe she should start writing a book, as Andrei had suggested, it would give her something to do when everyone else was out having fun. She could go through her trash and pull out all the notes they'd been scribbling and try to get some ideas. She smiled to herself as she contemplated what some snoop would make of the disjointed scribblings. She imagined him putting a big red mark on the door to tell all the crooks to stay away from this place, there's a mad woman living here.

There was a bump from another customer.

"Sorry," she mumbled.

"Any time," he replied.

It took a few moments for the reply to sink in. She looked up to see that the man was smiling at her.

"I take it you're waiting for inspiration too," he said.

She gave him a puzzled look.

"You don't seem to be reading the covers, and not many people have such a pretty smile on their face in the horror section."

Tracey looked again at the movies and realised that she had, as the man said, moved to the horror section. "Oh."

"I always find it hard to find something good to watch on my own," the man said. "Romance is out, it just reminds you you're alone. Comedy rarely seems very funny on your own. Same thing with action, the thrills just aren't there, so I thought I'd try some horror. I don't usually, but without any other ideas it seemed worth a go. Sorry, I'm babbling."

Tracey smiled at the man. He was young and slender, maybe just a couple of years older than herself. He had dark hair and the unshaven movie-star stubble that so many young men affected these days, but this man it actually suited. She thought he looked nice, pleasant and friendly – attractive. "It's fine," she told him. "I agree with you. None of the movies are much fun on your own."

"But you can't be on your own – no, wait. Don't answer that. It sounds like a pick-up line," the man laughed easily.

Tracey laughed with him. "Okay, I won't answer, but it's probably pretty obvious." She stopped suddenly and stared down the aisle.

"What is it?" the young man asked her.

"I just saw someone I thought I recognised," she said. "But I can't remember where from."

The young man looked down the aisle. "Which one?"

"No, he's already—" Tracey stood on tiptoes to look over the display racks, trying to see the man again. Short and balding. Was he someone she knew from work? Maybe one of her boss's clients. She turned away again rather than be caught staring. "He's gone. It doesn't matter."

When she looked up she saw the young man was giving her a strange look.

"I ..." He hesitated and then continued, "I don't usually do this sort of thing, really I don't. But I'll never forgive myself if I let you walk away without asking. Would you like to have a drink with me sometime? Obviously I'm free tonight, but any time. Only if you feel like it. If you'd like to. I don't want to be pushy. I mean, I know this is forward and all, but who knows when I'll ever see you again. I could just start coming here every night waiting for you, but that'd be like stalking or something and then you'd think I was really strange. You probably think I'm strange anyway ..." he trailed off as Tracey began to laugh.

"I'm sorry," Tracey said, "but I talk too much when I'm nervous too."

The man smiled at her. It was a very attractive smile.

- - -

John and Tracey stood out the front of John's house and waved as Jason drove off. It had been awkward, at first, introducing Tracey to Jason. John knew all the assumptions that Jason was likely to make. John tried to make it clear that Tracey was just a friend, just someone that was going to look after his house while he was away, and that – of course – entailed a whole new explanation.

"I'm going to Asia to get help with this brain thing," John had explained to Jason. "I could be gone for a while. And since you're now busy with your new bouncy baby boy, Tracey kindly offered to check on my house when she can, check my mail and pay my bills and so on. I thought you two should meet in case Tracey needs any help out here, you know, what plumber to call and that sort of thing."

By the time Jason left they had all been chatting easily. Tracey had a kind and open face and was difficult not to like, and John thought she had made a good impression on Jason.

When John started to turn to go back in, Tracey touched his arm. "Can we talk?"

"What is it?" he asked, curious.

"I've met someone. A man. He's really nice."

"Not still picking up battered strangers in the street are you?" John asked with a grin. "You know I warned you about that."

Tracey smiled at John's attempted humour. "No. We met in a video shop, both searching for movies to watch on our own."

"What's his name?"

"Mike. We've been out a few times now and I really like him."

"That's great, Tracey. I'm pleased. I was worried that all *this* may have disrupted your life too much."

"It's all this that's worrying me now," Tracey admitted.

"The world in which the aaranya exist, and then the human world in which they don't," said John. "I know what you mean. I face the same thing. I go to work and try to sort of switch off my personal life

34

and everything that's happening there."

"But that's the thing, John. I think everyone has that who-you-are-at-work and who-you-are-at-home. But now I've had to split my home-self into two as well, and it's hard. Something will happen while I'm with Mike that reminds me of you or the aaranya, but I can't say anything to him. Even today, I'm here and Mike doesn't know where I am. I haven't told him anything about any of this. I'm hoping it doesn't come up. He's busy this weekend, family commitments or something, but if he asks what I did, I don't really know what to tell him."

John had never really considered himself all that different at work to the way he was at home, not until these months with the aaranya, but he had seen it in others so he thought he understood. He certainly understood that it must be even harder for Tracey because she had a relatively normal personal life outside all this. As far as John was concerned his normal personal life had died with his wife, his life with the aaranya was his life now.

"Are you asking if we can introduce Mike to the aaranya?" John asked eventually.

"I've thought about that, but this is all too important to risk on a hope. Mike's nice, I like him, and I trust him – I think. But I guess that's the point: I only *think* I trust him. He's almost too good to be true after the dodgy dates and boyfriends in the past. The way I thought about it last night, when I stayed awake thinking about it, was that if he asked me to marry him now I would have to say *no*, because I just don't know him well enough yet. And if I don't know him well enough to want to marry him, then how can I know him well enough to risk betraying my friends."

John nodded. "I don't want to sound patronising, but I am pleased you take this all so seriously. It means a lot to me. As for Mike, I suggest you tell him about me, matching up your story with what I've told Jason. That way, if the two meet, everything will seem above board and consistent. Tell him I'm just a sick friend you met a few months ago, someone you're helping out. That also gives you something to tell him about this weekend, if he asks. Bring him out here some time so he can see that I'm an old codger who couldn't possibly be a threat to him."

Tracey laughed at that. "I may call you dad sometimes, but you're not old enough to convince anyone you're out of the competition. Meeting you is not likely to reassure him, not if he's inclined to get jealous or suspicious."

"I'm lost," John admitted, but he couldn't help being flattered by Tracey's assessment. "Do you want us to meet to see if he's the jealous type? Or not want us to meet in case he is?"

"I think I'd rather keep the two parts separate as much as possible. I just think it would be too hard to say all the right things if I try to mix the two."

"You're probably right. I just hope it doesn't spoil things with Mike."

* * *

John felt Asha's presence come up behind him. Her hands gently massaged his shoulders and neck and he felt the tension start to melt away. He leant back into the massage. "Oh that feels good," he said, and breathed out slowly.

"Your head will explode if you keep this up," she said softly. "You need me here to take care of you." She kissed the top of his head.

"I have missed you," he said. He turned the chair away from the computer screen he had been staring at for so long. He stood up stiffly, his muscles complaining after so much time sitting still. Asha stood against him and put her arms around him, running her hands slowly up from his buttocks to his neck. John felt the warmth of her touch permeating his muscles and easing away the discomfort. "Oh God," he said in relief, "I've missed that too."

She snuggled against him and he wrapped his arms around her. "You only love me for my healing touch," she accused.

"I can think of one or two other reasons," John assured her. He gently turned her head upward and kissed her passionately.

"Cough, cough," said Andrei from the doorway. "Cough, cough."

John pulled away from the kiss very reluctantly and tried to slow his heartbeat. "You didn't come back alone," he whispered to Asha as he drew back.

"Sorry to interrupt," Andrei said, although his grin left some doubt as to how sorry, "but there's the smell of something hot and burnt downstairs."

John stared at him for a minute and then remembered. He glanced at his watch. "Oh shit! That'll be dinner, it's been hours."

Downstairs he pulled from the oven the lump of charcoal that was to have been his dinner. He opened the kitchen windows to try and release the smell of burnt food and then looked around to see what else he could eat. It ended up being yet another microwave meal.

"So much for my efforts at cooking for myself," he said as he picked at his food.

"I should have noticed the other meal was burning when I came in," Asha apologised, "but I had my mind on other things."

"And much more important things," agreed John, smiling at her. "Anyway it would already have been a lost cause, if it ever had any chance at all."

"I don't think you're going to build much muscle from this stuff," said Andrei, studying the box from John's meal. "Very low in protein."

John just shrugged, it filled the gap and that's all he was worried about for now. "How's Ellie?" he asked Asha. Asha, Andrei and Senna had just returned from the Glade. Milla and the others were also away so the last couple of weeks had been very quiet in the house.

Asha sighed. "Not much change. Until I can learn more there's not much I can do."

"I'm sorry, Asha. I don't mean to prevaricate and delay our getting away – but I still haven't worked out how to get us all into Myanmar or China." It was this that had occupied John for weeks. The few people he knew that had been overseas had all done it in the conventional way, commercial airlines and organised tours and the like. He guessed he probably needed some illicit solution, but he had no idea how to approach any sort of criminal underworld that could smuggle his friends out, and the hazards of that seemed too great for someone with his lack of experience.

"I think we should just go," said Andrei.

"What do you mean?" asked John.

"It's not like you had any great plans the last time you set out from home on a quest, and that turned out okay." Andrei looked at Senna, thinking of his first meeting with her in the city. "Better than okay. I think we should head as far north as you can take us and then try to get help from the locals." He grinned at Senna. "The natives can be very friendly."

37

"Don't forget, I'm coming too, Andrei," warned Senna. "Don't go getting ideas about a girl in every port."

Andrei tried to look shocked and offended, but it wasn't very convincing.

"It was different before," said John.

"Why?" asked Andrei.

"Well ... it was," John answered lamely. "We know where we want to go this time, I've just got to work out how to get us there."

"But you've been at it for weeks already, and unless there's something you haven't told me, you haven't made any progress."

"I've got things sorted with Tracey and organised money." John was feeling defensive.

"I'm just saying that may be the only way to find the solution is to start and see what we find as we go." Andrei grinned to pull the sting on his next words, "I know it goes against the grain for Mr Responsibility."

"There's a lot to think of," defended Asha. "We don't want to go into this blind."

"I know that, Mrs Responsibility – did I mention that I think you two are really well matched? But it seems to me that we've come to a point where, if we're going to do anything, we have to do something. If you see what I mean."

John stared down at what was left of his meal, his appetite was disappearing with the thought of once again plunging into the dark. Last time it had just happened, he didn't remember ever really deciding – anything. But to consciously choose to take that leap? Andrei knew him very well, it went against everything he was.

"You could be right," said John at last. "I'll sleep on it."

Upstairs in the bedroom, he and Asha sat on the edge of the bed. John called Casseta out and she scampered around the room and over their bodies, enjoying the attention from the two of them. Over the time that John and Asha had spent together Casseta had grown to treat them as one, apparently equally content to stay with either – except when Asha returned to the Glade, then Casseta always returned to John as if sensing his need.

"You think Andrei's right," John said. It was a statement.

"I don't like it much more than you do. But, yes, I think it may have come to that. I'd be getting very worried if I thought you were going to spend more weeks getting as worked up about it as I found you this evening."

"It's just such a big step. I've got to resign and get ready to give up this life for God knows how long." He looked at her. "It's not that I mind doing it, I'll do whatever it takes to get Ellie back, but it's not an easy step to reverse. What if it's a mistake and I need my normal life back to make different choices?"

Asha put her hand to his face. "My love, some things can't be thought through. Sometimes it's because we don't have the knowledge, and sometimes it's because we don't have the capacity – some things are just too big. Sometimes the only way forward is to act."

Casseta ran along Asha's arm and nuzzled at John's face. Asha smiled with affection at the tiny, furry creature as it ran lightly over his face and onto his shoulder.

"You're right. Andrei's right," John said at last. "I'll start putting things in motion tomorrow. I've got to give notice at work so that gives us our departure date. We'll drive. It's a long way, but if we're going to explore parts of northern Australia looking for help we'll need transport." He gave a deep sigh. "It is almost a relief to make a decision, but there's still a lot I have to organise. If we're going to explore I'll need to study the areas we might want to go. It might be worth asking Milla if he or the other elders can give us some leads for the best places to try."

As John rambled on with the thoughts that flooded his mind, he watched Asha get up and pick Casseta off his shoulder. She carried the brevi to the open window and whispered to it briefly. Casseta climbed nimbly out the window and off into the night.

"I'll need to contact Tracey and let her know, make sure it fits in with her," John continued to ramble as more thoughts occurred to him.

Asha returned and stood in front of him. She placed her fingers to his lips. "You need to stop thinking about this for the night," she said softly. "You need a break from it."

John nodded reluctantly. "I know, but there's just so much to think about, so much to plan. It's hard to switch off."

"Perhaps I can take your mind off it for a while," she whispered, very softly, but John heard her clearly in the quiet room.

The room was dark, just some faint moonlight coming through the window. But that didn't matter. With vedana, his sense of life, he could have seen any narun clearly. His hyper-awareness of Asha meant that she was always clear to his senses. She was standing right there, close in front him. He watched as her clothes grew indistinct, gauzy, and then faded away completely.

Asha laughed gently, happily, at the expression on his face. She reached forward and gently pressed on his chin until his mouth closed. She pulled him forward off the bed and helped him to undress. Thought didn't stand a chance, sometimes the only way forward is to act.

3. Journey

Disturbed by the most recent email, Tracey flicked back through the past messages to read over their progress to date. Most of the messages had been written by Andrei and Senna, and were sent to Tracey as well as Tilvy and the others back at John's house. At the start the messages had come almost every day.

> Base Camp, this is Search Party.
> The forest here is very strange. Trees taller than ours, with ants scurrying around apparently randomly. No sign of life, but it does have rhythm. love Andrei.
> Translation: We're in Sydney. John went music shopping, I think he was hoping it would give Andrei a rest - some hope! love Senna.

The next day's message confirmed Senna's guess:

> Tree people, I'm singing for you too. love Andrei.
> Translation: Another day on the road. Today's music was Neil Diamond, Hot August Night. John's pick, he said it was a classic (I thought he meant violins and stuff!). Darnu and Garjae studiously ignored it, but Asha and Andrei both loved it and sang along very loudly every time it was played - which was very @#$%@#$ often!

John promised to let me hide the discs so we can play something else tomorrow. I just hope he bought something a bit more modern. love Senna.

Then came:

Enterprise, this is the Away Team.

The commander won't relinquish the controls so progress is slow and we've been forced to abide with yet more Klingons.

Translation: Andrei wanted John to teach him to drive, but John refused (phew!). But it does mean another overnight stop in a town (small this time). More time for Andrei to catch up on his TV - as if he needs it. love Senna.

A few days later they had made it to the top of Cape York.

Team Green Leader, this is Team Discovery Channel.

Tomorrow sees us venture forth in search of the lemon tree. We may be out of radio contact, but don't worry, our burly protector is with us. love Andrei.

Translation: Andrei watched another Simpsons rerun last night. We're here. You probably won't hear from us for a few days, John's coming part of the way with us. Keep well and we'll try to do the same. love Senna.

And when they got back:

Command Module, we have contact.

Your mission planner is a genius. Not only are the aliens friendly, they have exactly what we came looking for. love from your humble Mission Planner.

Translation: Andrei is gloating. We found

the Glade very easily, thanks Milla, and they spoke of people coming from Myanmar that may be able to help us. Those people went south, so we have to backtrack a bit to try and catch up with them. Wish us luck. love Senna.

A few days later it was good news:

Goslings to Mother Goose,
We're about to get our feet wet. Ready to set sail to the promised land. Sailing into the sunset to be one of the ships that pass in the night. Wish us a bon voyage and keep a fair-weather eye on the horizon.

Translation: Enough already Andrei! The people we met were travelling with a human!!! The man, Dengali, can't see us or hear us, but he knows we're here and we can talk to him using a computer with a screen that you can write on. Anyway, he's got access to a ship that's going to take us to Myanmar. We leave tomorrow. love Senna.

Tracey thought she might not hear from them for a while, not if they were stuck on a ship somewhere north of Australia, but the next day another message arrived:

From the Ship of Fools,
One of our crew has succumbed to a dreaded malaise, but the rest of us continue to battle on against the elements. Only this fragile electronic link keeps your brave crew sane while we float adrift so far from land. Writing with a shaky hand, your Andrei.

Translation: John is seasick. Dengali says it should only last a few days, but Asha doesn't seem so certain. Dengali has a computer with a satellite connection and seems happy for us to use it – which is how Andrei had time to look up words like "malaise". Being out on the open ocean is really amazing, but a bit scary too. love Senna.

The messages had continued in a similar manner as their voyage continued, until a few days ago when the messages had stopped. Then tonight's message had turned up:

From The Bounty.

I fear there could be mutiny brewing, Captain. The crew are getting restless and short of temper. The weather continues fair but that only means there is nothing to distract them from their low murmuring. I think we should mount an around the clock watch.

My translator has gone on strike, she could even be the leader of this uprising. John continues unwell, which of course means Asha is not in a good mood either. When you look around the ship they all seem to be finding places as far away from one another as they can. I think floating on the ocean is getting to them, we might be better off swimming. Time I went back on watch, say prayers for us all. your loyal servant, Andrei.

Tracey didn't know what to make of that, so she wrote to Tilvy to see what she thought. Tilvy's response tried to be reassuring:

Hi Tracey, Don't panic! Andrei can go a little strange when he's cooped up for too long with nothing useful to do. Senna's probably just keeping out of his way.

Are you coming over here next weekend? love Tilvy.

Tracey hoped that Tilvy was right. She considered next weekend. She had stayed home this weekend hoping to go out with Mike but, too late for her to change her plans, he told her that his weekend was full: visiting his folks, studying and working nights. She wasn't going to waste another weekend like that, so she wrote back to tell Tilvy she would be there.

- - -

Andrei climbed back on deck, he had gone down intending to offer comfort to the infirm, but John was sleeping. Andrei looked to the starboard – he'd been studying his nautical terms online – and could see Asha there, staring out across the sea. Garjae was next to her. He decided not to disturb them, and looked around, still restless. Ah. There was Senna, standing like a figurehead at the tip of the bow, her often donned cap was missing and her hair streamed away to one side in the wind.

He made his way along the deck, careful to avoid the few crew. Apparently some of them knew of the existence of the narun, but none, other than Dengali, could sense their presence, and it wasn't approved of to get in the way of a hurrying seaman.

Coming up behind Senna, he reached forward and raised her arms out to the side with his.

"I'm King of the World!" he yelled. But his triumphant call was cut short as her arm jerked back and elbowed him in the side. It was not the usual gentle tap. "Ow!"

"I'm not in the mood, Andrei," she told him without looking back.

Andrei turned and sighed. Just like the Titanic, he'd sunk. He wasn't having much luck. Everything he did lately seemed to be wrong. When he tried to be affectionate she turned him away, when he tried to be funny she spurned him – sometimes very roughly, he rubbed his side.

He made his way back along the deck and was surprised to see Garjae leaning against the rail near the stern, his eyes down, looking glum. Apparently Andrei wasn't the only one having trouble finding compatible company.

"Thar she blows, me matey," Andrei said as he came up to Garjae's side.

"Where?" Garjae asked, looking out.

Andrei shrugged. "Bound to be somewhere."

"Why are we doing this, Andrei?" Garjae asked, not looking at him.

"What?"

"Chasing rumours around the world. Mixing with humans."

"I know why the rest of us are doing it," said Andrei. "Guess I'm not so sure about you."

Garjae glanced at him and then looked away. "You still gloating?"

"I prefer the word *basking*."

Garjae acknowledged this with a short chuckle. "You don't think it's all been a bit too easy?"

"You complaining?"

"No. Just wondering what it is these people want."

"Dengali seems nice," observed Andrei.

"But what's he want?" Garjae insisted. "John got sick before he got around to finding out very much. Are we sure they're going to help us? It's John they seem most interested in. What's to stop them taking John and leaving the rest of us to fend for ourselves when we get there?"

"Us, for a start," defended Andrei.

"What about the aaranya that Dengali left behind in Australia?"

"They wanted to stay, they wanted to keep contacting other Glades. Anyway, Dengali says he's going back for them eventually."

"I just think this is all a mistake."

"It's not like we dragged you away from anything more interesting."

Garjae didn't answer, just stared out with his face set in an unhappy expression.

Andrei tapped his fingers on the rail in a restless tattoo. "Where's Darnu?"

Garjae pointed. Giving Garjae up as a loss, Andrei decided to try his luck with Darnu.

A few days later, around midday, they approached the Myanmar coast. Dengali asked the aaranya to come together in a cabin below deck.

Dengali was a strange mix. Generally Asian in appearance, he was a sort of blend of people of many lands, but more heavily boned than most and of no very distinct origin. He appeared to be

46

somewhere around middle-age, and spoke English very well, but slowly, carefully enunciating his words. He seemed very well educated in many areas, and yet curiously ignorant of modern human customs. Most significantly, he could sense the aaranya. He couldn't see them or hear them as John could, but he could sense their presence over small distances. Friendly and very enthusiastic about meeting John, Dengali had quickly offered them assistance to get to Myanmar. Now, with John ill in his cabin, the aaranya could only speak to him via a tablet computer that he carried around for that purpose.

"At some stage after we arrive there will be men entering to search the ship," Dengali told them, "and it may be better if you are on deck at that time, and try your best to keep out of their way. To draw their attention could present great difficulties with the government."

"I know, I know," said Andrei, feeling the absence of John's regular reminders to behave himself, "that means me."

Oblivious to Andrei's input, Dengali continued, "After that we will dock, make some preparations, and then move you all to a house in the city."

Darnu acknowledged this with a quick, "OK," scribbled on the tablet.

It was very late in the afternoon by the time the promised inspection happened. Andrei watched with interest as Dengali haggled with one of the inspectors. It looked like money changed hands, not Australian money, but crisp green bills. The inspection was quickly over and John's slumber in the cabin below was not disturbed.

Apparently there was still much to be done after the inspectors had gone, so it was after midnight by the time Dengali fetched two of the crew to carry John up onto the deck and then to shore. The aaranya followed.

Near the dock was a vehicle. Andrei didn't know what else to call it. It had probably been a small truck at one point, but was now such a mass of repairs, deletions and additions that *vehicle* seemed the only appropriate description. The back was divided into an enclosed area near the cabin and an open tray at the back. John was lifted onto the tray and then into the enclosed back. After the crew had left, the aaranya got up and Asha hurried to try and make sure John was comfortable. He had barely stirred, obviously still very weak and unwell.

The truck was noisy and the fumes from its exhaust were thick and smelly. They saw very little of the city as they were driven through dark streets that were probably quiet, if they could have heard anything over the noise of the truck. Sometimes in the distance Andrei would catch sight of a golden spire lit up against the night, a stark contrast to the closer, mostly drab, rectangular buildings. Many buildings looked run-down, perhaps deserted. There were few people or other vehicles at this time of night. The only pleasing part of the trip, for Andrei, was that Senna held his hand in nervous anticipation, though she didn't speak to him.

Eventually the noisy truck pulled into the driveway of a house on a large block. Unfamiliar trees spread themselves wide to fill most of the yard, the two-storey house was almost lost amid their vigorous growth. When Dengali turned off the motor it was as if someone had suddenly removed walls of noise from around them.

Dengali got out of the cabin and came around to the back of the truck. "I apologise," he started, speaking much too loudly after the noise. "I apologise," he repeated more quietly, "for the noise of our conveyance, but it is old now and has had much use. This house we can use until we are ready to travel further. Make yourselves comfortable. These trees are available for your use, or you can travel more widely if you want. It is unlikely you will meet other aaranya near here." He proffered his writing pad in case there were questions.

On Asha's behalf, Darnu asked about John's accommodation.

"There should be a room prepared on the lower level," assured Dengali. "Let me assist you." He climbed onto the tray and entered the small cabin area with Darnu and Andrei. Together they carried John out to the tray at the rear. They were preparing to lift John down from the tray when they heard the front door of the house open. They all turned.

Andrei couldn't help himself, he stared. It was not that she was stunningly beautiful, although she was certainly elegant. She was a mature human, perhaps a few years older than John, with very straight and very black hair hanging to her shoulders. Chinese

48

perhaps, Andrei thought, though he was no expert on the subject. She had a slender but strong build and an erect, purposeful walk. Her face carried a slightly stern expression, but not unfriendly, and a smile formed slowly as she approached them. But none of this was what held Andrei silent with astonishment. It was the intensity of her presence. If it weren't for the evidence of his eyes, he might have thought it was a narun approaching them.

"Samv—" began Dengali, bowing.

The woman interrupted, speaking loudly over Dengali, "I am Doctor Jia Tou, but just Jia is fine, there is no need of formality among us. Ben sent me. He said that one of you was ill and may need my help before you could continue the journey." It was obvious that she could see them all. As she spoke she locked eyes with each of the aaranya in turn, her gaze came to rest on Asha, who was hovering over John.

"Thank you, Jia," Asha replied. "I'm Asha. John has been ill – seasick. He hasn't been able to eat or drink properly for many days."

Jia nodded. "Bring him inside and I'll take a look."

It was only when Asha nudged him that Andrei realised he was still staring at Jia. He realised that the others, too, had been struck dumb by the woman's appearance. Only Asha seemed unperturbed, too concerned about John to pay much attention. Still too surprised to say anything, Andrei helped to carry John into the house.

John was laid on one side of a large bed, in a room at the front of the house. The room was quite large for a bedroom. A fan hung, unmoving, from the centre of the high ceiling. On the polished wooden floor were a few small, thin rugs. The walls were a plain cream colour and in need of paint. The door to an en-suite bathroom had been left open.

Jia spoke softly with Dengali outside for a few moments before coming into the room. "You don't have to stay," she said dismissively to the aaranya, who were crowded, silent, near the bed.

Darnu and Garjae left the room, Senna hesitated and then followed them. Asha remained hovering by John's side, clearly not intending to leave. Andrei decided he would rather stay and watch.

"Please wait on the other side," Jia told Asha, and moved past her to take a closer look at John. A tray of equipment had already been laid out near the head of the bed. Jia went to work. Some of it

Andrei understood: taking John's temperature, checking his pulse, and so on. He even understood the blood pressure cuff, because he had seen such things on television shows. Other things the doctor did were more puzzling. Jia spent time tapping, pressing and pinching at various points around John's body, apparently testing his reactions.

"He is quite dehydrated," Jia said eventually. "We'll start him on some fluid."

Andrei watched in fascination as the doctor attached some sort of small tube to the inside of John's arm, and then joined that to a longer tube. This longer tube connected to a bag of clear fluid hanging from a stand. Andrei could see the drip, drip of the fluid in a small cylinder beneath the bag.

"A hell of a way to get a drink," Andrei observed.

Jia glanced over, apparently surprised that Andrei was still there.

"Will he be all right, doc?" Andrei asked.

Jia turned back to John before answering. "Yes, he should be ..." Her voice trailed off as she began to repeat some of her tests.

"Has he reported any disturbance with his vedana?" Jia asked Asha.

Andrei found it strange hearing a human, if that's what she was, speak of vedana.

"He was complaining about—" Asha paused. "He speaks of a crack inside his head that seems to be related to his vedana. The seasickness upset that somehow, and it made everything worse for him."

Jia nodded. "And you came from the tropics in Australia?"

"Yes."

"There are some diseases that can affect the vedana in humans," Jia explained. "This may be more than simple seasickness."

"He was fine before we got on the boat," Andrei put in.

"It takes time for most diseases to incubate," Jia answered without looking at him. "We need to get him back to my hospital so I can run some blood tests. For now I'll just give him something that might help to fight off whatever it is he's picked up." Jia turned back to her tray and selected a small bottle. With a syringe she extracted some of its contents, and then she injected the fluid slowly into the tube in John's arm."

50

"Is your hospital close?" Asha asked. "Can I be with him?" Her eyes had barely left John's face throughout the proceedings. Andrei thought she looked drawn and very tired.

"That is where we were taking you all, so of course you can stay with him. But it is not close, we will need to stabilise his condition before we move on." Jia studied John's face, as if trying to discover what Asha was seeing. "I don't think he is in any danger now. He should make some recovery just from the fluid and rest. I'll give him something now so that he will sleep more soundly for the rest of the night. But I still want to get him back to our hospital, there is nowhere else that can offer him any assistance with vedana related illnesses."

The doctor injected something more into John's intravenous tube and then carefully packed away much of her equipment. That done, she turned back and looked down at John again.

"If you need me, if anything seems to be wrong, you can find me in a room at the back of the house," Jia told Asha.

Asha nodded absently, not taking her eyes from John.

As Jia was leaving the room, Andrei spoke, "Doc?"

Jia stopped at the door and looked at him, an eyebrow raised in question.

What was he going to ask her? He wanted to ask her what she was, she didn't feel human, but that felt a little rude in the circumstances. At a loss for anything else, he said, "Thanks."

Jia nodded, smiled slightly, as if guessing his thoughts, and left. She closed the door behind her.

When Andrei looked back to the bed, Asha had gone back around the other side and was studying where the tube entered John's arm.

"Why don't you go out to one of the trees and get some rest?" Andrei asked her.

"I don't want to leave him alone," Asha said, not looking up.

"I'll watch him. You heard the doctor, he's supposed to sleep soundly now. Let me take the sleep watch so you can be with him when he wakes."

Asha looked up, her eyes were red. "I thought I'd been doing enough for him," she whispered. "I didn't think he was this bad." Asha indicated the tube entering John's arm.

"He's human, Asha. You can't know everything."

"I'm supposed to be some sort of healer."

"He's human," Andrei repeated. "He's a nice guy, but he is still human. Anyway, I think the doc is just being cautious, she doesn't seem that worried." He tried to sound reassuring, though he too had found all the proceedings with the doctor a bit of a surprise.

After a pause, Asha looked up at Andrei. "Don't you want to go out with Senna?"

Andrei shook his head. "This Romeo's been singing the wrong love songs lately, Juliet closed the window."

Asha smiled at him gently. "Anything you want to talk about?"

"Nah. We're back on land, she's bound to open up again soon. I think she likes my dry humour better."

"You don't *always* have to be on, Andrei."

Andrei shrugged. It wasn't like he could explain his compulsions.

"I would like to rest," Asha admitted. "I can't seem to think straight, nothing's making sense. If you're sure?"

"Go," Andrei insisted. "This is one audience I can't annoy." He stepped to the door and opened it, waiting to let her out.

Asha leaned over John, swept the hair from his forehead, and kissed him, first on the forehead and then on his lips. She whispered something that Andrei couldn't hear and then quickly left.

Andrei closed the door gently behind her and went to the bed. He sat up against the pillow beside John and looked down. John appeared to be sleeping peacefully. The drip was still dripping and the world outside was quiet. Andrei tapped his fingers on his leg, he was still restless.

"Well, John, we made it this far. What's next, do you think?"

John, predictably, made no response.

"So far so good, it seems to me. The natives are not only friendly, they even provide free medical care. At least, I suppose it's free." Andrei looked down again. "This wasn't in my plan though. You're supposed to be here to help us past all the human stuff. At least, I suppose they're human. That doctor's mighty odd. Pretty, in a severe sort of way – more your type than mine, I think – but still very odd."

Andrei slapped his hands against his thighs and jumped up. When he looked back he saw that he had rocked the bed. "Sorry," he whispered, and then paced around the room. He investigated the doctor's things, he checked out the drip, studied the few pieces of furniture in the room, even checked under the bed. "The cleaning staff have done a good job," he noted. It was only now that he realised the room was still brightly lit, all the lights had been turned on while the doctor studied John. He turned off the main lights, leaving just a dim bedside light glowing on John's side of the bed.

With all other activity apparently exhausted, Andrei climbed back onto the bed with John. He patted John on the arm. "Sorry if I rocked the boat a bit." He thought for a moment and then chided himself in an English accent, "I say, that was in poor taste, that man."

Andrei didn't know how much time had passed, it felt like a lot. The dark and quiet inspired him to start humming some classical music under his breath, something from a late-night horror movie he had watched back at John's house – The Return of the Abominable Dr Phibes Rises Again or something. Some noise or movement had him look across to the door, the handle was turning. At first he stopped humming, in fright, thinking he had somehow conjured up the horror movie, then he sensed who was on the other side of the door and grinned.

"Yes, yes," he spoke in deep sinister tones, a passable imitation of Vincent Price, even if he said so himself. "I call on you once more, Vulnavia, come, my trusted aide." He followed this with an eerie laugh.

Senna stared at him from the partly open door and hesitated. Oops, Andrei thought to himself, I've blown it again. Then Senna closed the door behind her and came across to him.

Reassured, Andrei continued in the same voice, "Thank you, my dear, for answering my call." Before he could get to the part about the Pharaoh's tomb, Senna had reached across and placed her hand over his mouth.

"You don't have to fill every silence," Senna whispered at him.

That was the second time he'd received such advice tonight, perhaps there was something in it.

Senna climbed up beside Andrei. "Is he asleep?" she whispered.

"Either that or doing a very good impersonation of a log," Andrei answered. "The doc gave him something to help him sleep through."

"You've got to come out and try these trees, they're amazing,"

Senna whispered. She pushed herself up against him.

I don't recall Shakespeare's Juliet being quite so forward, he thought, but said, "Can't now, I got the sleep watch. Can you ... are you staying?"

Senna kissed him, hard.

I'll take that as a yes, he thought.

- - -

Outside, Asha chose a tree close to the house but away from the others. Before she merged, she whispered to her arm until Casseta emerged – the brevi had been staying with Asha while John was unwell. "Go now, have some fun," she urged the creature and Casseta bounded off. Asha laid her hands gently against the trunk of the tree and felt the pulse of its life. She stayed like that for a few minutes trying to relax, trying to let her worry and sense of failure leach away before she merged. Then, slowly, she let her hands submerge into the flow and the rest of her body followed. At first the relief of merging with a familiar flow of life, after weeks atop the ocean, overwhelmed other sensations. She let her essence spread out, stretching after too long confined.

Later, after the latent hunger of her being had been assuaged, Asha began to notice other things about the tree she had entered. It was not as large as the trees of her home, and it branched widely in confusing currents of life, but it felt very healthy, active and intense, particularly for a tree growing away from a forest. Its life was effusive. There was an enthusiasm and abundance that contrasted sharply with the more sedate and conservative forests she grew up in. Against this intrusive energy it was difficult to relax. Eventually she did manage to find a quieter part of the flow and settled down to rest as best she could.

Sometime later she woke to feel a light mist wafting against her leaves and felt a restlessness in her roots as if impatient for the day to begin. Asha drew her essence more tightly together and emerged onto the ground beside the tree. As she often did, she left one hand partly merged for a few moments in a gesture of thanks.

Casseta joined her, the brevi had apparently been waiting, and quickly nuzzled her way back into Asha's arm. Fog had drifted in and there was the scent and feel of salt in the air. Normal vision was down to only a few yards. Closing her eyes, Asha touched the tree behind her again, sunrise was not far away. She made her way to the house and through the wooden front door. She opened the bedroom door and entered before she realised that Andrei and Senna were occupied and turned quickly away from them.

"It's okay," said Senna quietly, after a moment.

Asha gave them a moment more before she turned back in. "I didn't mean to interrupt," she apologised. Rather than dwell on it longer she looked across at John. "Has he woken?"

"No," said Senna. She looked, embarrassed, at John lying quiet beside them on the bed. "He's hardly moved."

"Thanks for watching him. You'd better go and get some rest yourselves."

The two of them left with grins on their faces, they had obviously forgiven each other for whatever had gone on between them on the boat. Once they were gone Asha sat gently on the edge of the bed and looked across at John. He really did look peaceful for the first time in weeks. She pulled herself across next to him and satisfied herself that all was well: the bag of fluid was well down but not yet empty, the drip still dripping steadily. She pushed a stray lock of John's dark hair out of the way and studied his face. Once again it was gaunt and pale skinned, but rough and dark with the beginnings of a beard.

Over the past eighteen months she had watched dramatic changes take place to John's demeanour and his build. He had started, not soft exactly, but rounded, gentle in form and expression. Asha remembered thinking, back then, that the apparent softness was hiding a greater strength. You could tell that it was there, but in the comfort of his home, and the love of his family, it had no need to exert itself. But then the loss of his wife, his entire family he'd thought at the time, had drained the softness from him and he began to waste away. When he and Asha had started to see each other he began to make a slow recovery, but then Asha had been imprisoned. When he had come to rescue her, his body was gaunt and bruised, but through that showed his true strength. It seemed that in finding her, John had also found himself. There had been uncertainties, and there would be more, but the quiet confidence that had been central to his character had mostly reasserted itself. Given more time, given more luck, he would eventually be whole again.

An unwelcome thought made Asha shudder. Could John survive losing Ellie for a second time? John thought Asha was doing all this because she loved Ellie, and she did, she loved her as if she were her own. But she had another reason too, one she only admitted to herself with great reluctance because of the selfishness it exposed: if she lost Ellie, she knew she would lose John too.

As she had been thinking, her hand had continued to absently stroke John's face and hair. She looked down and saw that his eyes were open, he was watching her with a small smile on his face. "A penny for your thoughts?" he asked in a croaky whisper.

"Is that all?" she whispered back with a look of mock disappointment.

A bigger smile, one that almost broke her heart with the love that it expressed. "How about everything I own?"

She leaned down and kissed his forehead. "That could be a bit extravagant."

John struggled to move and Asha realised he was trying to turn to face her. She helped him to turn, making sure the drip-feed tube didn't catch or tangle, John didn't seem to notice it. Asha pressed his head against her breasts, and rocked him gently in her arms. His arm wrapped around her tightly for a minute or so, and then his breathing steadied and she felt his grip relax as he drifted back to sleep. She kissed the top of his head and continued to rock him gently. "Sleep, my love," she whispered. Through her mind one thought repeated itself over and over: we must not fail, we cannot fail.

- - -

The sun was shining in the window when John woke to find himself still wrapped in Asha's arms, his arm still draped across her.

"You're awake," she said softly against the top of his head.

John wrapped his arm more tightly around her and pulled himself up to kiss her lips. He was surprised to find how much effort even this small activity took. He tried to think about how he'd come to be here, but his memories were hazy. He remembered the headaches, the nausea and the dizziness, but now all that felt distant. The crack in his head was no longer swishing noisily, as if caught in a storm, now it felt as if a gentle and warm breeze were caressing it. As the memories caught up with him he realised how long it must be since he had last showered or cleaned his teeth.

"I'm sorry," he muttered and started to turn away. "I must stink."

Asha just laughed and drew him back against her. "If you're well enough to worry about that you must be feeling better."

Self-conscious now, John withdrew from her embrace and started to try and get up. It was then that he noticed the tube in his arm. "What's this?" He glanced up at the stand holding the bag of fluid and then turned to look at Asha. There was a disconcerting view of the sunlit pillow *through* Asha, and he had to blink a few times before his vision cleared.

Asha explained about the doctor.

"And she can see you too?"

Asha nodded. "I got the impression that there may be others like her, wherever it is they're taking us."

There was a knock on the door. It opened and the doctor came in.

"You're awake," Jia observed.

Introductions were made.

"Jia, can you unhook me so I can have a shower?" John indicated the tube in his arm.

Jia raised her eyebrows and studied him carefully for a minute before answering. "I think another injection first." She made her way to her equipment and drew out some fluid into a syringe. As she slowly pressed it into the tube in his arm she continued, "It will be best if the fluid continues for another few minutes after this."

John felt a hot flush spread out across his body. "What is that stuff, Jia?"

"There is a chance you caught something nasty in the forests of northern Australia, I am hoping this will see you clear. Let me know if you experience any unusual symptoms."

John wondered what she meant.

"Do you think you will need help in the shower?" Jia asked.

"I'll help him," interjected Asha.

"As you wish," agreed Jia mildly. "I was thinking that Dengali could provide stronger support if John needed it – he would be less likely to fall."

Asha didn't respond, but the expression on her face was determined.

Jia asked John to lie back and she went through the same procedures as the previous night. When that was complete she detached the tube but left the cannula in his arm, explaining that it would make it easier to administer further injections if they were needed later. Jia left to organise some appropriate breakfast.

Asha helped John to stand. Together they walked slowly to the bathroom and Asha assisted John to shave and shower. By the time they were finished John was exhausted, though he felt better for being clean. Asha led him back to the bed and helped him to drink the liquid breakfast that Jia had prepared. Soon after he had finished, he drifted off to sleep again in Asha's arms.

John woke again in time for a light lunch, and felt well enough to sit up for a while. The aaranya all came into the room. Dengali and Jia had gone out to purchase supplies.

"Any guesses on what she is?" Andrei opened the conversation.

John looked carefully at his friend. There was something not quite right, as if Andrei wasn't all there or something. He shook his head to try and clear it.

"Are you okay?" Asha whispered in his ear.

John nodded.

"You haven't asked?" Garjae said to Andrei.

"I couldn't come up with a polite way to ask."

"Since when did you care about polite?" Garjae retorted.

"I am a master of taste and timing," Andrei said in indignant tones, "thank you very much."

Garjae snorted.

"Maybe you can find out, John?" Darnu said.

"Find out what exactly?" John wanted to know, he still wasn't sure what they were talking about. As he looked around he thought all his friends felt a bit ... thin. Only Asha, her presence intense beside him, felt right, complete. The change, whatever it was, was disturbing and distracting.

"The doctor, John. She's a bit odd," said Senna from beside Andrei.

"She has a very strong presence, John," Asha explained. "She doesn't feel entirely human."

"Or not just human," added Darnu.

"You might want to pick your time," said Andrei. He picked up a

58

large syringe from the doctor's things. "While she's coming at you with this may not be the best time to ask if she's human."

"And while you're at it, find out what plans they have for us," said Garjae. "Where are they taking us?"

That evening John suggested Asha should go out to the trees with the other aaranya while he ate dinner with Dengali and Jia in the dining room. The first course of soup had really sparked his appetite, he looked on hungrily as Jia presented him with a small serving of rice, it was served with a spicy chicken and vegetable dish.

"My compliments to the chef," John said when he was finished, "that was delicious."

Jia bowed her head demurely. "Thank you."

Now that his hunger was satisfied, John remembered that he was supposed to be finding out what he could about Jia, and where they were going. He looked back and forth between Dengali and Jia. He thought he could sense some of what Asha had meant about Jia's strong presence, though it didn't feel so distinct as to cause him any great wonder. He didn't know how to ask what she was, so he thought to try the easier part first.

"What happens now?" John asked, looking at Dengali. "Do I have to go somewhere to sign papers to get a visa or something?"

Dengali looked uncomfortable. "Your entry into this country was not exactly ... orthodox."

"You mean, I'm here illegally?"

Dengali shrugged. "This country no longer pursues the isolationist policies of previous decades, it accepts tourists readily enough."

"But?"

"But not without papers showing how you arrived."

"So where does that leave me?"

Jia interjected, "We can provide paperwork that will be adequate once we move inland, but until we move on it will be as well to maintain a low profile."

John decided not to ask where such paperwork came from, instead he asked, "When will we be moving on? And where to?"

Dengali looked to Jia, who in turn studied John. "I am concerned about your condition, John," Jia said eventually. "Are you sure you haven't had any disturbances in your vedana?"

John tried to recall that feeling of unease from earlier in the afternoon, but it eluded him. "I don't think so."

Jia got up and came around the table to stand beside John. She felt his forehead and looked into his eyes. "I'm still concerned. I'll take you back to bed now and give you another booster shot and something to help you sleep." She turned to Dengali. "I think you should organise things to start our journey as soon as possible, I want to get John back where we can study this properly."

As John drifted off under the influence of whatever it was that Jia had given him, he realised that he hadn't managed to get the answers he wanted. He would have to try again tomorrow.

A dream disturbed his sleep, but this one felt more like a memory. He was speaking with Asha across the kitchen table in his home, admiring her beauty while she spoke to him. She was telling him things that he hardly believed. "The change isn't always permanent," Asha was saying to him. He was staring at her, trying to understand what she meant, and feeling as though the words were prophetic – and ultimately tragic.

He woke to bright sunshine coming through the bedroom window, and Asha's comforting presence beside him, holding him, touching him. He looked down at his arm, expecting to see her slender fingers resting there – but there was nothing! He pulled back with a start and turned to look at her. His vision flickered: sunshine and pillow, Asha, sunshine, Asha ... Asha. He stared at her in fright, his heart beating wildly.

"What is it, my love?" Asha asked, her voice soft, but urgent with concern.

John reached forward and stroked the side of her face to confirm that she really was there. She looked faded, like a photograph left too long in the sun. He remembered, now, the feelings from yesterday as he looked at his other friends, and he remembered Jia's constant querying of his vedana. This must be what she was expecting.

"I'm losing my sight," he whispered, barely daring to speak the words.

Asha looked back at him, silent, not understanding.

"You're fading from my sight," he repeated.

"Vedana?" she queried.

John nodded.

"I'll get the doctor," Asha responded. She had rolled back and off the bed before John had a chance to stop her. He didn't want her to go, he was worried he would never see her again.

Jia came into the room, dressed in a light dressing gown that emphasised the strong figure underneath. John breathed a sigh of relief when he could still see Asha as she came back in – faded, less substantial than she should be, but still there.

"Asha says your vedana is disturbed?" Jia queried.

"It's like Asha is fading from my sight. It started yesterday, with the others, but the effect was so subtle I didn't connect it to what you had been asking me."

"Can you still hear them?"

John turned to Asha, who came to the side of the bed and said quietly, "I'm here, my love."

John smiled and nodded. He turned to Jia, "There may be some fading in what I hear, but the change is not so obvious as with my sight."

Jia had already prepared a syringe and asked John to lie back while she slowly injected it.

John felt his body flush warm as the injection took effect. He turned his head and watched Asha. Like some magical studio special effect, her faded appearance deepened until at last she looked as she usually did. He smiled at her. "You're coming back."

Asha slid carefully onto the bed and touched his face.

"Whatever that stuff is, Jia," John said without looking away from Asha, "it seems to be working."

"Hmm," Jia agreed vaguely. "Good."

They weren't able to leave until the next day. Jia encouraged John to get some exercise to try and regain his strength. John asked Dengali to accompany him on a gentle walk. Asha, reluctantly, let John go while she went to rest in one of the trees.

John and Dengali wandered the streets at a slow walk. At least it was flat, John thought to himself, he wasn't up to hill climbing yet. He was still feeling weak and even this quiet walk was an effort. To John it felt like the city around them had been carried forward from the past, that it had lived through many years in some sort of stasis. There were small pieces of a more modern world laid over this historic city, but those pieces looked alien and out of place.

John didn't even recognise the language or languages being spoken. Most of the people looked bright and friendly, John thought it sad that he knew so little about them. He tried asking Dengali something of the people and the area, but Dengali replied, "I am sorry, John, I am a poor guide. I rarely stay here long."

They passed a spired pagoda, and that prompted John to ask about Dengali's religion.

"Much of this country is Buddhist, or Buddhism mixed with nat worship."

"Gnats?" John asked, "Like little wasps?"

Dengali explained, "Nats are spirits. There are the Great Nats, and many others, many local to a village or place – spirits of trees and water and so on. Of course, being aware of the narun, my own people do not worship nats."

"But your people are still Buddhist?"

"No."

John didn't pursue the subject further, Dengali seemed reticent to speak of his beliefs, and John didn't want to offend him.

"What about Jia?" John asked eventually. Having contrived to get Dengali on his own, John had hoped to find answers to questions that somehow never got asked when Jia was present.

Dengali glanced at him in question.

"My friends feel that she is different," John noted. "But we haven't known how to ask."

"Samv-" Dengali stopped himself, and then started again, "Doctor Jia Tou is one of the special people. You will need to ask her, or ... Benjamin, when you meet him."

John felt the awkwardness in Dengali's normally careful speech, this conversation was making him uncomfortable for some reason.

"But Asha, and the others, say she feels different," John insisted.

Dengali shrugged, and repeated, "She is one of the special people."

John didn't know what to make of Dengali's response, it wasn't an answer. He shrugged and moved on to the next question. "What am I getting my friends into, Dengali?"

They kept walking but Dengali looked across at him. "What do you mean?"

"I think you know. You were very pleased to find me, and even more pleased to escort me back to here – and further. But this isn't some casual pick up of a hitch-hiker, you've made a special trip just for me. We needed to get here so I didn't make a big deal of it before now, but before we go further I'd like some assurances, particularly with regard to my friends. What is it that you actually want of us?"

"Your concern was anticipated," said Dengali.

"And?"

"As we discussed when we met, the aaranya near my people are concerned about losing contact with Glades far to the north-east, and now some even closer. That is how we came to be in Australia. I was helping the aaranya to travel there – to spread the news of these strange events, and to receive what news they could from the Glades of that land."

John nodded, he'd heard all this.

"But my people have always been interested in meeting humans that are aware of the narun, so finding you was serendipitous. Benjamin was very excited, he very much wants to meet you. That is all we want, that is why we have been happy to assist you to come to our country."

John wondered if his questions made him sound ungrateful, but pressed on, "He could have come to meet me here, as Jia has."

"It is our firm belief that our interests coincide. You are searching for a healer and want to contact Glades in our country. We can assist you in that endeavour, especially those nearer to our home."

John nodded. "This is sounding better and better – for us – but is all this help just for the pleasure of meeting me?"

"Finding someone of your capabilities is very rare," Dengali answered.

John shook his head, not quite believing it, and started walking again. Dengali followed. John thought about what Dengali had told him. The lack of certainty bothered him. He had no idea if he could trust Dengali or his *special* people, whoever – whatever – they turned out to be. And even if he could trust them, if everything Dengali had told him so far was the literal truth, there were still huge gaps in his understanding of where this was headed. John had unconsciously picked up his pace as the frustration of his thoughts increased.

"John!" called Dengali.

John slowed, then paused and looked around.

"If you are ready to return to the house you need to go that way," Dengali pointed to a street that John had just walked past.

John nodded his thanks and walked in the direction indicated. His thoughts picked back up, but from the other side of the argument. Could they really afford to try and do this on their own? Just where would they go? He didn't speak the languages. None of them knew the region. Hell, he was in this country illegally, just walking away wasn't really an option. Wasn't it true that they really did need Dengali and his people? Andrei's earlier advice still seemed to hold good: they needed local help. Added to all that, John reminded himself, were the problems with his vedana. Where else could he find the help that Jia so freely offered? To have found exactly the sort of medical help he needed, just when he needed it was – what was the word Dengali had used? – serendipitous. It was good fortune that almost beggared belief.

John slowed his walk until Dengali was walking beside him. "Sometimes the natives really are friendly," said John.

"Pardon?"

"Nothing. We've trusted you this far, Dengali, and you've given us no cause to doubt you. We need your help – *I* need your help."

* * *

John didn't remember very much of the journey into the north of the country. He was conscious of the noise and smell of the truck during the days, and the relative quiet and peace of the nights. He was aware of the lush broad valley where they started, and then days later the intense green growth of the mountain jungles, and the water – more water than seemed credible to anyone that had grown up in southern Australia. All these things John knew, not for himself, but from the aaranya and how they reacted to their journey. Throughout the journey his mind, his every waking moment, was concentrated on his friends.

He would wake each morning in alarm, the feeling of loss hard upon him. Only Asha's presence, the firm hold of her hands, the warm embrace of her arms, kept him from crying out his despair.

He would wait impatiently for Jia to rise and inject the drug that would restore his vedana. A warm rush and then Asha would appear before him as if someone slowly turned up the light that illuminated only her. Moments later the others would begin to show. The truck would continue its noisy journey again and John would look from friend to friend, trying to cement their images in his mind. As the day progressed his friends would begin to fade from his sight until, as night approached, they were little more than obscure flickers at the edge of his sight, and he would wait impatiently for his next dose of the drug that would return to him those that had become his life.

Each day John's vedana would be worse when he woke than it had been the day before. Each day the recovery was less when Jia injected more of her drug. And each day the fading progressed more quickly as the day grew old. Sound had been slower to go. John could hear Asha's voice even when he could no longer see her at all, but each day even that receded. Soon he would be left with only touch. He had almost begged Jia to let him have more of the drug. He felt like a heroin addict pleading for his next hit, but Jia was firm that he could have no more until they reached their destination.

John knew that Andrei and Senna were keeping up their email contact with home, using Dengali's satellite link, but he had little to add for himself, he didn't know what he could say. He wrote just often enough to try and keep Jason from getting upset by the lack of news. It was ironic, John thought, that he had told Jason he had come to Asia to find a cure for what had gone wrong with his head. It was supposed to have been a lie. But now it seemed that it was exactly what he had found, a cure that he did not want.

John didn't try to count the days. One day, shortly after midday, Dengali stopped the truck where the road had been widened into a clearing. They were on a ridge that overlooked a long valley stretching away to the east of them. Silence fell around them, only slowly replaced as the wildlife of the forest began to make itself heard. Dengali climbed from the truck and called to those on the back, "I thought you might enjoy this view."

John and the aaranya got off the truck and followed Dengali and Jia to the edge of the road. Together they looked out across the valley. It was certainly a beautiful sight, thought John. The sounds of the birds and other wildlife came to him across the distance, and the exhaust fumes blew away and made room for the smells of the jungle. He breathed deeply and sighed.

He looked to his friends, already they were fading, translucent to his sight. He moved closer to Asha, placing one arm around her for the comfort it gave him.

Asha leaned into him. "Can you feel it, my love? Close your eyes."

John tried to let what remained of his vedana expand, and sensed out into the valley. He still found enough of his life sense that he could feel the jungle, like an immense sea of life spread before them. But this sea was warmer and more comforting than the sensations he had felt on the ocean. It didn't swirl and swish around in the dizzying fashion of ocean currents, it was steady and calming. It breathed and pulsed like some huge, mountain sized creature. Sparks of intensity marked particular patches of the forest. And there was something more, something he couldn't quite work out. It felt like there was something bigger, something underlying the sea of life that filled the valley. He opened his eyes and looked at Asha, but she was lost to her other senses.

John heard, very faintly, Darnu murmur, "Gayatri, I never thought to feel her so near."

John looked to Dengali, who walked up to him and spoke quietly. "Your friends like this place?" he asked.

John nodded but looked puzzled.

"I thought that you would sense it too."

"I do feel something," said John, "but I don't understand it."

"Gayatri," said Dengali.

"What's that?"

"Gaia; mother-earth. There are some places in the world that seem nearer to her than others, where she is more exposed. This valley is one of those places."

"Oh ..." murmured John, and looked out in wonder. He closed his eyes again and tried harder to understand the sensation he had of something beneath the life of the valley, but he couldn't make it any clearer.

After John had finished eating his lunch, he and Asha walked a small distance from the truck and stood with their arms around each other, looking out over the valley. They stood that way for a few minutes, not speaking, and then Asha pulled back and looked up at John with a speculative expression.

"What?" he asked quietly.

Asha didn't answer. She murmured to her arm until Casseta appeared. The brevi sat upright and looked out across the valley, as enraptured by the experience as the aaranya had been.

"I was thinking," Asha spoke at last, "that maybe Cassey should be staying with you. Maybe she can help more than those drugs the doctor keeps giving you."

John hadn't thought of it like that. He had missed Cassey's presence in his body, but she hadn't returned to him since they had landed. He put his arm out and the brevi ran across and up to his shoulder. She twittered softly in his ear. He turned to her, rubbed his lips gently into her fur, and told her softly how much he had missed her. John lifted his arm higher and continued to murmur to Cassey, trying to convince her to merge with his body. The brevi moved onto his arm and put her nose down against his forearm. She began to nuzzle as if she intended to merge, but quickly pulled back again and twittered loudly – to John, she sounded annoyed or alarmed. Casseta leapt from his arm and landed on Asha's breast, ran quickly upward and then merged into Asha's shoulder without waiting to be greeted or comforted.

John and Asha stared at each other, at a loss for words.

4. Samgha

The last part of their journey was very slow. The road wound itself through the jungle and deteriorated into little more than a vague, twisting path that was less overgrown than the rest of the forest. The day was almost over when they emerged at the top of a gentle slope. Beneath them was a clearing that contained a small village.

On this side of the clearing was a patchwork of fields. Beyond the fields was the collection of dwellings. These were open timber and bamboo houses with thatched roofs, all on raised platforms. It was, mostly, much like the other villages they had passed along the way through these mountains.

Beyond the village the forest began to close in again but was quickly interrupted by a tall cliff face, it reached up over twice the height of the tallest forest trees. The late afternoon sun shone brightly against the exposed rock, and faint lines of greenery revealed ledges in the face where lichens and creepers from the forest were doing their best to gain a footing. The lower ramparts of the cliff were obscured from John's current perspective by the narrow bank of trees near its base.

Dengali stopped the truck at the top of the slope. They all got out and approached the village on foot. Dengali breathed deeply of the air. "This is my home," he said.

"So this is it, this is the end of our journey?" John asked.

"Almost," Dengali replied. He pointed across to the cliffs. "There."

They walked into the village and a short, stout woman ran out from between the dwellings and almost threw herself at Dengali. "Dengy, Dengy, Dengy," she kept repeating as she smothered him with kisses.

Dengali looked like he wasn't sure whether to be embarrassed or pleased.

"They didn't tell me you were coming back so soon!" she accused him. She stood back and looked him over carefully. "Is everything all right?"

Dengali assured her that everything was fine. She turned her attention to John, and then looked at Asha, who was standing next to John holding his hand. She looked to each of the others and then back at John and Asha. She queried her husband, "Samvaya?"

Dengali glanced around and saw that Jia had kept walking, apparently not paying attention to them. "Not now," he said quietly. Turning to John he said, "John, this is my wife, Resineta." To his wife, "This is John. He is from Australia."

John wasn't sure of the appropriate etiquette, so just gave a slight bow. "Pleased to meet you, Resineta. Can you see my friends? Should I introduce you?"

"Oh, no," she mumbled, and looked down, embarrassed. "I didn't mean to stare."

"You weren't staring, it was just apparent that you knew they were there. I wasn't sure ..." John stopped with an apologetic shrug.

"I don't mind being introduced, if it'll stop you two apologising to each other," put in Andrei.

John laughed, and then had to explain. Since he was doing that he ended up introducing his companions. "I've never gotten around to asking Dengali," John continued, "but can you tell my companions apart? I mean, now you've been introduced, would you recognise them again?"

Resineta seemed hesitant to answer so Dengali explained. "I could not tell your friends apart unless I was touching them, and even then my senses are not totally reliable. My wife hesitates," he looked at her with affection and pride, "in order to spare my feelings. She is quite exceptional among my people, and much more sensitive than I. I believe she is not far from being able to see them. She would easily recognise your friends at this distance."

John felt a twinge. This late in the day his own senses were not much better; his friends were not much more than hazy figures to his sight, barely visible. Only Asha, close by his side, her presence ever strong in his mind whatever his other senses may report, felt real to him. Her hand in his was a tangible link that he clung to ever more tightly as she faded from his sight.

"Resineta asked if I was ... Samvaya? What is that?" John asked.

"It is best that others explain," said Dengali.

A young man came up behind Resineta. The resemblance was obvious, though the young man was taller than either of his parents.

"This is Reyndani, my eldest son," Dengali said.

The young man nodded his head at John and then the others.

"He has inherited his mother's talents, for which I am most grateful," Dengali explained.

"But my husband's intelligence," added Resineta, "for which I am grateful."

Dengali explained to his wife that they had to keep moving and she reluctantly let them go.

"She speaks English very well," observed John.

"Most of this village have at least a smattering of English, and some families, like mine, make a point of using English as much as we can so that we can more easily converse with the outside world."

"I wouldn't have thought they'd see much of the outside world from here," said Senna, her voice coming to John faded, as if overheard from a distance.

They came out from the village and followed a well-maintained path across a clear area toward the trees beneath the cliffs. There were buildings partly hidden under the trees. The buildings didn't look new, but they appeared to be more modern in construction than the huts of the village.

They followed the path past the buildings and beneath some trees from where they could see the base of the cliff. A sort of embankment had been formed by centuries of debris falling from the cliff, and a scattering of fallen rocks, both large and small, marked it out as a potentially dangerous place to stand. Despite the apparent danger, the well-worn path led up this embankment. Standing at the top, still and silent, was a man. Jia stood beside the man, looking suddenly slight and frail in comparison.

Dengali had walked a few paces before he realised that the others had all stopped, he looked back to see what was wrong.

John stopped because he was struck by the man's appearance. The man's skin was that of a well tanned European rather than the more typically Asian tones that John had seen since entering this country. Like Dengali, this man was attired in Western clothing, trousers and shirt, rather than the skirt-like longyi used by most villagers. But there was more. The heaviness of bone that John noted in Dengali and the others was much more pronounced in this man. A heavy brow-ridge extended across his forehead, and there was a heaviness of jaw and shape to his head that seemed, to John, to be very primitive. He was short and stocky, and his stance, with arms held away from his sides, demonstrated that the same heaviness and strength of build continued beneath his clothes. Even considering the obvious strength of the rest of his body, the man's hands were huge – massive paws dangling from his wrists.

Everything, the stance, the strength, the strangely primitive head and face, cried out in warning to John: here was an alien, an aggressive stranger, here was someone he had to defend against. Before he was aware of what he was doing, John had stepped in front of Asha and assumed a slight crouch as if expecting an attack.

The man laughed, a deep, echoing sound that filled the space between them. "Old instincts die hard I see," he called to them.

Only now did John recognise the smile on the man's face, revealing teeth as substantial as the rest of him. The voice, deep and powerful as it obviously was, managed to convey a friendly aspect to the man. John slowly straightened and relaxed slightly. He turned to look at the others, but his fading vedana only permitted him to read the expression on Asha's face. She didn't look frightened, but she did look surprised and awed. "What?" he asked her quietly.

"What is he?" she asked.

When John looked puzzled she added, "His presence, John. He feels even more like a narun than Jia."

John tried to see what she was saying, but his fading vedana couldn't feel any difference.

"Is it all right if I come down now?" the man asked, aware of the impact he'd had on all of them.

John looked at his friends, they had unconsciously drawn closer together.

"You don't have to wrestle him as proof of worthiness do you?" Andrei asked John.

"Not unless you want to," boomed the man's voice, accompanied by another deep laugh.

"That answers one question," said Darnu, "he can hear us."

"It wasn't the one I had in mind," said Senna.

The man walked slowly down the path. Asha stepped around John's protective stance and looked at the stranger carefully. "What are you?" she asked.

John barely caught Senna's murmured, "That's the one."

"Ha, that is an interesting question. Dengali, what would you say I am?" Much closer now, the man spoke quietly, conscious of the deep volume of his voice.

"Samvaya," said Dengali with a deferential nod of his head.

"I don't think that's quite what our friends are looking for."

Dengali looked puzzled.

The man reached the bottom of the embankment and stood still. He held his hands out in as submissive a gesture as his body seemed capable. "I am human – mostly," he said. "For proof I offer Dengali. He is a cousin. What is it Dengali, second cousins or something?"

"First cousin, once removed," said Dengali with the same deference.

"Close enough. As for the rest ... it gets complicated. I'd rather we found somewhere more comfortable to sit and talk about it. I came out to meet you to avoid such surprises in enclosed spaces. Believe me, John, your initial reaction is quite usual."

"I apologise for that, but ..." John didn't quite know how to finish.

The man laughed. "No worries. Isn't that what your people say? It is a very old instinct, you'll understand better after we've talked more. Ah, that is rude of me. I've not introduced myself. I'm Benjamin. You'll hear some call me Samvaya Benjamin but just Ben is fine." His great right hand was held forward in greeting.

John hesitated, surprised by many things, not least the name. He had been expecting something different, alien like the man's appearance.

"Don't worry, John, I'll be gentle," Ben chuckled quietly.

Embarrassed at his own rudeness, John reached out and shook hands. Ben's large hand almost swallowed his, but as promised the handshake was gentle. Ben greeted Asha warmly, seeming to linger over their handshake, and then he moved along and introduced himself briefly to each of the others.

"Now then. Are you happy to come with me into the Samgha?" In response to John's puzzled expression Ben went on to explain, "We call our home here the Samgha," he pointed to the cliffs, "we also refer to ourselves, our central group of samvaya, as the Samgha."

"So there are others like you?" asked Darnu.

"Some, but no longer very many. Physically we are a diverse group, though none of the others now have features quite as distinct as my own. But to your vedana most of us, the ones referred to as samvaya, will feel quite similar. You've already met Jia." He indicated the doctor still standing at the top of the embankment. "Come along, time is passing and it will be dark soon."

They followed Ben and Dengali along the path up the embankment to Jia, and then they walked along the line of the cliff for some distance. At the back of the group, Garjae stared up at the rock face as they walked. "I wonder if they have a special word for falling rock?"

"Ouch?" suggested Andrei.

Ben chuckled and said, "It looks more dangerous than it is."

The path became a ledge on the cliff that rose slowly. As they gained some height the trees formed a loose green curtain on one side, the granite cliff-face remained a hard grey wall on the other. The sun was sinking below the horizon and fingers of light, red and gold, filtered through the canopy of the forest. Above the line of the tree tops, the cliff face glowed a deep red in the sunset.

Not long before they would have reached the same height as the forest canopy, the path widened and then disappeared into a fold in the cliff-face. John followed Ben into this fold and found an immediate turn that opened into a tunnel leading deeper into the cliffs. The first twenty metres was lit only by the indirect light from the entrance, a blood-red of the disappearing sun. The corridor turned slightly and subtle interior lighting took over, not bright but adequate. The light came from patches of rock that glowed.

Outside the temperature had been warm and humid, not the swelter of the south, but enough to ensure that any exercise worked up some sweat. As they got deeper into the tunnel the temperature dropped noticeably and John shivered as the dry, fresh and cool air of the corridor swept over him. And corridor it was, he realised. This was no primitive mountain cave, this was a very human looking passageway that just happened to be carved in what appeared to be faultless natural rock.

The corridor descended gently at first and then levelled out. After that John had little sense of rising or falling or turning. When he looked into the distance, either way, it was apparent that the tunnel was not straight, but its contours were subtle. He had no idea just how far they had come or where they were relative to where they had started, but it felt like a long way. Asha had, at first, clung to him, venturing underground like this was too much like the months she had spent in the cavern prison. Then, slowly, the texture of the rock around them changed and Asha began to relax.

"Do you feel it too?" asked Asha.

"I feel ... something," he admitted.

"It's Gayatri," she said.

"Indeed," Ben agreed from in front of them, "our mother watches over us here."

"Would anyone like to explain it to me?" asked John.

"Soon, John," assured Ben. "Let us get comfortable first."

The corridor began to meet with others, some branching off at strange angles. There seemed little logic to the layout.

They saw a few people along the way, but other than deferential nods toward Ben, no conversations were started. The people he saw reminded John of Dengali more than Ben, certainly no one else had the same visceral impact on his senses that Ben had.

Ben walked them past an opening into a large hall. John caught only a brief glimpse of many people that had gathered to eat. "We'll start in more private quarters," was Ben's only explanation.

Not far past the hall they turned down another corridor and then Ben ushered them into a large room. The ceilings were a little higher here than in the corridor and sculpted with irregular patterns. Here and there a patch of the ceiling glowed, providing a soft warm light that filled the room. The walls were decorated with large, bright tapestries, most were a blend of natural and abstract scenes. The scenes suggested something of the forest outside, though the imagery was often obscure and sometimes, and quite strangely John thought, gave the impression of violence. The furniture in the room was a mix of soft lounge chairs, sofas and a few wooden pieces. There was a low table in the centre of the room. For what John could only think of as a cave, the room would have felt very cosy if it wasn't for the disturbing imagery of the tapestries.

Ben spent a few minutes arranging the furniture to try and make it comfortable for everyone to sit and speak as a group. His immense strength was apparent in the easy way he moved even the heavier items.

"Some food for myself and John," Ben said to Dengali.

Dengali bowed his head and left.

John looked down at his hand clasping the vague outline of Asha's warm hand. He looked up at Jia, feeling more like a drug addict than ever as he pleaded, "I know it's early, Jia, but could I ...?" He held up his arm. "I feel so blind."

Jia looked to Ben, who nodded.

Indicating that John should sit, Jia opened her bag and prepared the injection.

The warmth spread through his body and John stared eagerly at Asha as she became clear to his senses, a reassuring visual confirmation of her presence. She smiled up at the relief on his face. Soon his other friends appeared too. Andrei waved at him and grinned, John smiled back.

"It's not you he wanted to see," John heard Senna whisper to Andrei. It reminded John just how much he had been missing of their interactions in recent days.

"Thank you," John told Jia as she finished up and packed her bag, "very much."

Jia smiled at him. There was sympathy in her expression, but also distraction.

"You should probably check in at the hospital," Ben told her. "I'll entertain our guests."

Jia nodded to Ben and then the aaranya. To John she said, "I'll see you in the morning for another booster shot. Tomorrow we can make a start at getting on top of it."

"How long might that take?" John asked.

Jia studied him briefly in silence, and then answered, "It is difficult to say, but it will probably take several weeks of treatment, perhaps more." She glanced at Ben and then back to John. "I will see you in the morning." She turned quickly and left the room.

John stared after her, stunned. Several weeks!

Ben waited for the door to close behind her and then settled back in his chair. "Is everyone comfortable? If there's anything anyone wants, just ask."

The door to the room opened again and Dengali came in carrying a tray that he sat on the table between Ben and John.

"If you will excuse me," Dengali said, interrupting John's still dazed thoughts, "I am going to return to the village for now, to spend some time with my wife."

John stood and shook his hand warmly. "Thank you, Dengali, for taking such good care of me, of all of us."

"It was a most propitious meeting, John. I have been pleased to be of service." With that Dengali nodded once more to the occupants of the room and left.

"A good lad that one," said Ben after Dengali had gone. "A trifle formal, perhaps, but that's to be expected with our educational environment I think." He sat forward in his chair and poured water from a jug into two glasses. He handed one to John and raised his own. "To your good health," he toasted.

"I'll definitely drink to that," John agreed, and took a deep swallow of the clean, cold water.

"Don't you worry," Ben assured him. "It may take some time, but Jia will see you right." Ben looked to Asha and then Darnu and the others. "I hope you will excuse us eating while we talk, but John and I have material bodies that must be sustained."

John followed Ben's lead in filling a small plate with cold cuts of meat and salad from the tray. The meat smelt and tasted like pork, but the salad items were unfamiliar.

Ben watched as John sampled the items. "Not exactly traditional Burmese cuisine, but convenient for an improvised meal. You approve?" he asked.

"Very good," John said. "I assume this is all local produce."

"Yes. We carry in some luxuries, but we're long used to catering for our own needs in the way of fresh food."

Ben looked to Asha. "Perhaps, while John and I eat, you could tell me more of how you all came to be here. Dengali has passed on some of it, but I would like to hear it from yourselves."

John listened as Asha, and at times Darnu, gave Ben a brief explanation. It was apparent from Asha's terse phrasing that she was wary of Ben, and she offered little that they hadn't already told Dengali. The tale ended with the journey by ship and John's illness.

Putting down his now empty plate, Ben asked John, "Other than the problems with your vedana, you are well now?"

"Yes, I think so," John answered. He'd spent so much time worrying about the loss of his vedana that he hadn't really thought about anything else.

Asha corrected him, "John has still not regained his strength after the stress of the sea journey, and there is more. I can't tell what it is, but his body is struggling against something."

"And you are the one that would know," Ben said, looking at her with interest.

Asha just shrugged, not ready to open up further.

"Never mind, Jia will get on top of it," Ben assured her.

John put down his plate and sat back on the sofa. Asha curled up against him and her arms wrapped around his – possessively, defensively, it seemed to John. He broke the stretching silence, "You have very large and elaborate – I was going to call them tunnels, but I can't think of an appropriate word that really does them justice."

Ben shrugged. "It has been the work of a great many generations. Modern appliances, particularly the lighting and refrigeration, have made a big difference. Things are easier to maintain now – which is as well, there are so few samvaya left. The lighting down here was installed mainly for the benefit of those like Dengali, for ourselves it is not essential."

John raised his eyebrows in question.

"Down here we are protected and nurtured in the care of our mother, Gayatri. Vedana is all you need to find your way."

John looked to Asha.

She shrugged. "He may be right, although I think it could take some time to get used to."

"It's got to cost you a lot to maintain all this," said John, "especially when you're so far away from everything. It would cost a lot just in transport."

"We have been around a long time and accumulated resources – the Lord has been good to us."

"You're Christian?" asked John, surprised.

Ben laughed. "Not exactly, although we are familiar with Christianity."

"So your religion is something based on Christianity?"

Ben laughed even more loudly. "Based on Christianity? I shouldn't laugh, of course, you are not to know. Christianity is just a fledgling, little more than a rowdy child. Our history, like that of the narun, goes back much further than any offered by your people."

Ben's expression became more earnest as he continued, "We do believe in one God, the Lord and giver of Life here on blessed Gayatri, but ours is rather more tangible than the Christian God." With these words Ben unbuttoned the front of his shirt revealing a broad, well tanned and darkly haired chest. Hanging from a chain around his neck was a large gold medallion in the shape of a flattened orb. Its circular edge was delicately shaped to the appearance of curved flares, and the convex curve of the orb was a mass of swirls like satellite images of savage storm cells.

"The sun?"

Ben nodded. "The Sun. The giver of Life. The source of all prana. The father of all life here on our mother Gayatri."

"You said you believed in one God," said Senna, "but you speak of Gayatri with equal reverence."

"Yes, Senna. One God and one Goddess. The eternal balance maintained, even in the heavens."

"And the moon?" asked Andrei.

"Troublemaker," murmured Darnu.

"Our beliefs, our religion, if you want to call them that," said Ben with a smile, "see the moon as a sister to Gayatri, but has never raised her to the same status. She is revered, but as a lesser being, a little sister if you will. She has not mothered life herself, though she obviously influences the life that exists on Gayatri."

"A doting maiden aunt?" suggested Andrei.

Ben laughed.

"And the other planets and the stars?" asked John.

"They have a place, yes, but not as significant as many human beliefs give them. Our people have always been aware of prana, of life, and so our faith has always concentrated on those things that truly affect life. We have never tried to read patterns in the pseudo-random ramblings of the more distant heavenly bodies."

"Take *that*, astrology," said Andrei.

Ben smiled at him. "We are not competitive."

"You don't feel human," said Garjae abruptly.

The others fell silent. They'd all been thinking it, but had been reluctant to open this line of conversation.

"I am a bit of a throwback," Ben admitted with a smile. "But DNA tests happily catalogue me as Homo sapiens."

"You make it sound as if there is a reason why they shouldn't?" said John.

"My ancestors, the ones responsible for the differences that you are asking about, were not Homo sapiens sapiens – the subspecies classification for modern humans. My ancestors were still the same species, still Homo sapiens, just as yours were, but they had more in common with the Neanderthal subspecies, though it does get confusing."

"What do you mean?"

"Modern humans and Neanderthals have a common ancestry, and DNA suggests some interbreeding back when they shared the world. But there were other subspecies too, including my ancestors. As far as I can tell no modern human has recorded our particular branch of the family tree, so we don't have any formal classification in your systems – and it's probably too late for that now anyway."

"Why?" asked Senna.

"We've been mostly bred out. Many generations ago our community here was getting too small to sustain itself, and so we were forced to mingle with humans. At first just with villagers of this region, which explains Dengali and his family, but later we searched more widely. We tried to be selective, we wanted to maintain some of our more special attributes, but gradually what we were has been fading. Aside from myself, the last true throwback to the time of our ancestors, most now appear to be just heavily boned humans. Within another generation, maybe two, I imagine our origin will be lost, along with everything else.

"My own dear father was a European, an Englishman. So you can see how I ended up with my English name, and perhaps this skin tone, but it doesn't really explain the rest of my looks. He was not a heavily built man, he was strong but slender. He was a young and ambitious explorer when he came here after touring many other places. My father was particularly sensitive, perhaps brought on by the drugs he used to experiment with, and my mother convinced him to discard his ambitions and stay. My mother was a remarkable woman, beautiful and strong willed."

Ben paused and looked at John. "Your initial reaction to me, John, appears to be built into the Homo sapiens sapiens instinct. I think our peoples must have been deadly enemies in the distant past and that hostility got built-in, as it were. I rarely leave the Samgha for that reason. The others could wander the world with barely a second glance, but everything about my appearance invites unwanted attention and hostility from your people."

"And that explains why your presence feels more like a narun than a human?" asked Garjae in the same flat tones.

Ben looked at Garjae and hesitated briefly before responding, "My ancestry is the reason for the differences you see, yes."

- - -

It was late, she should be asleep, but Tracey couldn't relax. She had hoped to drift off to the memory of the lingering kisses in the car when Mike brought her home, but her mind kept fast-forwarding to Mike's refusal to come inside. She was a grown woman for God's sake, but Mike was acting like a school-kid in his reluctance to spend time with her mother. Not that Tracey was sure she had what it took to invite Mike to stay the night while her mother was home, and the knowing looks she would get in the morning, but the option might have been nice. As it was he had driven off, leaving Tracey feeling as if their relationship was something to be ashamed of.

Admitting defeat, sleep wasn't coming any time soon, she put on her dressing-gown and went into the room where her computer was set up. She had left it running again, she was doing that a lot lately. There was an oddly brief message from Andrei and Senna saying they'd arrived somewhere:

```
From the Wanderers,
Our hosts are friendly and helpful. love
Andrei.
Translation: We've been made welcome here
and they are ready to help us in our
search. love Senna.
```

The message lacked the flair of their usual attempts and didn't really say anything about what they'd found, or even where they were. It struck Tracey as very strange.

Tracey checked to see if Tilvy was at the computer at John's house.

"Anyone home?" she typed.

A few moments later a reply appeared on the screen, "Hi Tracey, I didn't expect to hear from you tonight!"

"Who's this?" Tracey typed back.

"It's me!" came the reply.

Tracey grinned and waited a few moments.

"Tilvy!!!" appeared on the screen.

"Just checking," Tracey typed back, "I didn't want to start pouring my heart out to someone else." The exclamation marks were as good as a signature, it was definitely Tilvy.

"Not a good night?"

"Most of it was good, just wish he wasn't so shy with my mother."

"Your mother or Brian?"

Tracey nodded, that might be it. She got the impression that Mike didn't much like her mother's boyfriend, and Brian was obviously in tonight, Mike would have seen his car in the driveway. "Who knows?" she wrote back.

"I think you're very brave!" Tilvy's message came up on the screen.

Tracey laughed to herself. "Not me," she typed back, "I get scared silly every time he asks me out."

"I've known Barma since we were kids. I can't imagine what it must be like to try and start a relationship with a stranger!"

"It's scary. I keep expecting something to change, for him to turn ..." Tracey stopped typing, not certain just what she was frightened of.

"Turn what?" Tilvy wrote back.

"I don't know. Turn nasty. Lose his temper ... something."

"I thought you said he was nice."

"He is. He's been ... perfect."

"Isn't that good?"

"No one's perfect."

"You said he's a good kisser, that's got to count for something!"

81

Tilvy had written.

Tracey laughed and typed back, "Sure."

"Have you found out if he's good at anything else yet?"

From anyone else Tracey might have found the question presumptuous, but Tilvy had become her best friend, there wasn't much they didn't talk about. "No. We still haven't had that much time together."

"So ask him out more often!"

"He works most nights and studies and works on the weekend."

"So we've found a fault with Mr Perfect," Tilvy wrote back, "he works too much!"

"It shows diligence and dedication," Tracey responded.

"Priorities?"

Tracey wasn't sure how to respond to that, she'd wondered the same thing. She wondered whether it simply meant that Mike didn't want to spend more time with her. Things hadn't gone much further than kissing after more than three months – she couldn't believe it had been that long already – not that they'd seen each other that often thanks to Mike's other commitments. It was sort of reassuring that he wasn't pushing her to go further, he wasn't just trying to get into her pants like some past boyfriends, but it also made her worry that he didn't find her attractive. But if that was the case, why did he keep asking her out?

"Perhaps we shouldn't look so hard for faults," Tilvy had typed.

"Good idea," Tracey answered.

"Even my Barma is not totally perfect. He has gotten a bit clingy since all that stuff we went through."

"That's understandable ... sweet."

"Yeah, I know, but it can get a bit much!"

There was a pause as they both considered what to say next.

"Is everything okay there at the house?" Tracey wrote.

"Very quiet! Milla's gone back again, someone's seen a stranger or something, so it's just me and Barma here at the moment. I think Barma is missing Andrei – I'm missing Andrei!"

"The last message from them didn't say much."

"Makes you wonder what they found. Must be impressive if it could shut Andrei up!"

"I'd better try to sleep again, got work in the morning. Will you be there tomorrow night?"

"You bet, I still want to hear more about tonight – all the juicy bits!"

- - -

"But it makes perfect sense," argued John.

Asha nodded, she knew it did, but that didn't make her feel any better about it.

They were lying on a bed in a small room, not far from the room where they'd been talking with Ben. Ben had shown them to this room and then led the other aaranya out to the forest above the cliffs. Asha had remained with John, knowing they would argue, but knowing also that she couldn't stay away from him on what may be their last night together for a long time.

Asha wasn't watching John, her eyes stared at the sculpted ceiling, tracing its patterns, but she could feel John's eyes on her: watching, but not touching, as he lay beside her.

"Ben's offer is a good one. A guide to take you all to the Glades of this region while I stay here for treatment."

Asha didn't like Ben, didn't trust him, but it wasn't something she could explain. It wasn't anything in particular, it was just everything in general. The way everyone deferred to him, and the way he expected that deference. The self-satisfied smugness in the way he spoke and sat and stared. The glint in his eye when that stare was directed at her. The confidence with which he had assumed that John would accept his offer of assistance. She didn't trust any of it, but there was no logic by which she could refute John's assertion, acceptance of Ben's offer really did make sense.

"I'd rather we didn't split up, not while you're so ill," Asha said.

"I don't feel that bad, at least, not once I've had that injection and can see you again." John gently turned her face to look at him, his thumb brushing gently at her cheek. "Looking at you is a cure for all ills," he said softly.

Asha put her hand over his. "You can't look at me if you send me away."

"Don't say it like that. I don't *want* you to go."

Asha pulled his hand from her cheek and kissed it. "I know."

"And really, I don't feel that bad. It's just the vedana thing."

"It's not, John. I can feel it in your body. Something is very wrong, and whatever it is, it's getting worse all the time. I'm worried."

"I know," John squeezed her hand gently. "But you can't wait here for me to get better," he insisted. "You heard Jia, the treatment could take weeks. We can't afford to waste that much time. And it's not really any different to what we'd planned. Even if I was healthy, you'd still be going to the Glades without me, I would only slow you down in the jungle."

Asha nodded again, the logic was relentless. "But you're *not* well. We have no proof yet that Jia can help you. What if you need *my* help?"

"You know I don't want to be apart from you, Asha," John said gently. He pulled her hand forward, kissed it, and then held it over his heart. "But you said yourself that you can't help me with this. Ben and Jia say they can. Let them help me while you do what we came here to do."

Asha looked back up at the ceiling and nodded helplessly. She had been so certain that John's only trouble was seasickness, persistent and severe, but still something that would resolve itself when they reached land. But Jia had seen more. Asha could feel it now too, but she hadn't at the start, and she still couldn't tell what it was. She only knew that John's body was struggling against something that was attacking him from head to toe, from marrow to skin. It was affecting John's vedana, but as far as Asha could tell the cause was something physical, something to do with his material body – and that was Jia's expertise. Jia had seen it coming, had predicted John's symptoms even before he had felt them himself. The woman doctor obviously knew what she was doing, so why was Asha so reluctant to leave John here, alone in her care?

5. Search

The sun had not long peeked over the horizon, and John sat alone on the ridge above the cliffs. He was looking out over the forest to the south-east, where his friends had so quickly disappeared to begin their search for a rumour: a healer that just might be able to help his daughter. His friends were gone. Asha, however reluctantly, had gone. Even Casseta, who had so often comforted him at times like this, had refused to stay with him.

The ridge was a natural prominence of bare rock. It rose from the plateau to a height that overlooked the forest on all sides. The bulging granite formed a large, flattened summit. It would be a great spot to build a house, John thought, trying to distract himself from his depressed mood. The views were spectacular. To the west the ridge sloped down to an abrupt edge. There the sharp line of the cliffs stretched away to the north and south, it looked like this plateau had been sliced away from the lower lands just yesterday. The other three sides of the ridge sloped down to the lush forest of the plateau.

The air was warming now, and with his vedana reawakened by his morning injection, John could sense the effusive life of the jungle. The morning sounds of the forest creatures came to him, a cacophony, and yet somehow comforting.

John heard footsteps and looked around.

"Do you want to join us for breakfast?" Ben asked.

"Sure," said John.

On the north side of the ridge, just below the summit, the granite opened into a shallow cave. Inside was a well concealed door to a tunnel that burrowed down inside the ridge. John followed Ben through, and they descended the steep flights of granite stairs into the Samgha. After they had descended a few flights, John could again feel that slow change in the walls around him, the living rock of the Samgha. He reached out and touched it. The surface, smoothed by hands long gone, was glossy and warm to his touch. The pink flecked granite looked almost like flesh. On an impulse, John stopped and placed his cheek against the wall. That soft warmth ... and a pulse. Not the warm fluttering breeze he felt beneath the bark of a tree, but something harder, stronger, more resilient, but still very much alive.

"She is compelling, isn't she?" Ben said.

John pulled back, he had almost forgotten Ben was there. "Yes," was all he could think to say.

"My people have been here for many thousands of years. We have grown to know Gayatri as most humans would never understand."

They walked on. Ben stopped a little later to show John one of the glowing patches of rock. "We have developed our own way of embedding LEDs into the rock so we get a good dispersal of light. They don't need to be bright once your eyes have adapted."

John ran his fingers lightly over the glowing patch, it was dead, not part of the living rock, but visually it had blended very well. "How is it powered?"

Ben ran his fingers along a line. "In main corridors, like this one, we use a tape that is almost invisible."

John ran his fingers along the same line and felt the tape.

"In more remote areas we use batteries and motion sensors."

"And where does the power come from? You're obviously not on a main power grid."

"No," Ben laughed. "We use a mix of solar and hydro, I'll show you later."

Eventually they reached the large dining hall that John had seen the day before. He heard the busy sounds of people having breakfast. There was a brief quietening as the people of the room became aware of John and Ben standing in the doorway, and then they went back to what they had been doing. Ben led John to a table on one side of the room and settled down. Dengali's son, Reyndani, came through to them from the kitchen area with plates loaded.

"Thank you, Reyndani," John said.

Reyndani nodded.

"Reyndani is naturally quiet," Ben said.

Reyndani nodded again, and then smiled and shrugged.

John looked around the room. The high ceiling was contoured with irregular patterns that extended down the walls. The hard granite floor, polished to a shine near the door, had no covering except for thin mats beneath the dining tables. The tables were scattered, apparently randomly, around the large room. John thought that the room should feel cavernous, cold and echoing, but in fact it was comfortable, and the sounds were remarkably subdued, especially considering the number of people eating and talking in here now. The tables and the mats were all of a solid practical construction, with little obvious decoration, and all had a feel of great antiquity. At the far end of the room, more brightly lit than the main part of the hall, stood a surprisingly modern kitchen area with refrigerator and other appliances, and a sink with taps.

There must have been at least fifty people in the room, and there were still more coming in. They were a diverse group of men and women. Many were heavily boned and the majority had the skin and dark hair that John had come to associate with the natives of the region, but others were of less obvious descent. There were some that he might guess were European, Negro, Chinese and others.

As if reading John's thoughts, Ben commented, "As I told you last night, since we started to mingle with humanity the Samgha have always tried to find humans with the right sort of sensitivities, wherever we find them."

"How many people here are ... like you?"

"Like me? None. But there are several samvaya in this room. See if you can tell me how many."

John closed his eyes and reached out his senses. There, there, there .... He opened his eyes again to see the people that he knew must be samvaya because they felt like Ben, though none were quite so intense. He looked around the room and then back at Ben. "I count fifteen, other than you. ... Sixteen, another just walked in."

Ben looked around the room, then turned back. "Very good."

"But this isn't everyone is it?"

Ben shook his head sadly. "No, there are other food halls here, but close enough. The samvaya you see here represent more than half of the Samgha now. Just a tiny fraction of what we once were. We are not enough to sustain the community much longer."

John ate his breakfast quietly and watched those around him. He noticed the other thing that marked out the samvaya: they were given deference by others, they were served by others and they were tidied up after by others. The samvaya were the privileged class among these people.

"Why did you want to meet me, Ben?" John nodded to the other samvaya in the room, and continued, "I can't be that unusual for you."

"You are very unusual. The samvaya you see here are what they are because they share my ancestry. You are pure human, adult, but with vedana. I wanted to see you for myself."

"With fading vedana," said John, feeling depression start to settle on him again.

"Yes," agreed Ben. "If you're finished, let's go see Jia and see if we can't remedy that."

They left Reyndani to clean up after them, and John followed Ben down more long granite corridors.

"Our hospital," Ben announced at last.

The corridor opened out into a large reception area. A nurse behind a desk stood and bowed her head to Ben, and then did the same to John. Ben barely acknowledged her, leading John further into the hospital.

It seemed strange to John to see the normal accoutrements of a hospital laid out against naked granite. The ceilings here lacked the sculpted patterns of the other rooms in the Samgha, and there was more ductwork that John assumed must carry the necessary cables and pipes. There was also more sound, the hum of various electrical equipment, and the muted voices of conversations that carried here more than in other rooms and corridors.

"The granite certainly looks better than hospital green," John said, "but is it hygienic?"

"This is one of the oldest parts of the Samgha, but its use as a hospital is only recent. We had to tidy things up a bit. It was something that my father started and I expanded. At first we tried to cover the granite, but we had trouble. In the operating theatre and recovery rooms we go to more trouble to hide these," Ben pointed to the ductwork, "but even there the bare rock has proved to be better than anything else we tried."

They saw Jia attending a patient in one of the wards they passed. "When you're ready, Jia," Ben called to her, and continued leading John through the hospital without waiting for a response.

They came to what appeared to be the other end of the hospital. Two corridors stretched to the left and right, and a third went straight on. "Our Isolation Rooms," Ben said. He indicated the side corridors, but offered no further explanation. John glanced down them, they weren't very long. There were a number of solid looking doors on either side and one at the end. It had the look of a prison facility.

Ben continued down the third, narrower, corridor that led straight on for a short distance, and then bent slightly to the left. There were no other rooms or connecting corridors, just this one long passage – tunnel seemed a more apt description here. The lines of the tunnel flowed gently up and down and side to side, to what purpose John couldn't tell.

The latter part of the tunnel narrowed further until they could no longer walk comfortably side-by-side. They reached the end and Ben opened the door and led the way into a room. To the left was an open space with a couple of chairs and a small table. Then there were two beds, one in front of the door, and another to the right, near a partition wall that gave some privacy to a bathroom area. John noted that his few belongings had already been brought down and placed on the bed to the right.

"We call this the Initiation Room," said Ben.

"Initiation?" John queried.

"We'll get to that. Take a seat." Ben indicated the chairs to the left of the room.

John looked around at the grey and pale-pink swirling patterns of the granite. The walls and ceiling of this room were not flat and smooth like the rooms of the hospital, but neither were they engraved with the irregular patterns of the rest of the Samgha. They had a flowing appearance, as if the walls and ceilings were the surface of some large body of water – a lake or the ocean. The visual effect, combined with the strong impact of the living rock on John's vedana, made him feel like he was deep inside some immense living

89

creature – Jonah inside the whale. The effect was ... uncomfortable.

They settled in the chairs, and Ben sat forward and looked at John intently. "How badly do you want your vedana?"

John stared at him in surprise. He didn't know what to say, surely it was obvious.

"I ask because the treatment we are going to suggest ... well, some of it may seem strange, and some of it will get very intense."

"You're a doctor too?" John asked, surprised that it was Ben starting this conversation.

"No. But due to my nature, what I am, I have some special insight into what we will ask of you. For this to be successful you must accept what we ask of you and give it everything you have. What we have in mind won't work unless you go along with what we ask, unless *you* put in the effort."

John looked back at Ben, silent for a few moments, still trying to gather his thoughts. "Ben," he said at last, "you heard my story last night. Yes, my first priority is to find help for my daughter, though there has been precious little that *I* can do. Beyond that it is hard to see anything *except* that my life is now irrevocably entwined with the aaranya – with Asha. I don't want to be blind to that world again, Ben. I can't be. Whatever hope you can give me, I'll grab it with both hands and hold on tight."

Ben nodded slowly and sat back in his chair. "Good," he acknowledged.

John looked up and saw that Jia had come into the room.

"I'll leave you to it," Ben said brightly and stood up. To Jia he added, "I'll send Reyndani down to fetch John – in an hour?"

Jia nodded.

Ben left, and Jia had John lie on the bed in the centre of the room while she took some blood samples. She then took his blood pressure, his temperature, and stared into his pupils with a small light. She went over his body, pressing here and pinching skin there. When she was done with that she had him go to the bathroom to collect a urine sample.

"All this is going to tell you what ails me?" John asked, trying to keep his tone upbeat.

Jia nodded non-committally.

She had him lie down again while she gave him an injection. This one spread through his body like a gust of chilled air. John shivered. A few moments later he felt suddenly restless.

Jia leaned back on the second bed and watched him. "That should give you back a bit of energy," she said.

John sat up and returned her gaze. "Feels good. Ready for anything. I could have done with some of that earlier. I feel dangerous," he finished with a grin.

Jia smiled back, her expression slightly shy, or embarrassed, which was unusual.

"Is everything okay, Jia?"

Jia's expression tightened and she looked down at her watch. "Reyndani should be here soon," she said, and looked back up with her usual slightly stern expression. "He's to start you on an exercise regime so you will need that enthusiasm – and more. Your body needs to build its strength for what is to come." Before John could ask what that might be, she stood up and walked to the door. "I'd better get back to my other patients, I'll see you again this evening."

Reyndani turned up soon after Jia had left. He raised one eyebrow, which John interpreted as asking if John was ready. "When you are," he responded. Reyndani led John on the long walk up to the ridge above the cliffs, and then through the jungle for a while before retracing their steps back into the Samgha again. John was exhausted by the time Reyndani led them to the food hall. John collapsed onto a chair and waited while Reyndani prepared lunch for both of them. After a small break Reyndani repeated the morning's routine.

The pace he set was not fast, but it was relentless, and it was all done with few words from Reyndani, just the occasional, solicitous, "Do you need to rest?" or "Do you want to stop?" as John huffed and puffed his way along another steep ascent. John, remembering Ben's advice, stubbornly shook his head at such questions, he wanted this to work. Reyndani would just smile in return and lead him on. They stopped for dinner and another break. When they got going again John groaned to himself, it appeared that Reyndani was going to start it all over again. But this time the routine stayed within the Samgha and soon led them back to the hospital.

Reyndani left John in the Initiation Room, departing with a brief, "See you in the morning." To John, feeling so weary after the day's exercise, those parting words sounded like a threat. He sat on the centre bed and considered lying down to sleep fully clothed. John made himself stand and clear his things from the bed on the right, it seemed to be where they expected him to sleep. Then he visited the bathroom. Showered and toileted he walked back into the room, naked, looking at the bed as if it were a long-lost friend.

"Eh-em."

John looked up. Jia was standing in the doorway, she had been waiting for him. John quickly backed into the bathroom and grabbed a towel to wrap around himself.

Jia smiled. "I have seen it all before."

"Not quite the same as me seeing you seeing it all."

She smiled. "Just a few more things, John."

She put John through a series of physical reaction tests, blood tests, breath tests and more. At times one young assistant or another would come in and help, but she would send each away again when no longer required. Finally, she had John climb into bed ready for sleep and gave him another injection.

A burning heat ran quickly through his body and he gasped.

"This is a stronger dose of what you've already been getting," Jia explained. "Your dreams may be more vivid than usual, but otherwise your sleep should be normal. If you wake and feel anything to be wrong, just press that button on the side table and one of us will be with you within a few minutes."

John barely heard her finish the last sentence before sleep took him. He did dream: Asha standing at the top of an almost vertical flight of steps urging him to climb faster, but as hard as he climbed, the distance never seemed to close.

- - -

Andrei looked at their guide. Seriyani was still a mystery. She wasn't aaranya, she wasn't anything that any of them recognised, and that really only left yaayaavara, who were known to be a strange mix of people. Ben had introduced her as their guide, saying only that she was Saarvaya Seriyani. Darnu's query, "Half?" had gone unanswered. Seriyani was short, squat, and powerfully built. Her yellow-blond hair stood out in stark contrast to her dark skin. Her manner was bold and in your face, and what humour she showed seemed cold and disinterested.

Whatever else she was, she was certainly strong and fast. She had set a hard pace through the dense forest for the last three days. There were animal paths, and Seriyani took these when she could, but such paths didn't always go where they needed.

"We should rest here," she told them. "The Glade is only a couple of hours that way, and it will be better if we arrive in the morning and relatively fresh."

Asha wandered off to one side, away from the others. Garjae turned to go to her. Darnu touched his arm and shook his head.

Andrei turned to Senna. "Share a tree?"

Senna studied him and seemed to find something she didn't like, or didn't want right now. She turned away without answering, her expression had said enough, and walked off.

"Still not forgiven," Andrei mumbled to himself. He had made another wise-crack earlier in the journey that Senna had taken the wrong way.

Senna wasn't enjoying the jungle. It was wondrous, it was exciting and intriguing, but it was also strange and overwhelming. Her senses, finely tuned for the city where she had grown up, had difficulty keeping the flood of sensory input in perspective. And, as Andrei had discovered to his detriment, this had made her especially touchy.

Andrei looked around restlessly. Seriyani was talking to Darnu and Garjae so Andrei went to join them.

"The Glades are closer together here than in most places," Seriyani was explaining. "The valley of Gayatri near the Samgha has attracted them, but the aaranya are simply not that populous, even here."

Seriyani was sitting next to Darnu, watching him closely. Andrei thought Darnu looked uncomfortable under such scrutiny. On the other side of Darnu, Garjae continued to look out toward Asha, who was sitting high in a tree off to one side. Andrei thought she looked lonely, a little lost, but he didn't think it was the company of anyone here that she craved.

The conversation between Darnu and Seriyani continued in much the same boring line. Andrei rapped out a restless tattoo on his legs and looked around. Despite the days of activity he couldn't settle, so he got up and walked around for a while. He found a tree that looked inviting and climbed up into it. From high in its branches he glanced down and saw that Senna had not merged with the tree she had chosen. She was sitting on a branch and staring out into the forest, apparently lost in thought. Andrei found himself a comfortable spot where he could watch over her.

Taiza, Senna's father, had told Andrei to take care of her, but he wasn't doing such a good job. Since the boat ride things had gone topsy-turvy between them, as if they were still being tossed around by the ocean. He knew that sometimes he had been stupid. There was so much new to experience, and so many new people to meet and study – and Andrei's own moods sometimes caught him by surprise. But now it felt like his relationship with Senna had become precarious. He was self-conscious around her as he tried hard not to offend her, and that only seemed to make things worse. With John and Barma missing as well, Andrei was feeling like he'd been set adrift.

Movement made him pay closer attention. Senna had turned her head and was staring fixedly at a point on the ground back past Andrei's tree. Did she know he was here watching her? After a few moments she shook her head, as if dismissing whatever she had felt, and went back to staring off into the distance, lost in other thoughts.

Andrei looked down where Senna had been staring, but could see nothing, so he turned his attention back to Senna again. A few minutes later she turned and stared off to one side of where she had looked before. As before, after a few moments she gave up and looked away. A short time later Senna gave up on whatever thoughts had been occupying her and merged into the tree. Andrei wished he was with her.

To distract himself, Andrei turned his attention to where Senna had been staring. If there was one thing he'd learn to respect, it was Senna's ability to sense things that others could not. She had complained to him that she felt blind out here in the jungle, that it was too busy to see anything, but still he'd rely on her senses over anyone else's.

Following a line from the two places that Senna had been looking, Andrei kept a careful watch. Eventually he thought that he could feel something. A presence ... maybe. He looked around the branches of the tree he was in and saw that, if he was careful, he could make his way to the next tree, closer to that possible presence.

Slowly Andrei worked his way forward, determined to investigate whatever it was that Senna had felt and then dismissed.

- - -

As she sipped her coffee, Tracey looked over the table at Jason. He had phoned this morning to see if she was at John's house and said that he wanted to come over and chat. His sandy coloured hair was dishevelled, as if he hadn't taken the time to brush it this morning, which she could well imagine because he seemed restless, almost bouncy like a pup. He looked much younger than John, and his gangly build and enthusiasm only exaggerated the puppy resemblance. He was so little like John that she wondered at how the two had ever come to be friends.

"I hope I didn't interrupt a phone call or anything," Jason said, "I heard you talking as I came to the door."

Tracey lowered her coffee and glanced down at it. "No, probably just talking to myself." She had probably been saying goodbye to Tilvy and Barma, they had decided at the last moment to leave the house while Jason was around, so as not to distract her.

"You want to be careful, it could be catching," Jason said. He smiled to show it was a joke. Seeing Tracey's puzzlement, he explained, "That's where it started with John – talking to himself."

Tracey smiled weakly.

"You don't get lonely out here on your own?" he asked her.

"No, I like the quiet."

Jason took a sip from his coffee and then asked, "I was wondering if you'd heard anything more from John than I have? His last messages have been very vague."

Tracey wasn't sure how to respond. They probably should have prepared something for this, had some story ready. John did copy her in on the messages he sent to Jason, but she was having trouble remembering what he had said in those, from what little she had heard from Andrei and Senna before they departed on their search. There wasn't much in either of them.

"John did say something about being on some sort of fitness thing," she replied vaguely.

"Yes, but he didn't say where he was or what the place was like or anything."

"I know. I found that a bit odd too," Tracey admitted.

"So you don't know where he is either?"

"I don't think John's told me anything he hasn't told you." That seemed safe enough, and it was close to true. So far she hadn't received much from John directly, and none of the messages had said much about where they were.

Jason got up with his coffee and walked across to the kitchen window and stared out. "I just worry that this brain thing's coming back, and now he's off in another country with no friends to fall back on. No one to help him if he needs it."

"I'm sure he's okay. He would have said something if he needed our help."

Jason turned back to her. "He didn't before. He just up and disappeared."

Tracey shrugged helplessly. What could she say?

"And why the stuffing around, driving all that way north and getting a boat? Why didn't he just fly over and be done with it?"

"I think he wanted a holiday – time away from everything." It was the best she could come up with.

"He did warn me that things might go peculiar," Jason admitted, "but I'd hoped you might have more idea what was going on. Why go running off to Asia anyway? Why couldn't someone here help him?"

Tracey shrugged again. "You'd probably have to talk to the doctors he was seeing."

"I would if I knew who they were. Do you?"

"No."

"They probably wouldn't speak to me anyway. Patient confidentiality and all that, and I'm not a family member. But he doesn't have any family. Did you know that?"

Tracey nodded.

"No one to look out for him. No one he can trust."

"There's us," Tracey defended.

"It's not the same as family, especially when it comes to doctors and legal stuff." Jason turned back to look out the window. "I'm sorry, I don't mean to take my frustrations out on you."

"You're worried, I understand that."

"It's been building up. The few short messages as he was

travelling and now he's got somewhere we're hearing even less. I've known John for a long time, and I have never known him to be so vague and so ... I don't know, what's the opposite of deliberate? With John it was always: this comes first, and then we do this and this, until we get the result we want.

"I miss that. Our work's fallen off. No one's said anything, but I know what we do now isn't as good as when John kept us on track. It's all gone a bit airy or something. Megan's okay, but it's not the same."

Jason sighed, his shoulders slumping. After a moment he turned back. "I'd better be off home. Liz will be wanting me to mind the little tacker while she gets some stuff done."

Tracey saw Jason out to his car. "I'm sorry I couldn't tell you anything new," she said.

"It's okay. Whatever John's up to, he's obviously keeping a lot to himself. Thanks for listening, I feel a little better just for getting it off my chest."

Tracey smiled at him, and waved as the car drove off. She went back inside and composed an email to John, telling him about Jason's visit.

- - -

John didn't see much of Ben over that first week, it was just Reyndani every day from dawn until late, and then Jia and her tests in the evening. Reyndani's apparently endless excursions filled the day with motion: walking, jogging, sprinting, lifting, carrying and helping to clear the always encroaching forest from around the village. At times their activity led the pair among others, and sometimes Reyndani would pause to allow conversation – not that John was up to much in the first days. Everyone they met was friendly and appeared to be very interested in John, but John was very tired and barely remembered who he had met.

John did see Dengali and Resineta a few times as Reyndani led John through the village.

"Your son is a hard task-master," John would call to Dengali each time.

"He is a good boy," Dengali would call back.

The least favourite part of this routine was in the depths of the Samgha, and the cold black river that flowed through the caverns beneath it.

On the first visit John couldn't believe what was happening when Reyndani stripped off and entered the water. The river flowed very strongly, John had already seen that one branch of it was used to power generators. Surely he would be swept away if he went in there, or frozen – the water was very cold.

"You want me to go in there?"

Reyndani lifted his head and nodded, but kept up his regular breaststroke against the current.

John seriously considered refusing, but he wanted this to work. He didn't want to live without vedana, to never see or hear Asha or his daughter again. He remembered Ben's words, that he must accept what was asked of him. So off came the clothes and he stepped cautiously into the river. The cold took his breath away and he pushed himself the rest of the way in a burst. The current grabbed at his body and started to sweep him back. Reyndani reached out and grabbed his wrist, pulling him strongly forward.

"Swim," Reyndani demanded of him, and released his wrist.

John tried breaststroke, but couldn't keep up against the current, so he changed to freestyle. That worked better for a minute or so, but the cold rapidly sapped his strength and he started to fall back again. Agony gripped one leg – cramp! His head submerged as his body curled over with the pain. He felt the current sweeping him away and he was powerless to fight it.

His body ran up against an obstruction with a bruising jar. One foot passed through a hole, he felt the skin of his leg scraping as it slid through, but in the cold water the pain from that couldn't compete with the cramp in his other leg. His body twisted in the current, he could feel the water sweeping past him, pressing him against the obstruction. He could also feel his breath running out. He tried to ignore the pain of his cramp, to stretch up for the surface and air.

A warm strong grip latched onto his wrist and pulled him up. John's foot caught painfully, then the grip hauled him forward against the current and his foot pulled free. Moments later his head was above the water and he gasped desperately at the air.

Reyndani drew John to the edge and carried him up onto dry rock. A towel was wrapped around his shoulders and then Reyndani rubbed at John's leg. The cramp slowly eased. John looked back to the water, to where he'd nearly been swept away, and saw that there was a metal grating across the river where it exited the cavern. That was what he had been swept up against. He might have panicked a little less if he had seen that earlier.

"I am sorry," Reyndani said, "you slipped away before I could catch you."

"I never was a great swimmer, Reyndani, don't worry about it."

John tried to lay back, he wanted to relax and get his breath back, but Reyndani lifted him to his feet.

"You must stay active." He handed John another towel. John looked and saw a small stack of them. Are there so many others that find this an enjoyable pass-time that they even keep a stack of towels down here? he wondered. Or maybe the long excursion down here to keep it stocked with dry towels was something Reyndani did when he wasn't busy torturing John.

John finished drying off and dressed.

"Come," Reyndani told him, and started back up the steep corridor to the main part of the Samgha.

John took a deep breath and reminded himself how important this was to him. Okay, so he didn't realise how difficult it was going to be, but that was his own fault, not Reyndani's. And if it worked, it would be worth all this – and more. He drew together what strength he had left and started after Reyndani's straight back. John's limp slowly evened out as his leg warmed up again.

That night Jia tenderly applied some antiseptic to the areas of his leg that had lost skin. The damage was minor and healed very quickly.

After days that blurred together in their routine, even swimming in that dark river was not the torture it had been. It was still a part of the day that John dreaded, he found the cold very hard to cope with, but he could now swim next to Reyndani in that dark cavern for long periods, or what felt like long periods to John, before tiring.

Reyndani was leading John by yet another steep corridor up from the river cavern. The Samgha was a maze of interconnecting corridors, many of them rarely used any more. This tunnel was well lit and a good width, and John was enjoying the fact that he was at last managing to walk side by side with Reyndani without the noisy panting of just a few days ago. He looked across at Reyndani and then called out in surprise, "Thank God!"

Reyndani glanced at him in question.

"You are mortal after all. That's sweat," John pointed to Reyndani's temples.

Reyndani nodded. "You have improved. Now I must exert myself."

John laughed. It felt good to be healthy enough to make Reyndani exert himself.

That night Ben and Dengali came to John's room.

"You've come along well," said Ben.

"My son is impressed," added Dengali.

John looked at Dengali in surprise. "Impressed? He rarely says a word."

Dengali smiled. "A father knows his son."

"To what do I owe the pleasure of tonight's visit?" John asked.

"Tomorrow we will be changing your routine," announced Ben.

"I'm getting better?" Without the constant company of the aaranya, John found it difficult to determine how his vedana had been functioning. Occasionally he would stop and try to consciously reach out, to try and feel the life around him. The results had been very inconsistent, but without Asha's guidance he didn't feel that he could trust his own responses.

Ben smiled. "Your material body is much stronger, you have progressed rapidly, but now you must work on your mind before we can progress further."

John stared at him warily. A fitness regime was one thing, but fiddling with his head?

"Now you must start your own search," Ben continued. "Tomorrow morning Reyndani will lead you on exercises as usual, but after breakfast he will leave you with Samvaya Triveni. Triveni will give you mental exercises designed to help you in your search."

"What do you mean by search?" John asked. "Is this some sort of mystical finding myself?"

"It is best if you try not to think of this in terms of magic or mysticism. What Triveni will teach you produces a real and tangible result, and you will learn better if you keep that in mind. Various human teachings speak of finding your centre, that point of balance within yourself where everything is in harmony. Something like that is what you are searching for. A point within you where your mind, your spirit if you prefer, is in balance between the two halves of your being: your material, flesh-and-blood self, and your praanin, living-energy self. Triveni will tell you more as needed."

The three of them chatted for a while longer about the things that John had seen when Reyndani was leading him around the Samgha and its environs. Their conversation was interrupted when Jia arrived for her nightly routine.

After Jia left, John lay awake for a while wondering how things were going for Asha and the others. When sleep did come, John's dreams were even more vivid than usual. Asha was being swept away down the dark underground river. John was caught in the grate, reaching through and calling desperately to her as she disappeared into the darkness. It was a relief to wake up.

After breakfast Reyndani led John down deep under the Samgha, John thought they might be returning to the river cavern, but found himself outside what appeared to be an unfinished room. The rough, raw granite made John more aware of being deep underground than the refined corridors elsewhere. Reyndani smiled at John when they reached the entrance to this room and indicated he should enter. Reyndani then turned and disappeared back the way they'd come.

John entered the room and found that even the floor was rough and scattered with rubble, and he had to tread carefully to avoid turning his ankle on loose rocks. It was darker in here than elsewhere, but the living rock was comforting and John thought he could see clearly enough – until one of the shadows moved. He looked across in surprise.

Triveni turned out to be a woman, an old Indian woman in appearance, with dark grey hair and a deeply wrinkled, uncompromising face. At least, he assumed it must be Triveni, she felt like a samvaya, but she never actually spoke to him on this day.

"Hello," John said.

She indicated a low rock near the side of the room.

John made his way carefully to it and then looked back at the woman. She indicated he should sit, so he sat.

The woman picked up some things in front of her and came

across to John. She showed him a piece of rock, about the size of a dinner plate. It was heavy and had a complex shape. She grabbed his hand and made him feel the contours of it. The surface of the rock had been polished smooth, in a brighter light John guessed it might have looked to have a bright glassy finish. Then she took the rock away, placed it out of his reach, and handed him a new rock. This one was of a similar size and complex shape, but when she pushed his hand across it he felt the roughness of it threatening to tear his skin. Next she placed a piece of paper in his hand. John felt it: a piece of wet-and-dry abrasive cloth. The woman pointed to the rock in his hand and then at the one she had placed out of reach. Then she pushed his hand and the abrasive paper over the rock he was holding. The meaning was pretty clear.

"Uh-ha," said John. "I think I've seen this in movies. Lots of menial labour to concentrate the mind."

The woman held her fingers to her mouth to indicate he should be quiet.

"Right, no talking," he muttered.

She reached across and flicked his lips.

John managed to stifle an "Ouch" of complaint. He nodded his understanding and began to sand the rock.

It was more difficult than he had first thought. The complex shape of the rock meant that he could not get up a good rhythm or stroke with the cloth. Instead of the mindless task he expected, he had to concentrate on what he was doing to avoid hurting his fingers. There was a pool of water next to him where he could wet and clean the cloth. He proceeded slowly, wondering if there was really going to be any point in this, or whether he was just helping them to create pretty ornaments for sale at the next market.

He thought that he was finally making an impact on one part of the rock when he heard the woman start singing or chanting. It wasn't really one or the other, it felt dissonant, broken and distracting. He looked up.

The woman was sitting on another rock on the other side of the room. John decided that it wasn't just her voice but the shape of the room that distorted the sound somehow. The woman looked at him sternly and pointed back at the rock in his hand. The song – for want of a better description – didn't falter. John turned back to his task.

He couldn't find the place that he thought he had made an impression on and was forced to just start again on another. Try as he might he just couldn't concentrate. The voice came at him from one direction and then another, it stopped and started, it swapped back and forth between perfect tones and discordant noise, it contained hints of words and meanings but never anything he could grasp. And always, always, it dragged at his attention. His fingers kept slipping on the cloth and stubbing into rough bumps in the rock that seemed to move by themselves.

John could feel his temper rising. He very much wanted to stand up and shout at the woman to just shut up! But he didn't. He forced himself to remember what Ben had said, that there would be a real and tangible result from this. He reminded himself of what he had to lose if he failed. So he pushed himself back to his task and tried to cut out the sound of the woman's voice.

He hadn't really made any progress, the rock felt as rough now as when he started. His temper was still sitting on edge when he heard a voice call from the doorway, "Lunch?"

It was Reyndani. John looked around but couldn't see the woman anywhere. "Where—" he started, but stopped and decided it must be the way they wanted to run this. So he stood, feeling the stress in his joints and in his buttocks from having sat on the low, cold rock for so long. After lunch Reyndani led him out into the jungle, and they came back soaking wet after a heavy downpour. When he was returned to his room John was feeling very tired and frustrated.

The next day was a repeat, except that after lunch he was taken back to the woman in the cave. This time the distractions included strange, often repellent, smells, and at times odd flashes of light. And the same the day after that. But on the following day, after breakfast, Reyndani led John to a small room not far from the hospital. It was a bright pleasant room, furnished apparently as a television room, including a sofa and two recliners. John walked in, as indicated by Reyndani, and found Triveni sitting back in one of the recliners looking at him.

Gone were the dark clothes of the cave, she was brightly dressed, her grey hair pulled back neatly into a casual pony tail. Her expression was still that of a strict schoolmistress, but it didn't seem so daunting here in the bright, modern setting.

"Hello, John," she said, and stood up as he walked toward her. "I am Samvaya Triveni. We have met," she finished, her face allowing a small smile. Her voice had the clear elocution of someone educated in a posh English school.

John accepted her outstretched hand, shook it, and then sat on the other recliner when she indicated. Triveni went to the door and closed and snibbed it before returning to her recliner. She sat back to look at him once more.

"Ben warned me you might be a quick study," she told him.

"Does that mean I'm ready for some sort of test?" John asked, feeling wrong-footed by the change of situation.

"That was the test," she told him, and smiled at John's look of surprise.

"You still have to sit the lessons. I was hoping to take the smile off Ben's face, but I lost that bet. You were succeeding on the second day, but the testing always goes for three days so we let you see it through.

"I am not convinced you are a quick study, I think you are just bloody minded. Are you bloody minded, John?"

"I prefer determined."

"But is that how others see you, do you think?"

John shrugged. "I don't understand the test. Did I get the rock shiny enough?"

"It was never about the rock, John."

"So what would have constituted a fail? Just yelling at you to be quiet, or maybe if I'd tried to brain you with the rock."

Triveni laughed. "I did see when those thoughts went through your mind, that is why I think you are bloody minded. You didn't take out your frustrations on the rock and damage your fingers," she glanced down at the nicks and bruises on his hands, "or not too much. You got angry but you just turned that into determination and concentration. And *that*, John, is what the test was all about, concentration. The test is intended to distract a person by any means short of physical intervention."

"Why short of physical intervention?"

"Because that is unfair, and probably irrelevant to our purposes."

John raised his eyebrows. "Our purposes being?"

"What you are going to learn now is how to put yourself into a trance that you can use to put your body into a very deep sleep – a form of hibernation. There is more to it than that, but we will get to that. The point is that you must learn to exert control of your body, both your bodies. Both the material and the praanin elements of your existence must be under the control of your mind. And you must learn to do this without being distracted by things going on around you."

John tried to take in what she had said. "That all sounds pretty complicated."

"It is. It may be something that you take a long time to learn, if ever. Or it may happen quickly. Everyone is different."

John nodded.

"All right. We start with a combination of autogenic training and autohypnotic trance instructions."

At first John felt pretty silly with the relaxation techniques. Counting in, imagining this limb or that to be heavy and so on. Again he had to remind himself that the results of this were supposed to be real and effective, that this was the only way he might retrieve what he was losing, so he pushed the feelings of foolishness away and tried to concentrate on the instructions he was given.

He was to have several sessions with Triveni each day, and in between these Reyndani returned to keep John active.

On the second day Triveni hooked up a series of sensors to various parts of his body and turned on the television screen. The images on the screen meant little to John, but Triveni explained that it was a form of biofeedback that may help to speed up his learning of the relaxation and trance techniques. He shouldn't try to interpret the images on the screen, simply be aware of them and how they changed as he used the various techniques.

At first the images seemed to do what they would regardless of what John did or said or thought, but by the third session of that second day he began to see correspondence between what he willed and what he saw on the screen. Triveni raised her eyebrows at this but said nothing.

Four days later and Triveni called their last session for the day to a close early.

"Quick study turns out to be an understatement, John. What you have achieved is astounding. I do not know what is driving you, but it is working."

"So what's next?"

"I want you to take tomorrow off." She stopped John interrupting. "You might not need it, but I do. Go keep Reyndani company or something."

- - -

"Do you mind?" Senna's voice stole past the sounds of the forest.

Asha looked down in surprise. She was perched on a branch that stretched over a small stream. She had been listening to its gentle burbling and to the many noises of the lush forest, while she thought about John. She wondered if he was all right. Was he recovering? How were those people treating him? She was worried – and she missed him.

"I know you wanted to be alone," Senna called up, "but I really need someone to talk to."

Asha indicated that Senna should climb up. She wasn't entirely happy with having her reverie, her sulking if she was going to be truly honest, interrupted, but Senna looked upset. "You two still not getting on?"

Senna didn't answer, just climbed up slowly and made her way to Asha, trying not to disturb the dozen or so small birds that had congregated around her. "Do they come to talk to you?"

"Mostly just to show off, I think. They can be a nuisance sometimes, when you just want some peace and quiet."

"I'm sorry—"

"No, I didn't mean that. Of course you can talk to me, though I'm not sure I can help."

Senna turned suddenly and looked out into the forest behind them, then she shrugged and turned her attention back to the birds. Senna reached out and a small parrot stepped onto her hand. She lifted it up and blew gently at it. The parrot turned its head into the draft, apparently enjoying the sensation. "The most I usually saw in the city were a few sparrows," she said.

"The abundance here can be overwhelming, even to someone like me that grew up in a forest. I have trouble imagining what it must be like for you," Asha responded. She looked back the way Senna had glanced but saw nothing.

"I think that's probably part of it. I'm always on edge here because I can't see very far. There's just too much life here, it gets in the way. You can't get outside of it to see it properly. In the city I could spot a bug on the footpath, in the dark, at a hundred paces – city kids used to play that sort of stupid game, and I always won. But here I can't even see elephants until they're right on top of us."

Asha smiled, the first elephants had come as a bit of a surprise. That the animals were so aware and curious about the aaranya was also a surprise.

"It was different back in your forest. Back there things were never so intense, and we'd visit John regularly, and sometimes he'd take us back to the city. I have never felt so closed in as I do here."

"I do miss the openness of the forest back home," admitted Asha. "This was different, fun, when we first got here, but now – like you – I find it all a bit oppressive."

"The people here, the aaranya, are different too," Senna said. "They're short-sighted or something. They only care about the immediate area of their Glade. It's as if growing up where they can't see any distance has stopped them from accepting that there is anything beyond it."

Asha nodded, she'd had similar thoughts, although she'd put it down to being surrounded by such an abundance of life, and so isolated from human interference, that they never imagined there may be places that were different. But she was older than Senna, old enough to be wary of such first impressions.

Their group had been accepted and greeted amiably enough at each Glade, but they never felt exactly welcomed, merely tolerated as visitors that would soon be gone. An elder would meet with them and their queries answered in a polite, but not all that friendly, manner. "A healer? Yes, there was one here many years ago. No, we don't know where she went, or even if she is still alive." These responses were too vague, and too consistent among the three Glades they had visited, to really be believable. But there was nothing to be gained by accusing them of lying, they could only accept what they were told and move on and try again. It was very frustrating.

"I think this place is affecting Andrei too," Senna said, staring out into the forest again.

Asha didn't reply, just watched the stream and waited for her to continue.

"Hell, I think it's affecting everyone. What is it between you and Garjae?" The question seemed to have slipped out without much thought, and Senna looked across at Asha, concerned that she'd said more than she should have.

Asha glanced at her then looked back down at the stream. "There is nothing between Garjae and me."

"But he'd like there to be?"

Asha shrugged, and then agreed, "I guess so."

"Does John know?"

Asha nodded.

"Is he worried?"

Asha thought about John's reactions to Garjae. It wasn't that he was indifferent, at one time he even told her that she would be better off with someone like Garjae, rather than lumbering herself with an oaf of a human – his words, not hers. She was pretty certain that she had convinced him where her affections lay. No, John was not jealous, she felt sure of that. "If anything, I think he is sad for Garjae."

After considering this, Senna said, "Probably best if you don't tell Garjae that."

Asha smiled down at the stream. "Probably."

"I get jealous of Andrei."

There seemed no good response to that, so Asha remained silent.

"It's not that I think he's really looking in that way .... but he *is* always looking to be the centre of attention. And I see the way the girls look at him. Everyone likes him."

Senna said nothing more for a while, just played with one bird or another as they came close to the pair of them sitting on the branch. Eventually she continued, "I think, if we let Andrei be the one to approach the Glades we might get more answers."

"And what do we tell Seriyani?"

"Get Darnu to distract her."

Asha looked up at Senna. "I didn't think he paid that much attention to her?"

"He doesn't really, but I think she'd like him to."

Asha looked back down at the stream. She'd never really thought about Darnu in that way, nor Garjae. It was always just a matter of wherever Darnu was, there was Garjae. It had been that way for as long as she could remember, like an older and more serious version of the pairing that used to exist between Andrei and Barma. "I can't really see him getting involved with her."

"No, probably not. She is a bit strange."

"And what about your feelings – if we let Andrei garner even more attention?"

Senna shrugged. "I miss my Dad. He could always make me feel special when I'm feeling down."

"And Andrei?" Asha prodded gently.

Senna looked out into the forest. "Usually, but lately he—"

"Ahoy up there," Garjae's voice floated up to them. "Seriyani wants to get going. Are you two ready?"

Asha looked to Senna, her eyebrows raised in question.

"It's fine," Senna said abruptly. "Let's go." She jumped down next to the stream before Asha could ask any more.

6. Separate

Ben and John were sitting in the Initiation Room. Jia had just left after her usual morning routine, John thought she had looked worried, her expression one of concern that didn't fit with her usual professional bedside manner.

"You've been progressing very well," Ben said. "Certainly faster than the others had expected, better than even I had hoped."

"Fast?" It hadn't felt that fast to John. He'd lost count of the weeks, and he still couldn't tell if it had made any difference.

Ben nodded and smiled at him. "Everything you've been doing up to now has been preparation. The next step, if you take it, will give back your vedana – and more."

"More?" John leaned forward in surprise.

"You must have wondered about the samvaya, why we feel different."

"You explained that. Your ancestors were a different subspecies."

Ben nodded. "That explains how we came to be what we are, but it doesn't really explain the difference you can feel – why we feel like narun to your vedana."

"But Garjae asked you that."

"And I didn't give a complete answer. We haven't kept our existence a secret from the world, humans and narun alike, for thousands of years by being open to everyone that lands on our doorstep." Ben's tone was smug.

"But the aaranya do know. Those that were with Dengali knew of this place."

Ben sat back. "Without giving you our full history you won't understand how our people's nature varied from humans back when the Samgha were pure, the distinctions are much less obvious now. I may look strong and aggressive, but *my* people were not aggressors. Defensive and secretive, *that* was always our nature. We saw the Aeonian War of the narun and we survived it by staying hidden, but the aaranya were decimated, and the Glades near here were destroyed.

"When the forests recovered the aaranya began to return. My ancestors approached the elders of the new Glades that formed, and agreements were made. They promised to keep our secret, and they promised not to pass on news of our existence to others. Given their past, the horrors of the war, how could they deny our request? They formed a buffer between us and the rest of the world. Those agreements have lasted through the generations.

"So yes, the aaranya near here know of our existence, and their elders know what we truly are, but they have kept that secret from the wider world."

John nodded slowly. "And you're about to reveal your secret to me?"

Ben nodded. "It is the way to retrieve your vedana."

"And the others? When they return, can I tell them?"

"It will be obvious. You won't be able to keep it from them."

John raised his eyebrows. "This will be the *more*, that you spoke of."

Ben nodded.

John frowned as he tried to work out what he was missing. "You've certainly gone to a lot of trouble to get me this far," he said slowly.

"You do want this, don't you?" Ben spoke over him. "You want your vedana back? You want to be able to see your Asha, and you want to be able to see and hear your daughter?"

- - -

Tracey stared at the computer screen, she couldn't quite believe what she had read. Most of John's messages had been brief, just assuring her – and Jason, on those messages sent to both of them – that he was doing fine, getting very healthy and being treated well. But tonight's message was different. It was all too personal and worrying. There had been no hint before now that anything like this might be coming. What was he doing? She re-read the message:

Dear Tracey,

I thought I should write this in case
what I am about to do goes wrong. It
shouldn't. I'm well prepared, they've done
everything they can to make sure I am.
They're not pushing me into this, it's my
choice, my decision. The procedure

What the hell was the procedure he was talking about? Tracey
scanned the rest but saw no further explanation, so she came back
and read on:

The procedure should either work and all
will be fine, or it will fail and I will be
exactly as I was. But there is a chance it
could go wrong, in which case this will be
the last you hear from me.

Crap! Was he serious?

Asha and the others are still away, it's
better this way. Please make sure they know
this was my choice, it was just something I
had to try – for Ellie and for me. I will
send Jason a suitably edited version of
this to prepare him too, just in case – and
it is "just in case". Please don't worry,
it will almost certainly all be fine.

Don't worry? She had already seen what John would put himself
through, and hold himself responsible for. Who were these people
he was with, and what had they talked him into? Oh boy, as if Jason
wasn't worried enough already. He would be on the phone to her as
soon as he got his version of this message.

The people here assure me that, if it
comes to it, they will make sure you get
appropriate documents, death certificate
and so on, so that you will have everything
you need to wind things up there.

He was serious! Tracey had never imagined that the responsibilities John had left on her could possibly include this.

> I don't want to get all maudlin, this
> will most likely come out fine, but if it
> doesn't … I wanted to say: thank you. Thank
> you for everything you've done, for me and
> for the others. You're a very special lady,
> and you've been a wonderful friend.

Tracey paused and wiped her eyes. He didn't want to get maudlin. Didn't he?

> I'm not religious, how could I be? But
> the preparations for this have brought to
> mind a childhood prayer, I don't even
> remember learning it:
>   Now I lay me down to sleep,
>   I pray the Lord my soul to keep,
>   If I shall die before I wake,
>   I pray the Lord my soul to take.
>   I can't imagine ever asking Ellie, or any
> child, to say such a prayer, but it does
> seem to describe a peaceful end, and that
> is all that I hope for if this goes wrong.
>   If all goes well, you will hear from me
> again in a few days. Take care of yourself.
>   love John.

What the hell was he up to? Jason would be furious, and like her, worried out of his mind. What a thing to send by email. There was no way to argue with him, no way to find out more. Perhaps that was the point. He didn't want anyone to talk him out of it, whatever *it* was. What was she supposed to do?

- - -

"What is the rush, Ben? Why not give John another week? Even better, a month?" asked Triveni.

"But you say he's ready."

"He is."

"And he's willing."

"That is one of the things that worries me. He should be more concerned about the risks."

"Convince me that the risks will be less in a month and I will delay the attempt."

"I cannot. He is at least as good as any other initiate we have ever tried. I can think of nothing else we can do to prepare him better – other than give him more time."

Ben turned to John. "Would you like to make Triveni happy and take more time?"

John looked back and forth between them from his place on the bed. What Ben was offering him was astounding, but it came at a risk. "You may, in effect, go to sleep and never wake up again," Ben had warned him. But this was John's choice, and for once it was an easy choice.

He could choose to do nothing – and lose everything. He could become deaf and blind to the world of the narun. He could choose to never see his friends again, to never see Asha's beautiful green eyes, to never hear the compassion in her voice. And, if they found a way to heal Ellie, he could choose to never see that miracle. He could choose to have his last memories of his daughter as a shrivelled grey being in torment.

Or he could take this risk – and gain more than he had ever imagined possible. As far as John was concerned there wasn't really a choice at all, this was simply his only option, his only chance.

"If I'm ready according to your normal procedures then I would prefer to try this now," he told Ben. Before Asha is here to object, he added silently.

Ben turned to Jia. "Do you have any objections?"

"Physically there is no reason we cannot proceed."

Ben looked back and forth between the women and then back to John, his eyebrows raised. John nodded to him.

"All right then," Ben declared, "let's get on with it."

John lay back and waited while Jia prepared her syringes. These drugs entered his system like ice, freezing lines that crept down through his body. He drew a breath and tried to calm himself.

"When you are ready, John," Triveni told him. "You have practised this."

John nodded and moved to one side of the bed. He closed his eyes and began his relaxation techniques. After just a few minutes he could feel his body slowing down. Parts of his body were going numb, he was already starting to feel cut off from it, but he knew this was only the drugs, the important process had not yet started. He waited.

As he waited he considered, yet again, whether he was doing the right thing. He was not by nature an impetuous person. But what he was doing now was impetuous, wasn't it? Irresponsible even? No. The only responsibility he had now was to Ellie. He loved Asha, he didn't want to hurt her, but he wasn't responsible for her. This was his risk and his choice.

He sent his vedana out along his body, the sense felt strong now, clear and precise. He could feel the life in all parts of his body, it was the only way he could feel his body at all now, the drugs had taken full effect. The time had come. He began the silent chant that would place his mind into a trance, primed with autosuggestion triggers. He finished the chant with a final thought and confirmation, "For Ellie."

The first trigger kicked in and the process started. Flames lapped at his fingers and toes. Fire burned along his limbs. Tension built and pulled, tearing at every cell. The body he thought was numb now screamed its agony at him. He had been told it would be painful, but this? The second trigger kicked in and his mind went blank.

"Are you sure there's not a more direct path?" Senna asked Seriyani.

"If you want to see all the Glades then the way will be long," Seriyani replied.

"We don't seem to be getting anything useful," said Darnu, "and it's taking a long time. Are you sure you want to go on?" he asked Asha.

"We've come this far, we'll go on," Asha replied impatiently, this wasn't the first time they'd had this conversation. She desperately wanted to get back to John, to make sure he was recovering, but she didn't want to return without some positive news for him, for Ellie. They had nowhere else to go. She couldn't give up yet.

"There's no reason to expect we'll get anything new from other

Glades here," argued Darnu.

"There was no reason to expect anything from any of these Glades. We didn't come here expecting anything – just hoping."

"But time is getting away, maybe it would be better spending our time looking elsewhere," put in Garjae.

"Where?" Asha demanded, glaring at him.

Garjae turned away.

"John wouldn't be happy if we returned without trying all the Glades we can," said Andrei.

"John's not the one—" Garjae glanced back at Asha and stopped himself from continuing.

"I am happy to keep guiding you for as long as you need," said Seriyani. "You shouldn't give up too quickly."

"A case of the blind leading the blind?" suggested Andrei.

Seriyani scowled at him.

"If you tell us the way to the next Glade we can manage from there," Andrei added.

Asha nodded her agreement. "They can direct us on to the next one." She turned to Garjae. "This is the only lead we have, we have to see it through." Then back to Seriyani again. "And we can certainly find our way back to the Samgha."

Seriyani looked at Asha, silent for the moment. Asha knew there was no love lost between the two of them. Seriyani had consistently been in agreement with Asha, insisting that they should keep trying, but Asha didn't think this was really an interest in what they were searching for. Seriyani didn't seem particularly interested in anything other than herself, with the possible exception of Darnu. She looked away from Asha and turned to Darnu. "There's no need for us to separate yet."

"I need some time out," Asha said, and looked around the group. "I think we all need some rest. I suggest we take a day out to rebuild our strength."

No one raised any objections, although Senna and Andrei gave each other some strange looks. Their tumultuous relationship continued rocky, but Senna hadn't tried to talk to Asha about it again.

Despite saying that they all needed rest, Asha couldn't settle and spent much of the afternoon walking the forest. Evening was falling when she sensed someone ahead. It turned out to be Andrei.

"I thought you said we should be resting," he told her.

"If you're so willing to accept what I say, why aren't you resting in a tree somewhere?"

Andrei grinned. "Keeping an eye on you."

"Who says I need keeping an eye on?"

"I do, ... well, Senna does."

"You two are talking again?"

"Sometimes."

Asha studied Andrei's face as she asked, "Why does Senna think I need keeping an eye on?"

"She doesn't actually, or doesn't realise that she does."

"Andrei, you're not making sense."

"Did you know we're being followed?" Andrei asked, looking smug as he watched the surprise appear on Asha's face.

Asha looked around her. "For how long?"

"On and off since before the first Glade."

"Why haven't you said anything?"

Andrei shrugged. "I don't think he means any harm."

"He? Who? Have you met him?"

"No, just brief glimpses."

Asha walked up to Andrei and looked him in the face. "Are you going to make me drag this out of you a word at a time?"

Andrei grinned widely. "Sounds like fun."

"Andrei!"

"All right," he held up his hands in surrender. "It wasn't me that noticed him, it was Senna."

"She hasn't said anything."

"She doesn't know."

"Andrei."

"Come and sit down," Andrei told her, "and let me tell it."

They settled in the leaf litter at the base of a large tree.

"I've been fidgety and unsettled ever since we got into this jungle," Andrei started. "I don't sleep much, and I spend a lot of time trying to take it all in." Asha nodded, she'd felt much the same. "One of the things I noticed early on was that Senna kept looking around, as if she felt something or someone nearby. She would always end up giving up on it, I think the jungle is hard for her, but I decided to investigate. That's when I first saw him."

Andrei paused, so Asha asked, "Who?"

"Well I don't know that, do I?"

"Andrei!"

"He's aaranya. I think he might be an elder, he certainly looks ancient."

"Why haven't the rest of us seen him?"

"No one else has been looking. I only started looking because of Senna."

Asha looked at him curiously. "Why didn't you say something to Senna?"

"Well, at first, she wasn't talking to me."

"And then?"

"And then, when she started talking to me, I thought she'd just get angry with me again when she learned I'd been keeping something from her, so I stayed dumb."

There didn't seem any way to refute such logic so Asha asked, "You know she's worried about you?"

Andrei looked surprised. "Why?"

"I'm not sure really. She started to try and tell me something a while back, but never quite got to it."

"Yeah, I know that one well enough. She often doesn't quite tell me things, and then complains that I haven't paid attention."

"Andrei, I'm serious."

"So am I. Don't I wish I weren't."

Asha thought about what Andrei had told her. "If he's an elder he couldn't have stayed away from his Glade for so long."

"I thought about that. I told you he was only here on and off, as far as I could tell anyway. I think maybe he returns to his Glade and then comes back to us."

"But how could he catch up? We haven't exactly been dawdling."

"But we've not been going in a straight line either. Senna thinks Seriyani has been taking the long way a lot of the time. If this man knew where we were going he could take a shortcut and catch up."

"Which leaves the obvious question of why," Asha thought out loud.

"Maybe he wants to make sure we don't pinch the silver."

"Around here I think it's jade they're worried about," Asha

corrected him.

The sun was not long up and the jungle was noisy with the dawn chorus of creatures greeting the day. Asha drew herself out onto a branch and stretched.

Casseta bounded down the trunk of the tree and jumped to her shoulder. Asha kissed the head of the creature. "Good morning, Cassey, did you have a good night?" There was a faint twitter of response. Asha expected the brevi to merge then, but she stayed perched on Asha's shoulder, enjoying the morning.

Asha leant back against the trunk of the tree and stared up into the canopy. She might be sick of the jungle forest, but at times like this it really was quite spectacular.

"Dawn is always a special time," a voice spoke softly from one side.

Asha looked around in surprise. Andrei had returned to be near Senna, so she had expected to be alone. On the branch of a tree next to hers, at about the same level, stood a man. An ancient man. Presumably the man that Andrei had spoken of last night.

"I am he," he said, guessing her thoughts. "Your friend Andrei is persistent, but he's not really a tracker. Now Senna, yes, Senna could be a tracker if she were trained to it."

"None of us are used to the intensity of this jungle."

"I understand. You are not the first foreigners I have met."

"Spied on."

The old man raised his palms. "It was rude. I apologise for the necessity."

"I hardly think it was necessary. We were looking to speak with others, you could have approached us at any time."

"It was necessary that I know your relationships, particularly to the Samgha. Such cannot be told, they can only be observed."

"It seems an odd job for an elder to undertake. You are an elder?"

The old man nodded.

Asha considered him carefully. He did appear to be very old. There were only wisps of white hair on his head, he was very thin, and his eyes were a very pale brown, as if the colour had been bleached from them by time.

The old man leapt up to a smaller branch that reached toward

119

Asha's tree, and then down onto the branch near Asha.

On the other hand, thought Asha, looks can be deceiving.

"I am Litak the elder," the old man introduced himself.

Asha opened her mouth to introduce herself, and then closed it again, realising such an introduction was redundant.

"Yes," the old man acknowledged, "you are Asha the healer."

"I have not adopted such a title."

"It was a statement of identity, not of title. I am an elder. It is not something I can claim or reject, it simply is. And you are a healer." He indicated the branch. "Can we sit and talk?"

Asha looked at him doubtfully, then at the brevi. Casseta didn't appear to be disturbed. Asha murmured to her and the brevi merged without any apparent qualms or hesitation. Asha sat on the branch and rested her back against the trunk of the tree. Already some birds were flying in to be near her.

The old man sat a small but comfortable distance from her and watched the birds with a smile on his face. "If I had any doubts as to who and what you are, these birds would have soon removed them."

"The birds have done this from the start, so you must have known what I was then."

Litak nodded. "But I still didn't know, wasn't certain, of your relationship to the Samgha."

"Why is that so important to you? Our quest is what it is, and has nothing to do with them except for the help they have offered."

"For what price?"

Asha felt disarmed, it was exactly the question that bothered her. "They wanted to meet John."

"So the price is to be paid by the human. That could be as well."

Asha looked at the man sharply. "John is my—" She stopped, uncertain how to complete that sentence to a stranger.

"I understand. You have affection for the human," said Litak.

Asha just stared back at him.

"You are looking for a powerful healer that once stayed here. You are hoping for help, for someone to teach you how to heal a preta, the daughter of this human."

Asha nodded.

"What makes you think such healing is possible?"

"What makes you think it is not?" she retorted.

"I have never heard of it being done."

"Have you ever heard of it being attempted?"

"No."

"So we don't know that it can't be done."

"Perhaps."

"Do you know of the healer?" Asha asked, looking the man directly in the eye, trying to read his reaction.

Litak returned her gaze calmly, and then turned away, looking out into the forest. "Age does not bring infallibility, not even great age. My compeers think I am mistaken. Some think my time is almost over – they may even be right about that. But I think they are wrong in judging you by the company you keep. I think you are sincere and truthful."

Asha remained silent, waiting. This had to be leading somewhere.

Eventually he continued, "The Glades here no longer trust the Samgha. Since Samvaya Benjamin has taken control, and even before that, when his human father exerted such influence over them, we have felt that the Samgha had turned from the hidden ways of their forefathers, and adopted the ways of so called civilised humans. We don't trust what this will mean for us.

"Do we have cause?" he echoed Asha's unspoken question. "Perhaps not. We cannot approve of all their activities, especially not now, but those that affect us out here in the forest have changed very little. But their attitudes have changed. They have become more peremptory in their dealings with us, the manner of your guide is an apropos example. They are not what they were when our agreement was first reached."

"What agreement?" Asha interrupted.

Litak didn't look surprised, but still asked. "So they really sent you out here without telling you?"

"Telling us what?"

Asha listened as Litak told her the history of the Samgha, how it had survived the Aeonian War, and how the aaranya elders eventually agreed to keep the secret of the Samgha.

"What secret?"

"What they are. Do you even know who, *what*, your guide really is?"

"I don't know what you mean."

Litak sighed and looked out into the forest. "To tell you more is to break an agreement that has lasted for generations, many thousands of years. I've already told you more than I should. I had hoped that you already knew, or had guessed from what you had seen of them."

"We weren't there long."

"Samvaya Benjamin had you bustled out the door before you could ask too many awkward questions? Sounds like him," Litak observed, and looked back at Asha.

"I know Jia and Ben both feel ... strange. Like a narun in a human body," she said.

"And you can't guess what that means?"

- - -

John woke to his body panting heavily and the memory of fire roaring through his body. "Fucking hell!" he swore out loud.

There was a loud booming laugh. "I think that means he made it."

John opened his eyes, he was staring at the sheet. The third trigger must have worked, he was awake. He was lying mostly on his side but tilted to the front. He started to roll back.

"Not yet," came a woman's voice and a hand restrained him.

He felt warm hands on his torso, and another pair on his legs. His body was lifted, carried a short distance, and then deposited gently on his back on the second bed. He saw Jia discreetly bring the sheet up and gently settle it over the lower part of his body. She moved to the top of the bed and adjusted it to lift John into a slightly more upright position. John saw Ben and Triveni looking at him with interest from the foot of the bed.

"You did make it, didn't you, John?" Ben asked.

"I think I must have," John replied. His voice felt weak and husky.

"That's better. You had me going for a moment. I thought perhaps your swearing was some sort of reflex behaviour, you do hear some strange things about Australians."

"Sorry. You told me it was painful, but I wasn't prepared for the burning."

"Some things are best not gone into in too much detail."

"Why am I so weak?"

"To be expected, John, it's a big ordeal for your body, both of them," Jia told him.

"A few things missing from my education," John observed.

"You were the one in a hurry to try this," Triveni reminded him.

Ben put a hand on Triveni's arm to stop further comment, and told John, "There's a lot of things that it wasn't worth going into in detail until we knew whether it was even an issue for you. Yes, you are weak, and it will take time to build your strength."

Jia continued, "And you are fragile, John. You spoke of the burning sensation. Think of your newly exposed body as all new skin, as if you truly had been burned. It will take time for your exposed praanin skin to thicken and strengthen."

John looked back and forth between them, and even that much activity took a lot of effort. He turned his head to look past Jia, and could see himself lying quiet and still on the other bed. He let his head roll back and peered down. With some effort he lifted one hand and looked at it.

He stared in wonder, then moved his fingers to be sure it was indeed his hand. So strange. His skin was translucent, almost trans-parent, but instead of seeing veins and flesh beneath his barely visible skin, there were swirling patterns of gold. He lifted his hand closer and gazed in wonder at the intricate flows. In one moment the flows looked like roiling lava, in the next it was the surface of the sun, now they reminded him of fractal images animated in endless shades of gold. Fascinated, John stared closer still, watching as the swirls inside his hand formed patterns that grew in complexity and variety the further he delved into their depths.

"Ben, it looks like those details are an issue now. Want to start filling me in?" he whispered.

"Not now," Jia interrupted. "You need to rest, John. Ben will answer your questions later. First, I need you to relax."

John looked up at her in surprise, he hadn't thought of himself as particularly tense.

"Take a deep breath, John," Triveni spoke softly from the end of the bed. "Remember the techniques you learned. Relax your body."

John thought to question, to argue that he wasn't in the mood, but found that he didn't have the strength. So he put his hand down and went through his relaxation exercises in his mind. Something about his body changed as he did so and he roused himself back to wakefulness. He opened his eyes and looked around him, everything seemed to have grown. He suddenly felt very small. "What's happened?" he asked, frightened by the change.

"Shhh. It's nothing, John," Jia reassured him, her hand large on his shoulder. "Your body is adjusting. It reduces in size to consolidate its strength."

John lifted his hand to look at it again. He could see that the skin was more apparent, thicker, he could barely see the patterns any longer. "It looked prettier before," he murmured weakly. He heard Ben laugh from the end of the bed.

"It's better this way, stronger," Jia assured him. "Relax now, you need to sleep."

Jia was right. There were questions rising in his mind, but he was too weak to deal with them now. He began his relaxation exercises again. He dimly heard Ben and Triveni leave the room. Jia stayed to lay John's bed back flat and then she turned to check his material body. John drifted into sleep and didn't see her leave.

- - -

"Samvaya, saarvaya, saardha. None of these words mean anything to you?" Litak asked.

Asha just looked at him.

"Samvaya means union. Samvaya is the union of the saarvaya and saardha."

She returned his questioning gaze with a blank look.

"Animals, including humans, are really two bodies overlaid, yes? The praanin body, what they call the saarvaya, over the flesh-and-blood body, the saardha."

Asha's eyes widened.

"Yes," Litak said as he saw the realisation dawning. "Saarvaya Seriyani, who has been your guide out here, is truly only half of the being known as Samvaya Seriyani. Back in the Samgha there will be a Saardha Seriyani, the flesh-and-blood body to which she must return."

"So Samvaya Benjamin?"

"Can separate his praanin body from his flesh-and-blood body, and exist like a narun."

Asha tried to sort through the flood of thoughts that swarmed through her mind. "But ... but this is the stuff of children's tales."

"Scary tales, if Samvaya Benjamin is in them," said Litak.

"You know what I mean. Our legends speak of such people, but only in ancient times."

"The Samgha has been there a long time."

"How? How do they do it?"

"They are different. Their ancestors were not all human," said Litak. "In generations past, those of the Samgha were more like Samvaya Benjamin than the others that remain."

Asha nodded. Yes, Ben had told them that much, just neglected to explain what it really meant. "So John ... they wouldn't?"

Litak shrugged. "I do not know. He doesn't share their ancestry, it may not be possible."

Or it might be, Asha thought to herself. And if there was *any* possibility, was there any doubt that John would try?

Litak continued, "We have not spoken word of their existence to others in all these years, but I doubt if it matters any more – which is why I have been willing to speak with you now. Samvaya Benjamin has been dealing with humans more than he tells us. The existence of the Samgha is truly not a secret any longer – not from those least to be trusted.

"I refer to humans, Westerner humans. And you come in the company of one, giving us yet another reason to doubt you for the company you keep. We have not met this human, this John, and have no cause to feel whatever trust and affection for him that you have so obviously found. And, I must tell you, that even if I answer your question there is a good chance that it will not aid you – not while this John remains aloof from those of whom you seek help."

Asha, still overwhelmed by the news of the samvaya, and what that might mean for John, had to struggle to catch up. "John didn't want to remain aloof, but he feared that he would slow the search too much, and that his presence would not be welcome among the aaranya."

"That much is probably true," Litak admitted. "It is a difficult dilemma." He looked at Asha with sympathy. "Meanwhile, he remains with the Samgha, perhaps paying a price that I see raises fear in your eyes."

Asha could only nod.

"But none of that changes what you came here seeking. Obviously you would not like to leave without obtaining what you may have already paid for."

"Will you answer our question?" Asha asked, pushing away her fear for John. Litak was right, she couldn't turn back, and the elder must know something or he wouldn't be here.

Litak ignored the plea and said, "We do have other reasons to be disquiet and untrusting at this time. We were not always such a suspicious people, and we are not all so short-sighted as Senna seems to think."

"You heard that?"

"Yes. It was a big risk getting that close while Senna was there, but she was distracted with her own troubles, and not paying much attention to what was going on around her. I almost approached you at that time, but decided to wait a little longer."

"Not exactly a *little* longer."

Litak shrugged. "Did the Samgha tell you of strange happenings at other Glades?"

"Some. They offered few details."

"Most of what they know comes from us. For their own part they have so far showed very little interest in helping us to find out more."

"They helped you send messages south," Asha commented, remembering the aaranya she had met visiting Glades on Cape York."

"True enough. I admit that they surprised me in that."

"Is there more?"

"All we know is that Glades are going silent, and when people try to learn what is happening, they go missing. It is very disturbing. If a Glade can just go silent like that, what is to stop it happening to us? And whatever it is, it is getting steadily, if slowly, closer.

"And you think the Samgha could be involved?"

Litak remained silent for a few moments before admitting, "That thought is, perhaps, my own imagination. Over recent years there have been some strange comings and goings at the Samgha and it has left some of us concerned."

"How is it you know anything about what comes and goes at the Samgha?"

Litak looked away. "We watch, and as our trust diminishes we watch more carefully."

Asha looked out into the jungle. If their search led them further north they might run right into this mysterious shadow of silence. She turned back to Litak and asked again, "Will you answer our question?"

"Will you promise not to involve the Samgha further in your search?"

Asha considered this. "I'm not sure I can make that promise. Depending on where the search leads us, we may need their help to get there, if they will give it."

After a few moments he nodded. "I will have to trust you to be discreet. As a woman of obvious strength and honour, I ask you to honour my request, to respect a foolish old man's sense of paranoia, and keep the exact details of what you discover from the Samgha while ever that remains possible. If this healer is still alive, if her home has not gone silent, then I believe her home is a very long way from here."

"You don't know where she is?" Asha asked, her hopes fading.

Litak shook his head, "No."

"Then how can you help us?"

"Will you promise?"

"What about John? I must be able to tell John. As you say, he will have to come with us."

Litak nodded. "You may tell him on this same condition."

"Then you have my promise. While ever it remains possible we will keep the Samgha ignorant of any details they do not need to know."

Litak sat there thinking. Eventually he resolved some internal struggle and told her, "You have been asking the wrong people. The healer was not aaranya. She was jalaja."

Asha stared at him in surprise.

He continued, "She was wise and generous and good, and she treated aaranya and jalaja, and even yaayaavara, alike. For a time her influence improved the relations between our peoples and made us ashamed of how poorly we had acted in the past. Mostly that positive influence has since faded. To discover more you must find some jalaja, but you will need to do so without your current guide. The jalaja have never formed any sort of trust or compact with the Samgha."

- - -

John woke and a sensation of convulsive movement made him open his eyes. Above him the stomach of the great beast heaved as it prepared to digest something not entirely palatable. The lining quivered and pulsed, and peristaltic waves flowed down the walls. John gripped at the sheet of his bed, waiting for the inevitable movement that must cast him into the digestive juices that would feed his life to this immense creature.

He blinked, and the ceiling and walls returned to stone. The pink flecked granite was still, the contours frozen in time. He turned his head and saw himself lying there, almost as still as the granite walls. He watched carefully for a long minute and thought he could detect the slow, shallow breath that indicated the body was still functioning. He continued staring, fascinated to see himself from the outside, to see himself as others must see him.

At last he turned back to his other self, his new self, the being in which he now existed. He lifted his hand and studied it again. It looked like the hand he remembered, it even carried the small scar on the palm from some forgotten childhood mishap. There was no sign of the patterns he had seen earlier, he wondered if that had been a dream or some side effect of the drugs. The bed, the room, everything, appeared to be very large, as if it had grown – that much at least had not been a dream. He lifted both hands and felt his face and hair, it all seemed familiar. His eyes could see that he must be smaller, but to himself he felt the same. A curious thought made him lift the sheet and look down: all looked to be in order, although he didn't feel much like making use of the fact.

The sound of the door made him put the sheet back down quickly and look up. Jia was looking in at him from the doorway, there was a knowing smile on her face.

"Just checking I didn't leave anything behind," John joked, embarrassed.

Her smiled widened. "You haven't, I checked," she told him, "it's my job." She raised the top of John's bed so he was sitting up and patted his shoulder gently, her touch lingering, and then she went back to the door. "I will let Ben know you're awake. Stay quiet on the bed for now." She left, closing the door behind her.

John rearranged himself on the pillows, noting that he wasn't

128

making as much of an indentation as he was used to. He considered ignoring Jia's suggestion, but when he started to move his legs off the bed the floor looked a very long way down, so he decided to wait.

He looked to the other bed, his other self. He had trouble believing that this had actually worked. As soon as he was able, he would have to send off news of his survival to his friends, and his apologies for worrying them. And he'd tear up the letter he'd written for Asha, she didn't need to know how much of a risk he had been willing to take for this.

He turned to the other side of the bed, and the chair from which Ben had shown him this was possible.

"Please sit quietly until I say otherwise," Ben had warned him.

So John had watched as Ben settled himself back in the chair and closed his eyes. It was only seconds later that Ben's body appeared to settle deeper into the chair, as if falling into a very deep sleep, something John now recognised as the deep trance state he had been learning to achieve. Nothing happened for a while and then John blinked to see if his eyes were playing tricks on him. It looked like Ben's body had started to vibrate. A moment later Ben stood up and stepped forward slightly. At least part of him did. There were now two of him. One remained sitting silent and still in the chair, the other was standing. The eyes on the standing figure opened and grinned at John.

John stared up at him, not quite believing what he'd seen.

"You can speak now," Ben, the standing version, had assured him.

John wasn't sure he could. He continued to stare, trying to take it in. The standing figure was noticeably smaller than Ben usually was, and naked, but it was certainly him.

"Ah," the standing Ben said, "some clothes for modesty." He appeared to concentrate for a few moments, there was a faint blurring around his body, and then the standing figure was clothed to match that of the seated figure.

John began to understand. The standing figure had a praanin body, just like a narun. He leaned to the side to get a better view of the seated figure. Its eyes were closed, its body was unnaturally still, and it lacked something – the presence that had been so strong before.

"Which is the real you?" John managed to ask, looking up.

"You can feel it for yourself. This is my life," the standing figure said, indicating itself, "this is my presence, and where it goes so does my self, my spirit. So, in the sense that you mean, this is the real me."

John looked back at the figure in the other chair.

Ben continued, "When I came into the room I was samvaya: the union. This," he touched his chest, "is the saarvaya, and that," he stepped aside and indicated the material body sitting silent in the chair, "is the saardha. The two halves of the body that, together, make Samvaya Benjamin. Separated like this, I am now Saarvaya Benjamin, and that," he pointed, "is Saardha Benjamin."

"But ...?" John couldn't continue.

"Some call that the physical body, but as you know this praanin body physically exists too, just in a different form. Calling that the material body works, but I prefer the old language: saardha means exactly that without ambiguity or imprecision."

"And you can separate ... just like that?"

"I can, yes, but most samvaya require assistance, the same drugs that you have been using. Yet another sign of our decline."

As the reality of what John had seen began to sink in, a new thought came bursting through. "If you can do this *you* can help my daughter!"

Ben shook his head sadly.

"She was separated from her body, just as you have done. You *must* be able to help," John insisted.

"I am truly sorry, my friend, but we can't. Your daughter is a preta, she was forcibly removed from her body. *If* the damage done by that can be repaired, it is a skill beyond the Samgha."

Ben walked across and sat on the side of the bed before continuing, "The risk we face when we separate the two halves of our being, the risk *you* will face, is to be left stranded, to be unable to waken the saarvaya after separation. If that happens the two halves cannot be rejoined and both, eventually, die."

Ben looked pensive, apparently wondering how much to say.

"Go on," John urged.

"The real issue is that your daughter no longer has her saardha. A preta is incomplete, just the saarvaya, just half, and one half cannot survive without the other."

Ben leaned forward. "You must know this already. Asha must have explained it. You know that to damage the material body is to damage the praanin body within, and to damage the praanin body is to damage the material body that carries it. We of the Samgha can separate the two, but we cannot undo that most intimate tie."

John slumped back. The sudden hope suddenly dashed.

Ben continued, "When the saardha dies, the death of the saarvaya usually happens very quickly. Sometimes it takes longer, even months, but it *always* happens, and it is not a pretty end. In the long history of my people there have been no exceptions. I'm sorry, John."

"I thought you would be happy," Ben's booming voice brought John back to the here and now. "It worked."

John looked over to the door. "I was thinking of my daughter."

Ben looked grim, and then his expression brightened and he asked, "How does it feel, Saarvaya John, to be separated?"

"Weak, but otherwise I feel fine. How long have I been out?"

"A day, close enough. Jia tells me you slept it away very peace-fully."

"Almost a whole day," John whispered.

"That's good," Ben assured him. "While you rest your body gains in strength and resilience."

"How? I'm not eating anything, I thought I'd be getting weaker," he looked down at his body on the bed, "and smaller."

"It's this room. Feel the life from the rock around you. The only place you will feel it stronger is when you're standing against a large tree, or swimming in a lake or the ocean. It's why we use this room. It's safe, protected and predictable, but it still gives you access to the life you need. Before my ancestors found this place, initiation would happen out in the forest, but being so fragile on first separation many initiates were lost."

"So I just lie here and soak it up."

"For now," agreed Ben. "For this first separation we usually recommend you stay separate for a full three days, but then return and merge back with the saardha, remaining whole for at least two days. We repeat this cycle, adjusting the timing as needed. Eventually you will feel strong enough, and confident enough, that separation will just be a matter of arranging for aid from Jia, or one of the other doctors here."

"Will I always need help from your doctors? You don't."

"I've had years of practice. I'm also different. I was born to this more so than almost anyone else here. You will always need the drugs and assistance."

John considered this, and his desire to see his daughter inside the Glade. He would have to work something out, he'd come too far to be blocked now. Maybe Asha could help him.

"How long until I'm strong enough to get around on my own?"

"We encourage activity as soon as you are up to it, but you won't be up to much more than moving around this room until your third or fourth separation. You need time for your skin to toughen up before it is safe to venture far."

"And what do I do with myself in the meantime?"

"You can watch movies on the computer screen there, or read some books. Someone around here has a reader with a huge collection of titles on it."

"I'd like to learn more about the narun – and the Samgha. Do you have any books on that?"

"Some, but they're mostly dry, scholarly texts. I'll ask Samvaya Nayati to come down. He is a wealth of information and much more entertaining than our books on the subject. He will be pleased to have a brand-new audience."

John sat himself a bit straighter on the bed.

"You look restless," Ben observed. "Would you like some assistance to try and stand while I'm here? Jia tells me you are a little shy in front of her."

John responded eagerly, "Please." He carefully slid his legs out and then pulled the sheet back. He stared down in surprise. He looked to be wearing underpants, something very like his preferred black briefs. "They weren't there before," he managed to say.

Ben laughed at his reaction. "I am impressed. Clothing doesn't usually come so quickly. Jia might be right, maybe you are a prude."

John rubbed his fingertips over the material. There was something a little odd about it, not least that he could sense his touch on the cloth. He looked up at Ben. "I've seen you do it, and I've seen the aaranya do it, but I'd always imagined it would take some thought or effort."

"Usually it comes about as a deliberate choice," Ben explained, "but there can also be an element of reaction, where your mind makes choices for you depending on your predilections."

"But how does it work? I don't remember thinking of these, or even feeling them appear."

Leaving John sitting on the edge of the bed, Ben leaned against the back of a chair and explained, "Without the exigencies of flesh-and-blood, your praanin body is much more a creature of your will. In time you will learn that you can control various aspects of your appearance: clothing, as you see, but also colouring and to some limited extent size. I have never known a saarvaya to gain the sort of flexibility enjoyed by the narun, but we get along."

John hesitated, then said, "I've told you of my daughter's appearance. Asha thinks that might be because her mind is not awake. What you say seems to bear that out, that if we can restore her mind we might restore her appearance."

"That may be part of it, but I keep coming back to the loss of her saardha. When you separate from the flesh-and-blood body you do not leave it completely empty of life, some residue must remain to prevent the flesh from dying. While both halves live the saarvaya remains connected to the saardha in ways we don't really understand, but we do know that when the saardha is lost something crucial to the saarvaya is lost too."

"But my daughter is a preta, she was pushed from her body. We have no reason to believe that anything was left behind."

Ben nodded slowly, doubtfully. "That's true. ... You may be right. Perhaps there is no reason to assume that our experience here directly reflects your daughter's situation." He stood up. "Come on, let's get you up and see how you feel."

Ben, while thickly built, had always been much shorter than John, but now he stood there large before him, making John feel like a child. John reached out and placed his hands on Ben's large, rock-steady forearms. He pulled himself forward and managed, with considerable effort, to slide his feet to the distant floor and to pull himself upright. He stood there swaying.

"Good," Ben encouraged. "Very good. Want to try some steps?"

John nodded.

Ben stepped backwards slowly and John followed, one slow step at a time. The weakness was the first thing he noticed. He didn't feel himself to be all that heavy, and yet his legs were having trouble holding him steady. There was also a change in sensation, all his sensations. Ben's arm was large and strong, and warm and living, but there was an intensity beneath John's fingers that he had not felt before. And then there was the floor. It felt harsh against the soles of his feet, as if he was standing on shards of rock. He could tell the floor was cold, but it wasn't chilling his feet as it had with his other body. Some background part of his mind marvelled over his casual use of such terms as his *other body*.

"Where to?" Ben asked him.

"How about the bathroom?"

"You shouldn't need that, not in this body."

"But there's a mirror in there."

"And you won't see anything in it."

"I know. That's what I want to see. I'm not sure I'll really believe it until I do." John was thinking about the first time he hadn't seen Asha in a mirror. It was that experience as much as anything else that made him want to see this – to *not* see this.

When they drew level with the foot of the other bed, John asked Ben to stop while he turned to look at his material body, his saardha, in the parlance of the Samgha. The expression on the face of his other body looked calm, serene in a way he guessed it rarely, if ever, looked when he was present. He laughed as a thought occurred to him.

"What?" Ben wanted to know.

"I was just envying the peace and quiet my other half was enjoying. That struck me as a rather silly thing to do. Let's go."

Eventually they made it to the bathroom, and John watched in the mirror as Ben led apparently nothing and no one into the small room. He carefully let go of Ben and reached out for the bathroom cabinet. Leaning his chest against the cabinet, he reached one hand out and tried to touch where his reflection should be. He could feel the glass but there was no reflection, nothing, not the faintest shadow or blurring. He rapped the glass lightly with his knuckles, still not really believing what he wasn't seeing.

"Any surprises here I should know about?" John asked, looking at Ben in the mirror. "My back is not purple with yellow spots or anything?"

Ben looked John up and down. "I didn't see this much of you before, but it all looks normal enough to me. The only thing you may not be aware of are these contours down your back." Ben reached forward and drew his fingers from beneath each shoulder blade, in lines down that almost met at the base of John's back. "They're perfectly normal and will fade as you spend more time separated."

John started to turn, to try and see his back in the mirror, then laughed at himself and twisted his arm back. Yes, he could feel them. Like two long lines of scar tissue from some long ago injury. "What are they?"

"There's a lot of debate as to their origin. In the narun this is where the wings of their children sprout from. In narun and saarvaya, this is where our clothing usually remains attached to the body. They are just a fact of our existence, like a vestigial limb left over by evolution when no longer needed."

John felt how his underpants were apparently joined to his body at the base of his back where these two lines almost met, he wondered what it looked like. Maybe he and Asha could demonstrate for one another – the thought brought a smile to his face. He wondered where she was at the moment.

- - -

"A jalaja ... a naiad?" Andrei asked, incredulous.

Asha nodded. "That's what he said."

The group of them were gathered high in the branches of a tree. Asha had waited impatiently for a chance to get the others away from Seriyani so she could tell them what Litak had told her.

Asha continued, "The frustrating thing is that if we had asked at Glades outside the influence of the Samgha they may have answered our queries more openly, having no reason to distrust us."

"But we only got to here thanks to them," Andrei reminded her.

"Did he suggest where we should start looking?" Darnu asked.

"There's a river to the north-east. He said there's some jalaja there that he believes will have memories of this healer, and they may still be friendly enough to speak with aaranya."

"But we're supposed to keep the Samgha ignorant of the details," Garjae said.

Asha nodded.

"Any idea how we do that?"

"We separate," said Senna. The others turned to look at her. "Andrei and I go to this river and meet with the jalaja, meanwhile you all go with Seriyani to the next Glade and pretend we expect answers. After you visit the next Glade or two, you tell Seriyani that you have decided that there is no more help to be had, and then we all meet back at the Samgha."

"Shouldn't Asha be the one to go to the river?" asked Darnu.

"Seriyani is not likely to swallow that," Senna replied. "Andrei and I can say we just want time to ourselves, but Asha is the one supposed to be qualified to meet any healer we find."

"Which is why she should be the one to meet with the jalaja."

"We're only looking for more information on how to find the healer," Senna argued, "we already know that we don't expect to meet one here."

"What if you don't find what we need from the first jalaja?" Asha asked.

"We keep looking, with their help if they'll give it, and you wait for us."

"Please," added Andrei. He was looking both surprised and pleased at Senna's suggestion.

- - -

Tracey sat at the traffic lights and tapped her fingers to the music. She was feeling pretty good. It had been a good day at work, quiet. Last night Mike had taken her out and she had worn the lovely bracelets he had given her. He had even come in afterwards and said hello to her mother – Brian wasn't home. He hadn't stayed very long. Still, it felt like a good start.

She glanced in the rear-vision mirror and noted the car and driver, they seemed familiar. The lights changed and she moved off.

She had received the expected phone call from Jason last Saturday. He had become quite nasty on the phone, but had called back later to apologise. It had taken three days until an email from John had put them all out of their misery: he was okay. Whatever he had done had apparently worked. John sounded happy, though the message was brief. Jason's response had been much longer and very strongly worded, Tracey wondered how John would respond to it, he hadn't yet.

At the next lights the same car was behind her, it seemed to be following her. She turned off the main road, down toward her house, and the car remained close behind. When she eventually pulled in at her house it was still there, she watched as it went slowly past. The car turned down a dead-end street. It must have been a local, that would be why they were following, and why they were familiar.

She got out and noted Brian's car in the driveway. When she went inside he was sitting on the sofa watching television, he lifted a hand and waved to her. He had been laughing at something on the screen. He was a tall, dark-haired man. He had probably once been athletic looking, but was now starting to spread around the middle. He had a round face that was always smiling, always in a good mood. She could see why her mother liked him, though Tracey found him irritating rather than likeable.

Tracey found her mother in the kitchen going through the fridge, sorting out what she wanted to cook for dinner.

"Good day?" her mother asked as she straightened up. Tracey envied her mother her slender figure. People said they looked alike, but, to Tracey, her mother always looked more elegant and together than Tracey ever felt.

"Quiet," Tracey replied. She grabbed the fridge door before her mother closed it and grabbed the orange juice.

"Brian said you left your computer on again this morning," her mother chided.

"What was he doing in my room anyway?"

"It's not like it's your bedroom or anything. He saw the computer was on and went in to shut it down for you."

"Hmm." Tracey wasn't particularly happy about Brian fiddling with her things. Technically the computer was in a spare room, it was just that in practice she was the only one that ever used it, and she had come to depend on that. What if he'd gone through her stuff?

"You home for dinner?"

"Yep."

"I didn't scare Mike off, did I?" her mother asked. She was smiling but looked concerned too.

"No. Last night was good, I think, but he's working tonight."

"He does that a lot."

Tracey nodded, she didn't really need the reminder.

"I picked those up today, on sale," her mother said, pointing to the other end of the table.

Tracey looked over and saw a stack of blankets. She looked back puzzled.

"They'll be much better than those old things you've got in the car now."

"Oh." Tracey understood. Her mother had been at her since Tracey had started going up to John's. Her mother had it in her head that everything outside the city was savaged by bushfire every weekend. She had found leaflets telling Tracey how to cope if she was caught in one, and made sure she read them. Tracey already had woollen blankets in her car, old ones that she had found in the back of the linen cupboard; she used them to make her car more comfortable for her aaranya friends. But now, apparently, her mother had decided those old ones, not much more than picnic blankets, weren't good enough for bushfire protection.

"They're pure wool," her mother said, thinking perhaps that Tracey thought there was something wrong with the new blankets. "Very good quality."

"They're great, Mum, thanks," Tracey said, there was no point arguing, it was easier just to go with the flow. "I'll put them in the car tomorrow."

"You can throw those old ones out," her mother said. "They're not much good for anything any more."

Tracey finished her drink, picked up the blankets and tried to decide what to do next. She certainly didn't want to sit watching television with Brian, so she went to the computer room and started it up. Nothing more from John yet, and there was no one online at his house. She sighed deeply. She had fallen out of contact with her few other friends when she had started going to John's house on most weekends, and chatting with Tilvy whenever she was available. It was only at times like this that she missed her friends from before.

It occurred to her that it was pretty selfish to only miss people because the ones she really wanted to hear from were not around. That made her wonder where all this was taking her. Could she really keep up a life-long friendship with people that no one else could see? That she couldn't see! And what about Mike, or if it didn't work out with him, some other man? What if she had kids?

The more she thought about it the more surreal it grew in her mind, it began to frighten her. For the first time she began to wonder whether she should have walked away when John had suggested it – more than suggested. Maybe she should have. She could have told herself it was an elaborate joke, maybe even told others, in some distant future when she could bear to live with the embarrassment of having been the object of such a con.

But it wasn't a con. It wasn't a joke. It had been deadly serious. It still was, as that frightening message from John had reminded her. But she was involved now, it was too late to turn her back on it. Tilvy was her best friend, and the others, too, were closer to her than she had ever felt with her human friends. It was a world she could touch, she *knew* it was there, but she couldn't see it, she couldn't hear it – she was separate from it. She had once heard Uncle's voice, as he fought to save her life, and that was as close as she had ever come to being part of that world; it was something that Tilvy said even her elders were at a loss to explain, a phenomenon of acintya was the best they could guess, and it wouldn't happen again. At times Tracey felt that she was deaf and blind, stumbling through a land of those that could truly see and hear, and she longed for the beauty that she knew they must experience. She had dreamed, fantasised, about waking one morning and meeting all these people that she had grown to love. But it would never happen. Could she live with that?

How was she ever going to mix a normal life with all that she knew now? She hoped that John would hurry home, maybe he could help her find a way to make it work.

- - -

When next John woke it was Samvaya Nayati that came to him. Nayati was a strange old man, he was not particularly friendly and yet John grew to like him a great deal. The man's big bone structure was all too apparent under his now gaunt body, though much of his body remained hidden under monk-like robes. His bald head shone in the light of the room. He smoked a pipe and left a trail of pipe ash on the floor when he left, oblivious of Jia's disapproval. For the first visits John had difficulty remaining awake, but as his strength grew he looked forward to Nayati's coming, waiting impatiently for the next chapter that revealed more of the history of the narun.

Every few days John would merge back with his saardha. As difficult and painful as separation was, merging was like clicking into place. He just lay back over his saardha, relaxed and opened himself to it. He felt himself sink into his body, like lying down on a too soft bed, and his body simply accepted him – he couldn't think of a better description. There was no pain, just a few moments of disorientation as his senses adapted. Some senses, like vedana, sight and smell, went noticeably dull, while the sudden reappearance of taste came as a surprise every time he merged. Suddenly reacquiring a sense of taste wasn't completely a good thing since his mouth tended to be dry and sticky and not particularly pleasant after days away from it.

Though merging with his body was not painful, actually starting to move about in it was uncomfortable. It took a while for the body to warm up enough to respond more than sluggishly, and he was told that it was best to just lie still for an hour or so after merging while everything kicked back in. He was also told not eat or drink anything, other than a few mouthfuls of water, for at least two hours, as the digestive system tended to be the slowest part to restart. And since each separation was prefixed with at least a six-hour fast, this left him feeling very hungry by the time he was allowed to eat.

When John was awake enough to move, Reyndani would arrive to lead John out to exercise. "Keep active," Ben had told him. "That's the secret to making the initiation go smoothly. Keep active and healthy and your saardha will be there for you when you need it." And Reyndani appeared to have been employed for just that purpose. Exercise after waking but before food was necessarily light, and there was always a brief period of adjusting to being full size again. He was allowed some time for relaxation after that first meal, but soon Reyndani would be encouraging John forward again.

During the weeks preceding his first separation, John had thought that there had been a gradual warming of his relationship with Reyndani, a sort of growing camaraderie. He was disturbed to find that that closeness was now gone. He understood the change better after his first pass through the village.

He saw Dengali and called out his familiar refrain, "Your son is a hard task-master."

Instead of the expected, friendly, response, Dengali bowed his head and replied formally, "Samvaya John."

John stopped in surprise and stared at him. "Don't start that crap, Dengali."

Dengali looked up in surprise.

"I'm the same person that I was before."

"You are Samvaya."

John gave him a pained look.

Dengali's expression softened a little. "The samvaya have aided and helped to protect our villages for generations, it is only right that we offer respect."

And used you for labour and a readily accessible gene pool, John thought, but didn't say. "We are still just people – I'm the ultimate proof of that. Being able to separate doesn't make one person any more special than another. It's just another variation, like being able to touch your nose with your tongue, or wobble your ears, or something." John hoped that Reyndani was listening.

"It is hardly that prosaic," replied Dengali. "And some among the Samgha are not convinced that you are as normal as you appear."

"Huh?" John said in surprise.

Dengali explained. "I believe some are trying to research your family tree to see if there is some chance that your family may have come here before now."

"I wish them luck, there was never that many of us about."

"Samvaya John," interrupted Reyndani, his head bowed. "We must stay active."

"Okay, I'm coming," John agreed. "Catch you later, Dengali."

"Samvaya John," Dengali acknowledged, and bowed his head.

John groaned but didn't say anything more, there didn't seem any point.

His fourth separation remained a horrendously painful process.

He was told that it would get easier in time, he could only hope so, for it showed little sign of improvement yet. It was the anticipation of the pain that made it hardest to concentrate on the trance required to make it happen. He took some comfort from the fact that it had become routine enough that Ben did not attend, only Jia and Triveni were with him to supervise.

He stared down at the sheet for a few moments after separating, reorienting and recovering, and swearing under his breath in the aftermath of the fire. He felt Jia's hands touch his torso, preparing to move him to the other bed. "Wait," he muttered, and her hands left him. He gathered himself together and sat up on the edge of the bed. The world swirled about him, and then steadied.

"Very good," Jia said quietly.

John nodded acknowledgement. He looked at his hand, there was no sign of the translucence of his first separations, the swirling patterns of this new body were now hidden behind his thickening skin. He looked down at the rest of himself and saw that his body had already asserted a smaller size, though he was larger now than he had been after his first separation.

With his expression set in determination, he pushed himself upright and walked the short distance to the other bed and leant on it with his hands. He was breathing heavily, though the breaths were redundant to this body. He turned and leaned back against the bed for a moment before standing straight.

"And that is where you pass over from determined to bloody minded," noted Triveni.

John forced himself to grin.

"At least you aren't so shy now," added Jia.

John looked at her in question, then looked down and saw that he was naked. As he looked his underpants appeared, like a black mist issuing from his skin that coalesced into a material over him.

"Your choice of clothing doesn't hide all that much."

"No one's offered me any lessons on improving my dress sense yet."

"It will happen," Triveni said. "But however determined you are, you should rest for a while before trying anything more strenuous."

"Will Nayati be coming?" John asked.

"I think Ben is planning to visit after you have rested," Jia said.

142

"Lie down now, he will be along in a few hours."

John woke again when the door opened. He looked up and saw Ben come in. It took him a few moments to understand what was different. Ben was wearing a light gown, like a lightweight dressing gown or one of those covers that swimmers wear before a race, and he was carrying another. But that wasn't it. John realised that this was Saarvaya Benjamin, he was separated, and smaller; he and John were of similar height now.

"Are we going somewhere?" John asked.

"Your praanin body needs exercise, just like your material one. This room is exactly what you need at the start, but you won't gain real strength and resilience until you take yourself out into the world. We'll stay within the Samgha today, and for that these can be helpful." Ben held up the spare gown he was carrying. "Wearing these ensures that others here, those without much vedana, can see us, and that saves remembering to get out of their way."

John got up from the bed. The short rest had made a big difference, he was feeling good. He was starting to tell how much lighter he was on his feet in this new body. He took the offered gown and put it on. It felt strange, foreign, against his skin.

Ben led John down to the river cavern. Reyndani was waiting for them there. "Saarvaya Benjamin," he bowed to Ben, then "Saarvaya John," to John.

"You can see us?" John asked in surprise.

"He can see the gowns," Ben corrected him, "but he knows we are here and who we are, and would do so even if we were not wearing these. He can't see our bodies, nor hear us." Ben went across to the stack of towels and picked up a tablet computer that was resting there. He scribbled something on its surface and showed it to Reyndani, who nodded.

Reyndani entered the water and let himself be carried down to the grate.

"He is there to catch you if necessary," Ben told John. "Your skin is still fragile, so we want to avoid hard knocks if we can."

"Has anyone with partial vedana, like Reyndani, tried to separate?" John asked.

"In the past," Ben said, "but without success. There have been two theories: one that there was a genetic factor, which would give

143

someone like Reyndani a chance; the other was that full vedana was required. You would appear to validate the latter."

Ben took his gown off and indicated John should do the same. "Start slowly, stay here near the bank until you get used to the flow." Ben entered the water downstream of John, there to assist him if needed.

John made his way cautiously into the water. It was still very cold, but the chill of the water didn't affect him so badly in this body. He knelt down until only his head remained above water. His feet slipped and the water pushed him along until he felt Ben's warm hands catch him at the waist.

"How is it your hands are still warm?" John asked.

"Yours will be too," Ben replied. "These bodies do not absorb or emit heat in the way of a physical body, they only feel warm to another living body because of the interaction of the prana. You could stay here all day and not get chilled."

John pushed himself forward, staying in the shallows, as he considered this. A thought occurred to him. "But I've seen narun burn?" he called back to Ben.

Ben nodded. "That is a different situation. Contact with fire, any direct heat or energy source of sufficient intensity, will burn and destroy the substance of these bodies more quickly than with your physical body."

John began to feel more confident and pushed his way further into the river. The water caught him and tumbled his body, and he lost track of where he was. Moments later Reyndani's strong hands stopped him. John felt one of his feet strike the metal of the grating, and there was pain as he grazed his ankle.

With Reyndani's help, John was able to swim forward against the current, but determined or not, there was a limit to John's strength and he soon had to return to the bank.

Sitting exhausted on the bank, John looked down at the graze on his ankle, faint golden lines that were slowly healing even as he watched – evidence that this body was very different to his human form. He touched them in wonder.

7. Lies

Weeks passed and John fretted more and more about Asha and the others. Were they okay? Why were they away so long? The fact that they had not returned seemed, at the very least, confirmation that they had not found what they had come here searching for. But what if something had happened to them?

"You're worrying needlessly," Ben assured him as they walked through the forest above the cliffs. "The aaranya would not harm them, and there are few creatures left in the natural world that present any danger to narun – or saarvaya."

"But there are some?"

"Perhaps. It's been years since the last of the truly savage spret have been seen."

"A savage spret?" John queried. "The only ones I've seen looked like a cross between a squirrel and a possum. They looked anything but savage."

"Spret is a word like animal, it encompasses many praanin creatures. But you're right, most spret left these days are small and harmless. It was not always so. Personally, I think most reports we receive of dangerous forms of spret these days are like the reports that humans get of the yeti: amusing but not to be taken seriously."

"I thought you might be the cause of the yeti stories," said John with a grin. "You've got pretty big feet, all you'd need is a fur coat."

"And some extra height," Ben said with a smile. "I hear the yeti is a tall creature."

"No one wants to admit to being scared of a short-arse," teased John.

"You must be feeling good, there was a time you found my build intimidating, short as it is."

"I still don't think I'd like to arm-wrestle with you, but yes, I am feeling good."

And he was. The weeks of cycling through being separated or merged, and exercising almost constantly in both forms, appeared to have had the desired effect. Separation was still a very painful process, but the pain was less intense and his recovery times were much faster. He knew that he would never gain the full size nor strength of his material body, but even so, he felt quite strong enough for the smaller demands of his praanin self.

The other thing that helped was to be able to clothe himself. Just a light pair of trousers and a shirt, but even that had added to his confidence. He no longer felt so exposed, although his still bare feet sometimes concerned him – he couldn't seem to manage shoes. Jia had laughed at his response, she wore very little in her saarvaya form, revelling in the freedom of it.

Ben said that John could, if he wanted, now move his material body to one of the Saardha Isolation rooms. Those were rooms off the corridors near the Initiation Room, with doors that had reminded John of a prison-facility. Each was a small, secure room to protect the saardha during separation. Ben had shown John one of the rooms, in it the material body of Seriyani was attached to various medical equipment, and Jia had been giving the body some light physiotherapy, keeping it ready for Seriyani's return.

John had considered the move, but he had gradually become used to the intensity of the Initiation Room. He felt that it was somehow better, right, to share a room with himself each night he was separated, and there was little space for that in the Isolation Rooms.

On one separation John had been accompanied by Saarvaya Triveni, and on some recent separations it had been Saarvaya Jia. She told him that she didn't get to separate often enough these days and entertaining their celebrity was a good excuse. Of the samvaya that John had met, Jia was the only one whose personality underwent a distinct change when she was separated, becoming almost bubbly and quite extroverted. She put John in mind of some strange sort of Dr Jekyll and Mr Hyde figure.

But today was with Ben again, and he was really setting a fast pace. "Your body has toughened up well, John," he called back. "So

146

we can afford to push things a bit harder now. The harder you push the stronger you will get."

So John followed Ben through the thick jungle forest, up some trees, apparently just for the view, and then learning to jump down again. Animals and birds scuttled and squawked out of their way as the two men moved past them.

"Don't forget and try this in your other body," remarked Ben after a jump down from a particularly high branch, "or you'll drive your knees through your shoulders."

It was an exhilarating feeling to climb so easily, and to jump from a great height and fall slow enough that when you hit the ground there was barely any jarring. John looked forward to sharing all this with Asha.

"It still pays to bend your knees and try to absorb the impact," warned Ben. "Land as lightly as you can, it's better to be careful."

"Is there a limit to the height?"

"More a limit on the circumstances. Jump from too far onto a sharp surface, or land badly on a rough surface, and you could be seriously hurt."

Eventually Ben paused near the top of a particularly large tree and settled down on a branch.

"Time for a rest?" John asked, hopeful.

Ben nodded.

John looked up at the sun and realised that in his other body this would be about lunchtime. "Do we ever have to eat in this form?" he asked. "You've said nothing so far about merging with trees like the aaranya do."

Ben looked troubled by the question. "We can't merge with trees, we can't even merge with water, not in the manner of the narun."

"Oh ... then how—?"

Ben continued to study John, considering how much to tell him. Eventually he said, "Our saarvaya bodies do absorb some small amounts of energy in the right environment: in the Initiation Room, or if you sleep up against a large healthy tree, or stay immersed in the ocean."

"Is that enough?" John asked, although the answer was probably clear in Ben's tone.

"If you lived quietly and continuously in the ocean, it might *almost* be enough, it's not something we've tried. It's one of the reasons why my ancestors have remained here, where the Valley of Gayatri and the richness of the forest meant that their needs were better met than elsewhere."

"But still not enough."

"For my ancestors it was. The saardha, even in its deep sleep state, can only last so long without modern medical support. They were forced to return, usually within two weeks, or risk death or major complications. In just days it was possible for serious problems to develop. They didn't fully understand the importance of fasting before separation and some would return to stomachs full of rotting material. Some would be poisoned directly, others died as the decay spread beyond the food to their internal organs. And when they avoided such short-term problems, they would face the complications of muscles left unused for long periods, blood flow gets interrupted and limbs waste."

"I'm surprised they kept up with it."

"You've felt it for yourself now. Are you telling me you would stop this just because there was a bit of risk? Do your people stop driving cars even when there are thousands of fatalities each year? My ancestors learned how long they could remain separated in relative safety, and they had rituals of fasting that kept most of them safe most of the time, even if they didn't know why. They learned that they had to return to their saardha regularly, and once merged the body quickly replenishes itself. If you are healthy enough, and get out into the sun, it can be just a matter of a few days to fully rebuild your strength again, even after a long separation, and be ready to do it all over again."

"So what's changed? You're dodging around something."

Ben nodded, acknowledging the accusation. "What changed is our ability to keep the saardha viable for longer. Now we can stay separated for more than a couple of weeks with little danger to the saardha, and this has presented us with difficulties that our ancestors never experienced.

"Here in the forest the saarvaya can live separate from the saardha, without other sustenance, for about two weeks in reasonable comfort. That coincidence was ideal for my ancestors. In their saarvaya form they had a built-in indicator that it was time to return, and that need for sustenance would drive them back. Within those two weeks you start to feel uncomfortable, hungry, needy, for want of more appropriate descriptions. After a month you weaken and have trouble concentrating. Much longer and you are in serious trouble, starting to fade regardless of how well your saardha is managing. In less ideal environments the times would be less, sometimes much less."

John considered this, and then asked, "But I grew stronger in the Isolation Room. Can't we just go back there to rebuild our strength?"

"That only works for initiates," Ben explained patiently. "You saw how thin your skin was on your first separation. In that state you can directly absorb the life offered by the room, and it speeds your recovery. But as you grow stronger, and your skin thickens, your body no longer accepts the life that is offered – or not enough. While in the room you will stop fading so quickly, but you can no longer sustain yourself there. That is the price of gaining the strength to be independent in this form; like a young bird leaving the nest, you cannot return to what you were."

John was silent for a while. He had assumed he was becoming like the aaranya, that he could be with Asha wherever she went. But it wasn't true. The disappointment hit hard. Since learning to separate he had dreamed of being with her, of learning to flow into the trees as he'd seen her do. He had no idea what it must really be like, but that hadn't stopped him trying to imagine it.

The sounds of the jungle came up through the branches and across the canopy to the two men, the two saarvaya, sitting silent with their own thoughts. John could feel depression settling so he tried to distract himself. "There is something," he said.

"Hmm?" Ben responded.

"What happens now? You've done so much for me. Are you really this altruistic, or is there something that you want of me?"

Ben turned and looked at John, his expression remained troubled – this new turn of conversation didn't please him any more than the last. He turned away again.

When Ben didn't say anything, John repeated, "What do you want of me?"

Ben glanced back. "Seriously?"

"Seriously."

"We've got part of what we want already. We wanted to know if what you have done was possible. Demonstrably, it is."

"And what will you do with that information?"

Another glance, and then back to the forest. Ben said, "We will probably try out other human candidates."

"There are others like me?"

"We are aware of one or two."

"You've not mentioned them before."

"We don't tell everyone about you either. Not everyone is eager to part ways with their normal human life on a mere possibility – you did that before we met you."

John nodded. "You said that was part, what else?"

"We would like your permission to take some sample material from you, your material body."

"For what purpose?"

"Study mostly. To see if we can find things that might explain why you have vedana when most other humans do not. Ask Jia for the details, it's not really my field."

"Anything else?"

Ben turned back to John. "We'd like you to stay here."

John met his gaze, but couldn't respond. The thought of staying, of being asked to stay, just hadn't occurred to him.

"Is it that horrendous a thought?" Ben asked him.

John turned away. "No, not horrendous. Just impossible."

"Why impossible? You've already cut your ties to your old life."

"My daughter, Asha, my home." The implications whirled around John's mind.

"You can only be with your daughter, properly, if you separate. And you can only do that here."

John wasn't giving up yet. "If you give me the drugs I need, Jia can teach Asha how to administer them. I can do this at home."

"You misunderstand the situation. We will never let the drugs leave this place, John. We will never allow you to separate anywhere but here, under our control."

"But—"

"Under no circumstances, John. I will not allow it." Ben's expression turned softer. "But if you stay here with us, we could

150

allow you to separate and then fly you, as a saarvaya invisible to the customs officers of your airports, to visit with your daughter and the others. We have the resources to do that."

John turned away again. He sat there stunned. He'd thought his choice had been simple, he should have known better. Eventually he asked, "Will my vedana remain if I don't keep separating?" Since learning to separate, John's vedana had returned stronger than it had ever been. He thought he had been cured.

"For a while," Ben replied blandly. "The strength of your praanin body will slowly fade back to what it was if it doesn't get exercised outside the protection of your material body."

"So I might lose vedana again – if I leave here?"

"Yes."

- - -

Seriyani led them north-east for several days, so Andrei and Senna stayed with the group. They visited another Glade, no more helpful than the previous, and then turned west. After a discreet interval Andrei and Senna made their excuses – Andrei, perhaps, overdoing the star-crossed lovers bit – and parted ways. They had not gone far when the elder, Litak, appeared in front of them.

"You seek the jalaja," he said. It was not a question. "Follow me."

Andrei looked at Senna, who shrugged and started to follow the old man. Andrei shrugged too, though no one was looking, and started after Senna. Litak kept up a strong pace and he was soon disappearing from their sight amid the dense jungle foliage. A short time later they both stopped, unable to tell where the elder had gone.

"It's a test," said Andrei. "You heard Asha. The old man's impressed with you, Senna, and he wants to see how good you are."

Senna looked at him in frustration, then her eyes flickered.

"There! What was that?" Andrei asked.

"What?"

"You felt something, I saw you. Go with it."

"It was just ... nothing. Oh, I don't know, something over that way." Senna pointed to a place away from the line they had been following.

Andrei didn't say anything more, just started walking in the direction she had pointed.

"Andrei?" Senna called, and trudged after him through the tangled undergrowth.

After a short distance they found the old man sitting on a branch above them. He nodded down to them. "Good," he said. "Follow." Then he leapt back down and disappeared into the forest.

That night, when they stopped to rest after an exhausting day's travel, Litak sat with them for a while.

"How do you disappear so quickly?" Andrei asked. "One moment you're there, the next you're gone."

Litak answered looking at Senna. "An ant loses itself amid other ants, but still it is there. A bird hides itself amid the flock, but still it may be caught by the falcon that tracks it. Humans hide themselves among other humans in their cities, but still they can be found by those that know how to look. Here in the rich forest I can hide my life in the life that surrounds us, but still I can be found by those that can see."

He looked to Andrei. "If I lived in your dry forest," then back to Senna, "or your busy city, I would feel exposed and vulnerable. In such places you have only learned to see far, here you must learn to see close. You must become short-sighted." The old man grinned at Senna's reaction to his teasing. "First you must learn to look close, then you can learn to understand what you see."

For the next two days the old man kept up the same fast pace and the same constant testing of Senna's ability to follow him through the jungle. On the third day they found that they were keeping up with him, but not, Senna said, because she was getting that much better, it was because the old man was slowing down. A slow, steady rain started around midday, and just a few hours later Litak stopped and turned to them. For once he was moving as if he were old.

"I am tired," he told them. "I must return to my Glade. The river you seek is just a few hours that way." He pointed. To Senna he said, "You show great promise."

"Maybe we can come back one day," suggested Andrei.

Litak glanced at Andrei and then looked back at Senna, his expression sad. He shook his head and turned to go.

"Litak," Senna called.

He turned back.

"Thank you."

He nodded and then moved away again, and despite appearing to move slowly, was quickly lost to Andrei's senses in the dense jungle.

Andrei and Senna moved on in the direction the elder had indicated. They travelled in silence through the forest that was wet from the constant rain and only dimly lit in the overcast afternoon. The day was almost gone when they descended the steep slopes of a gorge and found the river. It was wide and deep and swiftly flowing. Trees and bushes clung to the sides of the gorge, and at the bottom the river constantly threatened to undercut those that clung to its narrow banks. There was a distant roaring sound that spoke of rapids or a waterfall further upstream, beyond a bend in the valley. They found a large tree on the bank and climbed up to sit, side by side, on a branch that reached out over the water.

They sat there in a companionable silence for some time before Andrei said, "I think you made a friend."

Senna leaned against him and Andrei felt her shoulders shuddering. She was crying. He turned to her and held her until the tears subsided.

Andrei wasn't certain he completely understood her tears. Their departure from Litak was obviously part of it, and he contemplated a number of different reassurances, but decided none of them were likely to help. He said quietly, "I expected you to be angry with me."

"I am," Senna replied, but didn't pull away.

"Oh."

"But I'm also sort of pleased."

Andrei wasn't sure what to say to that. "Um ..." was the best he could manage.

Senna sat upright and wiped her eyes. "You should have told me when you first found out I wasn't imagining things. Of course you should, so of course I'm angry. But it was nice to hear you have faith in me, even when we're not talking."

"I wasn't even sure you realised you were doing it," he said.

"I don't think I was, not after a while."

For a while they paid little attention to the river, the dull skies, nor the rain. Then, as night fell, they decided it was best to merge with the tree and look for jalaja in the morning.

The morning was well progressed when they emerged from the

tree. Andrei stared up through the leaves and into the bright sky, he had big smile on his face. Sometimes, he thought to himself, life could be very good.

"Andrei," Senna spoke quietly.

"Yes, my lovely paurakanya," Andrei said without looking down. He'd thought himself very clever when he had first thought to call Senna a maiden of the city.

"I think the jalaja found us."

"Hmm?" Andrei turned to Senna and then followed her gaze to the riverbank below them.

There, staring up at them in surprise, was a young woman lying back on the bank, just her feet still touching the water. Andrei could tell it was a woman without any doubt or equivocation. Not that the aaranya of these areas were particularly well covered or self-conscious about their bodies, but there was something about this young woman that spoke loudly of her nudity. Perhaps, thought Andrei, it was her skin, lighter than that of the aaranya they'd been with, or perhaps it was that her posture seemed wanton, almost beckoning to him.

The young woman relaxed at the sight of Andrei's astonished face and giggled.

Andrei saw that the giggling not only made her face more attractive as she smiled, it also did interesting, enticing, things to other parts of her anatomy. He felt an elbow sharply in his ribs. He started to turn, to look at Senna, when another voice intruded.

"Maya!" a man called.

Andrei looked just a short distance further along the bank and saw a well-built man standing on the bank. Again, it was very apparent that it was a man, and that he was well-built. He stood proudly and unselfconsciously naked, and glared up at Senna and Andrei. There was a splash as the girl entered the river. She was swimming gently against the current, easily holding herself in place as she continued to stare up at them.

"I hope we didn't disturb something," Senna whispered to Andrei.

"Certainly won't win us any friends," Andrei agreed. "Good morning," he called down to the man. "Sorry if we surprised you, we didn't realise anyone else was around." When there was no immediate response he added, "A beautiful morning, isn't it?"

The man didn't move, but didn't respond either, just continued to glare up at them.

"Do you mind if we come down?" Senna asked. "We'd like to speak with you, if that's all right. Ask you a question."

Andrei followed Senna down to the base of the tree. The girl had swum upstream and was now standing beside and just slightly behind the man. Once he was on the ground, Andrei realised that neither of the jalaja were as large as he had thought. Their proud stance gave them the feeling and appearance of much larger people, but even the man would barely have come to Andrei's shoulder.

"What would aaranya want with jalaja?" the man asked.

"We were told you might help us," Senna said.

"Another jalaja told you this?"

"An aaranya, an elder."

"Who?"

Senna turned to Andrei, she had to pinch his shoulder to gain his attention. She looked up and smiled at the jalaja and then turned Andrei around so she could whisper to him privately. "Things will go a lot better for us – and for you later – if you would stop staring at his girlfriend."

"She's staring at me," Andrei defended himself.

"That's his problem, you're mine."

"Not that you're staring at him," he accused.

"I'm talking to him, which is more than you're managing right now. Do we tell them who sent us here?"

Andrei thought about this. "Litak didn't tell us not to. He didn't say anything about keeping secrets from them, he was disappointed that things aren't better between them and us."

Senna nodded and they turned back. "It was Litak."

The man nodded. "We know him."

- - -

Another separation cycle had started this morning. John was accompanied by Saarvaya Jia, scantily clad as was usual for her in this form, through the irregular routines of exercise for the day. This morning had been time through the jungle below the cliffs, then time amid the tunnels of the Samgha – learning how to keep out of people's way when they couldn't see you, then swimming in the river cavern, and this afternoon she had led a hectic pace through the jungle above the cliffs.

"I had hoped you'd set a slower pace than Ben," John said.

Jia called a halt on the ridge above the cliffs and sat there to watch the sunset.

"Ben would not forgive me if I were to treat you too lightly, Johnny-boy." Jia smiled mischievously at him.

"Does it really need to be this intense any longer?" John asked. "I feel very good."

"I can tell. And you are *looking* very good too." Jia moved her eyes up and down over John, and grinned when she saw him wriggle uncomfortably under her gaze. More seriously she added, "Ben thinks that the routine might slacken when the others return, he wants to make the most of your time while you are not distracted by other concerns."

Jia was sitting very close.

"Megan," John muttered to himself.

"What?"

"Nothing, I was just thinking of someone." This situation had reminded him of Megan, a colleague back in the office of his old life. Some people were close, touchy-feely sort of people, Megan was one and now Jia had turned into another – at least while she was saarvaya. It was all the more disconcerting here because Jia was wearing what amounted to not much more than a bikini, and it seemed to John, one that was smaller today than he remembered from last time. He found Jia much easier to talk to in her samvaya doctor's attire.

"Anyone I should know?"

"No. I was just thinking about some work I'd left behind, not sure why," he lied. Looking to change the subject, he continued, "Ben tells me you want to collect some sample material from me."

"If you permit," Jia said.

"Can I ask what you'll use it for?"

Jia looked at John, not very happy to be discussing work in what she considered her time off. "Most of it will just be for study, to see how you compare to others, genetically, physically and chemically. We are still trying to piece together all the interactions between the saardha and the saarvaya."

"So you're not talking about clones or anything. No army of little

156

Johns running around."

Jia smiled weakly at his attempted humour. "No, cloning is not something we have anything to do with here, although we do study other forms of reproduction." There was a pause and then she smiled more brightly and continued, "That is one of the forms of genetic material we would like to obtain."

John looked up at her in surprise. "Some—" he pointed down to his groin.

Jia grinned. "You got it. A sperm donation. From your material body, of course."

"I take it that's not just for study."

"No. We hope to sustain the Samgha, which means going forth and multiplying. To do that we need to collect suitable reproductive material from as wide a source as possible."

"But I wasn't born this way. My vedana has come only recently."

"We know, but the consensus here is that you, and probably your wife, must have been carrying the right genes – whatever they are. Hence your daughter and your own situation now. Some have suggested that you might have had active vedana as a child, like your daughter."

"I don't remember anything like that."

"There's probably no reason why you should, growing up in the city it would have had less chance to show itself."

"So I could end up with sons or daughters here?"

"Of course. No army of little Johnny-boy clones, but maybe one or two John juniors."

"Would I have any say in any of this?"

"The Samgha would be responsible. It would probably be better if you thought of this as like an anonymous sperm donation. Of course we would know who your children were, but there need be no reason for you to know."

John dwelled on this for a while. He had never thought about sperm donations before, not in his old life and certainly not since losing his wife. It was one thing to let people pull his DNA apart, but it felt like quite another to let them put it together with someone else's. How would he feel about having children for which he was not responsible? The thought was alien to him and he couldn't quite get his head around it.

He realised that Jia was leaning in close, her expression quite serious.

"If you'd like to make a more personal donation, perhaps even stay here and raise a child directly ..." she said quietly, and left the statement hanging.

John stared back at her.

"John?" a gentle voice called from some distance behind them.

"Asha?" John turned his head quickly, almost colliding with Jia as he did. Asha and the others were coming up the ridge from the forest. "Asha!" He leapt up, the shock of Jia's suggestion completely vanished, and he ran down the ridge to meet them.

He went to sweep Asha into his arms, but she held him at arm's length and stared at him. "Is it you?" she asked, incredulous.

"Last I looked," he said. He shuffled restlessly under Asha's intense scrutiny.

"What happened?" Asha asked at last, though it seemed to John that there was less surprise and doubt in that question than he had expected.

"It's a long story."

Jia interrupted, asking "Will you be using the Initiation Room to sleep tonight, John?" Her tone was formal and businesslike.

"If that's still all right."

"Certainly. I just wasn't sure if you might have other plans."

John turned to Asha, his eyebrows raised in question.

"Wherever you are, is where I want to be." She smiled into his eyes.

John asked Jia, "Is it okay if I show them the Initiation Room?"

"If that is what you want, certainly. I will go with Seriyani now, and leave you to speak with your friends, you have a lot to tell them. You can find your own way back down?"

John said he would be fine and the two saarvaya women departed. He looked around the group with a wide smile. "It is incredibly good to see you all again."

"You didn't look to be too lonely," said Andrei. Senna elbowed him in the ribs.

John looked at him, puzzled, and then explained, "Oh, Jia. They always have someone to keep driving me on exercise routines. Sometimes it's Jia, sometimes Ben, and when I'm all-together it's usually Reyndani."

"You're in real trouble if you stop believing now," Andrei told him.

John grinned at him, then turned back to Asha. "Are you willing to give this stranger a hug?"

"John," she said at last and threw herself into his arms.

They stood there for several minutes, just enjoying the sensation of holding each other. It was Andrei that interrupted them. "Are you two going to finish any time soon do you think? Or do we have time to go and get a good night's sleep?"

John and Asha separated and John greeted Andrei and Senna with a hug, and Darnu and Garjae with handshakes. Garjae looked less than pleased to find John in this form.

Back holding hands with Asha, John asked, "And?"

"We had no luck with any of the Glades," Asha told him, and squeezed his hands as she saw his shoulders droop. "Andrei and Senna may have something, but they refuse to give us any details yet."

John looked back and forth between them with a puzzled expression.

"Andrei and Senna went off on their own for a while," Asha explained. "We were going to meet back here, but they found us this morning, so we came back together after all."

"We want to do some research before we share it," said Andrei, "make sure it's real."

The sun was below the horizon now, the west was a deep red and darkness was closing in from the east. The sounds of birds settling for sleep were fading and being overtaken by the sounds of insects becoming more active. Another advantage of this body, thought John, he didn't miss the constant fight with mosquitoes, they had no interest in his praanin body. A sudden thought occurred to him. "You don't seem that surprised to see me like this."

"Damn! There goes my career in acting," said Andrei.

"Someone told us what the samvaya and saarvaya really are," Asha explained.

"But Seriyani didn't know we knew," said Senna.

"So we were all supposed to be very surprised to find you like this," added Andrei.

"You knew I could do this?" John asked in surprise.

"No, John," Asha said. "But I knew you would try." She smiled at him sadly.

John smiled back, feeling a little embarrassed. "You want to see the rest of me?"

"You haven't put it down somewhere and forgotten where it is?" Andrei asked.

John shook his head. "Come on."

They descended into the Samgha, and John gave them a brief explanation of what had happened. They reached the Initiation Room and the aaranya looked around in fascination. Even after the wonders of the living rock in the main corridors of the Samgha, this room came as a surprise. They had never experienced such intensity of life from rock before. All of them, even Garjae, became animated as they explored the room, or just stood with their eyes closed and felt it.

Jia, now merged back as samvaya and acting as a doctor once more, came in and told them that Ben had heard of their return and he would meet with them all tomorrow after they'd had a chance to rest. He suggested mid-morning on the ridge above the cliff.

"Do you have everything you need for the night, John?" Jia asked.

John nodded absently from his place beside Asha, and Jia left.

Soon after that, Darnu and Garjae said they were heading back to the forest, but Andrei and Senna stayed to play with the computer in the room. While they were doing that, Asha walked back and forth around John's saardha. John followed, just to be near her.

"It's incredible, John," she said quietly. "I know you ... and this is you," she indicated his saardha. She turned back to him and put her arms around him. "And so is this. A bit smaller, it is nice not having to stretch to match your size. And this feels like you, more like you than ever."

"I'm glad," John told her. "I've been worried you'd be disappointed with the new insubstantial me."

Asha squeezed him tightly. "No. As long as it's you, and you're well, that's all that matters. You are well, aren't you?"

John nodded. "I feel great. Things were pretty rough at first, but I feel really good now."

Asha looked back down at the body on the bed. "There's so much

I want to know, I don't know where to start."

"Same here," agreed John. "But how about we leave the rest of the show-and-tell until tomorrow. Tonight I'm just pleased you're here."

Asha replied with an absent, "Hmm," but she wasn't really listening. She stepped forward to the saardha and touched its shoulder, then stroked its face and brushed the hair from its forehead.

"I felt that," said John in surprise.

Asha glanced at him, and then leaned over and kissed the lips of the saardha. She looked back up at him. "And that?"

John nodded and smiled. "Not quite up to the real thing, but yes, I felt that too."

"Come on, Senna," Andrei spoke loudly from across the room. "We'd better leave them to their odd little threesome." Then, "Ouch!" as Senna poked him.

Asha blushed but John looked across and grinned at Andrei. "You're just jealous. Now I'm twice the man I used to be."

"Maybe, John, but one of you is not keeping up his share of the conversation."

Senna started dragging on Andrei's arm, trying to get him to the door. "Goodnight, John, goodnight, Asha," she said.

"Wait!" Asha called. "Aren't you going to tell us what you found?"

"Nope," Andrei said with a grin, but considerately added, "We'll talk in the morning, but I think it's positive news."

Senna kept tugging at him, and Andrei pulled the door as they went out, saying as he left, "Night Asha, night John ... oh, and goodnight John." They heard him saying to Senna, "Aren't you going to say goodnight to the other John, he might get—" and then the door clicked shut.

John looked back at Asha and saw that she was staring at his saardha. "Who would you like to sleep with, him or me?"

Asha turned and hit him on the arm. "Andrei and you are a bad mix." She looked back at the body on the bed. "It's disturbing to see you lying there with so little life in you. I can see that there is still some, I can sort of see how this must work, but it's disturbing anyway. It's like seeing you dead or dying, and I can't think of anything more horrifying."

John turned Asha to face him. "Then don't look. We can go back up to the forest if you'd prefer."

"Can you ... can you merge like the aaranya?"

He shook his head.

"Then—"

"Tomorrow." He didn't want to go into it now. "Do you want to go out?"

Asha glanced at the bed, and then turned back to John and held him tightly. "No. It's okay. As long as I'm holding the real, *living* you, I know everything's all right."

John pulled her away from the bed containing his saardha, and as they went past the door he turned out the room lights, leaving just the faint illumination of a few LEDs on equipment around the room. He didn't need light to see Asha, nor she to see him. His saardha became a dark shadow on the far bed.

"You can do clothes and everything," murmured Asha, tugging at his shirt.

"Sort of. Not up to a tuxedo or anything yet." John stepped back and concentrated, and his shirt and trousers disappeared.

Asha smiled. "You even manage underwear."

John looked down and shrugged. "Old habits die hard." He concentrated again and the last traces of clothing disappeared. When he looked up he saw that Asha was naked too. He pulled her close. "Do you suppose everything still works?"

"It feels like it," she whispered into his ear.

Later, as they lay together on the bed, John took a deep breath. "Well, that was different."

"Hmm. It was, wasn't it."

"Is it always that intense?"

Asha shrugged, her body moving against his. "You ask like I know the answer."

John thought about that. "You mean?"

"No." She laughed, and again he enjoyed her body's movement against his. "But it was a long time ago, and I don't remember it being anything like this."

"I'm still having trouble adapting to the differences in the way everything feels in this body. It still feels like you, it still feels like skin against skin." He ran his hand along her side. "But there's so much more." He ran his hand down her back, and then added, "I don't have the words."

Asha smiled at him and rubbed her body against his. "You feel different this way too."

"Good different?"

"Just different different." She smiled and brushed the lines on his forehead lightly with her finger tips. "I'm not disappointed with either body, if that's what's worrying you."

"It is nice not having to worry so much about hurting you."

"You never have." Asha kissed him to forestall any further questions.

John ran his new hands over her body as she continued to move against him, at first still wondering at the experience, and then soon lost within it.

- - -

Tracey picked at her dessert. She was nervous.

It was a nice restaurant, posh. Mike seemed to know his way around such places, perhaps it came from his part-time work parking cars for them. How he could afford to go to them as a student she didn't know, and didn't like to ask. He never let her pay, she didn't even get to see the bill. She wondered if he noticed the dress she had bought for tonight, more daring and more elegant than she really felt. She didn't have much that was good enough for the places Mike insisted on taking her and she wanted something he hadn't seen before.

"So we ended up late for the lecture, but that's all right, the guy's a bore anyway," Mike finished up his story.

Tracey looked up and smiled at him. She had missed the start of the story and hadn't managed to catch up again, she hoped it wasn't obvious. Her mind had wandered off into thoughts about later tonight. Her mother was going to be away, and Tracey wondered if tonight she and Mike might get past just kissing and touching each other on the sofa. If maybe he might even stay the night.

"Are you okay?" he asked.

She looked into his brown eyes, they seemed genuinely concerned. She nodded. "Sorry, just daydreaming I guess."

"I've been talking too much again, haven't I?"

Tracey laughed. "No, I like to hear what you've been doing."

"But I don't give you time to say what you've been up to."

"There's not much to tell. Just the occasional stressed client to liven up the workday, it all seems pretty dull compared to what you do."

"No steamy office affairs, no hot gossip from cooking the books for a crime boss?"

"Not that anyone tells me."

"Then what about your weekends. Last weekend you were visiting that place up in the hills again. Is he back yet?"

Tracey shook her head. "No, last I heard it sounded like it might be a long while yet."

"So what do you get up to there? Lots of nightclubbing?"

She smiled at that, Mike knew that nightclubs weren't her scene. "It's quiet. A nice place on the edge of the forest. I just sort of slob about all day."

"I'm sorry, but a beautiful lady wearing a dress like that can *not* use the word slob," Mike told her. "It just won't fit."

Tracey blushed.

"So he doesn't have you cleaning the windows and chimneys, taking meals to his ugly stepsisters, the whole Cinderella thing?"

"I told you, I just sort of mind the place. Pick up his mail, air the house out a bit ... that sort of thing."

"Walk around nude?" Mike asked.

"No." She couldn't tell him that she usually had company, so walking around nude had never really been considered.

"Sorry, just my imagination getting the better of me."

Mike's expression turned strange, serious. "And this guy—"

"John."

"This John is just a friend you say."

"Yes. I told you. He's not well, so I'm looking after his place while he's away."

"I keep getting images of the phantom of the opera or something. Some elegant and sophisticated figure with ugly scarring hidden behind a mask, forced to seclude himself in the mountains to get away from the jeers of the crowds."

Tracey shook her head. "It's nothing like that." She tried to smile at Mike's imagery, but she was getting uncomfortable now. They hadn't spoken much about John before, it was always just the

164

explanation of how she spent her weekends, briefly passed over before the conversation moved on to other things. But there was something unsettling tonight in the tone of Mike's voice, and the way he was looking at her.

"And he's off looking for some miracle cure in Asia?"

"I don't know about a miracle cure, but yes, he's gone to Asia looking for help."

Mike stared off somewhere over her shoulder. With the way his mood had turned, Tracey was expecting the words, "Likely story," to emerge in sarcastic tones. Instead, he said, "I'm probably starting to sound like some jealous creep. It's just that you go a bit strange whenever the subject turns up, sort of evasive."

Because I always have to lie about it, Tracey admitted in her mind. Out loud she said, "It's just a favour for a friend, there's nothing more to tell."

"We see so little of each other, and when I know you've gone off to another guy's place for the weekend—"

"But he's not there," she defended.

"But you *have* stayed there when he is there."

"... Yes. But it's not like that. It's never been like that."

"And his wife is dead, you said, and his kid. So there's no one else there."

"He's just a friend," Tracey repeated.

"A pretty good friend, if he lets you use his house every weekend."

"It's not every weekend!"

"Pretty damn close."

"You're always busy on the weekends, work and study and—"

"And that's so fucking convenient isn't it," Mike said angrily.

Tracey stared down at her dessert, melted and runny, like her eyes. How had the night turned so suddenly into this?

There was silence for a while, then Mike muttered, "Come on, I'll take you home."

Mike continued his usual courtesies as they left the restaurant, opening the car door for her and closing it gently after her, but they didn't speak again until the car pulled up outside Tracey's house.

Tracey opened the door and then looked back at Mike, he was staring intently forward as if impatient to be away. "It isn't anything like you think," she told him.

Mike didn't answer or look at her, so Tracey got out. As the door closed she heard a low, "Right, and I'm—" There was more but the door closed and cut it off. His car moved off quickly and Tracey watched until it turned at the intersection and disappeared.

She turned slowly around and made her way to the front door, wiping her eyes so she could see clearly. She fumbled in her bag for her keys and scratched at the lock with them. The door suddenly opened and Tracey looked up in shock.

"Where's Mike?" Brian asked her.

Tracey looked down, putting her keys back in her bag. "He's gone home." When she looked back up, Brian was squinting at her red eyes.

"A bad night, huh?"

"I thought you and Mum were going away?" Tracey said, brushing past Brian to go inside.

"We were. Something came up and I had to call it off."

"Where's Mum?"

"Gone to bed already, but I wasn't tired so I stayed up to watch TV."

Brian followed Tracey through to the kitchen and watched as she got herself a glass of water.

"You two have a fight?"

Tracey nodded numbly.

"Don't know how anyone could pick a fight with you looking like that."

Tracey folded her arms, the glass pleasantly cool as she held it against her bare upper arm. She suddenly felt very exposed. She didn't look up, but she could feel Brian's eyes on her.

"What did you fight about? Has Mike finally realised there may be reason to be jealous?"

Tracey didn't answer, but she looked up at Brian, wondering what he meant, what he knew.

"You don't have to tell me. I just thought it might help to let it out."

"He got upset about the amount of time I spend minding John's house," Tracey told him, she turned her eyes away, studying the few things on the kitchen table.

"That place you go to on weekends?"

Tracey nodded.

"Then I'm not surprised."

Tracey looked up.

"You turn up tonight, looking like that, and Mike's bound to start wondering where you spend your time. The fool's probably only just realising that he should be spending more time with you, if he wants to make sure you don't start to look elsewhere."

"But it's not like that. John's not there anyway."

"You should have told him that John was your mother's friend, or an uncle or something. Make it sound like a chore rather than something you want to do. You always seem very keen to go, and you can be sure Mike's noticed that.

"It does seem odd that a beautiful young woman like you, who should be going out with friends on weekends, should want to go up into the hills every weekend on your own. I know your mother's been worried. Is it such a surprise that Mike should be dwelling on it too?"

Tracey shook her head. She could only repeat herself, "It's not like that." She could feel tears welling in her eyes again and looked away from Brian. She couldn't say what it was really like, that she *was* spending her weekends with friends.

"Maybe you should invite Mike up there. It might ease his mind to see for himself that there's no one else there."

Tracey had thought of that, but she couldn't imagine having Mike there while Tilvy and the others were around, and she couldn't ask them to leave; it felt more like it was their place than John's now. "Mike's always busy on weekends," she replied.

"Make the invitation, you might find how *un*-busy he can become very fast."

"I'll think about it," Tracey said. "I'm going to bed."

"Sweet dreams, sweet thing," Brian told her as she walked passed him out of the kitchen.

Tracey shuddered. Sometimes Brian gave her the creeps.

- - -

Asha woke later and they were still pressed against each other on the bed. It was still a few hours to sunrise, she could feel the sensations of the night far above emanating from the walls of this strange, living, room. She looked at the door. She thought about the doctor,

Jia, and what she had seen as they arrived. She knew, she could feel, that nothing had changed between her and John, but sometimes he could be quite blind to how others reacted to him. She disentangled herself from John and got up to get the sheet from the floor where it had fallen. If the doctor came back in it would be better if they were at least covered. She gently pulled the sheet over John and then crept under it with him, pulling it up and over them and then wrapping herself back around him beneath it. He murmured something indistinct and then drifted off again.

Another thought occurred to her. If John was going to spend much time in this form, they might have to have a talk about the birds and bees – narun style. While he was in his flesh-and-blood body that had never been an issue, but, as a saarvaya, who knew what might be possible? Up to now she had rarely considered a child of her own with John, it had simply been an impossibility. But now ... now she wondered whether it was possible, and how she felt about that. Actually, she *did* know how she felt about that, but she was trying hard not to get her hopes up.

At some point Asha managed to drift off again.

She woke again later as the rock called to her, telling her of the waking day above. The sun was coming up.

She nudged John. "My love," she whispered to him.

John, only partly awake, stretched and then closed his arms around her.

Tempted as she was to let this go where he so obviously wanted, she didn't want to risk being interrupted by the doctor or anyone else, and most people around here were early risers. "John," she said more loudly. "We should get up."

John's hands started to wander and Asha felt her resolve weakening. Before it went any further she slid out from his grasp and from under the sheet. As she stood she reformed her usual clothing.

John looked up at her, fully awake now. "You mean it?"

Asha nodded. "There's a lot to talk about before we meet with Ben."

John nodded his acceptance and pulled himself upright. It was interesting to watch how lightly he moved in this new body. "You may want to consider some clothes," she reminded him.

He grinned back at her. "I'd rather you hadn't." He concentrated and formed his trousers and shirt. "At least getting ready to go is easy in this body."

They didn't speak much as they walked up through the Samgha, John appeared to be deep in thought. As they stepped out onto the ridge above the cliffs he said, "There are some things I'd rather speak to you about privately, before we meet the others."

They stopped and Asha said, "Perhaps we should have talked more last night?"

"I didn't want to think about it then."

"That bad?"

He looked away. "Bad? Some of it, I guess. Disturbing anyway."

"What? ... John?"

"Good morning! We didn't expect to see you two up so early," Andrei called. They turned and saw Andrei and Senna coming up the ridge toward them.

"Later," murmured John.

Asha looked at him with concern, wondering what had turned his mood.

"You didn't bring your other half?" Andrei asked. "He was looking a bit peaky, could probably do with some sun."

John smiled back at Andrei. "You can tease him later. He'll have to get up in another couple of days. Meanwhile you'll have to make do with me."

Senna looked John up and down. "You look good."

John looked a little embarrassed. "Thanks."

"Are you going to tell us more about how you got your super-powers, John?" Andrei asked.

"I'd rather hear what you have to say."

Asha took John's arm and said to Senna, "I want to hear both stories. Where are the others?"

Senna pointed back the way they'd come. "They're both up, waiting for us."

The group congregated in the same place that they had used before they had left on the search. Each took the same places amid the branches, except this time Senna and Andrei sat together. Garjae studied John carefully from where he sat, and Asha wondered what thoughts were going through his head – they didn't appear to be happy ones.

"So, who's going to start?" asked John.

Asha briefly recounted their journey, and their unsuccessful meetings at the Glades. "I felt sure there was more they weren't telling us."

"We all did," added Darnu, "but none of us knew why."

"But there didn't seem to be anything we could do to find out," continued Asha. "We had to accept what they told us and move on. And then Andrei shared a little secret with us."

"Andrei kept a secret?" John said in mock surprise. "You astonish me."

"Hidden depths, that's me." Andrei grinned in response and took up the tale. Senna kept him from getting too carried away and eventually they told of meeting the jalaja.

"But I thought you said something about a yaayaavara?" John queried.

"That was part of our cunning ploy. A misdirection for those to whom these secrets should not be revealed," said Andrei pompously.

"We needed some reason for having the information we were given," explained Senna, "something the Samgha couldn't try to follow up on. They let us think Seriyani must be a yaayaavara, so it seemed fair."

"So what happened then?" Asha asked, impatient to discover what they found.

"They led us upstream, walking along the narrow bank. That trollop, Maya, kept flirting with Andrei."

"Who gallantly and bravely rejected her advances," put in Andrei.

"Who every now and then managed to tear his eyes away and remember I was there," corrected Senna.

"I did tear my eyes away long enough to notice you *sizing* him up. I got the impression you didn't think he came up as short as he looked to me."

"I think he carried himself very well."

"He was showing off, trying to impress you, probably wondering if he could cope with such a lot of woman."

"Speaking of showing off—"

"Sounds like you had a fun trip home," John interrupted.

Andrei looked across at him. "I think this lot of naiads might be responsible for all those stories and pictures you humans have about dryads and naiads. They give the narun a bad name." Andrei turned to Darnu and asked, "Are all jalaja like that?"

"I believe they are generally a smaller race than the aaranya," Darnu said. "But certainly not all behave as you would have us believe these did. The few I've spoken with near our home are much more conservative."

"We're not exaggerating," said Andrei, "they really were—"

"Anyway," Senna broke back in, "they led us to meet Larko's mother."

"Larko was the guy," put in Andrei.

"And his mother was worse than Maya."

"Lovely woman," said Andrei with a smile, "very attentive."

"To you!" Senna growled. "I asked the questions and Andrei got the answers, not that I'm sure he heard them."

"I heard them."

"Yeah, sure. I know it didn't do anything for Maya's ego to be outclassed by her boyfriend's mother."

"Is that why—?"

"Yep. She had the shits with you," Senna said, pleased. "Huffed off back into the water and we didn't see her again."

"It's a shame Larko didn't go to console her after her loss."

"He was like his mother in that respect," said Senna, "very attentive to their guests."

"So what did the jalaja tell you?" Asha asked, wondering if they were ever going to get to the point.

"Oh," Senna paused.

"We thought it wasn't going to be very helpful, more mumbo jumbo and vague hints," said Andrei.

Senna cut back in, "Larko's mother said that the healer's home was in the North Sea. That seemed strange, a jalaja in the ocean, so I asked her to explain. She said it wasn't the ocean, it was fresh water. A large lake, very far to the north. The Older of the Sister Lakes, she said."

"Which sounded like mumbo jumbo to us," said Andrei. "And that's why we didn't want to say anything until we'd researched it. Last night we looked it up on the Internet. She's talking about Lake

Baikal, in Siberia. It has been known as the North Sea in the past."

Senna added, "Lake Khövsgöl and Lake Baikal are considered sister lakes, and Lake Baikal is like really really old."

Silence fell over the group as they considered what they'd learned.

"Russia!" John said at last. "Why did it have to be so far away?"

"Actually, John, it's less distance than we've come already," Andrei told him.

"It is?"

"Yep. It's like ten centimetres, whereas we're at least twenty-five centimetres from home."

"Centimetres?"

"On the map on the screen, I wasn't going to pace it out for real."

"You realise there is a bloody great mountain range between here and there?" John asked him. "Not to mention deserts and God knows what else".

Andrei shrugged. "The map doesn't make it clear how big the mountains are. I guess we go around them."

"Which might stretch those ten centimetres a bit."

"Can't we just fly over the top?" Senna asked.

"You mean, ask Ben to help us?" Asha asked.

"Why not? We tell him the region we want, and let him think we're looking for more aaranya – there's got to be some Glades near there, surely. None of us had thought about the healer being a jalaja, why should he?"

"We don't know that Ben will help us any more than he already has," said John.

Asha took up another aspect that troubled her. "Litak seemed to think we wouldn't get far with her unless you were with us, John. If she's deep in that lake, how are we going to get you to her?"

"Have him separate and come down like he is now," suggested Andrei.

John looked troubled. He told them, "I can only separate here. They won't permit me to try it anywhere else."

"Why not?" asked Darnu.

"I need certain drugs to do this. They're a secret and they won't risk letting them out of the Samgha."

Asha didn't say anything. She was thinking of the other implications behind what John had just revealed.

172

"So separate here and come with us like you are," said Andrei.

"How long can you stay separated?" Senna asked.

John explained what he'd learned from Ben, that separation could only last a matter of weeks.

No one said anything for a time, then Garjae looked to Darnu and said, "But Seriyani? ... We were away for months."

"I did wonder," said Darnu. "I never saw her merge. I thought she must be shy about it for some reason."

"She didn't seem very shy around you," Andrei observed.

"No, she didn't really, did she," Darnu agreed, but didn't reveal what he thought of that.

"I don't like this," Garjae muttered. "If they can't merge, I can only think ..." He trailed off, and then looked to John. "Didn't you ask?"

"I started to, then—" John paused as he tried to remember what had happened. "I got sidetracked," he finished lamely.

Garjae looked around at each of them. "We should leave. John, you should just collect your human body and we should get out of here." When there was no immediate response he continued angrily, "Acintya! How else could they sustain themselves if they can't merge? Animals kill one another for food, that is the path of nature, but to push or tear the prana from a living creature is a horror, abhorrent to all – or it should be. John, you've seen what happened to your daughter. *Aren't you appalled?*"

John stared up at Garjae in disbelief.

"The Glades here would never suffer it," said Asha.

"They mightn't know," said Andrei.

"You met Litak," said Asha, "can you imagine something like this getting past him?"

"No, I suppose not."

"Supposing they did know, what could they do about it?" asked Darnu.

"They should have nothing to do with the Samgha, and they should tell everyone what goes on here," said Garjae.

Darnu looked across at him and said, "There's a long history here. From what Litak told Asha this behaviour, this use of acintya – if that is what they do – may be something quite recent, only since they've started having longer separations. It would not be easy to let go of thousands of years of cooperation, however limited it had been."

"It's not right," Garjae responded.

"No, it's not – if that's what it is. But it's not simple either."

"But what are *we* going to do?" asked Senna. "If we just up and leave, then how do we get to this healer? And if John can't separate, how do we get him to see her?"

"Maybe she'll come to him," suggested Andrei.

"And if she won't? If we do find some way to get close enough to ask her, we'll have made it all that way and fail when we might have succeeded if we weren't in such a rush to get out of here."

"Even with Ben's help, it could still take time to get there and to find her, I couldn't stay separated for that long," argued John.

"With my help you could," Asha said softly.

John turned to her.

"I could sustain you, like I sustained Ellie before she entered the Glade."

"I could never ask it of you."

"You don't have to ask."

"I've seen what it does to you. I know what it takes out of you. It's one thing to do it for those truly in need, but I won't have you hurt for something like this."

"It may be the only way," Asha pointed out.

John opened his mouth and then closed it again, a sullen expression on his face as he recognised the choices confronting him.

Asha looked up at Garjae, noting his still angry expression. "I'm as appalled by this possibility as you are, Garjae, but we don't know if that's what they do. What choices do we have? There's nothing we can do to change what happens here."

"The end justifies the means. Is that it?" he asked. "I thought your ideals were higher than that." He looked around the group. "I thought all our ideals were stronger than that!"

There was silence for a while.

"Can you scuba dive?" Andrei asked John.

"Even if I could, I suspect it would be complicated to arrange."

Asha saw that Senna was watching her and John, as if expecting more. Senna shook her head in frustration, and turned to Garjae. "Walking away achieves nothing. Not for us, not for Ellie, and not to

174

stop what these people do."

"What do you want to do?" demanded Garjae. "It's rock, we can't burn it down."

Asha shuddered at the memory of that horror, of believing she was going to burn, and of seeing the children die. She tried closing her eyes but that just made it worse.

Senna retorted, "I want to achieve what we set out to do. To find this healer, to find hope for Ellie." Asha saw that Senna was again looking at John, puzzled at his silence.

"Maybe it's not acintya," said Andrei. "If it was, why would Ben risk telling John what he did?"

"Because he thinks we have no choice," Garjae replied, "but we do. We can leave here, now!"

John sat forward, he looked at Asha and smiled sadly, and then looked around the group. "We've been talking as if Ben would agree to help me, us, to go further, even if we did ask. There's no reason to expect this is true. He's already got what he wanted, mostly, so there's nothing in it for him to help us further. Leaving here may be what comes next anyway."

Asha studied John as he said this. There was more there, would he tell them? She glanced across and saw Andrei watching John too, probably wondering the same thing. Garjae, though, seemed mollified by John's answer, if still not happy.

"Why don't we ask him?" Senna said.

- - -

Ben met them in his full samvaya form. John was unsurprised to see that Ben reacted calmly when Garjae came right out and demanded to know how the saarvaya fed, how Seriyani must have fed while she was away with them. The man rarely seem surprised or perturbed by anything.

"John was explaining why he can remain separated for only a limited time," Garjae explained.

"And you're thinking of acintya?"

Garjae nodded. "Isn't it?"

"Not really. At least we prefer not to think of it that way. Acintya is objectionable for the suffering it causes. We do feed on the life of animals, when we must, but what we do causes less suffering for the animal than being killed for its meat."

Garjae was unconvinced. "How can you access the prana of a living creature without acintya?"

"You've seen how a preta feeds?" Ben asked mildly.

"I have," Asha answered.

"I haven't," Ben said, "but I'm told that what we do is quite similar. Would you say that what the preta, these victims of acintya, do is itself acintya?"

Asha frowned and exchanged looks with Garjae. "What a preta does is involuntary, they are driven," she said.

"But is it acintya?"

"No," Asha admitted, "I wouldn't have said it was. But it does cause great pain."

"To a conscious victim. The very few animals we ever take are knocked out first, they have to be. They feel nothing." Ben looked around the group. "It is rarely done, not many saarvaya here have ever been separated long enough to need to feed this way."

When no one argued further, Ben said, "If you were discussing the need for John to stay separated for a long period, does that mean you have somewhere else you wish to go?"

"We were told that the healer's new home was in a Glade near Lake Baikal," said Andrei.

"This is from the yaayaavara that Seriyani tells me you met," Ben said.

Andrei nodded.

"A very fortunate meeting."

John saw Andrei start to say something, but then stop himself.

"We wondered if you might help us get there," Senna said.

"Or give us some guidance on how to," added John. "I can get access to money if there's something you can do that I can pay for."

Ben waved his hand at John's offer of money. "We have resources," he said vaguely, and then sat there nodding, deep in thought. "I think we can probably manage it," he said eventually. "It'll take a few days to organise. Maybe we target the start of your next separation cycle, John."

John wasn't sure he'd heard correctly. "Just like that?"

Ben looked surprised at John's response. "Certainly. You've been kind enough to go along with what we wanted to do here, and of course – for our own interest – we would like to see how things go for you over this longer separation. While we may not know your daughter, of course we want to do what we can to help."

"I've not said anything about those other—"

"Of course, John. I'm not bargaining. It's an earnest offer to help you find this healer, all you have to do is accept – if you want." Ben looked to Asha. "Given your concerns about our practices, I presume you will be helping John in your own way."

"I will take care of John," Asha said firmly.

John looked unhappy but didn't argue.

"So, what do you say, John? Do I start making the necessary arrangements?"

John looked around the group. Predictably, Garjae didn't look happy, but he didn't say anything. Darnu looked non-committal at first, but eventually nodded. Andrei and Senna nodded quickly. Asha met his gaze and he read in her eyes the conflict happening behind them. She didn't like or trust Ben any more now than she had at the start, maybe less, but this offer of help could mean the difference between finding the healer in time to help Ellie – or not. And the possibility of not being in time was just too much to bear. She nodded.

John turned to Ben and nodded. "Thanks. It's not enough, but thanks."

"No worries, eh?" Ben stood and dusted off his pants. "Well, I'd love to stay and chat more about your journey." He looked across at Andrei. "I'd love to hear more about the yaayaavara, we don't get many through here these days. Maybe later. First I'd better get things under way for this trip to Russia." He waved to the group and went back into the Samgha.

Garjae stalked off without saying anything, Darnu looked at the others and then followed him.

"That went well," said Andrei, obviously pleased. "My sweet paurakanya was right."

"No need to sound surprised," said Senna. She looked across and read the tension between Asha and John. "Come on, Andrei, let's go back to the stream we found last night."

"But I was going to—"

"Later, my witless wonder."

"Oh, charming."

The pair waved to John and Asha as they walked off, continuing to insult each other.

"I don't like this, John," said Asha.

John turned away from watching the retreating figures of Andrei and Senna and saw that Asha was looking at him intently. "You think Garjae was right?" he asked.

"It's not that, although I don't like the sound of it, however reasonable Ben makes it seem."

"He is good at that."

Asha nodded. "Why is he helping us – really?"

"You don't believe it was from the goodness of his heart?"

"I'm not sure he has one." Asha's tone was bitter with frustration.

"He's been very good to me through all this."

"Because there was something he wanted. When did he get around to saying that you could only separate here?"

John took a deep breath and looked away. "A couple of weeks ago, I'm not sure." He led Asha down from the ridge and they found a place where they could look down at the village from the cliff-top. "I'll tell you what happened here while you were away." He pointed out Dengali's house where he'd spent some of his time before he learned to separate. He talked of the preparations, and of the painful first separations. As he got to the end he remembered Jia's surprising offer, but decided it best to skip that part in his recital, telling Asha simply that they also wanted a sperm donation.

When he'd finished, Asha asked, "So they want you to stay here?"

John nodded. "Apparently."

"And you won't be able to separate again if you don't?"

"Apparently not."

"Shit!"

John turned and looked at Asha in surprise, it wasn't often she swore. "What?"

"Nothing," she replied, "it's not important."

John searched her face, but whatever had bothered her she didn't want to discuss.

"How do you feel about giving them a sperm donation?" she asked him.

"I don't know ... not good really. But after this recent offer of help I'm starting to feel obliged to give them everything I can."

"Including staying?"

"I can't stay. You know I can't."

Asha touched his arm and looked into his face. "But it's not that simple, is it?"

"No," he started, then abruptly, "Yes! It is that simple. It's where you and Ellie will be, there is nowhere else I can be."

"Even if it means losing your vedana again?" she asked softly.

"I've been thinking about that. It must take time for my vedana to fade, perhaps lots of time. Maybe Ben would let me come back here, once a year or something, and I could separate and recover again."

Asha looked doubtful.

"I can ask," said John. "When we get back from Russia, I'll put it to him as a sort of compromise."

Asha changed the subject, "Ben has left a great deal for you to find out after it was too late to back out. It makes me wonder how much there may still be that he hasn't told you."

"Ben explained that. It really would have been overload to go through all this and then discover that it wasn't possible anyway."

"Maybe. To me it sounds like Ben has not been volunteering the information you might need, but always waiting for you to ask the right questions. I can't help wondering how many of his explanations are still incomplete ... and how many are lies."

Finding

8. North

Asha leaned over John to watch the ground as the helicopter rose into the air. The exposed ridge dropped away and she could see people come forward to remove the landing markers, soon there was no sign the machine had been there. Further down, below the cliffs, she could see the tiny scurrying villagers watching their departure. She sat back and looked at John with concern and a certain amount of disbelief.

"I am all right you know," said John, pressing his mouth close to her ear so his soft reassurance could be heard over the noise.

Asha pushed deeper with her senses. He was all right. He shouldn't be, but he was.

"That felt strange," he said, as she withdrew her senses.

"Sorry," she said.

John kissed her cheek. "Not bad, just strange."

Asha kept looking at him carefully. He really did look fine now – but she had seen it happen! The life of the body didn't want to come free. It was ripped away by sheer will, leaving just ragged tails of prana that fell quickly back into the material body. John, in his trance, was effectively unconscious at the time, no person could have stood the full impact of the pain that coursed through both bodies. In the separated praanin body there had been a brief turmoil, like a storm in the flows of prana, and then John woke from his trance. Pain had swept across his face, but the prana quickly settled, and in just moments he appeared to have recovered.

She studied him carefully again, shaking her head, and then smiled. "I can still hardly believe it."

"Me or the helicopter?"

"You. It can't be good, healthy, for either body to do this. What they go through!"

"I feel fine. Better. I feel really good, especially now that you're with me."

Asha smiled in response but didn't try to continue the conversation. Now that she had seen it happen she was glad that John had already decided not to stay. He must not do this again. She was determined not to tell him of the nascent aspirations she had conceived, and hoped that he would never think of them for himself. She knew that John would want to return anyway, if his vedana began to fade again as Ben told him it would, but she would have to find some way to convince John that it didn't matter. They would find a way to make it work – together.

The helicopter flew low through the valleys, rarely rising above the ridges, and the occupants watched without much talk as the mountainous countryside swept past them. Eventually they landed in a small town and the engines stopped. Jia told them they were in China now – she had come along as samvaya, merged so that the group had a representative that could interact with humans and also with John and the aaranya. The helicopter was refuelled and they continued their flight.

Later in the day they landed at the airport of a city and changed from the helicopter to a corporate jet. Inside they found seating for a dozen or more people, including a long couch taking part of one side of the fuselage, and several large, widely spaced passenger seats. The cockpit was isolated from the main cabin.

"Ben wasn't joking about having resources," John noted as he looked around the luxuriously appointed interior.

"Much more considerate than most human vehicles," agreed Andrei. "Real woollen carpets and seat covers."

"And where it's not wool it's leather," added Senna.

"Are all aeroplanes like this?" Andrei asked. "We should fly more often."

"I've never been on anything like this," John said, "I usually fly cattle-class." He turned to Jia. "I didn't think your people would have much call for something like this."

"It is not ours, it is on loan. Ben has an arrangement with someone who makes it available when we need it."

"Nice friends," said Andrei.

Being smaller had it's advantages, Asha sat with John in one of the large luxury seats. Across from them, Andrei and Senna sat together on the couch. Jia sat on the other end of the couch, and Darnu and Garjae took seats further forward, looking back toward the others. They each wriggled around trying to become accustomed to their strange new surroundings. Asha draped her legs over John's, he wrapped one arm around her and she snuggled up against him. It was a very comfortable and comforting arrangement.

With Jia present they couldn't discuss plans for the lake, so they chatted about things of little consequence as they waited for the plane to take off.

At last it started to move and the pilot's voice came over the intercom requesting that Jia should put on her seatbelt until they were in the air.

"Do we need to bother?" Andrei asked.

"It is up to you," Jia told him. She went forward to a seat where she could put on a seatbelt.

Andrei looked across to John. "How much help is a seatbelt going to be if we crash?"

"I think it's more in case of turbulence. If things get rough it stops you shaking around," John answered.

"I'd really rather you didn't discuss such things right now," Asha said. It was strange, they'd been through the flight in the helicopter and she really hadn't thought about being frightened. It had all been so immediate, but here in the muffled, isolated cabin of the luxury craft, the very lack of knowing what was happening outside made her nervous. She held tighter to John.

Andrei grinned at her.

"I know that look, Andrei," she warned, "don't start."

Andrei looked disappointed and turned his attention back to the couch. He picked up the cushions from the other end. "These will do us, won't they Senna."

Senna pulled him against her. "You'll be my cushion won't you, my darling?"

The plane began to pick up speed on the runway, and Andrei pulled away from Senna and leaned against the back of the couch to watch out the window. The thrust kicked in harder and he called out in joy, "Yes!"

"You're like a child, Andrei," Darnu said to him. Asha thought it looked like Darnu was holding on to the arms of his chair pretty tightly.

"You say that like it's a bad thing," was Andrei's reply.

The front of the plane lifted and Andrei looked down to try and see if they'd left the ground. A few moments later he called, "We're off!" He bounced back around to look at the others, looking excited, fidgety and restless.

"Maybe I should get Jia to see if the pilot would let you into the cockpit," said John.

"No you don't!" Darnu said quickly. "He's not getting anywhere near the controls of this thing."

Jia responded, "It would not be a good idea anyway. The pilots are not aware you are here."

"It's fine, Jia," Darnu spoke out. "He doesn't need to see the cockpit."

Andrei looked disappointed.

The plane levelled out and the pilot called back to say it was safe to move around. Andrei was flicking around the stations on the television, obviously bored. Senna took the remote off him and switched it off. "I'm tired," she told him.

It may not have been an active day, but the noise and tension of the helicopter journey had been tiring so the group made themselves comfortable in their seats and tried to get some sleep. Even Andrei, eventually, settled down next to Senna on the couch. John had tilted the seat back and Asha curled up against him. He pressed his face into her hair. The low drone of the engines soothed them all to sleep.

Asha woke later and looked around, trying to remember where she was. She looked across and saw Jia sitting on the end of the couch, she appeared to have been watching John. She was wearing headphones, listening to some music. When Jia saw Asha looking at her, she smiled and turned away, closing her eyes. Asha drifted off back to sleep.

When she woke next Andrei informed them they were landing at Shanghai, he was watching some flight display on the television screen. Jia explained that they would be spending a few hours here.

She would have to leave, but it was best that they remained on the plane. When she eventually returned they flew on to Beijing where they had an even longer wait as everything was organised for the final leg of the flight.

\- - -

"You could bring him here," Tilvy had typed on the screen, "Barma and I could make ourselves scarce. Even Milla is willing to give up a weekend for a good cause. Anyway, it sounds like the others may be out of contact for a long time, heading off so much further north, so Milla probably won't spend as much time here as he has been."

Tracey was sitting upstairs in John's house, close to the second computer. Apparently Milla was at the other computer, the occasional rattle of the keyboard or click of the mouse was all that gave him away. Tilvy was sitting next to her, typing onto the screen in response to what Tracey said.

"It would seem too weird. We haven't even – you know – yet. It would feel like I was bringing him here for a dirty weekend or something."

"And what's wrong with that?" appeared on the screen, followed by a little smiley face symbol.

Tracey laughed. "Maybe nothing, but I've had a bad experience with first times, I really don't want it to happen where we can't get away from each other."

"Tell me more!!" Tilvy wrote.

Tracey glanced back at Milla's chair and mouthed, "Not now."

"Right," Tilvy agreed. "Anyway, if you feel like that about him, it's probably not a good idea."

"I don't, not really. But what if just coming here doesn't convince him? What if he's still in a shitty mood when he gets here? It's a long way home with a cold shoulder."

"You're probably right."

"Anyway, he still hasn't called me. I might never see him again."

"You could call him," Tilvy's suggestion appeared.

"And say what? That it isn't what he thinks? I've already told him that. There's nothing else I can tell him. He's either going to trust me or he's not. ... And so far it looks like he doesn't."

"Then he's an idiot!!!" Tilvy typed, and then Tracey felt Tilvy squeeze her hand.

They had been chatting, one way or another, all weekend. Tracey had offloaded some of her concerns about the future. Tilvy had sympathised, but the best they had come up with was Tracey getting a job in the same town as John, so she could be closer to her friends. But that didn't really solve the big problem: how she could live a relatively normal *human* life and still keep her non-human friends a secret?

Tracey sighed. "I'm really not looking forward to going back, but I'd better leave soon. I don't know whether to hope that Mike rings, or pray that he doesn't. I mean ... what am I going to say to him if he does call?"

"Ask him if he's gotten over his hissy fit yet."

"It's what I feel like saying, but it wouldn't make for a very long phone call. I really don't know what to expect – or want."

"Why don't I come back with you?" Tilvy wrote. "Barma won't mind. I can help you make up appropriate responses to Mike," this was followed by another smiley face.

"I still have to work," Tracey said, "the days will be pretty boring for you."

"So I'll go out for walks. I know my way around the city, remember?"

"If Barma came you would have company during the day."

"But then we couldn't have proper girl-time when you're home."

"Are you sure?" Tracey asked.

"Love to! Sounds exciting!!"

"It does. It'd be really great ... if you're sure Barma won't mind. I don't want to cause problems between you two just because I've got the sulks."

"He won't mind!"

- - -

Barma did mind, a bit, but he tried not to let it show. Since their experiences in the city he always worried when Tilvy was away from him. But Tilvy was excited about spending time with her friend. And she was probably right. Tracey had been depressed when she arrived, she could do with the company of a friend.

He hugged Tilvy tightly. "I'll miss you."

"You'd better," she whispered back. She kissed him and got into the car.

Barma watched and waved sadly as Tracey drove off with the love of his life. It was only going to be for a week, but it felt like she was leaving for much longer than that.

When the sound of the car had faded away to nothing, Barma turned and went back into the house. He closed and locked the front-door behind him and went upstairs. Milla was so engrossed in what he was reading on the computer that he didn't even notice Barma enter the room. Barma stared at him for a few moments, feeling suddenly lost and lonely, and then he shrugged and went back downstairs to the lounge.

He sat in one of the chairs and tried to get comfortable. He had the sofa and television remote control to himself so he tried to enjoy the unusual situation, but it all felt wrong. Tilvy was gone, and Andrei was who knows where now. He flicked around the stations looking for something interesting and eventually the room grew dark around him.

"Barma!"

He turned in surprise. It was Beenae, he looked wrung-out and exhausted.

"Where's Milla?" Beenae asked hurriedly.

Barma pointed upwards and Beenae ran off. Barma turned the television off and followed to see what the excitement was about.

Upstairs he found Milla trying to calm Beenae.

"Say it again, slowly this time."

"There's humans in the forest, and grey ones like they told us about, the dhumraka!" Beenae blurted.

"Coming here?" Barma interrupted.

Milla held up his hand to Barma, then spoke to Beenae, "Tell me what happened, what you saw and when."

"I was coming here to see you. You said you'd show me more on the computer." Beenae pointed to the screen. "But last night I was getting ready to rest when I saw people in the forest, so I snuck over to see who they were. There were lots of them, humans and some of those grey narun. The humans were setting up a camp. I think one of the grey ones saw me, so I ran."

"And this was last night?" Milla asked.

Beenae nodded. "I ran all the way here. I didn't stop."

"Could you tell which way they were headed?"

Beenae shook his head.

"Then we had better go and take a look."

Beenae looked almost as frightened as Barma felt.

Milla looked over to Barma, "You had better come too."

"What about Tilvy?"

"We'll leave a message."

"We could send her an email," Barma suggested.

"She might try to come back early," Milla said. "It would be better to know what is happening before we bring her back into the middle of it."

Barma scrawled Tilvy a brief message, and then panicked about where to leave it. At Milla's suggestion he left it on the keyboard, she would certainly come up here when she came back.

They left quickly but were forced to take a break late in the night so that Beenae could get some rest. They were moving again before dawn and didn't stop until the following dawn when they found the abandoned camp where Beenae had seen the strangers.

Milla studied the area for a while. It was apparent that there had been many humans, but they couldn't tell anything about their narun companions.

"They are heading north, further into the forest," Milla concluded.

"Toward the Glade?" Barma queried.

Milla looked thoughtful. "Perhaps."

"But how'd they know where it was?" Beenae asked.

"A couple of people have mentioned seeing strangers recently," said Milla.

"But they'd have said if they were dhumraka," argued Barma.

"They could have been disguised. You said the dhumraka felt like aaranya when you saw them in the city."

Barma nodded.

"But we'd know if we had been followed," said Beenae.

"They would not need to follow us, not if they were patient. We have been going back and forth to that house a lot over the last months. They would just have to wait near the lines we usually take to confirm where we were going. If they were careful we would never even know they were there," Milla finished absently, thinking out loud.

"So we have to get back and warn the Glade!" Beenae said, panic rising again in his voice.

Milla stood there thinking. Barma cast his eyes around and tried to think too. He wanted to warn Tilvy to stay away, but that meant going back to the house and he couldn't leave Milla alone. Beenae was right, they had to get back to the Glade. He looked back at Milla, who was now studying Beenae.

Milla came to a decision. "Beenae, I want you to go back to the house and wait for Tilvy to return. *Don't* stay in the house. Stay out in the trees and keep watch."

"Shouldn't we send her an email and tell her to stay away?" Barma asked.

"Do you think she would?" Milla asked in return. "Would you?"

Reluctantly Barma shook his head.

"So we say nothing to her and hope that it's over before she gets back, whatever it is. Have you got all that Beenae?"

"But I want to come back with you!" Beenae complained.

"I know, but we need someone to wait for Tilvy and I want Barma to come with me, he has seen these people before. I need you to do this for us." Milla put his hand on Beenae's shoulder. "Take your time getting back to the house. Try to stay hidden as much as possible, and *be careful,* there could be more of these people about."

Beenae didn't look happy, but he nodded his acceptance.

"Good. We will try to get a message back to you and Tilvy just as soon as we know what is happening, try to keep Tilvy away until then. Go now, Barma and I have to hurry."

Beenae left, dragging his feet. Milla called after him, "Remember what I said, *be careful.*" Beenae waved back and appeared to pull himself together a little more.

Milla headed off in the opposite direction and Barma followed him.

- - -

When they landed at Irkutsk everyone was keen to get out of the aeroplane, the novelty of the luxury had worn off. Their first sign that it was not going to go as they expected was when Jia pulled on a bulky parka from a closet behind the cockpit.

When she noticed the others looking at her in question, she told them, "For when the door opens. It is winter out there, it is cold."

"Winter must be almost over," said Darnu.

"The seasons run late here, I am told," Jia explained.

John looked at Asha. "Is this going to be a problem for us?"

"No." Asha seemed confident.

"Not unless the whole lake's frozen over," joked Andrei.

Jia looked at him strangely and said, "I think it is, or most of it."

John saw a flash of surprise and then realisation pass over Andrei's features. "I was just hoping to go for a dip," he said to her, trying to cover his slip.

"I hope you didn't expect a sun-drenched holiday," John said, joining in the joke. "How thick is the ice?" he asked Jia, "maybe he can go ice-skating instead."

Jia shrugged. "I have read that it can be a metre or more thick at times, I don't know what it is now."

"Last time I let you plan our holidays," said Senna, and poked Andrei in the ribs until he wriggled out of her way.

John and the aaranya went quiet when the copilot came through from the front and opened the door to the outside. John felt the cold rush in despite the covered stairway that had been pushed over the doorway. A thickly coated inspector came through to inspect the papers presented by the pilot and by Jia.

John and the aaranya silently followed the copilot as he carried Jia's bags down the stairs. When they left the covered stairway it was very dark. Faint light from the nearby buildings showed snow caught up in corners, though the ground around them was clear. The frozen wind swirled around them. It wasn't a strong wind but John felt as if he should be searching for a coat – or at least some shoes. Despite feeling that it was cold he was not shivering, his body registered the temperature but didn't seem to care.

"This wasn't what I had in mind," he said to Asha. She didn't answer. He saw that she and the others were staring about, apparently feeling as lost as he was. There was no life here but themselves. No life meant that their sense of vedana was of little use in this world of concrete and metal. The dark really was dark.

A large black limousine was parked not far away, it glinted wetly in the light from the buildings. The copilot was loading Jia's luggage into the boot. John led the others around to the side of the car and they waited.

The copilot returned to the plane. A short time later Jia jogged lightly across and opened the back door to the limousine and gestured for them to get in. She climbed in after them and sat down. She raised her fingers to her lips when John went to ask a question and then called forward to the driver. He acknowledged her instructions and then a dark window separating the front from the back was raised.

"We will go to my hotel suite tonight," Jia said.

"I hadn't thought about the weather," John told her. "I've almost no experience in snow." He looked around his friends, Garjae was looking at him accusingly. "I doubt if any of us have much. It might make the search difficult."

"Ben's friends have arranged a flight to take us on tomorrow. That will take you to a good starting point, from there it will be up to you. We have little experience with aaranya outside our own region, we cannot help you much more than that."

"I appreciate what you've done, it's more than we expected. What will you do? We may be gone a long time."

"I know that, I will not be staying with you. Ben has arranged for me to leave behind a computer and satellite connection that you can use to contact us when you are ready to be picked up."

"Wow," said Andrei. "The man thinks of everything."

"Someone's got to," Garjae muttered.

"I didn't see you—" started Senna, but John interrupted.

"Are you staying here in Irkutsk, or going back to the Samgha?" he asked Jia.

"Back to the Samgha," Jia confirmed.

The journey was only brief, it was after midnight and there wasn't much traffic. Even the expensive hotel was quiet, so there was no trouble getting to Jia's suite.

Jia didn't seem inclined to talk. She went through to the bedroom and said she would see them in the morning.

"Later in the morning," Andrei corrected.

She responded with a wan smile as she closed the door.

The others made themselves comfortable as best they could on the sofa, chairs and floor. In many respects it wasn't as comfortable as the jet had been, the materials of the carpet and upholstery were not pure natural fibres and they felt strange and uncomfortable to lie against.

"The cold could be a problem," Darnu opened the subject they'd all been wanting to discuss since leaving the jet. He spoke very softly.

Asha nodded.

"I thought you said—?" John started.

"Quietly, John. Remember, your voice in this form carries even through walls to those that can hear it," Asha whispered to him, and pointed to Jia's room. "I didn't realise just how cold it was going to be when I said that. I've never been anywhere this cold before. Darnu?"

"I've spent some time up in the alpine areas, they're not that far from home. And we do occasionally get snow even at our Glade."

"But not enough to freeze our trees," put in Garjae.

Darnu nodded. "And that's the point. If it's cold enough here to freeze the water of the lake to a metre thick then the trees too are going to be frozen through."

"But the cold doesn't affect us, does it?" John asked, confused.

"Not directly, although I've never been anywhere that gets this cold. But we can't go through the ice. We can't merge and we can't pass through directly because of the crystals it forms as it freezes."

"So we might have to wait for the lake to thaw, is that what you're saying?"

"Perhaps, but waiting could be a problem too. If we can't get into the lake then we'd be looking for trees, but if the tree's are frozen they're not going to help us much either." Seeing John was still confused, he continued, "We don't feel the cold, but the trees do. The life within them slows down as they freeze until it is barely moving. Even when we can still merge it happens very slowly and there is little the tree can offer to sustain us."

"And trying to help you may be impossible," Asha added with concern.

"So how do the aaranya here survive?"

"In the alpine areas at home they mostly retreat to their Glade during the worst of the winter, only coming out occasionally until things warm up. I imagine that's what they do here."

"Will the aaranya here help us?"

"That's a problem too. If most are inside the Glade then we have less chance of meeting one to guide us, which means finding the Glade for ourselves and that could be difficult."

"Especially considering the conditions," added Garjae. "And while they'd probably help us out, even if they think we're fools, it's less certain they'd welcome you."

"You are obviously not aaranya," Asha explained.

John slumped. They'd come all this way only to find they'd been frozen out.

"There must be some part of the lake that doesn't freeze over," said Andrei. "It's a huge lake."

"Six-hundred and thirty-six kilometres long, and an average of forty-eight kilometres wide," Senna reported. While the others had been talking she had started up Jia's portable computer. The others turned to look at her as she continued, "It carries about one-fifth of the world's unfrozen fresh surface-water." There was a pause as she scrolled down. "Lake Baikal usually freezes in January and the ice breaks in May. The ice is seventy to one-hundred and fifteen centimetres thick."

"May ... fuck!" John swore.

"Now now, John, there are ladies present," Andrei told him. To Senna he said, "Does it say it freezes right across? That's one humongous icicle."

There was a long pause as Senna kept looking through details on the computer. "It says here that during one of their wars early last century they laid a railway over the ice." She looked up. "That sound's pretty well frozen to me."

"We should have waited," said Garjae.

"If we wait for the lake to break up we could be too late, we mightn't get back to Ellie in time," Asha corrected him quietly.

"We can't even be sure the healer is there, or if she'll help us," Garjae returned. "We may be better off looking elsewhere."

"Where, Garjae?" Asha asked, her tone exasperated.

He turned away.

"What do the jalaja do?" John asked. "Do they stay imprisoned under the ice?"

"Six hundred kilometres is a pretty big prison. I doubt they care much about the ice," said Darnu.

"So what do we do?" Senna asked, pushing the computer aside.

"We could ask Jia for help," suggested Darnu.

"And break our promise to Litak?" said Asha.

"You did leave open the possibility that there might be no other way."

"We don't know there isn't yet."

"But if she leaves us there'll be no one to ask."

"We can use that computer she's leaving behind," said Senna, "we could still ask Ben."

"He might not be able to do much from where he is," said Darnu.

John listened as the discussion, sometimes bordering on argument, bounced back and forth in whispers. He felt guilty for the trouble his friends were going through, and the accusing glances from Garjae felt well deserved.

He shuffled uncomfortably on the sofa, drawing a concerned look from Asha. He was feeling the first pangs of needing something. It wasn't hunger, or not as he'd feel it back in his material body, it was more of an undirected craving, a feeling of emptiness, as if something was missing. He tried not to think about it. He remembered now that Ben had said he may have less time away from the lush life of the jungle. He'd not only been away from that for some days now, but even the life of the land they had come to was sleeping through a long winter.

"We do what we always do," said Andrei. "We push ahead and look for the answers when we get there."

John wasn't sure what to say.

Andrei met his gaze. "What? It's worked okay so far, hasn't it?"

No one argued with that. They'd made it this far almost entirely on Andrei's optimistic, "We'll find out when we get there," approach. John wondered how far their luck would stretch, but right now there seemed no choice but to try and stretch it a bit further.

With nothing much resolved, they slowly settled to sleep as best they could.

- - -

Senna was already awake when the sky started to lighten outside the windows. Andrei was sleeping, draped across one of her arms, holding it tight. They'd made themselves as comfortable as they could with cushions on the floor. She smiled. He seemed a lot better now they were away from the jungle and the Samgha, less moody – or was it her? She didn't think it was, or not entirely.

Darnu and Garjae were still asleep, one in each of the armchairs. Darnu had one arm out, as if reaching out to save Garjae from falling. Garjae was looking the other way, and looked tense despite being asleep; the scowl on his face was becoming a permanent fixture. Why does he do it to himself? she wondered. No one forced him to come. It was obvious that he wanted Asha, whether he truly loved her was less certain, or so it seemed to Senna. But it was equally obvious that Asha had made her choice, for better or worse, so why put yourself through that?

She looked up at the sofa and saw that Asha was also awake, stroking the hair from John's forehead. They exchanged smiles and then went back to their own thoughts.

John and Asha were both control freaks, wanting to know for certain what would happen next and next and next, and Darnu was just as bad. Andrei had the courage to explore, it was one of the things she admired about him. ... Walking out into a Siberian winter without a plan, however, was perhaps starting to push things, even by Andrei's standards. Still, she wasn't about to back out now. They would do what they had set out to do, however negative Garjae might be.

It wasn't much longer before Andrei woke and then the others. They heard the telephone ring briefly, Jia must have picked it up in the bedroom. A few moments later she came out dressed in a loose tracksuit and warned them that her breakfast would be delivered soon.

Senna and Andrei knelt on the floor, leaned against the windowsill, and looked out at the city. The light wind of the night before was gone and the sun was bravely shining in orange rays through a light fog that hung over the region. Two stories below them the street itself was mostly clear, but snow lay at the feet of the buildings and crowned any level surface.

"So this is what winter looks like," Andrei spoke quietly next to her.

"Didn't look like this back home," Senna replied.

"I've seen snow, it happens sometimes where we are. When it does it's a novelty, we all muck around in it and have fun; I've even seen old Milla playing in it. But it never hangs around long. It's hard to imagine living with it for months at a time."

"Last night was the first time I've even been near it. I still haven't touched it. All I know about it is what I've seen on human television, people building snowmen and having snowball fights."

"Excited?" he asked, still looking out the window, but Senna could hear the grin.

"No snowballs, Andrei. Not unless I get first throw." She pointed down to the street. "Some of that looks too dirty to want to play in anyway."

"Won't be where we're going."

Jia returned to her room to shower and dress, and while she was out the others picked up the conversation again from last night.

Senna didn't pay much attention, there wasn't anything new. She watched the waking city out the window. It seemed a very quiet city. The city of her home was rarely quiet, except for a short time in the very early hours of the morning. The buildings were different here too, even their colours were different, it made her wonder how the people of this city varied from those of her own.

As she watched people walk past below, heavily garbed against the winter, Senna tried to imagine how they might look in spring and summer. Andrei sometimes teased her about coming from a place with no seasons, but it did really. Andrei saw seasons only in the flowers and plants, and Senna saw those too, but she also saw the seasons in the people of her city. In winter they dressed more dully and they acted more conservatively. Spring was an upbeat time in which people often behaved and dressed extravagantly, as if looking forward to a bright summer that sometimes turned out to reward less than it had promised. Summer was a time when the people of her city were extroverted and optimistic, it was a season they stretched and stretched so that autumn often felt very short. What autumn there was, Senna usually remembered as the bright deciduous trees near the river, and the people beneath them still trying to pretend it was summer, but slowly, so slowly, letting go of their summer freedoms like so many dying leaves. She had made Andrei laugh when she had first given him this explanation, he accused her of treating humans as mobile plants.

Soon after Jia was ready the call came to say the car was waiting.

All went smoothly getting down to the car and out at the airport. The only mishap was when one of the humans loading a case into the back of the helicopter stepped back unexpectedly into Andrei and both of them fell over.

"Andrei!" Darnu scolded.

"I didn't do anything," Andrei complained. He got up and, with a limp, side stepped the human. He rubbed one shoulder before climbing up after the others.

The human got back up carefully, and brushed himself off, looking embarrassed at apparently having fallen over himself.

Sitting now safely inside the helicopter, Andrei lifted one foot and rubbed it. "Near squashed my poor foot," he grumbled.

Senna looked carefully at his foot and then kissed his cheek. "I don't think it's a mortal wound."

Andrei held his foot up higher. "Want to kiss it better?"

Senna pushed it away. "Not particularly."

This was smaller than their previous helicopter. Jia sat up front next to the pilot, but it was a close fit in the back as they had to share the space with some cases of equipment.

The helicopter lifted and in a very short time they had left the city behind. They were flying over a white landscape with patches of forest scattered below them.

Sometime later Andrei pointed out into the distance. "There's our lake."

The pilot pointed and announced the same to Jia.

Senna looked into the distance carefully. From here some of it looked like water rather than ice. Could they be lucky?

As if echoing Senna's thoughts Jia spoke to the pilot, "That looks like water, I thought it was frozen."

"Ice," the pilot told her. "Very clear water make very clear ice."

The lake stayed distant on their right as the helicopter continued to the north and east. This helicopter was also relatively quiet, but even so they didn't speak much, everyone was intent on watching the landscape. The pilot chatted on and off with Jia, pointing out landmarks below and reciting the history of the region, apparently feeling it was his duty to act as tourist guide even though Jia didn't express much interest.

It was still before midday when the helicopter turned more

directly north. The mountains that had grown steadily more rugged seemed to reach up to them now, swallowing their helicopter as if it was an insect. They flew into a long valley with steep sides and briefly circled an area of clear snow. As they descended, the area appeared to grow and Senna could see a cabin on one side of what turned out to be a large clearing.

Jia pointed to tracks in the snow. "Are there others here?"

The pilot looked down were Jia indicated and then explained, "My tracks. I come two days ago, make sure safe and ready. Not usual for winter tourist to come here."

"Whatever else Ben is," Andrei said, "he's certainly thorough."

Senna nodded. She couldn't help wondering if this was all Ben's doing. Why would he have any idea what was required this far from his jungle? Maybe it was just the usual courtesy of the service here.

The helicopter settled in the snow and the great blades slowed, but the engine was left idling. Senna and the others waited while the pilot got out and opened up the door to the back. A basic sled was pulled out and the cases of equipment were loaded onto it.

The pilot pulled the sled, his footsteps sinking deep into the snow. John and the aaranya followed carefully in the tracks of the sled, their footsteps barely marking the compacted snow. Jia came behind them making sure to obscure even those traces.

The cabin was a sturdy looking building made of round logs, their ends protruding from each corner. It sat on the edge of a forest of fir trees. Someone had cleared the area around the front and sides of the cabin.

Senna and Andrei followed the others to a place to one side of the cabin until things were arranged with the pilot.

"When your friends come?" the pilot asked after carrying the last of the cases from the sled into the cabin.

Jia shrugged. "My job is just to make sure the equipment is here when they want it."

The pilot grunted, not going to question the peculiarities of rich foreigners. The pilot began to pull the sled back and Jia told him to wait with the helicopter, she would be with him when she had checked the equipment was all working.

Jia gestured the others into the cabin and quickly went through how to set up and use the equipment. It looked modern and sophisticated, even by the standards of what Senna had seen in the Samgha. Extra batteries had been supplied, but Jia warned that they should probably be careful not to use the equipment more than necessary anyway.

Jia looked at John expectantly. "Is that all clear?" she asked him.

John looked at the equipment silently for some time, Senna could see him slowly checking things off in his mind, and then he nodded. "Guess so. It seems simple enough."

"Good," Jia said and started to shut it all off and pack it up again. "Someone from the Samgha will come back in a month or two to check anyway, just in case anything goes wrong."

Jia slid the now encased equipment under one of the bunk beds and stood and looked around the group, her eyes coming to rest on John. Senna found Jia's expression difficult to read. Some reluctance to go, and apparent concern, but other things were mixed up in there too. Andrei's digs had probably been all too accurate.

"Then we are done. Good luck," Jia said and looked back around the group, "all of you. I will see you all again soon." She gestured for them to precede her out of the cabin. Outside she locked the door and then pretended to put the keys in her handbag. When she was certain the pilot wasn't looking she handed the keys to John, who passed them to Darnu.

"Thank you," John called as Jia started to walk back through the snow to the helicopter.

She nodded her head in acknowledgement but didn't look back.

After the helicopter had lifted off they stood as a group listening to the slowly diminishing sound of the engine. In the still cold of the forest the sound carried back to them for a long time.

Andrei broke the falling silence, "That was easy."

John turned to look at him with disbelief.

"We've barely started yet," Garjae reminded Andrei.

"Starting is the hardest part of any job," Andrei stated. "Isn't that right, John?"

John just shook his head.

"Anyway, look what I found," said Andrei. He disappeared briefly around the corner of the cabin and returned carrying a small pick-axe. "I smuggled it outside while you were all busy watching Jia. Just the thing, don't you think?"

John looked blank.

Andrei made swinging motions with it. "There's ice between us and the water, we just chop it out of the way. Humans do come up with the occasional good idea."

John took it from him and weighed it in his hands. "Bit small."

"All the better for carrying it with us," Andrei responded.

"Might be hard to cut through that much ice with something this small."

"Hey, if you don't book ahead you can't complain about the service."

Senna walked to the nearest trees and the snow lying around and beneath them. The snow obscured what it lay over from both sight and vedana; the stark white of muffled shapes confused the eyes, and the covering of snow cast a fog that confused vedana. She felt the snow with her feet and then knelt down and touched it with her fingers. It was cold, of course, but it was also hard and brittle. Nothing like what she had expected. She looked up and saw John experimenting with the snow as well. "Television lies," she told him.

He looked at her, "Huh?"

"On television and in movies snow looks all soft and fluffy. It's not."

"Not always," said Andrei from the other side. "But you wait until we see some fresh snow, it's much nicer."

"Where do we put the keys?" Darnu asked.

They looked around and decided on one of the taller of the trees that no human was likely to climb, it appeared to have a useful hollow high up. Darnu quickly scaled the tree and hid the keys from sight. When he descended he merged his hand slowly into the tree and even more slowly pulled it back out again. He turned back to the others and said, "It's even worse than I had expected. There's nothing for us here. I hope we can get into the lake or we're all in trouble, not just you, John."

Asha walked to another tree and ran her hands over the trunk. "If the trees can't help then we'll have to find a Glade or water – even a river."

Senna looked up in shock. "A river."

"What river?" Andrei asked.

"I just remembered – on the map – there was a big river through the city we just left, it came from the lake."

"Wasn't it frozen too?" Darnu asked.

"I don't know."

"A lot of good that does us now anyway," Garjae said.

"Do you have any helpful comments?" Andrei asked him.

"We must be a long way from the city now," Asha said. "Let's get to the lake."

Garjae studied Asha, his expression blank, and then he said, "We won't get anywhere standing around talking about it." With that he turned from the group and started walking.

Senna couldn't help wondering how much of a mistake it might have been to have overlooked the possibilities of the river.

Andrei told her, "We couldn't have checked out the river without telling Jia anyway."

"But maybe we could have found out more about it."

Andrei put his arm around her. "Nah, where's the fun in that? Come on, before Garjae leaves us all behind."

- - -

They walked for several hours without a break. The day continued fine and John found himself enjoying the walk through the quiet forest. Much of the snow had formed a hard crust which meant their insubstantial forms rarely broke through. The snow was not as slippery as John remembered it from his few experiences in the past, he supposed that must be another advantage of his new body, or perhaps it was the advantage of bare feet that never got cold.

The day was drawing to a close, the sun sinking behind them, as they began to descend from a ridge. Asha called ahead to Garjae and Darnu that it was time to take a break. Garjae stopped, reluctantly, and waited for the others to catch up with him.

"We won't get far if we keep stopping all the time," Garjae muttered to no one in particular.

Asha flashed an angry look at him, but didn't respond.

Garjae and Darnu pulled themselves up into the low branches of a tree and brushed the snow off to sit there. John didn't feel that agile so he leant the pick-axe against the base of a tree and settled down next to it. Asha sat on his other side. Andrei and Senna settled at the base of Garjae and Darnu's tree.

"Not as unpleasant as it could have been," said Andrei, in upbeat tones.

"It's getting colder now though," Darnu observed.

John realised he was right. It had been cold all day, but now he could feel the cold pressing down on him like a weight. The sky was clear, he hoped that was a good sign. He pressed his hand down on the snow beside him for a minute and then pulled it back up: it was dry. Then he huffed his breath: there was no vapour. He sat back, shaking his head.

"What?" Asha asked.

"We don't melt the snow. We don't fog the air."

"So?" asked Andrei.

"So we don't warm anything up. I had this silly idea that we could build an igloo or something." John heard a snort from Garjae but ignored it. "But without body heat we can't make it any warmer."

"Does it matter?" Andrei asked.

"I might be the only one, but even if the snow doesn't make my body cold, it's still far from comfortable."

"Sit on my lap," Asha offered.

"That's hardly gallant," he returned.

"Climb up onto a branch," Darnu called down. "Knock the snow off, it's better."

It took a couple of tries, and some help from Asha, but eventually John managed to share a branch with her. Darnu was right. John could hardly feel the life of the tree within the branch, but there was enough that it felt warmer against his body. Andrei and Senna did the same at another tree.

Asha pulled John against her. "Better?" she asked softly.

"Always."

Casseta chose that time to make her presence felt and John called her out. It had been such a relief when she had been willing, apparently eager, to return to him when Asha had returned from the jungle. She had still refused to merge when John was in his human body, but having her accept his saarvaya form had been reassuring. John stroked her soft fur gently with his finger tips and murmured to her. She ran briefly over the two of them before nuzzling at Asha's arm. Asha looked at John, he could see the same fear in her eyes that he felt: was he being rejected again? He shrugged. "Maybe she thinks you're warmer than me."

Asha murmured to the brevi and Casseta merged.

John pushed down his fear, it wasn't that unusual for Casseta to spend time with Asha. If he was feeling so uncomfortable in the cold he couldn't really expect the brevi to be happy either. Asha put her arms around him and leaned against him, he leaned back and tried to relax.

They sat there quietly as the darkness and cold fell around them. As far as John could tell no one slept. Eventually there was movement and Garjae jumped down from his branch, he broke through the snow crust and stumbled before righting himself.

"Come on," he called, and started walking without waiting for a response.

The others climbed down from their branches. It was more difficult now, although John couldn't work out why. He and Asha walked close, holding hands, and followed after Garjae and Darnu. Andrei and Senna came on behind them.

The night wore on and the cold grew even more intense. This was nothing like the jungle, where the intensity of the life there kept everything clear and sharp to his vedana. Here in the darkness it seemed to John that they were walking on and through dark clouds. The snow was an indistinct haze beneath their feet and the life of the trees loomed before them like faint ghosts. They went through a clearing and John saw that clouds had come over, though he didn't remember it happening. He had no idea how long they'd been walking, it was all happening in a dream. Only the warm touch of Asha's hand kept him from feeling totally desolate and lost.

"Wait!" Senna's voice called from behind them.

It took pressure from Asha's hand to make John respond and come to a stop.

Senna and Andrei came up behind them. "Catch up with the others," Senna told them.

Asha pulled John forward.

Garjae and Darnu were well in front and it seemed to take a long time to reach them. When they did, Garjae asked in surly tones, "What?"

"Something's coming," Senna answered.

They stood silently. John couldn't hear anything or see anything other than the ghost images of the nearby trees. Something touched his hand, the one still clinging to Asha's, but when he looked down he could see nothing there. He looked around and then up, and saw faint smudges descending around them. It was only when a few cold blurs touched on his face that he recognised them as snowflakes.

"There," said Senna softly, and pointed.

John looked dully back down, everyone else was looking off through the trees to one side. At first it was like some alien floating light, but then his vision partly cleared and he could see it was a wolf, its life standing out brightly from the forest. Then another, and another; six in all. John wondered if he should be frightened, but couldn't quite make the necessary connections.

The wolves approached them cautiously, aware of them but uncertain how to react. A couple of the lead wolves came within a few feet and then worked their way from side to side, sniffing at them and then backing away. After a few minutes the wolves decided to leave well enough alone and they turned away and padded quietly off.

Garjae turned and started to walk again. Asha tugged on John's arm and he stumbled as he tried to follow after her.

"Wait," Asha called.

"What is it now?" Garjae asked as he turned back.

Asha ignored the question and studied John carefully. "Something's wrong," she said quietly, mostly to herself.

"There is," agreed Darnu. "I feel it too. I think it's the cold. It seems to be slowing me down. I feel clumsy and uncoordinated."

"Me too," volunteered Senna. "I should have felt those wolves much sooner than I did."

"Whatever it is, it's affecting John badly," Asha said, still not taking her eyes from him.

John heard all this but was unable to form any words of response.

"I think he's losing strength too quickly, and combined with the cold it's like he's going to sleep," said Asha.

"But the cold doesn't affect us," said Andrei.

"You're not feeling any different?" Senna asked him.

Andrei was silent for a moment as he thought. "I guess I am feeling a bit down or something, I just thought it was Garjae's mood rubbing off on me."

Garjae grunted but didn't say anything.

"I—" Darnu started and then stopped and crinkled his face in concentration. "It's harder to think. Maybe Milla said something to me years ago about extreme cold ... but I can't ... it never seemed that important."

"What can we do?" Senna asked.

"Group hug?" Andrei suggested.

"It won't make anything warmer," said Darnu.

"But it still might help," said Asha. "It might help all of us."

Asha pushed herself against John and he registered the life of her body against his, it felt warm and reassuring. Next Andrei and Senna wrapped themselves around them and then Darnu.

"Come on, Garjae," cajoled Andrei, "none of us smell that bad."

Reluctantly, Garjae joined the circle.

"I think maybe I should try feeding him," Asha said quietly as they stood there. "With the extra strength he may cope better."

Surrounded by the living bodies of his friends, John did feel better, he felt warmer, whatever the real temperature, and he began to feel that the dream state was receding. He managed to slowly form the words, "No. ... Asha ..." His words ran out.

Darnu picked up on John's unfinished thought. "He's right, Asha. If being weak means being more affected by the cold, then you might both get in trouble."

"But—" Asha started.

"No," John said as firmly as he could manage.

"Together we can help John to continue," Darnu said. "If you get in trouble then that's another person needing help and one less to give it."

"And what do we do now?" Garjae asked. "We're not getting far standing around like this."

"Garjae," said Andrei, "don't be a spoil sport. You can't tell me you don't feel better for this cosy little get-together. Admit it, this is helping us too."

Sometime later, Darnu asked John, "Are you any better? Do you think you can walk?"

John thought this was like having stayed up all night, that fuzzy time before the first light of a new day when the mind is refusing to operate, when every stimulus seems to come from far away. But now, surrounded by the warm-seeming life of his friends, he felt the same waking sensation when, at long last, the sun began to rise. Even the craving sensation was familiar; if he was in his material body he'd be making himself a strong coffee about now to try and extend this period of alertness, because he knew that, just like such mornings, this feeling wouldn't last. Belatedly he responded to Darnu, "Yes. It is better – for now."

"Good," Darnu answered. To Asha he continued, "We'll stop when we have to, but Garjae's right, it's not going to help anyone if we stay still for too long. With this snow, and cloud cover settling in, it's not going to get much warmer come morning."

They started walking again, continuing to follow along behind Garjae and Darnu. Asha walked close to John on his right and Andrei came in on his left. Together they caught him when he stumbled and helped to guide his increasingly unconscious footsteps. Senna would sometimes replace Asha or Andrei, and later Darnu helped too.

When they stopped again sometime later, and again wrapped John in their presence, he eventually woke enough to understand that it was still snowing, heavier than before. The group huddled against the trunk of the largest of the trees they could find, but it offered little comfort and no sustenance. Despite the snow it was apparent that the light of a new day was growing around them.

Andrei pulled away from the group. "I'll be back in a few minutes," he told them and was quickly lost to John's senses, fading into the snow as if he was falling into depths.

There was some conversation around John as Darnu and Asha asked Senna where Andrei had gone, but she didn't know. They could do nothing but wait.

Time passed and John began to feel slightly better again, enough to guide his own footsteps for a while, and be less of a burden – he hoped.

Senna was getting restless, worried about Andrei. He felt her relax and turned to see where she was looking. A minute later Andrei reappeared through the snow. Senna pulled him in quickly and pressed him into the centre of the group with John.

"Where did you go?" she demanded.

"You missed me?" he asked.

"Where did you go, Andrei?" Darnu asked.

"I think we turned north through the night," Andrei said. John noticed he was watching Garjae warily, perhaps accusingly, as he said this. "We have to be walking east to reach the lake. I just went up to a ridge to get my bearings better. I don't know how much further we've already walked than we needed to, and I'm not sure I'd like to find that cabin again in a hurry either."

9. Ice

Andrei studied Garjae. Garjae returned his gaze for a while, his expression unconcerned, almost blank, and then turned away. Andrei had a persistent, dull and distracting headache throbbing slowly in his temples. But Garjae? It was hard to tell how the cold was affecting him. His mood was sour, but that wasn't unusual.

"Let's go," said Darnu.

Garjae broke away from the huddle and Andrei watched him carefully, making sure the direction he took was due east. It was difficult to keep concentration in this foreign world of snow and sleeping trees, they would all have to pay attention.

Andrei walked beside John, at first just helping him to keep the right direction, and then joining with Asha in helping to support him. Most of the time John seemed unaware that there was anyone around him. Andrei wondered, if it came to it, how far they could carry John through the snow. And it really was *through* the snow now. The easy walking of yesterday was gone, each step sank deep into the soft fresh snow that Andrei had been so keen to show Senna.

Late in the afternoon it stopped snowing, but it remained deeply overcast and didn't get any warmer, if anything it was getting even colder. After each stop to huddle around John, he would improve, but the improvement got less each time. By the end of the day any improvement was barely perceptible.

Night fell and they kept walking. Andrei was finding it harder to make sure Garjae continued to lead them east, or even to remember that he should. His headache was growing worse, the pounding of his footsteps was loud and hurtful inside his head. He had to remind

Senna to relieve Asha on the other side of John.

They paused again, Andrei thought it must be about midnight. He gave his head a shake to try and clear it. His headache pounded loudly and then receded slightly. They had entered a grove of skeleton-like poplar trees. Up through their bare branches he could see that the sky was now clear, stars sparkled sharply against the black sky. The clear air felt almost frozen. Around him everyone was just standing there, apparently numb and unthinking in the cold. He waded through the snow and pulled the group together into their now familiar huddle.

As they shared the comfort of their contact, life against life, some coherent thought returned to Andrei. He recognised that they were in serious trouble. If they weren't careful John, or even one of the others, could collapse and fall behind and no one would even notice. They probably only had another day, maybe two, left to them unless the temperatures warmed appreciably or they found some way to rebuild their strength.

Garjae broke away from the huddle and started walking again. Darnu paused, as if unable to make up his mind what he should be doing, then turned and followed. Andrei, Senna and Asha shared a look and then together they started to pull John forward again – there was no sign that this pause had helped him.

Dawn was still a couple of hours away when Andrei tried to get everyone to stop again, but Garjae ignored his calls, and they were forced to keep going or be left behind. They trudged forward as fast as they could, pushing and pulling John into reluctant footsteps with them. Sometimes they could barely keep sight of Garjae and Darnu.

Later, as they struggled up to a ridge, Andrei could see the sky was lightening ahead. Staring, mesmerised by this prelude to a new day, it took Andrei some moments before he registered a light hissing noise that grew quickly louder. He had no chance to react, suddenly he was hit in the chest by snow and John was torn from his grasp. He heard Senna call out, but then he was rolling in the snow, blinded and disoriented.

When the snow stopped moving again, Andrei pulled himself clear and stood up. Not exactly an avalanche, he supposed, just a settling of the newly fallen snow, but still something they could have done without. His head was aching worse than ever.

"John! John!" Asha was calling as she waded back and forth through the snow.

Andrei looked around and saw that Senna was sitting up, but as yet she didn't seem to have pieced together what had happened. He went over and helped her to her feet.

"You okay?"

Senna stared at him blankly and then nodded slowly.

Andrei looked up to the ridge they had been trying to climb. He expected to see Garjae and Darnu coming back down to help them, but they were not in sight, and the newly swept slope revealed no footsteps. He turned his attention back to Asha, she was becoming frantic. He went over to her, pulling Senna along behind. When Asha paid no immediate attention he released Senna and grabbed Asha by the shoulders and turned her to face him.

"Shhh," he said softly but firmly.

"But John—"

"I know. We'll find him, just … stay calm. Okay?" Andrei tried to sound confident and reassuring, maybe he had a career in acting after all.

Asha nodded back at him.

We really are in trouble, thought Andrei to himself, Asha is never this submissive. He turned to Senna. "Can you feel him?"

Senna hesitated and then pointed.

Andrei wanted to laugh, but he couldn't find the strength, it was either that or give up now; they had almost fallen over him. There was John, lying mostly on top of the snow, curled on his side as if he had found a comfortable place to sleep. Only the fact that his body was covered in a dusting of ice crystals showed that he too had been rolled by the snow slide.

Together they raised John to his feet again and dusted him off. He seemed neither worse nor better for having been tumbled by the minor avalanche. They struggled out from the deep loose snow of the slide and made their way up to the ridge, Senna walked a small distance ahead of them, and to one side.

As they approached the ridge the sky grew lighter and lighter until, abruptly, they reached the summit and stopped in surprise. Ahead of them the ridge descended gently for a short distance and then just dropped away. From somewhere below that drop extended a flat, white plain that reached out to the distant horizon and as far as they could see to either side. As he looked out across this vast and apparently empty expanse, the first orange-yellow rays pushed through a light mist in the distance and a tiny arc of the dawning sun appeared. Of Darnu and Garjae there was no sign.

- - -

The weak rays of sunlight fell on Asha's face like a gentle caress, warm beyond mere heat. The sun was distant, the life it offered greatly diffused through the skies of winter and early morning, but for all that – especially for all that – its meagre offering was to be welcomed and treasured. She closed her eyes and opened her arms to the dawn.

How long she stood like that she didn't know, but suddenly she opened her eyes in alarm: John! She relaxed again when she felt him there beside her. He was standing silently, eyes closed as hers had been, but he was not aware of the sunlight, he had simply stopped because no one was compelling him to move.

The lake's vitality was masked by the layer of ice, and by her dulled senses, but it was too huge to have its impact completely hidden. Like the ocean this was a system of life so large and so *alive* that it overwhelmed the senses, even in this depth of winter.

"Where are Darnu and Garjae, do you think?" asked Andrei, breaking the still quiet of the dawn.

Asha looked around in surprise. They should be here.

"There," Senna said, pointing to the smooth slope that ended abruptly at the drop. "The snow slid away on this side too."

"Ay caramba!" murmured Andrei. He started forward.

"Careful," Asha warned.

Andrei waved a hand but kept going. He got to the edge and peered down. After a moment he yelled down, "Did you find the lake?"

"Where have you been?" Darnu's voice came back.

"The same thing that happened to you happened to us," Andrei called, "but we went the other way. Are you two okay?"

"Garjae's been hurt."

"I'm all right," Garjae's voice cut in.

Andrei wandered along the edge looking for a way down. He

called back when he found a place where he thought they could make it with John. It was steep and rocky and slippery, but Andrei went ahead ready to catch John if he started to fall. Slowly, and with a few scares as more snow slipped around them, they made it to the bottom of the cliff. They had to work their way out through the debris beneath the drop before they reached the flat ice of the lake and could make their way back to where Darnu and Garjae were waiting.

Garjae was holding one arm stiffly, but when Asha tried to take a closer look he pulled away. "I'll be all right. It's just bruised," he told her.

Darnu explained that they'd come over the ridge, and before they understood what was happening, the snow began to move under their feet and it had tumbled them over the edge. Darnu had landed in soft snow and received little more than some light bruising. Garjae, however, had landed against hard ice jutting up through the surrounding snow and was pounded against it by the snow that fell after him.

Asha tried again to see if she could help Garjae, but he turned away. "It's fine," he snapped. Asha gave up without saying anything more, she didn't have the strength to argue.

The sun was well up now and without any wind the morning was actually feeling a little warmer. Only a metre or so below them was a huge mass of water, only close to freezing temperature rather than well below it, and the life of that mass also had an effect.

Asha stared down at her feet. To be so close, not much more than an arm's length from the life they needed to rebuild their strength – to feel it and yet to have no way to reach it was unbearably frustrating.

"We made it to your lake," Garjae said to Asha when she looked up. Then he turned to Andrei. "Now what? Do you want to start digging?"

It took Andrei some time to understand what he meant, and then looked to John, and then to each of the others.

Garjae did the same. "Where is it?"

Andrei shrugged his shoulders.

"Who had it last?"

Asha remembered that John was carrying the pick-axe on that

first afternoon leaving the cabin, she couldn't remember seeing it since.

Garjae looked to Asha. "What do you want to do?"

Asha didn't know how to respond.

Andrei spoke up. "Well, it's definitely frozen solid here." He banged his foot on the ice for emphasis. "If there's going to be holes anywhere they're going to be closer to the middle. Let's head out onto Lake Garjae and see what we can find."

Asha wasn't certain Andrei's logic was sound, but couldn't think of any better ideas, and she didn't want to give up on the lake now that they'd reached it.

"Lake Garjae?" Darnu asked.

"I wasn't sure which of you hit it first," said Andrei, "but I thought you wouldn't mind giving the naming honours to Garjae, since he is suffering for his art."

Garjae didn't acknowledge this, he just turned and started walking out toward the sun and the distant horizon. It was obvious from his broken stride that he was in pain, but it was also obvious that he was in no mood to discuss it or relent to it. Darnu hurried after him, but Garjae shrugged off his proffered help.

Asha studied John. The sunshine and warmth had made her and the others feel much better, but so far it had had little effect on John.

"Is he going to be okay?" Andrei asked her.

Asha shrugged. "If I'm right then all we need is just a few feet below us, if only we could get there."

"We can," said Andrei. "Come on, let's race Garjae to the other side."

They set off again, pulling John along with them. It was much easier travelling here on the flat ice, it was level, and away from land there was less of the deep soft snow. It was also easier to keep up with Darnu and the injured Garjae.

Mostly they walked without talking, only the light crunch and squeak of snow beneath their bare feet broke the silence. The morning progressed and the sun rose further, glaring on the ice and snow. Occasionally one of them would stumble over some small imperfection in the otherwise level surface, Garjae more often than the others – Asha could hear his grunt of pain each time.

"This is worse than the jungle," Senna muttered.

Asha tried to reach out with her life sense, as she would in the forest. The life of the lake, so immediate and imposing beneath their feet that it was like walking on the ocean, rose up through the lake all around them, filtered and distorted by the ice and snow. It was like the air around them was shimmering in a heat wave. Combined with effect of the bright sun on her vision, Asha found it hard to clearly see even Garjae and Darnu just a short distance in front of them. It felt like she was going blind. She shook her head to try and clear it, but it made no difference.

"You too?" Senna asked.

"I hope it's not permanent," Asha commented, still tugging on John's arm, compelling him forward.

"Now there's a cheery thought," said Andrei from the other side.

John's foot caught on a patch of snow and he fell forward before either Andrei or Asha could catch him. Senna helped them to stand John back up. There was no damage, he didn't even appear to have noticed the fall, and they started forward again.

They stopped around mid-morning, the ridge behind them was now only a faint shadow on the horizon. Garjae sat heavily on a small mound of snow, one arm wrapped around the other and his chest. Asha made sure Andrei was taking care of John and went to Garjae.

"Show me," she demanded.

Garjae turned away.

Asha looked across at Darnu. "Can you talk sense to him? I might be able to help."

Darnu raised his arms helplessly.

"Threaten to tickle him," suggested Andrei. "If his chest is as painful as it looks that should be enough to make him cooperative."

"Garjae?" Asha asked again.

Garjae glanced around at the others and then back to Asha. "Just look," he said reluctantly, quietly, as if even speaking was painful. Garjae concentrated and his shirt disappeared, and then he lifted his stronger arm out of the way so Asha could see his injured arm, held protectively against his chest.

Asha gasped. Garjae's chest was a mass of dark bruising and she could tell that much of it went very deep. But, as bad as his chest was, his arm was much worse, even the shape of his forearm was distorted. She looked into his eyes with concern. "You should have said something. We shouldn't have been walking with you in this state."

"Sitting around in the snow is not going to help anyone."

"Jeez, Garjae," Andrei started, but stopped at a touch from Senna.

Asha sat closer to Garjae and touched him lightly at various places around his chest. It must be painful, but she didn't think there was anything too serious there. Then she placed her finger tips as gently as she could on his forearm, he winced even from this feather touch, and she pressed her senses into his arm. There was real damage inside, she thought it might have come close to bursting open under the pounding of the snow.

She tried to remember what she had done for Barma those months ago, the only other time she had seen anything as bad as this. She knew she had poured her life energy into Barma, but she couldn't afford to do that here – she just didn't have that much to spare. Her actions back then had come from instincts driven by desperation, but she was having trouble finding those instincts now. Since that time she had helped others with less serious problems, influencing the prana of the body to aid natural healing and to reduce the pain, but always by offering something of herself. There *had* to be a way she could help, she was supposed to be a healer.

Garjae began to pull away. "You've looked."

Asha snapped her attention from his arm to his face. "Sit still! This is serious, Garjae. I need to do something or it's just going to get worse."

"You can't afford to now," Garjae argued back.

"I can't afford not to. Now shut up and sit still."

"Good to have you back, Asha," Andrei said quietly from behind her somewhere, but she ignored him.

Asha arrayed her fingers along the length of Garjae's arm, and pushed her senses deeply into the damage. The normally tight and ordered flows of prana beneath the skin were a mess, some areas were pooling, the flows almost stopped, other areas spurted agitatedly through channels that shouldn't even exist. The hurt and pain and damage of it cried out against everything she was, she could not ignore this, she had to do something.

At first she tried to deal with the worst areas, but nothing she did made much difference, there was no order from which she could make a start. She moved her concentration back to less damaged areas, trying to calm and redirect the flows, and then slowly worked her way back toward the more severe injuries. She felt the energy flowing out from her, across her finger tips, it was the only way she knew. As she began to feel a slow improvement in the forearm she knew she could not stop – it was all she could do, it was what she had to do.

Slowly, so slowly, the arm began to knit itself together beneath her fingers. Occasionally parts would start to fall apart again and she was forced to return to them and wait for greater strength to form before moving on. It wasn't enough, there was still massive damage, but gradually the worst areas were starting to come together and form more ordered structures. It was all still weak, still so fragile, but with care and time the body's own healing could take over.

She became aware of a hand pressing on her shoulder, as it pinched harder she drew her attention away from the arm and looked up. "What?"

"Enough," said Garjae, and tried to push her away.

Asha tried to resist. "No! There's more I can do."

"Darnu," Garjae said, "make her stop. She's done enough, and she's fading before my eyes."

Asha felt hands grasp her shoulders and pull her back. She tried to shake them off but they held firm and slid her back away from Garjae.

"Now we have three invalids," said Garjae.

"A bit of gratitude wouldn't go astray," cut in Andrei.

Garjae looked up sharply. "We can't stop here. There's nothing for us here. But now Asha has been weakened too. Do you think I wanted that?" He looked back down at Asha, more softly, but still with angry tones, he continued, "Of course I'm grateful. The pain is a lot less now, and look," he slowly straightened his arm and then bent it back against his chest, "I can move it again. It is a lot better, but you shouldn't have given up so much of yourself."

Asha was barely listening, her gaze was intent on the arm, assessing from this more distant vantage how much damage was still there. The shape of the arm was mostly restored but it was almost black with bruising and her senses could tell there was still a lot wrong, and still a great deal of pain. "Try not to use it, Garjae," she told him. "It is still very fragile."

"I know, I can feel it."

"You should rest, Asha, and you too, Garjae," said Darnu.

Asha looked up and saw that it was past midday, she wondered where the time had gone. She felt sleepy and weak. She nodded in a belated response to Darnu's suggestion and tried to make herself comfortable where she was.

"Over here, Asha," said Senna, pulling gently on her arms.

Without paying much attention, Asha went where Senna led and lay down. Before she drifted off to sleep she felt the presence of others pressing in from either side, offering what comfort they could against the cold.

- - -

Senna woke to a tugging on her shoulder. She looked up and saw Andrei looking down at her, his face set in a worried expression. This was so unusual that she was suddenly fully awake. She pulled her arm gently from around Asha and sat up. The day had gone dark.

"What is it?"

Andrei pointed to the west, the way they had come from.

The sun had disappeared behind a dark bank of cloud. The leading edge of the cloud bank looked to be rolling forward like a wave, and even as she watched Senna could see it moving. A storm was approaching – fast!

As her eyes took in this sight her other senses felt the change in the air around them, the pressure had dropped dramatically.

Andrei woke Asha and then moved rapidly over to Darnu. Darnu woke with a start and looked where Andrei was pointing. Darnu tried to wake Garjae as tenderly as he could, but still Garjae cried out in pain as he woke with a start and tried to move his arm.

"We need to find shelter," Andrei said.

Senna looked around the vast flat plain of the frozen lake. Shelter? Already the air was starting to move around them. The closest shelter was miles to the west, into the face of the storm.

Beside her, Senna heard Asha making vain attempts to wake

John. It was no good. His movements were, if anything, even more reluctant than they had been earlier in the day.

They stood and looked around for anything that might offer some protection from the storm bearing down on them. Senna pointed out to the north-east. "There's a mound of snow over there, perhaps behind it ..." Her voice petered out, it seemed hopeless. Even if they got there in time it looked too small to help.

"Great!" said Andrei. "Come on, let's go." He grabbed one of John's arms and started pulling. John almost fell before Asha caught up and steadied him.

Darnu tried to help Garjae, but with the bruising to his chest there was little he could do without hurting Garjae more.

Senna saw that Asha was leaning on John more than she was helping to move him forward, greatly weakened by what she had done earlier. Senna moved in between Asha and John. She placed one shoulder under Asha's arm to help support her and with her other arm tried to pull John forward faster than the slow tread he was managing so far. They'd gone barely fifty paces before John stumbled and fell, pulling from their grasp and landing face down in the snow.

Senna urged Asha ahead. "I need both hands to help with John."

Asha looked liked she was going to argue, then nodded and walked on.

Andrei and Senna lifted John back to his feet. The sky was growing even darker, the cloud bank was almost over them, and gusts of wind swirled in confusion around them.

"Come on," said Andrei, "no time for sight-seeing."

Each supporting one of John's arms, Senna and Andrei half-carried, half-ran John after the others. The wind began to buffet them from one direction and then another, and the temperature was dropping rapidly. Senna could barely see the mound of snow that she'd pointed to before, it seemed impossible that they'd get there before the full force of the storm hit them.

They were gaining on the others. "Come on slow coaches!" Andrei called ahead. "You're holding up the works."

Darnu put an arm around Garjae to try and hurry him forward. Asha stumbled along behind them, glancing back often to see that they were following.

"We've got him!" Andrei called out to her. "Just keep going."

The words had barely left Andrei's mouth when a gust of wind knocked them from the side and the three of them fell in a tangle of arms and legs.

As they picked John back up Senna heard Andrei saying, "When you wake back up, John, we're going to have serious words about your sleeping habits."

The wind was getting stronger now, blowing hard against their backs and left side. If they leaned too far forward a gust would blow them over, if they tried to lean back into it a brief drop in the wind had them fall backwards. Senna heard a cry and saw that Garjae had fallen, and Darnu was struggling, fighting against the wind, to get him standing again.

Senna looked ahead and could just make out the mound of snow through the haze of ice blown by the wind. It wasn't big, but maybe it would help.

The six of them were almost in a group now. "Almost there!" Andrei yelled, his voice competing with the noise of the wind.

A few more paces and the wind renewed its strength as if determined that they shouldn't make it. Senna saw Asha turn to check on them and then lose her footing and fall to the ground. She was having trouble getting back to her feet, fighting against the wind. Senna slowed to help. Asha waved her on. "I'm okay," she called weakly, trying to right herself against the gusting wind.

The remaining distance closed slowly, but at last they made it. Senna and Andrei lay John down next to Garjae in the inadequate lee of the mound. The wind still tore around them, the mound wasn't making enough difference.

"Dig a cave," said Andrei, and started trying to dig at the snow.

Senna and Darnu joined him. The snow was hard against Senna's fingers, this mound was still here because it wasn't soft. Trying to dig your fingers into it was like pressing them into hard-packed sand. At first it seemed hopeless but Darnu managed to make a start, and from that beginning the three of them managed to enlarge the hole. Slowly the excavation grew until Senna could feel that it was blocking some of the wind.

"Darnu!" Garjae called.

The three of them looked around to where they had left Garjae and John out of the way of their digging. Garjae had a hold of John's shoulder.

"The wind is trying to move him," Garjae called.

As they watched the wind gusted stronger and John's body began to slide again. They reached out and pulled both John and Garjae closer to the hole they'd been excavating.

"Where's Asha?" Garjae asked.

"She was behind us," said Senna. She started to stand, to try and get a better look, and was knocked off her feet. Only Andrei's quick reaction, catching her ankle, stopped her from being blown beyond the meagre protection of the mound.

They looked at each other in panic. Garjae started to try and get up but Darnu pulled him back.

"You hold my leg," Senna told Andrei. "I'm going to try again."

Trying to retain as much of a grip on the ice as she could, Senna pushed her face out over the mound, squinting into the wind. She could feel Asha's presence almost at the base of the mound. Asha was now lying flat on the ground. One hand had found a precarious hold on the ice, and that was all that was stopping her from being swept away by the wind.

"I see her!" Senna called back to the others. "I think I can reach her."

Senna crept further out, feeling Andrei's firm comforting grip on her ankle. A strong gust blew her sideways and she had to paw her way back again, sliding her body and keeping it as low as she could.

"Asha!" she called.

At first there was no reaction, so she called again. Asha's head turned slowly and stared dully at her.

"Can you reach out?" Senna yelled to her.

Again that dulled-reaction delay and then slowly Asha's free arm began to move out from her body and toward Senna. Senna stretched out and waited for Asha's hand to meet hers. They had almost touched when a wind gust pushed against them both and tore Asha's other hand free from its hold on the ice. Asha began to slide, her body quickly picking up speed.

"No!" Senna screamed and pushed off with her hands, pulling her ankle away from Andrei's surprised grasp. The wind pushed and turned her body as Senna lunged across the ice toward Asha. She clutched desperately at Asha's outstretched hand and got only snow. She clutched again and caught Asha's finger tips. It was a tenuous hold but Senna pulled anyway, slowly bringing them closer together. As the wind spun their bodies on the ice, Senna managed to get her other hand around and grab Asha's wrist. With her free hand she clawed at the snow and ice beneath her looking for some traction, anything that would stop them sliding away.

Her fingers caught at something, a ridge or crack. The momentum of their movement threatened to rip it from her grip, but she held on. The wind slackened and she used that reprieve to push her fingers deeper into the crack, and to pull Asha up beside her.

The mound was lost in the swirl of snow, but she could hear Andrei calling her name. "Senna!" Andrei's voice came again. He sounded panicky.

"We're all right!" she called back. "Stay where you are! We'll come to you!"

"We hear you," Darnu called back.

"Can you hold tight onto me?" Senna asked Asha.

Another delay and then Asha moved the hand that Senna wasn't holding. It worked its way slowly forward and up their joined arms, managing to grasp Senna's shoulder.

Senna didn't know whether Asha's current state was due to the sudden drop in temperature, or the weakness from helping Garjae, perhaps it was a combination. Whatever the reason, it seemed that she was headed the same way as John. Senna knew she had to get Asha back to the small shelter of the mound soon.

"Hold on there," Senna told her, "I'm going to let go of this other hand," she pressed with her fingers to emphasise what she meant, "and then you can use it to hold my other shoulder. ... Do you understand me?"

A delay and then a nod.

Senna released her grip. Asha's hand moved away slowly, and slid across Senna's back, grasping at her side.

Senna closed her eyes to give them a break from the lashing wind and snow and tried to gather her strength, then she reached up and held the crack with both hands. She waited, conscious of Asha's grip on her shoulder and side. When the wind subsided a little, as if taking a breath for the next big blow, Senna pulled them both forward. When the crack was level with her face she reached ahead, feeling for another hold.

The next big gust of wind pushed at them and Senna held fast where she was. As that gust weakened she pushed herself further so the crack was now at her waist and continued to reach forward with her other hand. She found something. It didn't feel as strong as the ridge beneath her, but she managed to get a grip on the small rise in the ice and held on to it past the next gust. Then she pulled them both past this new hold and searched for another.

How long this went on Senna couldn't tell. The occasional extra strong gust threatened to tear them both away. Senna's fingers were aching with the strain of holding them to the ice. Regularly there would be another call from Andrei asking if they were still coming. Senna tried to keep the desperation from her voice when she called back.

She could make out the mound of ice ahead of them now, but off to one side, there would be no protection from the wind until she made it all the way there. She could feel the presence of her friends.

She ran out of holds. She pushed the last one back as far behind her as she could without losing it, but couldn't find another. Another strong gust rattled her and she slid back, certain she would be shaken loose. But she held on.

"You're almost here," Darnu called.

"Darnu will hold my ankle and I'll reach out to help," Andrei added.

"There are no more holds," she called back. "I'm going to try and come across in a hurry, get ready to catch us."

Senna moved Asha up beside her, making certain they both stayed pressed down against the ice. The wind howled over them, and Senna waited for any brief respite that might let them move.

Then, at last, a lull came. Senna didn't wait for Asha's dulled reactions. She hauled Asha forward under one arm, and with the other hand and her feet she pushed desperately at the smooth windswept ice, trying to propel them both forward without rising into the still strong wind.

The relative safety of the mound and her friends were just a few impossible metres away. She could see Andrei stretching out on the ice, his feet held by Darnu and Garjae. His body was being pushed to the side. He reached out toward her, willing her closer. It was taking too long. Any moment now the wind would pick back up and they would both be swept away. There was only one chance. Senna pulled one leg under her, she could feel the tiniest of ridges beneath her toes – that would help with what she was going to do next.

Andrei seemed to read her thoughts, "Senna, no!"

Senna pulled herself into a low kneeling position and pushed off against the tiny grip under her foot. Holding Asha pressed against the ice, Senna slid her forward like a toboggan. Senna brought her other leg up and pushed again. She tried to throw herself forward, hoping that she could slide the last distance with Asha, flat on the ice. But she had raised herself too high. The next gust came, stronger than any before it, and it caught Senna's body like a sail and blew her into the sky. She heard Andrei's desperate cry fading rapidly into the distance.

She tumbled through the blasting air, totally disoriented, not knowing which way was up. The stray thought occurred to her that she hadn't flown like this since she was a young child. Suddenly she was slammed back onto the ice and pain flashed through her back and head. She was vaguely aware of sliding along the ice and being rolled and turned. The wind picked her up again and when she next hit the ice everything went dark.

- - -

Andrei was in torment. He had only just managed to grasp Asha's hand as Senna pushed her toward him. Senna had been right there, he could almost have touched her, with his free hand he had tried to, but then the wind had ripped her away from him. He screamed her name and thought he heard her answer, but he couldn't be sure it wasn't the wind.

He wanted to kick his feet free from Darnu and Garjae. He wanted to leap into the wind and try to follow Senna – but he couldn't. Asha dangled from his other arm, the one that wasn't outstretched in a vain attempt to reach Senna. The wind swirled past him and Asha's body swayed back and forth across the ice.

He turned his attention to Asha and edged her nearer. Using his free hand he got a better grip on her arm and pulled her closer still. He felt himself sliding and at first he panicked, thinking the wind was taking him, taking them all. Then he realised he was sliding backwards, against the wind, as Darnu and Garjae pulled him back to their inadequate shelter.

Drawn back behind the protection of the mound he helped to slide Asha up next to John. Asha was murmuring something but the words were too soft to make out.

Andrei looked at his friends and then looked back out to where Senna had disappeared. He couldn't leave her on her own. "I've got to find her," he said, and started to push himself up.

Darnu and Garjae must have been expecting it, they each grabbed an arm and pulled him back down against them. Andrei was lying mostly across Darnu, he struggled and struck out. His head banged against Darnu's and one of his hands hit Garjae in the chest. Andrei heard his grunt of pain but it hardly registered. They had to let him go!

"No, Andrei!" Darnu told him and wrapped both his arms around him, trying to hold him still.

"Will you stop!" growled Garjae. He was holding his injured arm protectively against his chest. Garjae's face was screwed up against the pain all this movement was causing him, but still he held tight to Andrei with his uninjured arm, tightening his grip on Andrei's arm each time Andrei tried to lash out.

"You can't find her in this storm," Darnu told him, his face was pressed up against the side of Andrei's as he hugged him tighter. "When the wind slows we can look, but we can't now."

Andrei gradually stopped struggling and lay against Darnu panting. Slowly he began to accept it. Even if he'd gone out as soon as he saw Senna blown away, there was little chance he would have found her. Now it would be impossible.

"You won't help her by getting lost yourself," said Garjae.

Andrei could hear the pain in Garjae's voice and remembered hitting him. He tried to turn his head to look at Garjae, but Darnu was still holding him too tight. "I'm all right now," he spoke down past Darnu's shoulder, into the ice, "you can let me go."

"Promise?" Darnu asked into his ear. When Andrei was slow responding he continued, "You will stay with us until it's safe to go out. Promise!"

Andrei nodded his head against Darnu's. "I promise."

Darnu's embrace loosened and soon after that Garjae let go of his arm. Andrei slid off Darnu, going to the side away from Garjae because he didn't want to risk bumping him again. Darnu must have feared Andrei was going to try to leave again because he rolled over to keep one arm around Andrei's chest.

"It's all right, Darnu. I promised and I meant it. You're right ... you're both right." Andrei sighed with regret. He lifted his head enough to look across at Garjae. "I'm sorry, Garjae, I didn't mean to hurt you."

Garjae grunted in response and then lay back with his head up against the back of the shallow excavation they had made. On the other side of Garjae, Andrei could see Asha and John lying next to each other, apparently sleeping peacefully on the ice.

The wind continued to howl around them. It swirled into their shallow excavation, alternately covering them with ice crystals and then drawing them away again. This wasn't really shelter from anything except the main force of the wind. Garjae had had about as much as he could take and lay beside Asha with his eyes closed. Whether the grimace on his face was from the pain of his recent injuries or his usual unhappiness was hard to tell.

Darnu and Andrei spent some time trying to dig further into the mound, with only limited success. The cold began to creep up on them and Andrei felt his headache returning in earnest. Darnu's reactions were slowing too. When they could dig no more they tried to arrange everyone as close to one another as they could without disturbing Garjae's injuries. Darnu settled beside Garjae and Andrei carefully made his way across Darnu, Garjae, Asha and John, to press himself up against the other side of John.

"We'll have to stay awake," Darnu spoke across to Andrei, "so we can keep clearing the snow away, or we will all end up buried."

"Okay," agreed Andrei. Despite how dreadfully tired and weary and weak he felt, Andrei felt certain that sleep wouldn't come anyway. The pounding in his head was one thing, but above everything else was his worrying about Senna. Where was she now? Was she even still alive? How far had the wind blown her? He considered breaking his promise and leaving now to try and find her, but kept reminding himself how futile it would be.

He listened to the wind howling and watched the billowing clouds of ice and snow fly past over their heads, some of it settling down over their legs stretched out from their small hollow. Some snow swirled back and settled over his face. If they were humans they could bury themselves in the snow, use it to keep the heat in perhaps, though he had no idea how well that might work. If they had been human then Senna wouldn't have blown away like that. But they weren't human. The way the cold was affecting them, the way it weakened them and dulled their senses and slowed them down, if they let themselves be buried in their sleep they might never wake again.

"How long do you think it might last?" Andrei asked Darnu.

There was no response.

Andrei pulled himself up and looked across their bodies – lined up like sardines in a tin from John's pantry back home, back where it was warm. Darnu had rolled onto his side and placed one hand protectively on Garjae's shoulder. He had fallen asleep. Andrei thought it probably happened soon after he last spoke. There was a bruise on Darnu's forehead, Andrei guessed that he had put that there. Darnu's hand on Garjae's shoulder showed a golden glow of prana around the finger tips. Andrei looked down and saw that his own were the same – damage from digging into the hard snow, and it was taking a long time to heal.

He moved his gaze to Garjae. The grimace had relaxed a little now. Garjae's shirt obscured the bruising on his chest, but his injured arm looked bad, very bad, as if it wasn't healing at all.

Asha had a worried look on her face, and she looked weaker to Andrei than any of the others, even John. He guessed now that Garjae had been right to get upset with her. Then he glanced back at Garjae's arm and wondered how far Garjae would have come without her aid.

Andrei settled back lower and stared at John lying beside him. "Well old sod, this is a fine pickle we've gotten ourselves into." John's face remained blank. Andrei noticed that John too had some bruising, probably from one of the many times he had fallen into the snow. Andrei sighed. "I know that none of us wanted to see any more fire or explosions, but coming out here into the middle of nowhere to freeze to death might be taking things too far. ... I know, I know, it was my idea to come barging out here, but no one else had any bright ideas, and I didn't expect you to fall asleep on the job. ... Sorry, I guess that's not very funny.

"It's just ... I've gotten used to having you around to keep me going, keep me sane. It gets hard sometimes, you know? Being what everyone expects. Mostly I just sort of push past it, or try to. Barma knows, and Tilvy of course, but we grew up together. They know how to cope with me when I go a bit funny. ... Not funny, that's the problem. Strange. Peecuuliaar," he stretched out the word for emphasis. "Senna knows – of course she does. She tries to help, but I never make it easy." He sighed, his head was still pounding. "Talking to myself, that's not good, and I never laugh at the punch-lines."

Andrei rolled back and stared up into the night. And night it was now, he realised. It had been dark before, but that was just the dark of the storm. The wind still howled around them and in the blackness his vedana still felt the haze of the ice and snow being swept past them. Senna. Where was she? Was she awake and watching the storm? Was she thinking of him too? He wanted to promise that he would be easier to live with in the future if she'd just come back to him, but he knew it was not a promise he was likely to make good on. "Senna?" he spoke out loud, but there was no answer.

- - -

It was early Saturday morning and Tracey had made a quick trip to the local shops to pick up some milk for her mother. Tracey and Tilvy had decided to stay in the city for the Friday night too. Brian wasn't around, he had been gone all week, and her mother had gone out to some work do last night, so staying another night had seemed like a fun thing to do, a good way to finish off a fun week. Anyway, there was no one answering the computer at John's house, so there seemed no rush to go back. Tilvy was a bit put out, she had thought Barma would be waiting impatiently for her return, but apparently everyone had found something else to do.

Tracey walked back to her car, the milk in its flimsy plastic bag swinging from one hand. She was distracted with thoughts of the argument with her mother this morning. The weatherman said it was going to be hot this weekend, a high risk of bushfires, which – as it always did – fed her mother's paranoia on the subject. Her mother didn't want her to go to John's, she didn't realise that Tracey had no choice, she had to take Tilvy home. As far as Tracey was concerned it was just another hot day.

She reached her car and sat the milk on the roof while she scratched in her bag for her keys. She didn't pay much attention to the man getting out of the car on the other side until he spoke to her.

"We need to talk," he said across the roof of her car.

Tracey looked up. It was a small, thin and balding man. It took her a moment to realise that she had seen him before, that she had thought he must live close to her home. While Tracey was still taking him in, trying to understand the import of his words, the man was looking around him, obviously nervous.

"Not here," he said to her. "Can you follow me? Not far."

"Do I know you?" Tracey managed to ask.

"No, but I know John Caldor. This is about him. And about the others, about his place. Where you spend your weekends."

Tracey stared at him.

"The narun," he said, having to speak louder than he wanted over the noise of passing cars.

"What do you want?" Tracey asked him, not quite believing that she'd heard him correctly.

"There's something you ought to know," he urged. When Tracey still didn't look like moving he continued, "Gods be damned, girl! I don't know why I'm trying to tell you this, it's time I was gone." He stared back at her, waiting for a reaction. "I'm going. If you want to know what I've got to say then follow me, if not—" He shrugged and turned back to his car.

Tracey stared at the back of his head as the man opened his door, she caught a glimpse of his profile as he turned to lower himself into his car. She *had* seen him before! Months ago, as he scrambled to the lift in the basement of the Research Centre – before things had gone bad. Stunned, she opened the car door and sank into the driver's seat. She pulled the door gently closed behind her and turned to look through the passenger window.

The man was looking at her. He nodded at her and then concentrated on waiting for a break in the erratic morning traffic to let him reverse out.

A loud knock on the driver's side window scared Tracey. She jumped and turned, a small squeal escaping her mouth. An older woman, solidly built with a round, kindly face, was staring in at her, holding Tracey's milk in her hand, the plastic bag fluttering.

"You forgot your milk, love," the woman spoke loudly through the glass.

Tracey wound the window down.

"I didn't mean to startle you," the woman apologised.

"Thanks," Tracey said, taking the milk from the woman's hand.

"Could have made an awful mess," the woman told her.

"Yes, yes, thanks, thank you," Tracey murmured. She turned around to put the milk on the passenger seat and saw that the man was already reversing from his place. She got the keys into the ignition and started the car hurriedly, over-revving the engine.

"Are you all right, love?" the woman asked through the still open window.

Tracey ignored the question, concentrating on the traffic. The man was already pulling away, there were already cars between them. She saw a space and reversed out into it, receiving a beep from a driver that had to slow and wait for her. As she started forward, Tracey glanced to the side and saw the kindly woman staring at her. She waved briefly and mouthed, "Sorry," and then looked forward again, trying to find the man's car ahead.

It was blue, wasn't it? A large sedan. There! in the right lane. She pushed her small red car over into a space on that lane, receiving another beep from a car behind. She saw another blue car ahead in the left and panicked that she had picked the wrong one – but no, that was a smaller car.

A few blocks further on, the car she was following moved into a right-hand turn lane. Tracey flicked on her turn indicators. There were two cars between them, waiting for the lights to change, and she couldn't tell for certain if she was following the right car. She tapped her fingers nervously on the wheel. The lights changed and she caught a glimpse of the man in his blue car as it turned onto the side road. It was him.

Ian! That was his name. He was the man that had been locked in the room with Tilvy. If Tilvy had been with her then she would have recognised him straight away, but Tilvy was waiting back at the house.

There was only one car between hers and the blue car now. She saw the blue car put on its indicators and did the same – and so did the car between them. Another turn and then the blue car slowed and put on its indicators again, apparently intending to park. The car between them pulled out impatiently, accelerating past and disappearing ahead. Tracey had to go around Ian too, finding a free space a short distance in front of him.

She pulled over and saw that they had stopped next to a small open park area, a few trees with neatly kept lawn between them. There was a man walking a dog, he looked to be leaving already, but there was no one else this early in the morning. She knew this place. It looked safe enough.

Safe? Only now did it hit Tracey that she had followed the blue car without making the conscious choice to do so. She had been so surprised that she had just done it. What should she have done? What should she do? She glanced in the rear vision mirror and saw the man standing beside his car looking toward her. She didn't want him in her car so she got out.

With a jerk of his head the man, Ian, indicated that she should come to him. He didn't wait to see how she would respond. He walked around his car, opened the passenger side door and sat down, obscured again now inside his vehicle.

Tracey walked around the front of her car, looking to see if there was anyone else around. Nothing looked out of place. She made a wide circle and slowly approached Ian. He remained sitting in the passenger seat of his car, the door still open. His feet were on the ground outside with his elbows resting on his knees, hands loose between them. He was watching her.

She stopped a few yards away from him and stared at him, not certain what to say, and pretty certain that she shouldn't be there. She glanced around again and then looked back at Ian.

He nodded.

"What do you want?" she asked him.

"You're being watched," Ian told her.

Tracey glanced around her nervously.

"Not here. At home, and maybe other places too."

"You," Tracey accused him, "you've been watching me."

232

Ian shook his head. "Not really. Well, yeah, I suppose I have, but only to find out what Davies is up to. The man having you watched is also looking for me. He almost caught up with me, so I decided to get smart for a change. Best way to stay out of sight is to know where the eyes are looking, and mostly they've been looking at you. When they're looking at you they don't see me."

"I've seen you."

"Doesn't matter, you don't know me from Adam."

"I do. You're Ian. You were at the Research Centre the night it burned. I saw you."

Ian looked surprised and uncomfortable. "You were there?"

Tracey nodded.

"I guess that explains how come you know Caldor."

"If you're not watching me, why this?"

"Because I'm off. I've been watching Davies, and what he's been up to, who he's dealing with. I've been waiting for him to give up trying to find me, hoping I could finally relax, but the bastard's bloody persistent. I'm done waiting. Something big's coming down and this mother's son is taking his chances elsewhere."

"So who's watching me?" Tracey asked.

"The one I know about is Davies, Darren Davies, I don't know who's behind him, not any more."

"I don't know any Darren Davies."

"No, you wouldn't. But what do you know about Knight?"

"Brian?"

Ian nodded. "He's one of Davies' cronies, always smiling as if life's a joke, maybe it is to him. And that young bloke you've been seeing."

"Mike?" Tracey refused to believe it.

"I don't know anything about him, but I've seen him talking with Knight. Davies really has a hard-on over you. More likely it's over Caldor and his friends, and you're just a way to get to them."

"But John's—"

"Yeah, I know. Away in Asia, still looking for a cure for his daughter."

"How do you know that?"

"I can even name which of his friends went with him."

Tracey's mind seemed to freeze over.

"You kids really have no idea, do you? You think all these phones and computers and stuff are just there for your amusement. It's never been so easy to find out stuff about people. You leave a little bit here and a little bit there, thinking you're being so fucking clever and obscure. Christ! The Internet has just made it all too easy. Even someone like me could piece together the lives of most of you kids these days."

"You've been hacking my computer?"

Ian laughed. "Me? No. I'm no computer genius, I did it the easy way. I just walked into your house and read it off your screen whenever I wanted to know what was going on. But if I were you I'd be buying a new computer, a new phone, a new everything. Christ knows what cute bits they've added to your stuff."

Tracey continued to stare at him. *Everything* she had done with her friends had been written down one way or another, and some of it was very personal. She blushed thinking that total strangers, including this man in front of her, had read what she had told Tilvy.

A car drove past slowly. Both Tracey and Ian watched it to make sure it didn't stop.

Tracey walked away a few steps and then came back again. "Why are you telling me this now?"

Ian stared back at her for long moments before answering. "I guess I feel some sense of obligation to Caldor, I certainly feel sorry for the guy. It was him, on that night, that let me get out of all that. I doubt if I'd still be around if he hadn't turned up and started all that ruckus. So I'm repaying the favour. It's probably too late for Caldor anyway, but you're obviously a friend of his, someone he cares about. Get out now, any way you can. And stay clear of Caldor's friends, they're bad news."

"I can't."

"I told you, something big's coming down, this weekend I think. I wouldn't want to get caught in the middle of it. I should be gone already, but I've been waiting for a chance to talk to you. It's probably the best time for you to disappear too."

"Coming down where?" Tracey asked, her voice quiet. She was feeling very small.

"Back at Caldor's place, I expect. Out that way anyway."

"What? What is it?"

Ian shrugged. "No idea, but I wouldn't want to be out there."

"That's where I'm going now," Tracey told him. "I've got to take Tilvy back."

"You've got one of those things here?" Ian asked in alarm. He stood up and looked around nervously.

Tracey didn't disabuse him of the idea. His obvious alarm gave her more confidence and she stepped closer to him. "Can't you help us? There must be something we can do. Go to the police or something?"

Ian gave her an incredulous look. "And what? Tell them that there's an army of commando-wannabes and a bunch of invisible people holding a war. Just a moment officer, I'll point out which of the invisible guys you should be arresting."

"A war?"

"I don't think it's the teddy bears' picnic."

Tracey stood still, trying to make her brain work. There was a cold feeling in her back, like someone rubbing ice down her spine. Fear.

Ian closed the passenger door of his car and walked around the other side. "I've done what I came to do, you can make up your own mind from here." He opened the driver's door and looked across at her. "If you'll take my advice: don't use your phone or your computer to repeat any of this. I'd also appreciate it if you'd forget my name. In fact, forget you ever met me. No offence, but I'll be trying to do the same. Good luck." He climbed into his car, started up, did a fast U-turn and drove off quickly.

Tracey stared bleakly after him. A war.

- - -

Andrei woke with a start, something was nuzzling at his face, brushing at his eyes. He was lying on his side, leaning up against John. Whatever was in his face was too close, he couldn't focus. He drew back and recognised the brevi. "Casseta." And next to the deep ginger brevi was the pale cream of Nuttachen, Darnu's brevi, looking almost dirty against the clean white snow. "What are you two doing out?"

He sat up quickly, his head pounded in protest. He looked out. The storm had blown itself out and day had come. The sky was still overcast, dark and heavy looking, and it was still desperately cold. But however dull the early-morning light, it was very welcome.

Senna! He scanned the horizon and could see nothing but the flat

235

white of the frozen lake. She had to be out there somewhere. How far away was she?

He looked down at his friends. They were all shrouded in snow. The lower parts of their bodies, and his own, were completely obscured, but their upper torso and head formed person shaped white mounds like snowmen that had fallen over. There was a break in the shroud over Asha and over Darnu where the brevi must have pushed through. The two brevi were sitting on John's chest, or where it must be under the layer of snow. They were looking up at Andrei expectantly.

Swearing at himself for having gone to sleep after all, Andrei pulled himself out of the snow. When he managed to stand he stood still with his eyes closed for a few moments waiting for the pounding in his head to settle. Why had the brevi chosen to wake him rather than Darnu? He thought he could guess, but hoped he was wrong.

He looked down. "Thanks for waking me," he told the two twitching faces, "just ... just stay there for a bit will you."

Andrei stepped carefully around where the legs of the others must be and crouched next to Darnu. He carefully brushed the snow away from Darnu's face and called to him. There was no response. Less carefully he pushed the snow from Darnu's shoulders and shook him. Darnu muttered a few incoherent sounds, but that was all. Andrei grabbed Darnu's arm and began pulling him out from their shelter. After that struggle he got Darnu clear of the mound, but stayed kneeling, waiting for his head to settle. He tried shaking Darnu again, this time more strongly, but again there were just a few muttered words.

Andrei went back to the others. He was about to start sweeping the snow from Garjae when he remembered his injuries, so he left the torso alone and brushed carefully at Garjae's face. When it was fairly clear he patted Garjae's cheeks. After a few moments Garjae's eyes flickered open.

"Wha—?" Garjae said indistinctly.

"Good morning, Garjae," said Andrei in relief. "I never thought I'd be so happy to hear your cheery voice in the morning."

Garjae's eyes focused and he looked back at Andrei. "What's happened?" His voice was still husky, but clearer now.

"We all drifted off to the serenade of the wind last night. Cassey and Nuttachen just woke me, but we can't wake Darnu. Can you get up?"

The snow over Garjae's torso started to move and then Garjae gasped with the pain.

"I'd try to help but I don't want to make it worse," said Andrei apologetically.

"I'll be right," Garjae said, "just give me a minute."

Andrei sat back and waited. Garjae used his good arm to start to clear the snow. When the injured arm reappeared it looked no better than last night.

"Can you … can you give me a hand up?" Garjae asked reluctantly.

"Sure," Andrei bounced up, or tried to. His coordination still wasn't great and he swayed as his head tried to explode.

"Are you okay?" Garjae asked.

"Just a headache. Here." Andrei leaned down and offered his arm for Garjae to hold on to with his good hand.

Garjae reached up and pulled himself slowly upright. As far as Andrei could tell this was achieved by determination more than anything else. "Thanks," Garjae said without looking Andrei in the eye. Garjae made his way over to check on Darnu.

Andrei knelt down and began to clear the snow away from Asha. She seemed to be rousing for a moment, but drifted away again. He pulled her out near Darnu and went back to get John. He knelt down to clear the snow from his face.

"Okay you two," he spoke to the brevi. "Sit on my shoulders while I dig the rest of him out."

The two brevi quickly bounded up and sat either side of his head, where they braced themselves as Andrei worked around John. Andrei found he could get John to sit up, the strange catatonia continuing as it had been the previous days; John would move when pushed to it and hold his position, but made no movements of his own volition.

Garjae saw Andrei struggling and together they managed to get John standing, but when they tried to walk him out toward the others, his feet caught on the snow and he fell over again. They ended up dragging him out near Asha.

"So that's four and a half down," said Garjae in resignation.

"How's it feel to be the last whole one left, Andrei?"

"Senna's still out there somewhere," Andrei said.

Garjae looked out. "But she's not here."

Andrei didn't have the strength to start an argument so he left Garjae standing there and went back to the mound. From that small advantage in height Andrei scanned the horizon, but the snow and the ice and the lake continued to interfere. If Senna was all right she might have better luck. To the south Andrei noticed an area that looked shiny, like water reflecting in the dull morning light. He stumbled off the mound in that direction and started walking.

"Where are you going?" Garjae called.

Andrei waved an arm absently and called back, "I just want to see something. I'm coming back."

The distance was further than he had thought, it seemed to take him a long time to reach it. As he got closer it looked more and more like water and he started to run – or try to, he didn't manage much more than a slow shuffle. At last he got to it, and walked out across it in disbelief.

This really was like walking on water – or glass. He banged his feet against it until they hurt before he convinced himself that it was ice. He had vague memories of their helicopter pilot talking about clear water making clear ice, but he hadn't imagined anything like this. He was staring through a window into the lake, he even caught glimpses of fish, and in one place thought he could see the bottom of the lake far below. He could see the occasional fault in the ice, like a flaw in a crystal. He knelt down and pressed his hand against the ice, wondering if it was possible to merge through ice so clear that it looked like the cleanest of all water. But it resisted him, there was no path here. It was an amazing sight though, he could hardly wait to show Senna.

Senna! He stood and looked around him. Nothing but the empty flat ice, except back the way he had come. The now indistinct figure of Garjae was still standing, probably watching Andrei. Andrei couldn't see his friends at Garjae's feet, and could barely make out the mound.

Casseta twittered in his ear. He had almost forgotten the brevi were there. "You're right," he answered Casseta, "we'd better get back and see what happens next."

238

He traipsed his way back. Garjae was watching him as he got close, but didn't say anything until Andrei was standing near him, looking down at their friends lying on the snow.

"What did you see?" Garjae asked.

"Ice," said Andrei dully. "I thought it looked like water, but it was ice." If it had been any of the others Andrei might have tried to retrieve the feelings he'd felt while he was back there standing on the frozen water, but those feelings had faded as he returned, and Garjae wasn't the sort that encouraged that sort of sharing.

Andrei waited for Garjae to start saying what a mistake this all was, and he wasn't sure how he would respond.

What Garjae actually asked was, "Any ideas?"

Andrei looked up in surprise. Then looked out to the east. It was the way that Senna had been blown so it was the way that Andrei would go just as soon as he worked out how. But he couldn't just leave his friends here.

Both the brevi started to twitter and then Nuttachen nuzzled at his ear. "What is it?" he asked the brevi, trying to turn his head toward it. A thought started to form and Andrei put his hand up to Nuttachen, who scuttled onto it and stared back at Andrei. "Could you find Senna?" he asked it. The brevi twittered back at him. Andrei looked at Garjae. "What do you think?"

"He was always Darnu's, he never paid much attention to me," said Garjae.

"But is it safe, do you think?" Andrei pressed. "I don't want to send him out if he might get lost."

"If he will go then I imagine he will be at least as safe as staying here with us." Garjae paused and then looked at Andrei intently. "You could go too. There's no need for you to be stuck here with us invalids."

Nuttachen twittered again from Andrei's hand, and then Casseta joined in from his shoulder.

Andrei considered what Garjae had said, he had already been considering it. But perhaps this was a better way.

"I could never keep up with the brevi," he said at last. "They seem bright and strong, as if the cold is not affecting them." He paused before deciding. "If one of them will go then perhaps they can at least get a message from her."

"They are less likely to get lost than you are," Garjae agreed. "There's not much to lose in trying."

Andrei looked at Nuttachen still perched on his hand, its nose twitching. "Nuttachen, can you find Senna?" He paused trying to think what to say, wondering how much the tiny creatures understood. "Don't go unless it's safe," he told it. "If you can find her then tell her ... tell her that we're still here. Tell her to send a message back saying if she wants to come back here, otherwise we'll come to her. You can lead us to her when you come back."

"That's probably enough," said Garjae, "don't get too complicated."

Andrei nodded. "Can you do that, Nuttachen?" he asked the creature. He knelt down and put his hand close to the ice. The brevi twittered back to him, Andrei wished he could understand what it said. It leapt from his hand and bounded off across the snow. A moment later Casseta leapt from his shoulder and followed Nuttachen. Andrei was about to call after her, he didn't think he should be sending both of them out, but Garjae stopped him.

"Let them go," Garjae said. "Trust their instincts, that's what Milla always told Darnu."

Andrei watched the creatures bounding across the snow, they were too light to break through even the softest snow. Nuttachen, in his pale cream fur, was quickly lost from sight on the white snow, but Casseta's deep ginger stood out a little longer.

"Do you think it might work?" Andrei asked.

Garjae started to shrug, but then thought better of it and said, "They're as well off looking out for themselves as they are here with us." He continued, "You said to say that we would come to her, have you thought how we might do that?"

Andrei looked at Garjae and then down to his friends. There were three that needed carrying and only two to do it – or as Garjae had phrased it, only one and a half.

"Perhaps you should go anyway," Garjae said.

"Not yet."

"You won't get any stronger just sitting here on the ice."

"What about you? You can still walk. Why don't you go?"

Garjae looked down at the snow. "I'm only standing up because it hurts too much to lie down. I won't have any choice much longer."

Andrei looked around, trying to come up with ideas. He thought about Senna, sending the brevi felt right. He still wanted to go out searching for himself, but the brevi had a better chance than he did. His head was still pounding, and while he was better off than Garjae, he was far from strong; he could end up wandering around in a daze and walk right past her. If the brevi returned and could lead him to Senna, he would consider leaving his friends then, but not before.

- - -

Senna groaned and tried to move but her entire body was held fast. The back of her head felt as if it had been caved in, her back was just one big throbbing ache, and one leg felt as if someone had tried to twist it off. She eventually understood that she was buried beneath some snow. She pushed out with one hand, her back complaining at the effort, and managed to break through. She pushed away more snow and was able to work herself into a sitting position and look around.

It was still dark although she thought the sky behind her might be lighter, as if dawn was not far away. The wind had mostly gone, some soft gusts were still brushing past, last wisps from the tail of the storm. It had pushed her up against some mound of snow and buried her against it. She had no idea how far she might be from the others. She pulled free of the rest of the snow but didn't try to stand, she didn't think she could manage that yet. Her leg looked fine, but it was hurting badly, competing with her back and head. It was still desperately cold.

She shook her head to try and clear it before she realised what a mistake that was, pain ripped through the back of her head, trying to reach over the top and claw its way in. She groaned again and put her hands to her face, just sitting there quietly, hoping for some relief.

Senna struggled back from her torpor. She knew there were moments, perhaps minutes for all she could tell, that were slipping away from her. The cold and her pain were trying to drive her back to unconsciousness. She couldn't let that happen. What if the others were looking for her? If she fell asleep beneath the snow they might walk right past. Were they even all right? Had Andrei managed to catch Asha, or had she been blown away too?

241

She pushed herself to her knees and her right leg screamed at her. Another moment of blankness passed and she forced herself to try and stand. Movement by movement, pain by pain, she forced each limb to obey her until at last she stood, hunched and panting but on her feet.

She turned slowly and looked east. Before her was a large scattering of rough mounds and what looked like boulders of ice. Beyond that and above the horizon, was some faint brightness, the dawn trying to make its way through heavy cloud. To the north and south she could make out other areas of rough, hummocky ice, part of the fault-line against which she'd been blown.

Slowly she turned back to the west, her mind already turning to the question of whether she could try to walk back, and even if she could manage to walk that far, however far it was, would she be able to find it? Would they even still be there? Might they have given her up as lost?

Facing west, that last question still haunting her, Senna realised that something had tried to get her attention. She was thinking of Andrei and whether he could have given up on her, and now she thought about how he had known when something was tickling her senses. She turned back, grumbling to herself, and peered into the distance. There was nothing.

"First you must learn to look close," Senna heard Litak's voice in her mind. She pulled her eyes from the distant horizon. The rough mounds of snow and ice could be hiding anything, the ice and snow and the life of the lake beneath her feet confused her senses. She tried to concentrate. The mound against which she had been lying felt different, as if there was something beneath it, or within it. Something living, perhaps. It had to be something large. Did bears come out onto the ice to hibernate? It seemed a ridiculous idea, but she supposed it might be possible.

She stumbled her way painfully past the rough lumps of ice, her feet sometimes breaking abruptly through accumulations of fresher snow, jarring her leg and back and bringing new waves of pain. In places, jagged pieces of ice poked out of the snow, clear and shiny, like large shards of wet broken glass. She tried to push her senses into the other mounds of ice around her, but only this largest one returned that sensation of warmth, of life. With her back and leg

242

complaining all the way, she climbed around more ice-boulders to try and get closer to the mound on its eastern side.

As she came closer there was the definite sense of life, and even some movement not far beneath the snow on the side of the mound. She drew nearer and whatever it was moved away, as if it had sensed her presence.

It was lighter now, although the overcast sky meant the morning light remained dim. But whatever she had sensed had not been visible, it was only her vedana that had felt the presence through the wall of the mound. She knelt down next to the mound and pressed her hands against the snow. Again she felt something, but it was deeper inside now. There had to be a space there behind the wall. Senna pressed harder with her finger tips and felt the ice give a little. She pressed harder still and her hand suddenly went through into the cavity behind. She drew it out quickly. Coming from the hole was warm air carrying a musky animal smell and, curiously, what smelt like rotting fish.

Senna held still and wondered what to do. The warmth and life she could feel through that hole beckoned to her, but what about the creature that had caused it? The indecision held her for long moments, her mind trying to find some logic to follow. She needed the warmth if only so she could start to think clearly again; she felt there was something she was trying to remember but it wouldn't come. Whatever had moved behind the wall of snow knew she was there. As she stared at the small hole made by her hand another thought went through her mind: would she be endangering the creature by opening a hole into its carefully constructed burrow?

That last thought had her stand again. Maybe that was the thought that had been trying to make it through. Surely the creature had to get in there somehow. Senna again set off, climbing around the mound. She even climbed over the top of it. But despite the effort and pain this took, the only hole that she could find was the small one made by her hand. If there had been another hole it must have been covered by the storm.

Again she found herself kneeling in front of that small hole. She pressed her eye to it and tried to look in. Little light made it through the snow, but what there was showed her that the tunnel was small, it would be a tight fit trying to slide through it, even if she reduced her size as much as she could. If she met something coming the other way she might be in trouble. Animals that could sense the narun weren't usually aggressive toward them, but then she wasn't usually caught up with them in a tight burrow either.

She thought of the others and of trying to walk back to them. She didn't think she was up to that now, not that trying to slide through the tunnel was going to be fun with her back the way it was. Eventually she decided that she had to know what the creature was.

Senna began to break away more of the wall to the tunnel until it was just large enough for her to slide into. As she kicked away from the ground outside a jab of pain went through her right leg and she flinched. She hit her head against the wall and the pain in her leg was suddenly irrelevant. Sparks flew across her vision and pain roared across the back of her head.

She lay there for some time waiting for the pain to recede. At least it was warmer than it had been outside. Already she could feel awareness growing on her like a slow awakening. She began to push her way along the tunnel. The tunnel turned sharply and Senna thought she would be stuck. She made it around the turn and was faced with a fork, she chose the direction that felt warmest and followed that. It was only after she had gone through that tunnel and faced yet another fork that she began to worry about finding her way out. Should she back out now while she still could? If she still could. To return to the cold and that dull-minded existence of the open was an impossible choice, so she pressed on. The air grew warmer, and the animal smell stronger, as she progressed. Another turn and another fork and then suddenly it opened out.

It was a large low cavern in the ice, four metres or more long, and more than two metres wide. Senna had come out in the middle of one side. Down the wider end of this cavern was a seal, and Senna remembered what she had read on Jia's computer. There were seals in this lake, the Baikal Seal, known as nerpa – *that* was the word that had been rattling around in the back of her mind trying to get through. The dark silver-grey mother was staring in Senna's direction, its long whiskers twitching and its nostrils flaring as it sniffed in and out, trying to work out if Senna was a threat. In front of the mother was a seal pup bundled in thick white fur, its large black eyes stared at Senna in open curiosity. There was movement a second pup peered out from behind the mother. This wasn't just a cavern or burrow, it was a birthing den.

"I'm sorry to disturb you," she spoke softly. There was no reaction from the seals. They obviously knew Senna was here, but that didn't necessarily mean they could hear her. Even so, Senna felt as though she had to speak, if only to convince herself that she wasn't dreaming this. She continued, "I don't mean any harm. I just want to share some of your warmth."

The tunnel she had been following was too small to be used by the mother, it must have been created by the pups. As she looked around she saw more of these small tunnels, they must be incredibly busy little creatures.

Then Senna noticed something else, something even more surprising, the answer to what they had been searching for as they walked across the lake. There, on the other side of the den to where Senna was poking out of the tunnel, hidden from the world outside, was the way the mother came and went from the den. It was a hole in the ice!

10. Water

The dawn approached and light slowly crept down through the branches. The lush life around the Glade woke with a slowly building exuberance as the day began.

The dhumraka had not moved from their positions, but Kaia seemed not to see them now. The small, apparently frail, figure of the elder was looking up into the branches. As the sun brought its first rays down over them, Kaia stood and began to sing into it, as if meeting a great love that had been gone from her life for too long. It was a song without words, or no words that Barma recognised. Starting as a soft chant, it grew and spread in power and volume. It didn't compete with the chorus of life around them, it joined that awakening and celebrated with the birds and the trees the great power of the dawn that brought the sun, the giver of life, back to the forest.

Barma saw tears spilling down Milla's face, and then felt them on his own. These were not tears of sadness, of the loss they knew they were facing, but tears that came from the overwhelming joy and love of life. These were a greeting and acknowledgement of the great wonder that was a new day.

All too soon Kaia's song began to fade, and Barma came back to the harsh reality standing around them.

The circle of dhumraka and humans had closed around them yesterday. There must have been a hundred or more. At intervals could be seen pairs of the grey narun handling the complex equipment of ray-guns, like those Barma had seen, and felt, in the city.

Barma had wanted to leave then, even as the circle was closing, to try and get back to Tilvy. But Kaia had placed one hand gently on his chest and told him, "It is too late now. *They* will not let you through even if I were to permit you to try." Barma had tried to step past her anyway, and for the first time in his life he felt the power of the elders. It was gentle, from Kaia it could never be anything other than gentle, but it was firm and strong. It may have been possible to break past that restraint on his actions, but it would have been a break, a pain to both himself and to Kaia, and by extension to the Glade. Barma could not will himself to inflict that pain, so he had remained. He had sat with Kaia and Milla and a few others outside the Way, keeping vigil over the Glade as they waited for whatever was still to come.

Now the new day had arrived and there was a restlessness, a sense of anticipation, coming from the circle around them.

"Are many of our stand still out there?" Kaia asked of Milla.

"Tilvy and Beenae, as you know. There are perhaps a dozen others, mostly those on the outer. We brought back as many as we could."

"And it's too late now for any more."

"What is it the dhumraka want?" Barma asked.

"None of them have spoken," said Milla. "So far they have not hurt anyone, though I'm not sure what that means. They cannot bring that equipment into the Glade, and without their equipment I can't imagine they will try to enter and fight on more equal terms."

"I do not think they mean to enter the Glade," observed Kaia.

"They just want to trap us here?" Barma asked.

"No," Kaia answered. Her eyes wandered over the dhumraka in front of the Way, and to the few humans beyond. "I believe they mean to destroy us."

Barma stared at her, she couldn't be serious.

Kaia glanced at him and then looked back out again.

Barma followed Kaia's gaze. Beyond the circle of dhumraka were the humans that had come with them, doing the heavy lifting. Among the humans were a few smaller figures silently directing their actions – dhumraka encased in cloth. The humans were attaching small devices to the trunks of trees as high as they could reach – their figures dwarfed to insignificance by the massive trunks that surrounded the Glade.

"Is there nothing we can do?" Barma asked.

At first there was no response, Barma thought that might have been answer enough, but then Kaia said, "There was precious little our ancestors could do to protect themselves from such hatred. Against these new weapons I can see only one path."

Milla asked, "You think it will come to that?"

Kaia nodded, still staring out into the trees. "In different circum-stances there may have been other possibilities, but against all this, and being singled out ahead of the others in this way, I don't see any other choice that offers hope."

"Hope?" Milla questioned. "If it comes to that, is there really any hope?"

"I believe there is," Kaia returned.

"After everything Asha had to say about those twins, we should have known to expect this, perhaps we could have been better prepared."

"Those who anticipate battle, invite war."

"And yet we have war anyway."

"Perhaps not yet," Kaia said. "Not if we refuse to fight."

"So you—?" Milla started and then stopped. He looked out at the circle of dhumraka, contemplating what he now understood of Kaia's plans.

"I don't suppose there is any point in asking you to let me do this?"

Kaia turned to face Milla. She reached up and stroked his cheek. "Everything I know, everything I am, is already part of the Glade; your gifts are of greater value in this time. This risk is mine to take, dear Milla. Please, don't argue with me."

Barma watched in concern and confusion as the two elders stared silently into each other's eyes. "What are you going to do?" he asked, but neither of them answered him.

Eventually Kaia and Milla turned back to the forest, and Barma looked out too. Others emerged through the Way and watched with them. Some eventually returned to the safety of the Glade, others stayed to keep the vigil.

"What are they waiting for?" Barma asked.

"They wait for another," Kaia answered cryptically. "One who desires to lead this destruction."

It was late morning when they heard the noise of a helicopter overhead. It slowed, hovered still for a time, and then continued on its way. Some minutes later the pale figure of Sando came walking confidently through the forest.

"That's Sando!" Barma whispered urgently. "The one that was controlling Tilvy's mind until I hit him."

Kaia nodded, but said nothing in reply. She didn't seem surprised.

They watched Sando make his way past the dhumraka and come around to the front of the Way.

"You will be wary of his power?" Milla cautioned.

"I will. His power, indeed all of this," Kaia indicated the circle of dhumraka, "is best wielded against the unprepared. He may find it less effective against a mind grown inflexible with age."

"No one was ever foolish enough to say that your mind was inflexible, Kaia," Milla spoke quietly, "though some may have suggested that you can be stubborn."

Barma saw that Kaia was smiling as she responded, "Yes, my friend, I heard you."

Kaia turned her back on the dhumraka and dipped her hands into the rippling transparent surface of the Way. Barma stared in amazement at the small pool that lay glistening in the cup of her hands when she pulled them out, it shimmered like crystal-clear water in bright sunlight. He had never seen anyone take any part of the Way before. She splashed the liquid over her face, as if washing at a stream, but instead of splashing and falling to the ground, the essence of the Way quickly disappeared into her skin. She repeated this process a few times more, splashing her arms and torso. She dipped her hands one more time and drank the contents. When she was done, Kaia turned to face the dhumraka once more.

Barma stared at her. The cloud of white hair about her head moved slightly at the touch of a light breeze. So delicate and fragile in appearance, and yet such strength emanated from her that he felt almost as frightened of her as he was of Sando and the dhumraka.

"Good morning!" called Sando across the distance that still separated them. His voice was impossibly youthful, cheerful, seductive; a complete contradiction to the circumstances.

Kaia nodded but said nothing.

"I believe the usual practice in these circumstances is to ask you to submit," Sando spoke loudly.

"Submit to what?" Milla asked. Kaia placed her hand on his arm, but the question had already been asked.

"You see, that really is the problem," replied Sando cheerfully. He began walking closer to them, as if totally unafraid, as if there was nothing they could do to harm him. "Why bother asking for something I don't want."

"It is time for you all to return to the Glade," Kaia's voice came softly to those behind her, her lips did not move. There was a quiet but strong power behind this gentle request, and all those that had been watching began to turn back to the Glade. Even Barma found himself reluctantly having to follow the others.

"You're leaving before I'm finished, old man," Sando spoke out in cheerful tones.

That was the last Barma heard before the pressure of the Way closed around him and carried him into the Glade.

\- - -

Tracey drove as fast as she dared up the winding gravel road. It had been a tense trip, not helped by the speeding ticket she had received on the freeway coming out of the city. In the city, with so many stops for lights and other traffic, it had been possible to hold a conversation with Tilvy in the passenger seat, there was time to read the notes held up for her. But out of the city, on the freeway and now these country roads, Tracey couldn't spare the time for more than the simplest of messages from Tilvy. It made the trip very quiet, and that only increased the tension she knew they were both feeling. Despite the warning from Ian, and her mother's protestations, they couldn't have stayed away.

At last the driveway came into view and Tracey turned in. She drove the short distance through the trees and then into the large clearing in front of the house. She stopped the car in the middle of the clearing and watched the house. She hadn't known what to expect, but it seemed quiet.

She put her hand down to put the car back into gear. Tilvy's hand closed over hers and squeezed gently, then tapped once and released. Tracey looked across and watched the pencil and large pad wobble as Tilvy scribbled, "Wait here."

The passenger side door opened and Tracey saw the pad and pencil placed on the seat, the pencil rolled down against the back. Tracey turned the engine off, she wasn't going to be moving now until she knew where everyone was. With the motor and air-conditioning off, the heat was quickly invading the car through the open passenger door.

She wound her window down and looked out. The tops of the huge trees, far above, were swaying gently in a breeze that she couldn't feel down at this level. There was some insect noise, cicadas in the forest, but little else. In her visits here she had learned that much of the forest slowed down through the heat of the day, so the quiet felt normal, peaceful. She looked back to the house and studied it. Nothing seemed disturbed, except ... was the front door ajar?

There was a thump against the open passenger door. Startled, Tracey turned to look at it. The door wobbled on its hinges and then slowly swung closed with a light click.

"Tilvy?" Tracey called out.

There was no response. Tracey waited for a few moments, hoping the door would open and the pad and pencil would be lifted.

Tracey called out again, "Tilvy? What's happening?" She could hear the tremor in her voice. She didn't know what to do. She couldn't move the car, she didn't know where Tilvy was, or if there might be someone else around. Why had Tilvy closed the door? Except it didn't really sound like it had been closed, did it? It sounded like someone had bumped it. Who?

Memories of the attack those months ago, back at the Research Centre, came flooding into her mind. Who else might be out there? Tracey wound up the window.

Tilvy might be in trouble. Tracey cursed her own nervousness, she shouldn't have wound up the window. Rather than winding it down again she got out of the car and closed the door quietly behind her.

"Tilvy?" she called again.

She walked slowly around to the front of the car. Nothing. She took a few steps around toward the passenger side and then heard movement on the ground in front of her. She reached her hand out, as if groping around in the dark. She touched nothing so took a step forward, and almost fell over when her foot touched on something.

She pulled back and knelt down, reaching forward, her hand waving a few inches over the ground. A leg. She began to move her hand up. Her wrist was grasped, clutched at by a small hand. Tracey screamed in fright and tried to pull back. The hand held on tightly. Tracey put her left hand up over her face to try and shield herself from the expected blow.

- - -

Sando watched the frail old woman standing alone in front of the Way. His favourite Glades were those where the entire stand came out and stood silently before the Way, as if daring him to do his worst. He liked to watch the surprise on their faces when they discovered just how bad his worst could be. Not that Helix left much opportunity for such heroics these days, but Sando had had hopes for this Glade, especially when he saw the crowd that had been there just moments ago. Never mind. Time to find out what this one had planned.

"That was a bit rude, don't you think?" he mocked the old woman.

She said nothing.

"Come forward and speak with me," Sando told her. He pushed with his mind.

Nothing happened. He frowned and tried again. Still nothing.

"I speak for the stand, and for the Glade," the old woman spoke at last. "If you wish to remain here to talk, or simply to enjoy the life and peace of our home, then you are welcome."

"You *know* that is not why we've come," Sando said.

The old woman nodded. "Then I ask you to leave. I ask that you do not harm us, nor our forest."

There was a quiet dignity to the woman's simple request. There was also a power in her presence and her voice, Sando found himself almost willing to accede, and he felt the dhumraka around him stir uneasily. There was something else about that voice too. Though obviously old, there was something in the tone and delivery of it. He studied her face and her pale green eyes.

"You're related to Asha," he said to her, speaking quietly, almost a whisper.

The woman nodded.

Perhaps that explained her resistance, he thought. Sando shrugged, it changed little, and he could not let the dhumraka see any weakness on his part. If he could not control this woman directly, he would simply destroy her. He wanted to respond with some smart quip but, frustratingly, nothing came to him. He stepped back, and as he retreated before her steady gaze, he raised his right hand and let it fall.

The dhumraka to either side of Sando around the circle turned on their ray-gun devices, the antenna shapes directed at the Way.

The old woman should have collapsed where she stood. He had not been able to draw her further out, but that should not matter. But it obviously did. The woman ignored the rays, only a look of concentration on her face showed that this indifference was coming at a cost. She took a small step back and ripples in the shimmering surface of the Way showed that her back was pressed up against it, into it. She raised her arms out high on either side and rested them into the surface of the Way. Spreading out from her frail figure, the rippling, mostly transparent, surface began to turn milky, and the crests of the ripples flickered with silver streaks.

Sando had been anticipating some sudden rush of people from the Way, the rays were spread across the space between the two great trees to catch them as they came out, but now it appeared that the woman herself was the threat. He lifted his arms and waved inwards, indicating that the dhumraka should focus their fire on the woman.

Sando watched as the concentration expanded into pain on the old woman's face. He smiled.

Unexpectedly, she returned his smile and bowed. But instead of emerging from the Way, the glistening milk-and-silver surface came forward with her hands and fell around her, fluttering like a delicate silk scarf. The woman was quickly lost within the collapsing folds of the surface, and the folds continued to collapse as if the woman was no longer there. As the crumpling surface shrank further still, it turned more brightly silver. It glowed briefly with some inner light and then winked out of sight.

- - -

Tracey could feel her heart thumping as she knelt there waiting for the attack. More movement came from the left and she cringed to the right. There was a touch on her left arm and Tracey whimpered, anticipating the pain she remembered all too clearly.

The touch changed to a grasp and a gentle squeeze. It slowly dawned on Tracey that she recognised that touch, and the presence behind it. It was Tilvy. The unfamiliar grasp on her right hand released her.

"Tilvy?" Tracey asked, fear making her uncertain of her senses.

The hand on her arm squeezed gently once.

Tracey lowered her arm. "Are you all right?"

A wavy line was drawn on her arm. That meant "Sort of," in the sign language they had developed with Andrei.

Tracey tried to calm herself enough that she could think of useful questions. What had Tilvy meant, sort of? "Are you injured?"

Tap, tap – no. But this was followed by another wavy line.

Tracey stared at her arm, trying to understand. She gave up. "I'll get the pad."

She began to stand up, but Tilvy didn't release her hold. It took a moment before Tracey realised that Tilvy wanted help to get up. Tracey stood and helped Tilvy. There was movement on her arm as Tilvy did something, and then Tracey felt a second presence standing close. There was a tap on her arm that Tracey understood to mean she should get the pad and pencil.

With the pad resting on the bonnet of the car, Tracey held the pencil out to Tilvy and then stood and waited.

The pencil hovered uncertainly over the pad before an explanation slowly appeared. "Beenae is here. He came to warn us that something was happening at the Glade. I think something bad happened there – just now. Beenae and I were knocked over with pain and shock."

"Are you okay now?" Tracey asked.

"Think so. Still hurts, but going away."

"Can I do anything to help you?"

"No, am okay, I think."

"What do we do?" Tracey asked.

"Beenae says humans and dhumraka went into the forest. Must have attacked the Glade, must be what we felt – must be too late." The last was a hard to read scrawl. The pencil fell onto the pad, rolled off down the bonnet, and dropped to the ground.

Tracey felt Tilvy move into her arms. She could feel her friend trembling, her shoulders shaking as she cried against Tracey's shoulder. The second presence, Beenae, came up and leaned against Tracey too. She wrapped her arms around both of them and held them firmly. She couldn't think of what to say, she didn't really understand yet, if she ever would. "Oh, Tilvy, I'm so sorry," was all she could murmur.

They stood like that for a long time. Slowly the shaking subsided and first Beenae and then Tilvy pulled back. After a few moments Tracey saw the pencil rise from in front of the car and then hover again over the pad.

"Beenae says that men – humans – came here too. They left things on the trees around the house. They went into the house too. He doesn't know what they did in there. Then they left again."

"There's no one else here now?" Tracey asked.

The page of the pad flipped over and Tilvy wrote, "No," on the blank sheet.

"I'll go look in the house."

Tilvy grabbed her hand, tapping on it twice.

A few moments later the pad was held up with the message, "We should stay together!" Then the pad went back to the bonnet and another message was written and held up. "But Beenae and I need to rest first."

They made their way cautiously to a bare patch of lawn not far from the car and sat down. Everything was quiet.

Tilvy didn't write much for a while, Tracey guessed that Tilvy must be either resting or talking to Beenae, so Tracey lay back and tried to think.

She felt more separate from Tilvy's world now than ever. She had never seen the Glade, would never have been *able* to see it. She understood that it was Tilvy's true home, her sanctuary. They had spent a lot of time talking about it, but it was still unreal to Tracey, something from a fairytale. She tried to imagine what it would be like to have lost her own home, but she knew that wasn't big enough. Tracey's home was really just a place to live, it had never meant that much to her, it wasn't even where she had grown up. Tilvy's Glade was much more than that. And what about the people? What about Barma? Tracey felt tears forming and tried to draw back from the emotions welling up inside her.

Tracey sat back up and looked around again, trying to distract

255

herself. She realised how hot she had become sitting out here in the sun, and pulled at the material of her loose top.

The pad rose beside her and the pencil moved across it. Tracey felt that she could almost see Tilvy leaning the pad against her knees. "I think we'll be okay now," appeared on the paper.

"Do you know ... do you have any idea what has happened?" Tracey asked.

"Not really," Tilvy wrote back. "It must have been bad for us to have felt it like that but the Glade is still there somewhere, I can feel it." There was a pause, then she added, "It feels further away or something. Can't explain."

"So do you think ...?" Tracey trailed off. She didn't know how to ask what she wanted to know.

"I don't know. Just don't know," Tilvy wrote back.

The pencil started scribbling again, "Let's go. I want to look around here first and then Beenae and I are going to find out what happened to the Glade."

"What should I do?" Tracey asked.

But there was no response. The pad and pencil suddenly jerked and fell to the side. Tracey felt Tilvy clutching at her. Tracey pulled her close, Tilvy's body was quivering and twitching. Again Tracey was lost, she had no idea what must be happening. She held on to her friend, calling her name, "Tilvy, Tilvy."

- - -

It had all happened in some absurd slow motion, and yet it was over before Sando could react. He looked between the two great trees and there was nothing to see. The old woman and the Way were simply gone. He understood now that she had managed to close the Glade – so quietly and simply that he hadn't realised what she was doing until it was done.

Sando had wanted the Glade closed, but he had wanted the Way broken, ripped down and torn to shreds to maximise the damage to the Glade and those trapped within. What that old woman had done was tantamount to gently closing the door. Yes it had still locked them in, but it had also closed Sando out. He couldn't harm them now, not directly, not violently, and *not* to his satisfaction.

Maybe his brother had been right. He'd spent too much time planning this, looking forward to it, ready to feel the exaltation when it was over. But it hadn't come out as he wanted. The Glade was still there, somewhere, wherever it was that Glades existed. Closed, but not destroyed, perhaps not even damaged – and it could return.

Sando pulled himself out of his frustration. For now it was best to pretend that he wasn't surprised by this turn of events. He flicked his fingers and some dhumraka rushed to the two great trees that had held the Way. Charges were placed and everyone moved back. These were only small charges, shaped for a specific effect. After the loud, echoing reports as the charges fired the two great trees shuddered and slowly began to topple.

Sando nodded his approval and began to move away, not waiting for, nor acknowledging when it happened, the crash as the great trees tore past their neighbours and hit the ground. The work here wasn't done yet, but it didn't pay to stand too close to what was coming next.

The helicopter returned and Sando climbed the long rope ladder to the cabin. There was a clothed dhumraka directing the pilot, he looked to Sando for instructions. He indicated that they should ascend but wait.

Sando watched the tree tops fall away below him, and noted that a light wind had come up, only weak gusts as yet, but he nodded his satisfaction, it would help. On the horizon there were clouds forming, there might be rain later, but the water would not come in time to save this forest haven.

The helicopter rose to a safe height and Sando reached across to the waiting transmitter. He slid back the safety and put his fingers to the switch. His allies below would have made it to a safe distance by now and be on their way out – or not, it didn't matter much to Sando. He flicked the switch over. Muted by the distance and the noise of the helicopter, it sounded more like fireworks than serious explosives, but the flames that leapt above the canopy of the trees shortly afterwards confirmed that the blaze had started. These eucalypts would burn well on this hot, dry day, and the destruction would extend for miles.

Sando stared down in fascination, watching the flames consume the forest. Bright orange flares leapt higher, looking for more. He wished he was closer so that he could feel the heat. After so many months of waiting for the circumstances and timing to be right, Jaimee had finally agreed that Sando could have the first part of his revenge. And there it was. It wasn't everything that he had wanted, but in the hungry blaze of the fire Sando saw something of his own anger tearing at those that had dared to stand in their way. It felt right. It felt good. The Glade would not return soon, and when it did Sando would be ready to close it again. And again. He'd poison the ground if necessary, and there was nothing, now, that they could do to stop him. The Glade would fade into nothingness and take its occupants with it. It wasn't everything he had wanted, but it was a start. He could console himself that there was more to come.

- - -

Andrei woke from a nightmare in which fire had engulfed him, he could still feel the heat of it, and there was the memory of some sharper pain still lingering in his chest. He heard harsh bird calls and opened his eyes, groaning. He lifted his head, to be reminded of his throbbing headache, and eventually focused on two large black birds sitting on the mound of snow that had been their shelter.

"Crows," Asha said from next to him.

He turned in surprise. "You're awake."

Asha nodded. "I dreamt I was burning," she said softly, and then she tried to sit up. Andrei dragged himself into a sitting position and turned to help Asha, she was still very weak.

"Same dream," said Darnu. "I'm awake too."

"Great," said Garjae dismally from the other side of Darnu, "I'm happy for you all."

Andrei thought it must be close to midday. The sun had come out and the temperature had warmed a few degrees, that probably explained the partial recovery of his friends. Either that or the horror and pain of their shared dream. He pushed the memories of that dream from his mind and wondered how far his friends could walk. Come to that, he wondered how far *he* could walk.

One of the birds called again and Andrei looked up at them. "You normally attract a better class of bird, Asha," he commented.

"They're just curious," she answered.

"Yeah, well, they mightn't be interested in pecking at us, but they're hardly a bird of good omen."

"I'll try to do better next time."

Andrei looked at John lying still between Asha and Darnu. He could only hope that John was no worse than he had been.

"Where's Senna?" Asha asked.

Andrei turned and saw that her eyes were locked on him. He had to look away before he could answer. "The wind took her." He looked back. "But the brevi have gone to find her ... both of them." He told Asha and Darnu what had happened since the previous night, and finished, "so Garjae and I decided it was best if we all waited here for their return."

Garjae, still lying back – the effort to sit up was too much – added, "Something like that."

"I'm sorry," Asha started, "if I'd kept—"

"It's not your fault," Andrei interrupted, "Senna does what she wants to do. Anyway, she'll be all right. She's tough, probably tougher than the rest of us."

"I don't doubt that," Darnu agreed as he struggled to get on his feet. After a few tries he managed it and stood there swaying. "I don't ... I don't understand why I'm so weak. Garjae's injured, Asha has done her healing, John is – whatever. I feel like I've been drained."

"I'm not much better," said Andrei, also struggling to his feet. "Anyway," he added, "take a look at your hands." He held up his own in testament. "Too much digging in the snow, healing is really slow."

"Which means you're weakening much faster than you should," said Asha. "Help me up, Andrei, and I'll take a look."

Andrei put his hands behind his back. "No need for that."

"No," Darnu agreed.

"Help me up anyway," said Asha, reaching out to him.

Andrei put his hands out and pulled her up, though for a moment it felt like she was going to pull him back down. Asha was slow letting go of his hands, it wasn't until he felt a tingling in them that he realised what she was doing. He pulled away from her.

"They're not good, Andrei."

"But they're not that bad either." Andrei turned to Darnu. "If we start walking will the brevi still be able to find us?"

Darnu nodded.

"Then I think we should walk while we're all awake. It will get colder when the sun starts to drop, and I worry we'll all go to sleep and never wake up again."

"You lot go," said Garjae. "I'm not going anywhere."

"Come on," urged Andrei. "You can lean on me, I promise I won't tickle you."

"What about John?" Asha said.

Andrei realised she was right. Everyone else could walk – just – but they would never be able to carry John. "Darnu, help me get him up."

Even between the two of them it was a struggle. John didn't appear to have become that much weaker from lying on the ice, just slower to react. But he still moved when urged to, eventually, and they managed to get him upright.

"Your turn, Garjae," Andrei said.

Garjae looked up at him, preparing to argue.

Andrei didn't let him start. "We're not leaving you behind, Garjae, so you either try to move, or we'll all flop down beside you and make sure you're *really* miserable."

Garjae held up his good arm and Andrei grasped it and braced himself. Slowly Garjae pulled himself up, the pain obvious on his face. Finally upright, he leaned heavily on Andrei's arm as he tried to gather his strength.

"Well done," Andrei encouraged him.

Garjae just grunted.

They began to make their way east, Garjae leaning heavily on Andrei, Darnu and Asha pulling on John.

Their progress was slow and they paused often, but they didn't sit or lie down because it was too difficult to get back up again. The mound where they had spent the night gradually dropped behind them. The two crows had taken off and circled over them for a few minutes, but eventually went on their way. Andrei wasn't sorry to see them go.

- - -

Tilvy's writhing grew quiet and stopped. Tracey saw the pad twitch and then lift up. Tilvy rested the pad against Tracey as she wrote, and then waited for Tracey to turn the pad and look at it.

"Pain. Burning. The Glade, the forest, something is burning," was written in shaky letters.

Tracey stared at the words. "Are you okay?" she asked. "What can I do?" The questions felt inadequate.

The pad was pressed back against Tracey and more words were added.

"Will be okay ... think ... just hurts."

Tracey held Tilvy close. Beenae came closer and Tracey reached out to hold him too. She sat there rocking the two aaranya, feeling helpless and useless, and wondering what it was her friends were going through.

The slowly growing noise of an engine pulled at Tracey's attention. At first she thought it might be a car coming, and she wondered what she should do. As the noise grew she realised it was not a car, it was a helicopter. She looked up and eventually saw its tiny shape appear far above the trees. It appeared to stop, not much more than a dark speck hanging in the sky. Tracey wondered if they could see her.

A deafening crack and crash tore through the air and Tracey forgot the helicopter. Even as she was turning her head toward the house a series of loud booms went off all around her, as if someone was firing huge guns in rapid succession. The first thing that she understood were the flames pouring from the windows of John's house, and then she was surrounded by fire as the forest erupted around them.

The shock threatened to pin her in place, holding more tightly than ever to her friends with fright, not even recognising how tightly they clutched at her in return. The heat of the fires broke through her shock and she realised they had to move. There was only one possible shelter that was not burning, her car.

Clutching tightly to Tilvy and Beenae, Tracey rose into a crouch and stumbled her way to the car. Her mind was racing. Bushfire. Her mother's constant harping about Tracey travelling into the bush now felt justified. She tried desperately to remember what she'd learned from all those leaflets her mother had forced her to read and re-read.

Tracey clutched at the front passenger door, then realised there wouldn't be room for the three of them in the front. The first advice of everything her mother had shown her was not to be there in the first place. Too late for that now.

Tracey opened the back door. The second advice was that almost any solid building was going to be better than the car. Not in this case.

She ushered Beenae and then Tilvy into the back. The next advice was that if nothing else was available, then a car was marginally better than nothing. Tracey hoped so.

She climbed in after the others. You were supposed to have parked your car facing into the fire-front, but the fire was a wall all around them. You were supposed to park in a clear area. At least that much had gone right.

The wind picked up, embers were flying past the car. The fire outside was roaring, and the heat was radiating fiercely in through the windows. Wrap yourself in pure woollen blankets and curl up on the floor of the car. Her mother had made sure she had the blankets. Tracey gave Beenae and Tilvy each a blanket, then she pulled the third from the front seat and pulled it over herself.

It must have been Tilvy that worked out how to move the driver's seat forward, Tracey could see both, now very small, blanketed figures crouched there. She did the same for herself behind the passenger seat, wishing she could shrink herself down like her friends. The blanket across from her wavered and Tracey felt Tilvy's small hand grasp hers and squeeze.

"Are you all right?" Tracey called above the roar of the fire.

Tap – yes.

"And Beenae?"

Tap – yes.

The heat in the car was growing rapidly, it made it hard to think. What else had she read? You were supposed to turn off your engine and air conditioner. Fine, done. But you were supposed to turn on your headlights and hazard lights to stop other traffic hitting you. There was no other traffic here. Shit! Close all the vents. With the passenger side seat pushed forward, Tracey stretched into the front and flick the levers. Everything was so hot!

What else? What else was she supposed to remember? There was smoke in the car now, and fumes. Things were melting. Her damn car was all plastic! Tracey coughed, but that just made the pain in her lungs worse. Water. She was supposed to be drinking water, she *wished* she was drinking water. She felt like she was going to choke

262

to death, if she didn't cook first. What else?

Get out! That was what else. As soon as it was safe to do so. Get out and move to ground that was already burned. Something about only being able to survive inside the car for two minutes! She could only pray that some miracle would keep her and her friends alive.

- - -

Hours passed. Andrei could still feel the sun on his back, but it was low and he could feel the temperature dropping. He knew his mind was slowing down and he knew they didn't have much time left before the night took them.

Garjae had stopped grumbling some time back, and didn't respond to anything Andrei did, other than to stop when Andrei stopped and to start, reluctantly, when Andrei started. Andrei stopped now and waited while Darnu and Asha came up with John, they were only a few steps behind despite how slowly John was moving.

"Do we try to keep going through the night?" Andrei asked the others. When there was no response Andrei turned to them. Darnu was staring at him as if trying to remember the question, Asha was still staring down at the snow in front of her as if she hadn't heard at all.

When he did answer, Darnu spoke slowly, the words coming with great difficulty, "I think we should keep going until we have no other choice."

"That's what I was thinking," agreed Andrei, "if we can keep straight."

He looked ahead and surveyed the lake in front of them. There was an area of rough ice off to the right, and some of it stretched across in front of them. Andrei didn't want to try and lead their party of invalids through such obstacles, especially not in the dark. He picked out what appeared to be the clearest path, they had only to bend a little way to the north.

Andrei stood still with indecision, there was something more, something he should be looking for, but it was hidden behind the throb of his headache. The only thing still clear in his mind was the need to keep moving while they still could.

He looked again toward the path he wanted, past this line of broken ice and piled up snow, and pulled on Garjae's good arm.

There was a low grunt and then Garjae began to walk, leaning more heavily on Andrei's arm than ever.

They had gone several shuffling paces before it occurred to Andrei that he couldn't hear the sound of the others behind him, something he'd grown accustomed to hearing over the last hours. He turned his head to look behind him, still stepping forward with Garjae, and saw that the other three hadn't moved.

"Darnu!" he called back.

When Darnu failed to respond, he didn't even look up, Andrei tried to stop Garjae and turn back all at once, and in amongst it somewhere their legs got tangled and both fell down. Andrei heard a low howl rising around him. It was Garjae. He had fallen on his injured arm and the pain of it was trying to rouse him from his stupor, he was struggling feebly.

Andrei hurried as best he could to help, muttering repeatedly, "I'm sorry, Garjae, I'm sorry." He laid Garjae on his back and tried to gently place his injured arm on his chest where Garjae had been carrying it before. He couldn't tell if more damage had been done, but he knew it couldn't be good. The howl faded and so did Garjae, his eyes closed and Andrei couldn't get any response from him.

Andrei gave up and looked back for the other three. They stood still where they had been before. Andrei looked past them and watched the sun drop below the horizon, taking the last of their hopes with it.

He wasn't sure how long he lay there trying to think what to do, but eventually he struggled to his feet. He wanted to bring his friends together. He tried to take a step and fell over, probably his own feet, but it could have been Garjae's, he couldn't tell. He lay still trying to gather his strength, and then tried again. He thought he heard someone calling to him. "I'm coming, I'm coming," he muttered. He managed to stand again and took one slow step, but as he brought his other foot forward it caught on something and he felt himself starting to fall again.

Andrei resigned himself to hitting the hard ice, he didn't even raise his arms to break his fall – but it didn't happen. It took him a moment to understand that he was wrapped in warm tender arms. "Senna?" he asked weakly. It could only be his Senna.

"I'm here, Andrei," her voice came back to him.

"Senna?"

"It's me, my darling idiot."

"It's amazing what you can teach an idiot these days," Andrei muttered. He felt her arms tighten around him.

- - -

John woke with a start and tried to draw breath. Water filled his mouth and he flailed about, trying to find the surface. He was drowning. He tried to cough but there was only water.

"John! It's all right. John!" Asha called to him.

He felt her hands on his arms trying to hold him still. Asha! He tried to draw another breath and panic took him again. He slowly registered that despite being immersed in water he wasn't drowning, there was no pain in his lungs, there was no blackness encroaching on his mind. Slowly memories came back to him, who he was, and at this moment *what* he was. He didn't need to breathe. He didn't need the air. His movements slowed.

Asha was floating in the water beside him, watching him with that familiar warm compassion, but tinged with fear.

"Did I hurt you?" he asked.

Asha relaxed and smiled at him. "No, my love. I'm just pleased to see you awake at last. I was scared for you." She swam forward and they embraced.

"Is this—?" John asked quietly.

"The lake? Yes. Senna found a way in, and some help."

John thought back to the last things he remembered, stumbling numbly through the night. "Did you ... did you have to carry me here?"

Asha shook her head against his shoulder and then pulled back. "It's a long story, but I need to merge and regain some strength before I can help you – and Garjae's been hurt too."

John looked around. "Where are they all?"

"They've all merged." She came forward and kissed his lips. "Now I really must merge too. You're still weak and you need my help, but I have to merge first. If you want to get out of the lake the hole is just there." Asha pointed. She kissed him again and then faded into the water.

John had seen her do this before, back when he didn't believe she was real. He concentrated and could feel her presence in the water not far from him, and she slowly began to move away. He thought that perhaps he could see something of her, as if her presence in the water formed vague patterns. There was no human shape to this presence, just an area of the water that felt like Asha. It was a feeling that, not long ago, he might have puzzled over, but now he simply accepted it.

It occurred to him that he'd been speaking under water with no effort or problem, and no distortion. The telepathy of the narun could be really convenient. Some time he'd have to try it without moving his lips like he'd seen Milla demonstrate.

He swam up to the hole in the thick ice, and bobbed up through to find himself looking into a small ice-cave. It was very dark, just a dim haze of the snow and ice against his vedana let him pick out the dimensions of the space. There was a distinct animal smell to the air and it didn't feel much colder than the water. He tried to lift himself up inside, deciding it would be more comfortable out of the water, but he couldn't get enough of a grip on the ice to haul himself out.

He felt a tug on his foot and dropped back down below the ice. It was Senna.

"Would you like to get out?" she asked him.

John nodded.

"There's a trick to it. Watch this and then follow me up."

John watched as Senna dropped deeper into the water and then swam past him with gathering speed, her lithe body made it look easy as she cut through the water and disappeared into the hole and then out.

"Sure," he muttered, "some trick, superwoman."

John wasn't at all sure he could emulate her actions, especially feeling as weak as he did, but he had to try. He dropped a bit deeper and tried to swim as fast as he could through the water. As he entered the hole he reached his arms out and tried to keep his momentum going by pushing up from the edges of the ice. He felt his hands slipping and he started to fall back, but Senna grabbed him under his armpits and pulled him further in. At last he got a knee over the edge and was safe from dropping back.

"Thanks," he said, as he pulled back out of her arms, self-conscious of their intimate embrace.

He looked around the cave. "What is this place?"

266

"It's a seal birthing den, all those little tunnels you see are made by the pups. The mother took her pups away when the jalaja came, but they say she's got another hole not far away and she might return here after we've gone. They filled in the hole we made to get you all in here, to keep in some warmth, and it means it should still be all right for the seals."

"The jalaja?"

"The naiads, the people of this lake. That's the really odd thing: they were expecting us, just not here exactly. Anyway, they saw that we needed time to recover and thought this was the best place. So they left us here and said they'd come back in a few days to take us the rest of the way."

"So ...?" John began, and then stopped, not sure where to start.

Senna understood the unfinished question and started to fill him in. She hadn't finished her story when there was movement at the hole. A dark shiny head with large black eyes surfaced and there was a gush of warm, moist air as the seal flared its nostrils and took a breath.

"She's come back," Senna whispered. "Come on, move back and see if she'll come in."

Senna drew John back with her to the narrow end of the oval den, and they stayed there pressed against one another and watched the seal as it took more breaths and floated quietly, assessing her den.

"I hope she'll bring the pups back, I feel bad about having forced her from her home," Senna whispered in John's ear.

The seal spent most of her time looking in their direction, and John wondered what she made of them. Eventually she slipped silently beneath the water and was gone. They waited a few minutes but she did not return.

John put a little distance between him and Senna, and asked her, "You said that the brevi found you in the water, what happened then?"

"They gave me Andrei's message, and I tried to have one go back to get you all on your way here. I wanted the other one to stay with me and guide me to meet you when I was strong enough. But they had their own plans."

John smiled. "Yes, I've discovered they can be like that."

"Casseta took off deeper into the water. I've never seen them swim before, but those flaps of skin they use for gliding work really well, she was really moving. Nuttachen stayed with me, ignoring me when I asked him to go back to Andrei with a message. Eventually I merged back into the water, I thought I'd have to go back and get you myself.

"When I thought I was well enough to be of some use, I drew back out of the water and started to make my way back to this hole. Nuttachen was waiting for me and he came up and kept chattering at me, I've never heard one be so strident. I finally took the hint that he wanted me to wait. So I did.

"It wasn't all that much later that Casseta returned, leading a potamo – it's what the jalaja call their brevi, except they aren't quite brevi either – I won't try to explain, hopefully you'll see one for yourself. Cassey was exhausted and kept at me until I let her merge. It's the first time that's ever happened to me; a strange feeling, isn't it?"

John nodded. "You do get used to it."

"Guess so," Senna agreed and then continued, "Nuttachen and the potamo twittered at each other and still we waited. I'm not sure how much later it was that Novoi and his friends arrived, it felt like a long time. They had been searching for us further west but Cassey had gone to fetch them. I told them as much as I could as quickly as I could, I was impatient to get going. We went out and found you close by, Andrei was about to lead you past us. Novoi and his friends helped to bring you back here. They had to make a new larger hole to get you all through, the seal and her pups had vacated before then, and here you are."

"What about Garjae? Is he going to be all right?"

"I think so, when Asha is up to helping him again. I think entering the water was pretty awful for him, it woke him up to the pain. I hate to think what it must feel like, the arm looks terrible."

They sat in silence for a while, John reviewing what he'd been told. "I think I remember where I left that pick-axe," he said, "not that it's any help now."

"I don't think it mattered," Senna told him. "I'm sure we'd have lost it before we got to the lake anyway, we were all pretty out of it."

John nodded. He was feeling pretty miserable. Not just the craving – the needy sensation that he had felt coming on before he blanked out was stronger now than ever – but he was also very weak and tired. And now he had heard how much of a burden he had been to his friends. He closed his eyes. He didn't know what he could have done differently, but he felt that there should have been something.

"Will you be okay if I go out to find Andrei?" Senna asked him.

John nodded.

"You sure?"

"I'm fine, Senna, just tired. Go. I'll just sleep here until everyone's ready for whatever happens next."

He felt Senna touch his arm briefly, then heard a faint ripple from the water in the hole as she returned to the lake. He lay there and tried to sleep, but couldn't settle. He shuffled around trying to find a comfortable position, but guessed that you had to be a seal to be comfortable in here. As useless as it was, he kept going back through the events that had brought him here, looking for some way he might have avoided endangering his friends. After many fruitless iterations he drifted off to sleep.

When next he woke, Andrei was reclining near him. There was a faint glow to the ceiling of the cave that John assumed meant it was daylight outside.

"That's a relief," Andrei said.

John looked at him in question.

"We've been visiting on and off, making sure the hole doesn't freeze over again. I was starting to worry you'd gone all the way back to sleep, you know, like you were before."

"Just dozing," John replied, "there didn't seem much else to do." John pulled himself up on one elbow, he would have liked to sit up but there wasn't much room and he didn't feel strong enough.

"Pretty good doze, it's nearly midday outside."

"You've been out?"

"Not in a hurry to be out there again," Andrei said. "I was starting to think some very mean thoughts about this lake, but I've mostly forgiven him now. It's almost snug down here."

"First time I've ever heard zero degrees called snug."

"Zero degrees has never worried me before, but now I know that minus twenty-something does, I might not be so cavalier about such

269

jaunts in the future."

"Sure, Andrei, I'll believe that when I see it. Shouldn't you still be out in the water? I mean, how are you feeling?"

"Not bad, all things considered. We don't all have the amazing restorative powers of Asha, so it will take a few days to really feel better, but I'm not complaining."

"How is she?"

"She asked me to apologise for needing more time. Garjae was in a pretty bad way, so after she looked in on you, and found you snoring, she went back to help him. Now she's had to merge again. I doubt if you'll see her until tomorrow."

"And Garjae?"

"Still as happy as ever. It took considerable convincing from all of us to get him to let Asha treat him. I told him that the only good martyr was a dead one, but he didn't find it amusing – I think he's still pissed off at me falling over with him." Andrei had to explain that reference since Senna hadn't mentioned it. "Anyway the pain finally got the better of him and he let Asha do her magic, but we weren't allowed to watch. He's still a long way from perfect, but he is feeling a lot better now. You can tell because he's getting morose again, rather than just bad tempered."

Andrei chatted on for a while, telling John more of what they'd seen. Telling him of the glass-like ice that he'd found and of the wind that took Senna.

John felt his head starting to drop again.

"I must be slipping," said Andrei, "I can normally keep my audience awake."

"Sorry. Despite sleeping so much already, I still feel very tired and out of sorts."

"You'll feel better after Asha has sorted you out."

"I hope so, and I hope it's not too hard on her. Maybe we should just—"

"Don't you start. Asha's not going to go on without doing what she can for you, and the rest of us will do whatever she says is best, so you can save time and breath by not arguing about it."

John gave a weak grin. "Can't let Garjae take all the limelight."

"Sure you can, he's got the face for it. Look, go back to sleep. I'll head back into the water and see if a bit more time merged will improve my performance on the next visit." Andrei started to move away.

"Thanks, Andrei."

Andrei looked back, waved one hand and grinned, and then slipped head first through the hole and into the lake.

John fell back to sleep quickly, the hard ice floor no longer enough to disturb him.

He woke slowly, luxuriantly. He could feel Asha lying against him, firm and strong and soft and gentle all at once. He put his arm around her and pulled her as tight against him as his weakened state allowed.

"Andrei told me you weren't dead yet," Asha spoke softly in his ear. "It wasn't funny at the time, but all of a sudden it is."

John chuckled softly. "This isn't how I greeted Andrei."

"I should hope not, you're too weak for such activity." With that Asha pulled back a little. "We need to make a start on this, John."

"I thought we were."

"No, it's ..." Asha trailed off.

John could almost feel Asha thinking, so he stayed silent, waiting for her to continue.

"What I do for Ellie is different from healing open wounds. It's harder and more personal. More intimate. I've never done it with anyone other than Ellie ... and the other preta back—" Asha stopped there. John just held her and waited. She continued, "I don't think it will be possible if you resist."

"I'm not intending to resist."

"I know, but now it has come to it I'm nervous. We should have practised this before we left, made sure it would work."

"Maybe we don't have to do it anyway," John replied. "Maybe I can last until we get back."

"No, you need strength now or you won't get far."

John relented. "What do you want me to do?"

"I wish I knew. Relax and try to just let it happen."

"Sounds easy enough."

Asha looked doubtful but nodded. A look of concentration came over her face. John watched carefully, studying the lines he'd come to know so well. A frown appeared and her eyes turned angry.

"John!"

"What?"

"You're not letting me in."

"I'm not doing anything."

Asha looked frustrated, and then her flash of temper subsided. "Maybe it's me. Try to relax more, to empty your mind. Maybe close your eyes. I can feel you staring at me, thinking about me. I don't know whether that's distracting me or you, but something is getting in the way."

John nodded and closed his eyes, trying to relax as best he could, although there was a certain amount of tension between them now, and that made it harder. He thought back to being with Asha in her forest, the day they had sat on the dead tree trunk and he had learned to use his vedana. Feeling the trees around them, the trunk beneath them and the bright form of Asha in front of him.

With that thought he became aware of her bright form in front of him again, no longer just the woman he loved, but an intense form of life that was concentrating on him – on his mind. It was like there were tendrils reaching through his thoughts, touching here and there and bringing back memories: Asha crying in front of him, insisting she was real; with Samantha and Ellie at a picnic; meeting his friend Jason for the first time at college. Just random memories tripped as the tendrils reached deeper and deeper.

His first reaction was to push them away, and he immediately felt the tendrils receding. Then he remembered what was happening and tried to relax, tried to open the way. There was nothing in his life that he wasn't willing to reveal to her. He wasn't necessarily proud of every moment, but there was nothing that he wouldn't willingly entrust to Asha.

The tendrils probed deeper. He remembered finding his father dead on the lounge room floor; watching his mother and father together; roaming the streets with a gang after school; standing on tiptoes to watch out the window of the flat to the busy streets far below. Memories he had scarcely known still existed. There were more, but the images became vague, blurred and indistinct. The probing tendrils slowed and then went still. Everything stopped and John wondered if this was it, if this was what he had seen happening with Ellie. The tendrils tensed. There was a flash of pain and then the tendrils were gone, vanished as if they had never been. In his chest, above his heart, he felt a glow, like a still hot coal buried in cold ashes, and the heat began to grow.

John opened his eyes in surprise. Asha was staring into his face, her eyes unseeing, but with a look of such strength of love that he felt overwhelmed and inadequate. He looked down and saw that the front of her dress had opened and from over her heart came a thick, transparent beam, glowing gold. Life was streaming from her, across the small space between them and into his breast, into his heart. He felt the fire that was entering him spread out, warming his chest and his stomach, stretching out along his arms and legs to the very tips of his fingers and toes. The heat was burning up into his head and flaring beneath his skull.

He had seen this beam before, Asha had let him watch her feeding Ellie, but to feel everything that went with it. ... It was like burning with a fire that didn't cause any harm, that gave only life and energy and strength. A fire with its heart at his heart. A fire that carried love, not pain.

He wanted to pull Asha tight, to tell her how much he loved her. He wanted to cry out that he wasn't adequate to receive this, that he wasn't strong enough nor good enough to earn it. He wanted to cry with the joy of it. He wanted to leap up with the sudden strength he felt filling his body. But he held himself still, willed himself to be still. He promised himself that he would strive to be worthy.

His eyes drew back to her face and the strength that he had seen there was fading, the effort and cost of this sacrifice was becoming apparent. How long should he let her continue?

He closed his eyes and stayed still. He had to trust that Asha would know when to stop. Meanwhile the fire boiled through his limbs and he marvelled at the strength and warmth of it, he revelled in the exhilaration of the life that was filling him. Flashes of the memories that Asha had woken leapt past his thoughts, but he ignored them so he could concentrate on the sensations of his body. His libido was stirring, he could feel himself swelling where their bodies were still pressed together. He tried to ignore that too, but the heat of the fire made it hard.

The heat over his heart began to cool and he opened his eyes and looked down. The beam of life was fading and shrinking. As he watched, it faded further and then vanished. Asha sighed. He looked up and saw that she had closed her eyes. She suddenly looked drained, he supposed that was exactly what she was. He pulled her close and kissed the side of her head.

"Are you all right?" he asked softly.

There was a pause before she answered, "I will be. ... Just hold me."

John held her tightly and waited. The fire was still flowing through his limbs, he had to concentrate to stop pressing himself against her, the sexual urge strong with the heat.

Asha must have felt it and whispered, "I can't," she touched his hip to indicate her meaning. "Not now."

"I know. Ignore it. I think it's a reaction to the heat."

"Heat?"

"That's what it feels like, like you've filled my body with fire."

"Oh. I did wonder what it must be like on the other side." She pulled her head back and looked at him in question.

John tried to tell her, but felt that his words didn't really make it. "I can't help wondering how it feels to you," he said. "Does it make you feel cold?"

"Just weak and tired." Asha gave John a sad smile. "And not at all inclined to ... I'm sorry."

John realised he had been pressing himself against her again and pulled back. "Don't apologise, it's one of those things that will go away if you ignore it."

Asha smiled, leaned forward and kissed him.

"That doesn't really help," John admitted. He paused and then asked, "At the start ... was that really you in my mind?"

"Yes. I'm sorry, I know it's invasive."

"That doesn't matter. You mightn't like everything you see, but it's all me, it's what you've got if you still want it."

In answer, Asha stroked the side of his face and smiled.

"Could you actually see the memories that you stirred?"

"Some. Not much comes across very clearly, but certain flashes do. Did you really find your father when he died?"

John nodded. "I had trouble with that for a while, feeling guilty because I'd been spending so much time with Samantha and so little time at home with Dad. It was a very strange time when he died."

The wakened memory expanded and pushed out more words. "Samantha and I had been going out for months, but she had never actually met my father, not face to face. Not for any weird reasons, it just never happened. And he died not long after the September 11 attacks in America – not that it probably means much to you, but it was a big deal in the human world at the time – and that was all anyone else could talk about. It was like I was the only one that really noticed Dad had died."

"And you felt isolated."

John nodded, then changed the subject, commenting, "Nothing like a bit of morbid conversation to cool things off. You also stirred up a memory of my time as a member of a street gang, when I was a kid, did you catch that one?"

"Maybe. Some didn't make much sense to me."

"Some didn't make much sense even at the time, that was one of them."

They didn't speak for a while, just lay there holding each other. Asha snuggled her face into John's shoulder and neck.

Eventually John asked, "Is the memory thing just a side effect, or is it part of whatever it is you do?"

Asha reached her hand up between them and brushed her finger tips over his heart, as if looking for the place where they had been joined. "I don't really know," she said. "It's like ... like I have to reach inside to find the place to start, like looking for a trigger that will open up the connection. I'm not consciously trying to pry—"

"It didn't feel like you were prying, the memories just trigger as you reach past them."

"That's it. They just happen. I think it started that way because I was trying to find the real person within the preta, and now – now I don't know how else to do it, how else to make it happen."

John pulled back a bit so they could see each other's faces. "It's all right you know. I don't mind, not that. I only mind what it does to you."

"I'll be fine."

John studied Asha's face. "Do you want to go back to the water now?"

"If you don't mind too much. I am feeling very weak, merging again will help."

John kissed her. "It's fine. The sooner you feel right again the sooner I can stop feeling guilty about you having to go through all this."

Asha didn't answer that, just smiled, returned his kiss, and then exited into the water.

John lay still with his eyes closed and felt the subsiding heat still permeating his body, it felt a lot like the afterglow that followed good sex. Perhaps it was that association, or perhaps the process left him more tired than he felt, but whatever the reason, John drifted off to sleep.

When he woke next it was to see Andrei pulling himself from the hole in the ice. He appeared to be dry as he came free of the water, John wondered how that worked, it didn't seem to work for him.

"You're awake," Andrei observed. "Feeling better?"

John nodded. "Good, very good. I'm surprised I slept again."

"She's a magician is our Asha," said Andrei. "She even told me you'd probably sleep again. You feel like coming for a swim? You might want to get used to it before we have places to go."

John agreed and followed Andrei into the water. It was warmer than the den above, invitingly so; the den was cooling down without the presence of the seals to keep the temperature up.

It was bright under the ice and John looked around him, but there wasn't much to see other than the underside of the ice, rough along one line but smooth as they moved away. He couldn't see anyone else around.

Andrei was swimming below him and called up, "You'll want to come deeper. It's daytime and most fish go deep."

John tried to follow Andrei down into the darker depths of the water. Andrei was moving much faster than John could manage and before long the pressure of the water began to make him uncomfortable. "Andrei!" he called down. He saw Andrei stop and look back up. John stayed where he was, hoping that he might get used to the pressure. Andrei swam back up to him.

"You're holding out," Andrei told him.

"It's getting painful," John explained. "The pressure. I feel like it's going to squash me."

"That's what I mean," Andrei said. "You're holding out. You're

276

making a hole in the water and it doesn't like that."

"I don't know what you mean."

"It's like my mother used to tell me," Andrei said with a grin, "don't point, it puts holes in the air and birds trip over them."

"You're not making sense."

"Sorry, joke. My mother always got a laugh from us kids with that one. You're holding the water out, making a hole in it that the water is trying to fill – so you feel the pressure of it. Just let the water pass through you. No more hole, no more pressure."

"I still don't know what you mean." John tried to contain his frustration. "I can't merge like you can, I told you that."

"This isn't merging. You've seen us pass through wooden doors and the like, this is sort of like that, but water is special, anyone can do it, not just the aaranya."

"Do you think that *anyone* includes me?"

Andrei looked puzzled. "I assume so. If not we could be in trouble, I expect the jalaja will want us to go deep, and you can't swim very fast if you keep making holes in the water."

"Can we go up, this is getting painful?"

They swam back up close to the ice and John felt much better. "So how do you do it?" he asked.

Andrei frowned in thought for a minute before answering, "How do you stand upright without falling over?"

John shrugged.

"Well that's how we do it. It's like balance, it just happens when we need it." Andrei thought some more. "Milla tried to give some lessons based on human knowledge. He said you describe water as existing in three states: as a solid, ice; as a liquid, water; and as a gas, steam. Well the narun can only interact with water as a liquid, but we can do it in three ways: make a hole, like you, in which case we get wet, like you; or we can pass through it, like I am now, in which case the water passes through me and I through it, but we remain separate and I remain dry; or we can merge with it, become part of it, like the others are now, which is when we can draw life from it to sustain ourselves."

"Solid, something and liquid?" queried John.

"Okay, so the analogy isn't perfect, it's not my fault your lot don't understand about prana. When we get back you can ask Milla to try and explain it better."

"But before that I have to learn how to do this ... whatever."

Andrei looked past John and said, "Maybe our magician can help."

John turned and saw Asha swimming toward them. "Feeling better?" she asked.

John nodded.

"Except for one minor hiccup," Andrei told her, and explained what they had been talking about.

Asha studied John and thought about it. "Have you tried the relaxation techniques you were taught to help you separate? See if it will happen for you when you relax, when you stop resisting the water."

John agreed that it was worth trying.

"I'm not good with relaxation," commented Andrei. "I'll be off, if you two are okay."

John and Asha nodded and Andrei swam off. Asha picked another direction and led John away. "Just ensuring we have some privacy," she explained.

When they reached a place that Asha was happy with, they floated a few feet below the ice. John found himself mesmerised by the way Asha's hair flared out and floated around her head and face. He thought that this was more like floating weightless in space than being immersed in water. He brushed a hand forward and the movement of the water made her hair undulate gently.

"John, you're supposed to be relaxing."

He grinned at her. "Probably need to close my eyes." He tried that and began the routines that he had been taught. Slowly his body began to feel heavy ... and then his concentration was broken by the discomfort of the water pressure. He opened his eyes and found that he had sunk much deeper into the lake.

Asha had descended with him. "Doesn't seem to be working," she observed.

John could only agree as he began to swim upward again. He wondered why his body had been sinking, from what little he under-stood of buoyancy his body should either be knocking against the ice or finding some appropriate level in the water, even if it was the bottom. For some reason things didn't work that way in this body, and that thought gave him some hope that he could do this thing that Andrei had described. John guessed that his body must already be making some compensations without him realising it.

"What is it I'm trying to do?" he asked Asha, "I still don't really understand."

"You've got to stop resisting the water, you have to let it through. There is life in the water, but there are also spaces for more life, and our bodies can pass through them without pushing the water aside."

"But I'm not resisting anything, I'm just floating here."

"I really don't know how to explain it any better. This is something that we learn as young children, now it just happens automatically. It's how we can dry off so quickly, we just let the water pass through."

"I knew there must be some trick to that," said John. "Do you suppose Ben and the others back at the Samgha can do it?"

"I assume so. As far as I know it's sort of built-in to this form. But maybe they've never had to learn about, or to use it even if they do know about it. They may not think it's important."

"I suppose that's possible."

Asha stared at John for some time, thinking. John looked back at her, simply for the view. A smile grew on her face, turning slowly into a grin. John thought he knew that look, but hadn't expected it now.

"I've had a thought," she said softly.

"So it appears," John answered. "Looks like a good one."

"I think the problem is mostly with the skin. You have to learn to let the water past the barrier that you've built up since separating."

John nodded.

"I was wondering if a wash might help?"

He didn't respond. They were immersed in a lake, how much more of a wash did she want?

"You remember. We've shared a bath a few times at your home, you seemed to enjoy it."

John grinned. "When you're there I do. You like looking at yourself in the mirror, outlined in soap bubbles. I've wanted to take a photo of that, I'd call it *Beautifully Clean*."

Asha grinned back at him, blushing slightly. "It's fun."

"It is," John agreed. More seriously he continued, "But what's that got to do with swimming in a lake?"

"When I wash your hair and shoulders you say it's relaxing."

"Less so when you move lower."

Asha grinned back at him. "I thought we might try that here – the relaxing part anyway. I was thinking the combination of relaxation and having your skin rubbed might do the trick."

"All right. I'll enjoy it even if it doesn't work."

"Take your clothes off," Asha told him.

John looked around, suddenly conscious of how clear the water was.

"It's all right," Asha assured him, "there's no one close. If anyone comes close enough to see what we're up to they'll disappear again, you learn to be discreet when you have no rooms of your own."

John wasn't sure how he felt about that, and he was certain he didn't want Garjae watching them, things were bad enough for him as it was. As John hesitated, Asha's clothes faded from her body. "When you put it like that," John said. He concentrated and his clothes vanished too. He reached out to Asha.

"Give me your back," she demanded.

Reluctantly, John turned. He felt Asha come up behind him.

"It's a shame we don't have a ledge to sit on," she commented.

"And a mirror and some soap," added John.

He stopped talking as he felt her body rub gently against his back, he had to remind himself that he was supposed to be relaxing. Her fingers reached into his hair and started massaging his scalp. He tried to imagine that they were back in his house, immersed in warm soapy water, him leaning back against her as she scrubbed his hair and skin. Asha's fingers moved to the back of his head and neck, massaging deeply, and then slowly moved down to his shoulders and back. John groaned. This really was good. He hadn't thought about becoming stressed and tense in this body, but Asha's fingers were finding knots he didn't know were there, and she was smoothing them out one by one.

It hit like a bucket of cold water. The water swamped through his being, he felt Asha drawn against his back as the water flowed into the space occupied by his body. Moments later the sensation of cold had passed. John floated there stunned.

"It worked!" Asha exclaimed in surprise.

It took John a moment to answer. "Never had any doubt," he said slowly, he was still taking it in.

"I did," Asha admitted. She turned him around by his shoulders to face him, her smile wide. "We did it."

John was still feeling stunned and didn't answer her smile straight away. He waved his hand through the water. He could feel the water passing through it, and he through the water. The closest he could come to describing the sensation to himself was what people called a lazy wind, one that couldn't be bothered going around, that felt like it just swept the cold right through you, though this wasn't cold any longer, or no more than it had been. But that wasn't quite right either. He felt almost like he was floating in the air, but air that he could still feel passing through him. He shook his head, there were no comparisons to an experience like this.

He brushed his hand at Asha's hair and saw just the faintest of undulations result, his hand was not pushing the water, or not very much. He reached forward and touched Asha's hair. It still felt the same to his touch. No, not quite the same. It felt as it would have felt on land, as if it was dry, it didn't have that wet slippery feeling. He moved his hand to her neck and shoulder, it was like touching dry skin. He moved his hand back through her hair again.

"You want to wash my hair?" Asha asked.

John looked up at her face, she was grinning at him, obviously very happy. He grinned back. "The very least I can do, but can you get it wet?"

Asha paused before saying, "I can, but you can't."

"What do you mean?"

"To get wet I have to merge and then draw back out. Here, I'll show you."

John watched as Asha vanished into the water in front of him, and then a few moments later she reappeared. He reached out to her hair. It had that familiar slippery feel, her skin too had that slightly adhesive quality of clean wet skin.

"But you can't merge," Asha said. "It might sound a bit strange, but you'll have to wait until you get out of the water before you can get wet again."

John shrugged and then smiled at her. "Wet or dry, you're still beautiful,"

Asha let the water flow through her, and John's body was drawn against hers. "My hair is clean enough," Asha spoke into his ear, and she wrapped her arms and legs around him to keep him close. One of John's last coherent thoughts was that he had wondered what it would be like to make love in a weightless environment; it turned out to have its difficulties, but it was well worth the effort.

11. Zarana

Most of the next day, and some hours into the following night, John spent with Asha. They were joined for part of it by Andrei and Senna, exploring the water of the region around and beneath the seal den. They saw Darnu and Garjae for a short time, but Garjae was still nursing his injured arm, and he seemed inclined to stay away from Asha in case she insisted on helping him further.

For John it was like learning to swim all over again. Immersed in the water this way felt more like floating in air than water, and he had trouble gaining enough traction to get himself started. With practice he found that once he had made a start it got easier to build his speed, and he soon found it was possible to swim faster than ever before. He still couldn't keep up with the others when they put on speed, Andrei in particular liked to show off, but John was content that he could accompany them wherever they ended up going in this huge lake.

In the upper levels of the lake, during the day, John could see a long way through the clear water. Sometimes he saw shoals of salmon-like fish that he would later learn were called omul, dark on top but with silver sides. As they got deeper the light slowly diminished and his vedana began to take over, but he could no longer see or sense so far; the abundant life of the lake threw up a haze, like shining a torch into fog.

As they got deeper still they came across strange pale, translucent fish, called golomyanka. They met the fish mostly as individuals or occasional small loose groups, but the fish began to follow them, congregating around Asha, at times nudging at her. The four of them spent a lot of time floating in the depths playing with these curious fish. Most were less than twenty centimetres or so in length, the front of their bodies slightly bulbous while the tail was long and slender. They had long delicate pectoral fins, barely visible, like dragonfly wings; similar delicate fins rose in vertical lines along the narrow latter half of the body. Their heads narrowed into flattened, pointed snouts, and most strangely of all, to John's mind, was that they didn't appear to have any scales. At first John thought they were quite ugly, but as they spent more time with them, the fish insinuated themselves on his affections. They had a charm of their own, even individual personalities.

Night fell far above them and the movement of the golomyanka tended upwards, so John and the others followed them.

"She's coming!" Senna called.

John looked across and then followed Senna's gaze upward. A few moments later a seal appeared through the haze, dark and round, her stumpy torpedo shape belied her speed and agility in the water. The fish around them scattered. The seal turned, she was hunting the fish. John was starting to regret his growing affection for the golomyanka, since it appeared that at least some were destined to become dinner for the seal.

"Do you suppose she's moved the pups back?" Senna asked.

"Let's go look," Andrei said.

"I don't want to drive her away again."

"She's hunting, she'll be busy for a while."

So they swam back up to the ice and found the den. The pups were back, sleeping. They watched them for a short time and then left them alone, resisting the temptation to touch them.

Asha drew John away from Andrei and Senna.

"I want to feed you again," she told him. When John started to object Asha explained that it would be easier if they did it regularly, she wouldn't have to give so much at a time. "And anyway, the stronger we keep you the better prepared we'll be."

"For what?"

"For whatever. It's not like we predicted what was going to happen up in the cold."

Eventually John agreed. The experience overwhelmed John again, even doing it while floating in the water was not enough to distract him from the intensity of it. When it was over he looked around, the tiny life inhabiting the water had formed a dense cloud around them, and through that cloud poked the occasional curious golomyanka.

"We've a fan club," he observed to Asha.

Asha glanced around them. "Life attracts life," she said.

Despite having given up less of herself this time Asha was still tired, so she started to move away to merge with the water.

"Why do you move away so far?" John asked after her.

"I draw heavily on the life of the water, I worry I might damage you or the other creatures we've attracted. I try to keep moving to spread the impact." With that she faded into the water. Her presence moved away and John floated there in the water wondering what to do with himself.

He had been awake for hours and knew he should probably sleep, but the fire was still burning through his body and he felt restless. He looked around, fidgety, and realised that it all looked much the same to him. If he moved from this spot he would probably get lost. The others seemed to always know where they were, he wondered if that was another trick he could learn. His restlessness was partly fed by the thought of trying to sleep suspended in the water. It should be easy, the ultimate waterbed, but the freedom of it felt alien and he wasn't sure how he would manage.

To distract himself, and for something to fill the time while he waited for Asha, he picked out a pattern in the ice above him that he thought he would recognise again and swam down a short distance. He swam back up, checked he was right, and then swam down further; if nothing else the practise would do him good. After one extended trip it took him a while to find his place again and he was more careful after that. Casseta came back to him during one of these dives, she had spent a lot of time away, apparently exploring this new world for herself.

Asha reappeared out of the haze of life that surrounded him. "I thought you might be asleep," she commented.

"Not sure I know how to."

"It is a bit strange. We aaranya much prefer the snugness of our trees."

"Which means you normally sleep merged?"

Asha nodded. "But for preference I'll sleep wherever you are."

They ended up falling asleep still holding each other. When John woke later they were still joined gently by their finger tips.

They spent the new day in much the same way as the previous. John was slowly getting used to inhabiting this new world. The following day Darnu and Garjae approached with a group of strangers, the jalaja had returned.

"This is Novoi, Platov, Yeleney, Stasia and Yurim," Darnu introduced them.

The jalaja were mostly shorter than the aaranya, but broad shouldered and stockily built with wide, slightly flattened features. John had thought the aaranya were at home in the water, but the jalaja moved even more smoothly and easily, as if the water itself was obeying them. Their clothing was loose and billowy, often exaggerating their stocky appearance, but never inhibiting their agility in the water. Their hands and feet were large, perhaps, but John couldn't discern any webbing or other adaptations to their environment. He didn't know what he had expected, but such an ordinary, and to John's mind, human appearance was a surprise.

"Are you well enough to travel now?" Novoi asked. His tone neither particularly friendly nor otherwise. John wasn't sure how to interpret it, were they welcome or not?

"Garjae?" Asha asked.

Garjae stretched out his injured arm and flexed it. "I'll be fine."

Novoi stared with surprise at the arm. He turned to Asha with a look of respect. "Ulvanya wishes to meet you."

"Ulvanya," Asha tried out the name, "is that your healer?"

Novoi nodded. "She asked us to bring you to her."

"She knew we were coming?" John asked.

Novoi turned and studied him carefully. John got the impression Novoi didn't like much of what he saw. "She was told," Novoi said to him and then turned back to Asha. "Will you come?"

"It is why we came," Asha answered.

Novoi nodded and turned to lead the way. The other jalaja swam loosely back amid the aaranya. The jalaja were forced to reduce their speed to allow for John's lesser skill in the water. Novoi showed some impatience with this, but the others, especially the much younger Stasia and Yurim, seemed pleased that the slower pace would make it easier to converse with the strangers.

John heard Stasia ask Senna, "You are aaranya?" Stasia's face was round with wide innocent looking eyes, her hair a mass of dark curls.

"We are," answered Senna.

"He's not," Yurim stated. John didn't have to turn to know the young jalaja meant him. Yurim looked to be much the same age as Stasia, both of them younger than Andrei and Senna. Yurim's expression was one of self-importance, and John guessed he was feeling privileged to have been included on this expedition, and in that he reminded John of Beenae back at Asha's Glade.

"John's a bit complicated, wouldn't you say, John?" Andrei spoke across to John, making it obvious to Yurim that John would have heard.

John glanced across and saw Yurim looking back at him with a forced boldness. "That's probably a good way to put it." He had to turn his attention forward again quickly, he couldn't keep up the pace and look around as the others were managing. This was just as well anyway, because he didn't want Yurim to see him chuckling at the young jalaja's expression.

"What are y—?" Yurim started, but Stasia interrupted.

"Where are you from?"

"Australia," Senna told her.

"Where's that?"

"Somewhere a lot warmer than here," said Andrei with feeling.

The conversation progressed with Andrei and Senna trying to explain where Australia was and how different it was to this place. Stasia and Yurim were astonished to learn that Andrei and Senna could read and write. Yurim, forgetting his self-importance, begged Andrei to tell him more of the shape of the world and what they had seen. John smiled to himself as he heard Andrei reciting what he had learned from his time on the Internet.

Novoi continued to lead the way ahead of the others. Platov and Yeleney swam with Darnu and Garjae, occasionally looking back to see where John and Asha and the others were and, John suspected, sometimes just to get a better look at John or Asha.

Their progress took them gradually deeper and deeper into the lake. There was a slow change in John's perceptions as they descended, the life that filled the water around them took on a new clarity and brilliance, and colours slowly emerged as if the creatures they passed were glowing from within. Even the little golomyanka took on subtle colours that had not been apparent earlier. Asha explained that this was because his normal sight was less use now, and so his vedana was taking over, filling in the details with its own interpretation of the world around them. The effect was beautiful, if rather disconcerting because the colours, though muted, looked slightly surreal. Even the narun around him appeared to glow, particularly their eyes. The effect was subtle, only apparent when he looked for it, but it was consistent enough that he didn't think it was his imagination.

They reached the bottom of the lake, a vast flat plain of sediment that had been dropped over the millennia. Up through it reached the occasional peak, like the tops of mountains, leading John to wonder what secrets might lie beneath the vast layer of debris. When they reached a group of peaks, huddled together like children sharing secrets, Novoi stopped and told the group they would rest here for the night.

"How much further?" Darnu asked.

"Day after tomorrow," Novoi answered. He looked to Garjae. "Will you be all right to travel again tomorrow?"

John thought Garjae looked to be in pain, but he nodded.

"And you?" Novoi looked to John.

"After a rest I should be fine," John told him.

The older narun disbursed to merge with the water. Stasia and Yurim still had more they wanted to learn from Andrei and Senna, so John and Asha left them to it and wandered among the small peaks. There were fish even at this great depth, and also some long flatworms, tiny crustaceans, and many stranger creatures. There were growths of various sorts over the peaks, in some cases they looked to John's vedana like colourful summer garden displays.

Asha tugged on his arm and pointed: a couple of very bright creatures were chasing each other back and forth through the valleys. They looked to John like small seals, but glowing with a shining mauve colour that made them look more like toy-store animals than real creatures. "Spret," Asha told him, "or whatever the jalaja call them down here."

John watched them for a minute but found his concentration slipping.

"You're tired," Asha observed.

John nodded. "I was glad Novoi stopped when he did, I don't think I could have gone on much longer."

"Let's top you up ready for tomorrow."

"You must be tired too."

"Yes, but I can merge to help me recover. Come on."

Asha led him further from the others, and again she fed her life to him. After that she merged for a few hours, waking John briefly as she swam back to hold him through the night.

The next day was much the same, though this time Platov, Yeleney, Darnu and Garjae dropped back to swim more with John and Asha. Platov and Yeleney were curious about John and Asha, but more reluctant than the younger jalaja to show it. Novoi remained ahead, setting and keeping the pace and remaining aloof from the group.

"Will you be taking us into your Glade?" Asha asked Platov.

"Our zarana, yes, we must."

"That's quite an honour."

Platov glanced across at Asha. "Your Glade is a sacred place?"

"To the people of our stand, yes, obviously. But I was more thinking that we were aaranya. Back home, your people and mine do not mix."

"You are enemies?"

"No, nothing like that. We just don't spend time together."

"It is different here," Yeleney put in. "Different even for jalaja. In the past lots of people came to see Ulvanya: aaranya, jalaja, even yaayaavara. She accepts all, so of course we must accept all."

Novoi had been listening, he slowed to close the distance between them. "It is different for the jalaja anyway. Most jalaja never have a zarana, what you call a Glade. Only in very large lakes are there ever enough people for one to form, and most lakes don't live very long, not like this one. So we see our zarana differently from how you see your Glade."

"Is it not your home?" Asha called ahead to Novoi.

Novoi slowed again until he was part of their group. "Not in the same way that the Glade is yours. Our people are used to a mostly solitary life, if the zarana were not there we would continue."

John thought the words were spoken with thinly disguised disdain, Novoi apparently thought their way of life superior to the aaranya. Asha didn't respond.

John asked Yeleney, "You said there were lots of people in the past, do you not get so many now?"

"Ulvanya is very old now, not many people remember her or think she is still alive. In the last few years there have been very few, and none from the east."

Asha and John shared a look, both thinking of what they'd heard of Glades going silent.

That night Asha was moody, and John asked her what was wrong.

She gave him a strange look that he couldn't interpret. "You're going to think I'm silly," she told him.

"What is it?"

"It's just ... you're going to see their Glade tomorrow, their zarana."

"Yes. I'm sort of nervous about it. I've only ever seen the outside of yours, and that was strange enough, out of this world enough, to leave me wondering what it must be like. I never expected to enter one. What's the problem?" When Asha didn't answer straight away he asked, "Do you think I mightn't be able to go through?"

Asha shook her head. "That's not it."

"Then what? You've never really spoken of what it's like inside your Glade. Is there something I should be worried about?"

"Nothing like that. I've never wanted to talk about it because I knew you couldn't go in. But I've dreamt of taking you. ... I always thought ..."

"What?"

"I always thought it would be my Glade that you would see. Now, tomorrow, you will see a Glade, but it won't be mine. You'll never see mine and it doesn't seem fair," Asha finished quickly.

"Maybe I could do a deal with Ben," John suggested.

"No! Once you're back in your proper body I don't want you tearing it apart again. It's not right. It's dangerous, and I don't trust Ben."

"But to see your home, even just the once?"

"No. I'm just being silly, I'll get over it."

John pulled her close and held her. "Do you want to tell me about your home before I see the zarana tomorrow?"

Asha shook her head against his shoulder.

"Are all Glades, all zarana, the same?"

"No. A Glade forms around the people and the place where they live, it takes on a form that ... that matches them somehow. They can be very different, even those Glades closest to ours feel very different to my home."

"So you don't know what to expect tomorrow either?"

Asha pulled back to look at him. "I guess not."

"I'd love to see your home if I could, Asha."

"You've seen my forest, you've lived in my forest, that's enough. That's got to be enough."

- - -

Tracey woke slowly. The first sensations were pain. Her face and hands in particular, but also patches on her legs, her back, and the back of her head, all reported hot stinging, burning distress, but strangely muted. Every breath she took felt like she was sucking on sand. The next sensations to fight their way through to her attention were the smells: a subdued smell of something unfamiliar, a musky, thick odour, and beyond that the antiseptic smells of ... a hospital. She was in hospital? She could feel the comforting cool of the sheets on her skin. She tried to remember how she came to be in hospital, but everything was foggy and vague.

And then she heard voices. She hadn't opened her eyes yet, but she recognised the speakers.

"The fireman told me she was very lucky," her mother was saying in tones that suggested this had been repeated many times. "The worst of the fire went high into those huge trees very quickly, drawn up by the wind and heat, he said, and she was only on the edge, the wind took the worst of the fire away from her."

Tracey remembered the fire. Sheltering in the car with Tilvy and Beenae. She remembered the tortuous heat and choking on the fumes as her car melted around her. Where were her friends? Had they survived?

"Are the burns very bad?" asked a man's voice. It was Jason.

"It looks worse than it is, the doctors say. She is dehydrated and has some nasty scorches, but most of it's like a severe sunburn. The fireman said it was miraculous. Not many people survive a bushfire in their cars, let alone come through it so well. But I told him that Tracey was well prepared, she knew what to do and I made sure she had woollen blankets. The fireman said they probably saved her life, those and managing to get out of the car when the worst of the fire had passed."

Tracey tried to remember getting out of the car, but couldn't. The last thing she remembered was huddling down in the car, scared out of her mind, with Tilvy's hand squeezing hers. Had she managed to get out on her own?

"Do you know any more about what happened? I mean, how did she get caught in it in the first place?"

"I don't know."

"She still hasn't woken?"

Jason sounded surprised and concerned, Tracey began to wonder how long she'd been asleep.

"She's stirred a few times, and said a few words, but nothing very sensible and it hasn't lasted long."

Tracey didn't remember any of that.

"But the doctors don't seem concerned," her mother continued, "they said her body is still recovering from the shock."

"I saw police out there, Tracey's not in trouble is she?"

"No ... no." Her mother didn't sound certain.

"It was a strange fire, and not the only one," Jason said, "but they've not given much detail on the news. I tried to get up to see John's house, to see how much is left of it, but there's a roadblock and they wouldn't let me past."

"What did John say? Is he coming back now?" Tracey's mother asked.

"I can't reach him," Jason explained, the frustration obvious in his voice. "I've sent him emails about it, but that's all I can do, and I still don't know if he got them."

"Mum," Tracey tried to speak, it came out as a rough gasp.

"Tracey. Sweetheart." Her mother's voice a combination of surprise, relief and concern.

Tracey tried to open her eyes, they felt as if they were glued closed.

"I'll leave you to it," Tracey heard Jason say quietly, and a moment later the sound of a door opening and closing.

At last Tracey's eyes opened, she could feel some sticky substance on her eyelids making them feel strange, unnatural. The bright light of the room hurt her eyes and she blinked slowly a few times until they adjusted. Everything was still hazy, but she could see her mother leaning forward, watching her with love and concern.

"Mum," Tracey whispered.

"Sweetheart," her mother said again. Tracey couldn't see clearly enough, but she could hear that her mother was close to tears.

Tracey wanted to say something but couldn't find the words.

"You're all right now, sweetheart," her mother assured her. "You'll be up and around soon and I can take you home."

Tracey tried to smile but her face felt stiff, as if her skin had gone hard and brittle.

The next days passed slowly for Tracey, her thoughts often returning to her friends, and wondering what had become of them. The doctors assured Tracey that she was healing quickly and there should be no scars on her face, though there may be some scarring on her hands and a few spots on her legs where she had been scorched, probably when she got out of the car – something that Tracey still couldn't remember. The skin on her face and hands started to peel and that quickly expanded up her arms and into her scalp and down her neck; it looked dreadful and trying not to scratch at the itchy new skin was frustrating.

By Friday she could get up and get around on her own, still stiff and sore in many places but otherwise feeling much better. In the small wardrobe of her hospital room she found a large plastic bag that contained the few belongings that had been saved from the fire. Her clothes, her mother told her, had been discarded.

Tracey rummaged around in the plastic bag to see what was there. She found her phone and tried to turn it on, but it didn't respond, not even a flicker. She dropped it back in and pulled out her handbag and rummaged around in the accumulated rubbish, remembering that she'd been intending to have a good clean-out. She noticed a folded piece of paper that she didn't recognise and pulled it out to take a look. The paper was brown and brittle as if it had been held too close to a flame, though the rest of the contents of the handbag seemed okay.

She took it all back to her bed and sat down to study the paper. She unfolded it carefully and recognised Tilvy's writing inside, the pencil scratchings were smudged and not easy to read against the browned paper.

I know what your first question will be, Tilvy had written, *so here's the answer: We are both okay – singed in places, but nothing that won't heal. Thanks to you – you saved our lives! We got you out of the car after the worst had passed, but I don't know if we were in time. I can only hope so. There's still fire burning in the trees around us, so we're still using the blankets and we will stay here with you until someone comes. I can't think of anything else we can do to help you – if only Asha was here. You know where we have to go from here, after that I don't know what. I can hear a truck coming, hopefully it's someone that can help you. I hope you will be okay and I hope you find this. Best of luck my dearest friend. love T.*

Tracey felt her shoulders relaxing, at last she knew that Tilvy had survived. She studied the short message again. The last part of the message had obviously been written in a hurry. Tracey wondered when and how they might arrange to meet up again, there was so much she wanted to know.

There was the sound of a throat clearing. Tracey looked up and saw a stranger standing in the doorway, he was watching her. Without looking down she folded the paper hurriedly and fumbled with her bag, trying to put the paper away.

"Up to answering a few questions?" the man asked her.

Tracey's fingers froze at the opening of her bag. "Who are you?" she asked him.

The man walked into the room, the door closing softly behind him. He was a tall man, solidly built, but not fat, with an erect bearing. He wore a dark suit that looked a little tight on him. He had close-cropped greying hair and a steady gaze that watched her closely as he approached.

"Don't you know how to knock?" Tracey asked, feeling suddenly exposed and vulnerable in her flimsy hospital gown. She pushed the note into her bag and pulled the sheet over her legs and up as high as it would go. She glanced to the side looking for a call button.

"Relax," the man said quietly. "I'm with the police. Name's Raymond Cleaver."

He held out an open wallet. Tracey glanced at it, but only had time to notice the photo and something about Australian Security before the man flipped it closed again. He sat on the end of the bed.

"The doctors tell me you're doing well," the man said.

"What do you want?"

"We've some questions about the fire."

Tracey nodded cautiously, she didn't know what to think or say.

"What were you doing there?"

"I check on the house for the owner."

"John Caldor?"

Tracey nodded.

"You were in something of a hurry to get there on Saturday weren't you?" There was a faint smile on the man's face, as if he found all this amusing.

Tracey looked back at him, not understanding.

"The speeding ticket," he reminded her. "If you'd driven a bit more slowly you might have avoided all this trouble."

Tracey hesitated before asking, "Should I have a lawyer or something?" As soon as the words were out she cursed herself for sounding so defensive.

"That's certainly your right," the man said agreeably. "But these are just a few friendly questions. You're a witness to an unusual fire, that's all. You're not under arrest. You're not obliged to talk to me, not now."

"I can just tell you to go?"

The man nodded. "If you want, but I'd rather if you could help me understand what happened, how the fire started."

"I didn't light it." Again with the defensive tones.

"I'm not saying you did," Cleaver assured her reasonably. "Let's start at the beginning. Who was with you?"

"No one. I was on my own." Tracey couldn't stop her eyes glancing down to her bag.

When she looked up the man was still watching her steadily, though his posture was relaxed and his expression friendly. He asked, "And what time did you arrive at the house?"

Tracey answered this as accurately as she could, only to stumble when the man wanted to know what she had been doing with her time, since she had also told him that she had not entered the house. Even to her own ears her mumbled, "Just looking around," sounded lame.

The man nodded agreeably, apparently not perturbed by her answer. "And tell me about the fire itself. How did it start?"

Tracey told him what she could of the explosions she had seen.

"And you don't know what caused them?"

Tracey shook her head.

"And what happened next?"

Tracey told him as much as she could remember of trying to hide from the fire in her car.

"And you didn't see or speak with anyone else?"

"No," Tracey said as firmly as she could.

The man then asked her a few questions about her relationship with John, and whether she knew how to contact him. Again he accepted her vague answers as if there was nothing odd about them.

There was silence for a few moments, then the man asked, "Is there anything else you want to tell me?"

Tracey shook her head.

The man stood up, he hadn't even waited for Tracey's response, not expecting anything more.

"That's it?" Tracey asked, not quite believing it.

"Like I said," Cleaver confirmed, "just a few friendly questions."

"So what happened? What were those explosions?"

"Don't know," he answered, "still looking into that. We may have a few more questions for you later."

"Oh."

Raymond Cleaver paused at the door and looked back. "Good to see you're doing well, Tracey. Anyone that's been there and seen what happened are amazed that you've come through this so well. You're a lucky young woman." He nodded at her. "We'll be in touch." Then he slipped through the door and was gone.

- - -

The next day, about midday according to Asha, although from this depth John had no idea how she knew, they approached the zarana. From the distance it appeared to John as simply a brighter spot shining through the haze of life that filled the waters, it was glistening like a reflection of moonlight from some distant object. As they got closer the spot grew until it rippled before them like a great waterfall of mercury, constantly moving, five or six metres high and at least that wide.

John could see nothing beyond this dark silvery sheen. Peaks emerged from the sediment on either side, massive supports that appeared to support the surface draped loosely between them. The peaks were covered in a mass of brightly coloured plants. Beneath the rippling surface, in front of the group, was a thick layer of inter-twined growths and over those plants swam many creatures, some were familiar, like the golomyanka, others were very strange; so many almost random shapes and colours that he had trouble picking out individuals. John also had trouble picking which were material beings and which were spret, but every now and then there would be an extra ripple as one of the spret disappeared into, or emerged from, the zarana.

"Gaudy," Andrei commented quietly.

"It's amazing," murmured Asha. "Like it has spilled out into the lake."

John looked around at the others. Everyone had stopped to take in the scene, even the jalaja. Despite Novoi's earlier dismissal, it seemed that even he held this place with some reverence.

Novoi, as if feeling John's attention, turned to him and then turned back and swam on until he disappeared into the glistening expanse. A ripple rolled out from his point of entry but was quickly lost amid the constant movement of the surface.

"Was that our invitation?" Andrei wanted to know.

"Of course," said Stasia. "Come on."

The others followed her lead, disappearing with overlapping ripples, but John held back with Asha.

"This is it," John said.

"This is where we find our answers," Asha replied.

Still John hesitated. Before him was a way into another world. The aaranya called this entrance simply the Way, the jalaja called it the tiirtha, but to him it was like some last bastion between the existence he once accepted as solid and certain and predictable, and his new, constantly changing and surprising existence as part of the world of the narun.

So far, despite managing to separate from his flesh-and-blood body, he had remained part of the world he thought of as real, the world he knew. When he went through the Way, according to Andrei, he would enter a place that wasn't part of this world. It wasn't there, hidden in some space behind that glistening, silvery surface. The zarana was somewhere else, part of some other dimension or some other existence. He knew the words, as a child he had read science-fiction stories like most other boys, but when it came right down to it phrases like *other dimension* had little meaning. What must happen, what would happen to him, when he passed through that interface?

"My love?" Asha's compassionate voice broke through his thoughts.

He turned to her.

"Are you ready?"

He nodded.

Asha took his hand and together they approached the Way. He touched it first with the finger tips of his free hand, it was like touching the surface of some viscous liquid, then their momentum carried them on and he felt the pressure of the surface run over his arm, his head, and on down his body. There was no other sensation, no sight, it didn't even register as blackness, just void. There was no sound or smell or sense of passing through anything, just the faint pressure of the surface as it continued along his legs. The surface passed over his bare feet, and then there was nothing for some immeasurable time, only the reassuring touch of Asha's hand in his. Then, in a feeling like déjà vu, he felt the surface of the Way run over his outstretched arm. His head emerged and everything came back at once, his senses all working again as if they had been switched back on. He felt the surface of the Way run down his body again as the rest of him passed out from the surface.

He blinked. At first he thought it must not have worked because it all looked the same to him. He thought he must have passed straight through and on into the lake on the other side, just as Andrei had told him would happen at their Glade had he tried to go through the Way in his human body. He looked down at his hand still holding Asha's, and then along her arm until he came to her face. She was smiling at him.

"You made it," she told him.

In surprise John turned back. Yes. Yes, it was different. The cloud of tiny creatures that had filled the water outside had gone. This water was clear and he could see a long way, as if his normal sight had returned and the sun had come out somewhere far above the water. He saw that there were creatures in this water, some that looked mostly like fish, and he saw a couple of the shining mauve coloured seals, and in the distance there were others, some quite large, but he couldn't make out what they were.

"It's so much the same," said John.

Asha smiled at him. "You're disappointed?"

"I didn't know what to expect, but I thought it would be more ... different."

"It's a place that comes into existence for its people. It's like its own version of the world outside. Give it time, you will see that it *is* different."

"You two coming?" Andrei called to them.

The others were all swimming upwards, Andrei had turned back to see what was keeping John and Asha.

"Come on," Asha said gently, "let's see some more."

They started swimming up after the others. John looked down to where they'd come from: the Way looked much the same as it had on the outside, and the peaks on either side looked similar too, though between them was a wall that passed behind the rippling surface, there was no other side to it from here. It looked like they had come through solid rock to emerge from that interface.

John turned his attention back to the approaching surface, this water was apparently not as deep as the lake outside. Looking forward rather than up, the water continued beneath a dark shadow. It wasn't until they broke the surface and John saw the shore that he understood, they were swimming near a huge floating island.

He blinked in the brightness and looked up, the sun was shining brightly. The choppy waves made speaking awkward so he concentrated on his swimming and put his questions aside for now. He and Asha followed the others along the line of the shore and eventually into a small inlet that became a gently flowing river. The banks on either side were overgrown with grass of a faded green. Further up the banks were occasional groves of trees, they looked to be spruce and pine and cedar like the forests around the lake outside, but these were standing tall and green in the full flush of spring. Bright flowers grew amid the grass and in clumps beneath the trees. In the distance ahead of them the land rose and John could see rolling hills rising into more substantial peaks.

"You're right," John told Asha. "It is different. It's impossible for a start," he said, thinking of seeing the water stretching beneath this land.

"You're not going to start that again?" asked Andrei, swimming sidestroke as he grinned back at John and Asha.

"I'm not saying I don't believe it, I'm just saying it's not possible."

"You wanted different," Asha reminded John.

"You don't have a zarana?" Yurim asked from ahead of Andrei. His movement through the water looked effortless.

"No," John answered.

Yurim turned to say something to Stasia, John thought he heard the word "yaayaavara," the nomads of the narun. John didn't correct him, explanations could come later.

They followed the river for some distance as it wound among the hills, John was wishing they could get out and walk, this swimming upstream was exhausting him. At last they did just that. Novoi swam to the side and then walked up onto the firm flat mud near the bank and started to follow a small stream that flowed into the river.

John walked out of the river, and then stopped and leaned over, resting his hands on his knees.

"Are you okay?" Asha asked him.

"Just glad to be done swimming," he answered and stood straight again. He looked at Asha and then down at himself: he was dry, totally dry, he had emerged from the river dry. He knelt down next to the clear water of the stream and ran his hand through it, then lifted it out and stared at it. "And I can get wet again," he commented, noting the water sticking to his skin. Whatever the change had been in the lake, his body had reverted automatically when he emerged from the river.

"With practice you will be able to pick and choose," Asha told him. She knelt down next to him and ran her hand through the water, it came up wet. She did it again and it came up dry, the water barely disturbed by the passing of her hand.

John didn't remind her that he would probably never get the chance to practice, he would be returning to his human body soon. He looked up, the others were disappearing between the hills as they followed the stream. "We'd better try to keep up."

The streambed turned to loose stones as they got away from the river, so they walked along the bank on one side. The grass beneath their feet was short and even, though it got longer further up the bank and onto the hills on either side.

"Are there animals here ... I mean spret like cows or horses or something that eat this grass?" John wanted to know.

Asha looked around. "I doubt it. The creatures of a Glade are usually quite small, though this place had many in the water, more than I've seen elsewhere, and some of those were quite large. They're not all spret. Spret are creatures of the outside world, and they come and go from the Glade as they please. There are creatures of the Glade, we call them pazuka, although I imagine the jalaja have their own name for them. You've met the brevi, they're very special, they are of the Glade but can come and go with us. These others are part of the Glade and remain within it." Asha pointed to some bees hovering over a patch of daisy-like flowers. "Those bees are pazuka."

"We call them sarasa," Stasia said from above them. "The creatures like fish in the water we call matsya."

They looked up and saw Stasia and Senna standing on the hill above them, Andrei and Yurim were coming up behind.

"We thought you'd gotten lost," Andrei told them. "Taking time to sniff the flowers?"

"It's a new world for me, Andrei," John replied. "It takes some getting used to."

"Do we have far to go?" Asha asked.

"We're there already," said Andrei, "as you'd know if you'd kept up."

The four of them came down to John and Asha, and they all followed the stream around another bend between the hills. The valley opened wider, its floor rising in a gentle slope before them. The stream took a winding rocky path up the first part of the valley, and trees stood in groups on the grassy land on either side of it. The stream flowed from a small, tranquil lake in the centre of this wider valley. Beyond the lake the stream came down from the hills beyond. There were poplar trees, or something very like them, and some sort of pine, and there were others that John couldn't guess at. Two large willow trees hung over the left side of the lake. It seemed a strange and unlikely setting, but it was calm and peaceful, just the gentle burbling of the stream flowing over the rocks distilled the quiet.

Novoi, Darnu and the others stood on a clear patch of grass not far from the willow trees. The group came together with their attention centred on Novoi. Novoi said nothing, just turned and looked to the lake. The others turned and watched too.

For some moments there was nothing, then in the water just beyond the space between the two willow trees there was movement. The water rose and then fell back revealing a young beautiful face, her eyes large and dark, her long hair, black and shiny with water, lay flat against her head. She came forward slowly, leaning on a wooden staff. As she stepped toward the shore she rose out from the water, her flimsy robe clung to her body revealing ripe ample breasts, an impossibly narrow waist and then large rounded hips and thighs. At last she stood on the edge of the lake before them, the water dripping from her gown, her gaze surveying her audience solemnly.

John stared at her, unsure what to make of her. Was this their elderly healer?

"Wow!" said Andrei, and then, "Ouch," which John guessed was the result of another jab in the ribs from Senna.

The woman concentrated her gaze on Andrei, and then her solemn expression dissolved into a bright smile. The woman's form became indistinct, John blinked, feeling as though his eyes were not focusing. The water that had been clinging to her dropped to the ground with a quiet splash. When the woman's form slowly clarified, before them stood an old woman that appeared to have shrunk to the point of emaciation. Her dry gown no longer looked so flimsy, and it fell away to the ground as if there were little left beneath the still square shoulders that supported it. What little hair she had left was short and pale grey. So much changed, and yet her eyes kept their dark sparkle, large and young inside a face now grey and wrinkled.

"It is good to see I can still make an impression on the young," she said with a chuckle, her eyes on Andrei.

"Double wow," he replied. "They do say first impressions are important."

"Yes, I have heard that," she answered. "Did I make a good first impression?"

Andrei glanced at Senna standing beside him and then looked back to the old woman. "Do I have to answer that now?"

The woman laughed. Despite a voice that sounded as old and frail as the woman that now appeared before them, John thought it was a young laugh. She continued, "Stesha was right about you, a young man of great courage and resource."

The woman turned her attention to Senna, her expression now serious. "He is worth the effort ... and so are you I see." Her steady gaze moved to Darnu. She stared at him in silence for a few moments before saying, "Yours is a pain I cannot heal, I am sorry."

John looked at Darnu in surprise. Darnu's eyes had dropped to the ground, he said nothing.

When John looked back at the old woman she was watching Garjae, who glared back at her, as if daring her to say anything. John thought he detected a faint shake of her head before she moved on to John.

John could see that her eyes were a deep dark blue, like the depths of the lake outside. Her direct gaze felt like an interrogation and he wondered what she could see.

"Yes, Stesha, here is our human."

There was a gasp from Stasia, and a cut off sound came from Yurim.

John nodded to the woman.

"You seek help for your daughter."

It wasn't a question, but John nodded anyway.

The woman didn't say anything more to him, her gaze moved on to Asha. John felt Asha tense next to him as she accepted the woman's scrutiny.

The old woman hobbled forward, leaning heavily on her staff, and John realised how small this woman was. After peering up into

Asha's face the old woman went around and looked her over from the side and from behind. As she hobbled back around to face Asha again she was muttering, "Daiva, you say, Stesha. Are you sure? There's not much to her." The woman reached out and squeezed one of Asha's arms and then reached up and turned Asha's head from side to side.

Asha submitted, returning the woman's gaze calmly.

"Proud, I see. ... And stubborn. That much is good, she'll need that. A temper too, but that's not a bad thing if she can channel it." The old woman glanced toward John and then stared back at Asha again. "Passionate, but that much is obvious, she wouldn't be a true healer without passion. She must be careful though, let it go the wrong way and her talents will go with it. What was that, Stesha? Yes, yes, of course."

The old woman stepped back. "Stesha says you are a healer."

"I have healed some injuries," Asha replied cautiously.

"Show me," the old woman said.

Asha stared back at her in surprise and question, but the old woman turned to look along the line of visitors. Her eyes rested on Andrei. "Come here," she told him, and indicated that he should stand to one side between her and Asha.

Andrei came forward looking a little nervous. "There's nothing wrong with me," he said.

The old woman ignored him. One hand was still holding the staff, leaning on it, with her free hand she reached out and pulled one of Andrei's arms up between her and Asha. "Hold it there." Andrei obeyed. The woman released her grip on his arm and moved her fingers across his forearm, his skin split open and golden liquid prana began to spill out.

"Ow!" Andrei complained

The old woman held up her hand, indicating he should be quiet. Looking up at Asha she demanded, "Heal it." Asha glared back at her angrily. The woman just pointed to the wound she had made.

Asha glanced at Andrei in apology and then concentrated on his arm. She reached the fingers of both hands forward and John saw a look of deep concentration form on her face. Her fingers ran lightly back and forth along the cut, running through the liquid prana still spilling from the wound. It was difficult to be certain, but John thought he could also see a stronger golden colour emanating from the region of her finger tips, like the beam he was now familiar with when Asha fed her life to him. Slowly the wound began to close, up from the bottom and in from the ends. At last the final small opening closed over, all that was left was the prana that had bled out onto the skin, and that was quickly evaporating in a golden haze.

Asha held her fingers up before the old woman in accusation, their tips still golden with the prana from Andrei's wound. "That wasn't necessary," she told her.

"It was," the old woman returned simply. "A healer must learn, and the only way she can learn is to heal."

"What did I learn that time?"

"You? You didn't learn anything. That was for me. I learned that you are wasteful. Do you think your body is a never ending source of life? You must spare it. ... What was that Stesha? ... Yes, yes, I know that she shows great power, but what use is such sacrifice if it leaves her too weak to help those that need it? She must be conservative." The woman looked up at Asha. "I'm tired. Come back tomorrow and we will see how much you can learn." The old woman turned and began to make her way back to the lake.

"But—?" John called after her.

The old woman paused and turned back to look at him. "Your daughter?"

"It's why we came."

"Is it?"

John nodded.

The woman paused, frowning, and then said, "Stesha doesn't want to talk about it now. Tomorrow. We will talk tomorrow."

They watched as the woman hobbled back to the lake and slowly disappeared into the water.

John turned to Novoi. "That was the healer?"

Novoi answered curtly, "Yes, that was Ulvanya."

"Then who is Stesha?"

"Ulvanya will tell you if she wants you to know."

Senna had come up to Andrei and was studying his arm. "Is it all right?"

"Sure," he said. "Asha does fine work." He grinned at Asha and held his arm up. "See, nary a scar."

"I'm sorry, Andrei, I had no idea."

"It's fine. I won't say it didn't hurt, but it wasn't that bad. Cutting people open seems a strange occupation for a healer though."

"What do we do now?" Garjae wanted to know.

"Relax, explore," suggested Novoi. "Come back here at sunrise, Ulvanya prefers the mornings. I'm going back to the river." He walked off without a backward glance.

"He doesn't exactly invite conversation, does he?" observed Andrei.

Platov and Yeleney led the group up the valley past the lake and up onto the hills beyond. They found a hilltop, bare except for short grey-green grass, and settled down to rest and talk.

"Did Ulvanya really look like that when she was young?" Andrei wanted to know.

"I do not know," Platov said. "Seems like she's always been old."

Yeleney nodded her agreement. "Grandfather told me she was very beautiful, but she wasn't young, even when he knew her."

"She is an elder then?" Garjae asked.

It took some discussion to clarify what was meant, the jalaja had no elders as the aaranya knew them.

"I do not know," admitted Platov. "It has been a long time since she left the Glade, but I just thought it was because she was no longer very strong."

John looked out over the hills. To the west the sun was low, in the distance its rays were glinting off the water of the lake or sea from which they had come. To the north and south he could see rolling hills, some with small forests or clumps of trees, others bare grass like their own. From this vantage he could see a network of rivers winding among the hills. To the east the hills climbed toward low craggy peaks with what looked like snow lying in patches amid the rocks. He rubbed his eyes, trying to clear his vision, but when he looked again everything was just the same.

"What's wrong, John?" Andrei asked.

"It's so big ... and real looking."

"It is real. It's a bit open for my tastes, and their trees are underwhelming, but I suppose this is what the jalaja like." Andrei turned to Stasia.

"Your Glade doesn't look like this?" she asked.

"No, we're aaranya, we like trees. This is all a bit wet and open."

"I like it," said Senna.

"You're human," Yurim cut in, looking at John.

John nodded. "I was … am … will be. Something."

"You don't look human," said Stasia.

"He left a bit of himself behind," said Andrei.

"And that's why you're here?" Stasia asked. "To ask Ulvanya to get it back for you?"

John smiled. "No. I know where my human body is, I'll go back to it when we leave here."

"What is wrong with your daughter?" Platov asked. "If she needs help, why is she not here?" John looked at the older jalaja, trying to work out where to start.

"Best leave it for tomorrow," Yeleney spoke, placing her hand on Platov's arm.

John nodded his thanks to her and looked back out over the hills. "Just how big is this place? Is it a whole world, or something smaller?"

Platov followed John's gaze. "It is not complete like the world outside, but it is very big."

"Glades vary in size," added Darnu, "sometimes quite dramatically, and they change over time."

"Nayati told me stories," John said, remembering the old man back at the Samgha. "One of them spoke of connections between Glades, that you could walk from one to another."

Platov looked to Darnu. "Is that true?"

Darnu nodded. "Back in ancient times, before the War, when the forest covered much of the world."

"I was never really sure if I believed all that," said Andrei.

Darnu shook his head sadly.

"I do not think the zarana of jalaja were ever connected like that," said Platov, "not that we ever learned."

"Ulvanya once said something like that about the samudraka," said Yeleney, "that out in the ocean their zarana are connected like the rivers of a flood plain."

"Like arteries between hearts," said John. "That was how Nayati described it. That each Glade was the heart of the region in which it formed, and that the Glades helped to sustain one another by pumping life from one place to another. I was imagining that I'd see something like a tunnel, just over there somewhere, that I could wander into."

"It sounds like a tale from the history of the aaranya," said Darnu.

"I wonder who told him," added Garjae.

"What happened to them?" Stasia asked.

"Many Glades closed during the War," Darnu said, "and the life of the region was destroyed or reduced until they could not open again. They faded, and the connections with them. When new Glades formed they were smaller, or more distant from one another, or the forests had died back too much, and the connections have never returned."

"But what's it like, on the edge of the Glade?" John asked. He pointed to the sinking sun. "If I walked to where the sun is—"

"Swam," Andrei corrected him.

"Swam then. Would I reach a wall, some sort of barrier?"

Asha leaned against John and whispered into his ear, "You are still human then, you still want to know the how and why."

John turned to her and she smiled at him. John shrugged helplessly, he was getting better but there were still times when he couldn't stop his curiosity.

"There are no edges, John," Darnu was saying. "I don't know how large this zarana is, but if you kept going then eventually you would find yourself coming back again."

"Like you've turned around?"

Andrei put in, "No, it's more fun than that. You head out and keep going and then sooner or later you find yourself coming back from somewhere completely different. Things start to look familiar and you realise you've arrived back again. It's almost never the same path two times running."

John stared at Andrei in disbelief for a few moments and then looked back to Darnu, who nodded his confirmation. John sat there silent, trying to get his head around the idea. Eventually he asked, "But what about these arteries that Nayati told me about, they sounded more like tunnels or something."

It was Andrei that jumped in again. "Me and Barma used to play in them. There are some places that sort of close over—"

"What do you mean, close over?" John interrupted.

"It varies. You'd have to see our Glade to really know what I mean. The branches intertwine and form large tunnels, but you can't push or even merge through to see what's beyond them, so you follow the tunnels. Some go a long way and split and merge, others barely seem to go any distance at all, but you find yourself somewhere completely different in the Glade."

"There are places like that here too," said Yurim. "Rivers that flow in underground and come out somewhere far away."

"Makes playing hide and seek really fun," added Stasia.

Yurim put on a serious expression, trying to appear as if such children's games were well past him. "They're interesting places to explore."

John noticed that Senna looked as lost as he felt, and he remembered that she, too, was new to the world of Glades and zarana, although at least she had seen Andrei and Asha's home. "Have you seen any of these places?" he asked her.

"Not yet."

Andrei said with a grin, "Our games of hide and seek have been more about the finding part than the hiding part."

Senna nudged him.

The sun dropped below the horizon and most of the others got up to find somewhere to spend the night. Platov and Yeleney headed back to the river, Darnu and Garjae wandered off further into the hills. Andrei, Senna, Yurim and Stasia ran off to something that Yurim wanted to show the aaranya, leaving John and Asha sitting quiet and alone on the hill.

"So you've seen all those things Andrei was talking about?" John asked eventually.

Asha, leaning against John's shoulder, nodded. "But not all of us started as young as Andrei. From what I heard, the parents trying to keep track of him had a hard time of it, more than one child took a long time to find after trying to follow Andrei and Barma on their escapades."

John chuckled. "I can imagine that."

Casseta chose that moment to make her presence felt, and she emerged from John's forearm. He spoke to her affectionately and she twittered back. A few moments later she bounded away, in search of Nuttachen was John's guess, off to explore this new world.

As the glow from the sun faded and night fell around them, John found that he could still see clearly although there was no moon. Two milky bands of stars stretched across the sky above them and he could see nothing in them that looked familiar to him.

"Are they real?" John asked, pointing up to the stars.

"Real enough."

"And the sun? Was it the same sun?"

"Always with the questions," Asha said in soft exasperation, then, "I don't know. Ours keeps much the same time, if that's what you mean. Nighttime in our Glade is nighttime outside. I suppose it's the same here."

"When is a world not a world?" John muttered.

"What was that, my love?"

"Nothing really. It sounds like some silly kid's riddle. I still can't quite get used to this place. So much looks so normal, but it's not. This huge land or island apparently floating on some great lake, and who knows how many more lands around it, and all of it inside another great lake. It's impossible, but here it is. A world that is not a complete globe but neither does it have edges. A world with impossible tunnels, and its own sunshine and starlight. I feel like I must be dreaming."

"But it's not a bad dream?" Asha asked and placed her hand against his chest.

John covered it with his own. "While ever you're here beside me it can't be a bad dream."

They kissed and made love beneath the stars. Later, Asha fed some of her life to him and then they moved to a small grove of trees. Asha merged with a tree to rebuild her strength, and John made himself comfortable sitting at its foot. He leant against the trunk and watched the stars in a blissful daze. When Asha emerged, they lay down on the soft grass and she wrapped her arms around him. Together they slept peacefully through the remains of the night.

They walked down the slope toward the lake the next morning and could see that Ulvanya was already standing before her willow trees. She was speaking with Novoi in the pre-dawn light. There was a call, and John looked back to see Andrei and the others angling down toward them.

"Top of the morning to you," said Andrei brightly as they got near.

"Good morning, Andrei," John answered. "Staying out of trouble?"

"What sort of question is that?"

"A good one," said Asha. "How about it, Senna, has he been good?"

Senna grinned back at them. "Not too embarrassing."

"He's funny," defended Stasia.

"You can't have been too bad if you still have a fan club, Andrei," said John.

"Don't believe these miscreants," Andrei told Stasia and Yurim, "they would have you believe the worst of me."

Senna grabbed at him. "Someone's got to offset your bragging about being called courageous, it's going to your head."

"I just think she must be a very discerning woman."

They were getting close now so Senna spoke a bit more softly, "Say too much and she'll be sure to pick you for practice again."

Asha looked away, not happy to be reminded of what happened with Andrei the previous afternoon. John put his arm around her but didn't say anything. Senna looked apologetic.

As they were saying good morning to Ulvanya, Platov and Yeleney came up from the direction of the river, and Darnu and Garjae came down another slope.

Ulvanya spoke to the group. "I must apologise for yesterday. I get tired easily these days, and my grand entrance took more out of me than it should. When I was young I was told that age would give me freedom from the vanity and impatience of my youth, but if anything I've become more vain and less patient."

"But you've got to have fun," Andrei told her. "Anyway, maybe you just haven't gotten old enough yet, something to look forward to."

Ulvanya smiled at him. "Thank you for defending an old woman. I am pleased you haven't held a grudge."

"I don't think Andrei is the type," Asha said.

"He doesn't have the patience for it," added John.

"So a lack of patience can be good you think?" Ulvanya looked at John, and again he was struck by those young eyes in the old face.

311

John had a flippant answer prepared but under her direct gaze he responded, "We wouldn't be here without him."

Ulvanya turned her gaze to Asha. "Are you ready to learn what I can teach you?"

Asha hesitated. "What I want to learn is how to heal John's daughter."

"And nothing else?"

"I didn't say that," Asha responded curtly. More gently she continued, "We have only limited time before it will be too late. It took us a long time to find you."

The old woman's shoulders dropped and her expression turned sad. "Yes. Stesha forgets that you came here for your own reasons. Daiva, she said, and I believed her." To John's puzzled expression, Ulvanya explained, "Daiva, is a gift of the gods. Stesha believes you have a larger purpose, one that you know of but don't yet understand. It is my vanity again, thinking that you sought me out just to learn what I could teach you. I wanted a protégé, someone to whom I could leave my wisdom." Ulvanya looked out across her small lake, as if seeking answers there. "The folly of such thinking, the vanity. I told you, it gets worse with age, not better."

"Who is Stesha?" Andrei asked.

"What? ... Oh. ... We are in for a long morning. We had better get comfortable."

In addition to the main stream leading into the lake from where the valley narrowed, there was also a tiny trickling stream, little more than a gutter. It ran across the widest part of the valley floor and entered the lake on the downstream side of the willow trees. The water made the faintest of tinkling sounds as it ran over the small stones of the insignificant streambed. Ulvanya led them along beside this runnel until they walked beneath a small grove of poplar trees in full leaf. Under the trees the ground rose slightly on either side of the trickling stream, and Ulvanya made herself comfortable sitting on the bank with one foot dipping in and out of the water.

She laid her staff on the ground beside her and looked around at her audience. "Well? Make yourselves comfortable, we are likely to be here for some time." She looked to John. "I want you to tell the story of your daughter, do you mind if these others hear?" She indicated the jalaja.

312

John shook his head.

Between John, Asha and the others, they told the story of how they came to be sitting before Ulvanya. When they had finished silence fell over the group. They watched Ulvanya sitting quietly with her eyes closed, nodding occasionally to herself as if listening to an inner voice.

Ulvanya opened her eyes, she stared directly at Asha, and asked, "What makes you think this Jaimee and this Sando have finished with you?"

Asha opened her mouth to speak, but nothing came out.

"We've seen nothing of them since," Darnu said, "and until we came here, we were in contact with our friends back home. There has been no report of them."

Ulvanya turned to him. "And these are the sort of people that will walk up and introduce themselves?"

"We would have heard something," Andrei spoke up.

Ulvanya looked over the group. "Maybe you have, maybe you haven't – but you will. Stesha says you will."

"Who is Stesha?" Asha repeated Andrei's question.

Ulvanya settled her gaze on Asha. "Like you, I am a twin. Stesha is my twin sister."

"But—" Andrei started.

The old woman held up her hand and Andrei stopped. She continued, "I was not born here. I was born in the mountains to the east. A peaceful place in which great power came from the earth, like this Samgha and its valley of life that you spoke of. We lived along a stream and a small lake not unlike this one." She waved her hand over the valley, and then smiled as she added, "Though the willow trees here came just for me.

"My family was happy, but most jalaja don't stay together long. We are happiest on our own or in very small groups. You may have noticed how few of my people you have met since coming here, we rarely congregate. You see Novoi there shuffling in his seat, uncomfortable around this many people, but he makes an effort – for me.

"My sister left before me, something disturbed her. I know now that it was her talent. She saw things, felt things that she did not understand. She left to explore what it was she saw, and it led her here, to this old man of a lake.

"Months later I had still not left my home. I think my father was getting impatient, he wished to have his wife and his lake to himself, but I was experiencing strange feelings here in my breast and here in my fingers. These grew into my talent for healing, but back then I had no idea what they meant, and we had no elders to pass on the knowledge of such things. One day I was struck down, as if a bolt had come out of the clear winter sky and struck me dead. My mother told me I was unconscious and delirious for days. I remember only this feeling of great confusion and cold, of suffocating as if the water had turned to poison. Toward the end I felt as if I was being torn apart and then I woke – and I knew that my sister was dead.

"I knew it, but I refused to believe it. She tried to speak to me even way back then, to explain that it was all right, that she was dead but she would never leave me, but I shut her voice out. I would not listen. I roamed the world in search of her, but for many years I stayed away from this lake, where that voice kept insisting I go. My ability to heal would show itself at unexpected moments, but I was too angry to see it, too angry to let that voice in my head be heard. And so, I wandered, and I saw more than I could tell you in a month of such sittings.

"Finally I had no choice. I know better now, but back then I thought I had seen all the world that there was to see. I thought this was the only place left that I had not explored, so I submitted and came to this lake. Here I found and accepted the truth and found my sister. At last I would listen to her voice. Stesha helped me to recover from the long delayed grief and then to develop my neglected talents as a healer. Together we explored the world once more, but I was a different woman. To do it in the company of my sister made all the difference to what and who I am."

Ulvanya stopped then. She closed her eyes briefly and then opened them again and looked to Asha. "I am sorry, Asha. Such a story cannot be easy for you to hear."

John saw that tears had welled in Asha's eyes, but still she responded determinedly, "Sarva is not dead."

"No," Ulvanya agreed, "you would know if he was, but you do know what it is to be parted from your twin."

Asha nodded.

"What happened to Stesha?" Senna asked.

Ulvanya looked across at her. "Shall I tell her, Stesha?" she asked the voice in her mind. "Yes, yes, I suppose they have." She paused and waved her foot through the trickling water and then rearranged her seating.

"Stesha was young, she didn't understand what was happening to her. ... No, I'm not making excuses for you, it's the truth. ... At that time she still thought that she must have been given these visions so that she could change what they showed her. When she saw a vision of a family caught in the snow she thought it was her duty to save them. She came here in the summer and learned to love this old man of a lake. She met the young family she had seen in her vision and knew that she had come to the right place. She made friends with them as best she could, it is always difficult between jalaja, and tried to stay close as winter came on.

"Winter was almost passed before it happened, Stesha starting to wonder if her vision had been false, though they never had been before. She never found out how or why, and the child didn't remember, but the family was caught out on the ice when a storm hit. I don't have to tell you what they can be like. This one blew them against an outcropping of ice. They might have survived that if, after being trapped there, they had been left exposed until the warmth that eventually followed could reach them, but the end of the storm was accompanied by snow that buried them deeply with the intense cold. Outside that cold snow the weather turned suddenly warmer, and that can be a dangerous time on the ice.

"Stesha sensed the family's location and began digging for them. The snow had frozen hard and it hurt her greatly to do it. ... No, I'm not dragging things out, Stesha, this is what happened. She found the head of the man and dragged him free. She looked for the boy but didn't see him at first so she pulled at the woman and dragged her clear too. She went back into the hole she had dug and saw movement. The parents had huddled the child between them, and he was still awake. She had just grasped him when there was a great boom and the ice beneath her began to move. Unable to think what else to do, she threw the child toward his parents as the ice around her exploded. A wall of ice hit her and knocked her unconscious.

"When she woke she found herself in a small space between

blocks of ice. It was a miracle that she had not been crushed, but perhaps not a kind one. The intense cold that had buried the family was still with her, and she could feel her mind descending into confusion. She worried about the boy she had thrown, whether she had thrown him far enough to be clear of this ice. She didn't know how long she lay there, her mind was not working well, but eventually she began to hear more sounds through the ice, the booming thunder that tells of great cracks and movement. She thought she would either be crushed or set free, but it turned out to be neither.

"Her small hollow in the ice was pushed down into the lake and water began to fill the cavity. At first the warmth of it helped and her mind began to clear, and then she realised that the water would quickly freeze and expand and crush her where she lay. She thought she saw her chance, and it was a good idea. ... Well it was, Stesha, it could have worked. Stesha merged with the water, hoping to flow out through the cracks where it had entered. But she was too late. The water had had to flow through many long narrow cracks, and as Stesha tried to flow back out, the water was already freezing. She was trapped. She couldn't flow out, she couldn't flow back, and there wasn't enough space for her to emerge from the water. The water froze and as it crystallised it tore my poor sister apart."

Ulvanya stopped there, her eyes wet, and she stared down at the trickling water.

The group sat stunned. Asha leant against John's shoulder and he put his arm around her. He tried to stop himself imagining what it must be like to have every minute part of your being twisted and torn apart in the inexorable process of ice crystallising.

Ulvanya pulled herself straighter. "Stesha says I shouldn't be so maudlin, this was all a long time ago."

"What happened to the family?" Senna asked gently.

"They survived, all three of them. By the time I relented and came to this lake the boy she had saved was an old man – I had taken that long to submit. He remembered Stesha, not well, he was only very young when it happened, but he remembered her. It was meeting him that finally convinced me. Stesha recognised him and when I spoke to him I realised that her voice was real, that she had been with me all that time."

Darnu asked, "Why does the cold affect us like that, the slow minds and the weakness?"

Ulvanya raised her eyes to look up through the leaves above them. "Because life wants to wait for the warmth and the sun," she answered. "When you are strong and fresh you can withstand a great deal of cold, but when you weaken, the life in your body conserves itself to wait for a more fertile time. Like the trees and the bears and much other life of the outside world, the life in your body begins to go dormant and waits for the spring."

"It could ask," muttered Andrei. "It's not like we're waiting to burst into flower."

"It is a consequence of our nature," Ulvanya told him.

"You've obviously lived a long life," Garjae spoke to Ulvanya for the first time. "And yet you've also travelled. Are you an elder of this zarana?"

"A delicate way of calling me ancient, Garjae dear," Ulvanya smiled at him. Garjae didn't rise to the bait. "No, I am not an elder as you aaranya know them. I do not know why I have lived so long. Stesha thinks it might be because of my healing talents, perhaps I heal myself without realising it."

"That's convenient," Andrei observed.

"It is not really a blessing," Ulvanya corrected him, "though I doubt it will be a problem for much longer."

John felt Asha sit up straighter beneath his arm. When she spoke her voice was firm, "Can you teach me how to heal John's daughter?"

Ulvanya looked sadly back and forth between John and Asha. "No," she said at last, "I can't."

12. Healer

Asha slumped. She felt John's arm tighten around her and turned to look at him. His eyes were closed and his head bowed. She couldn't stop the selfish question that fired through her mind: was she going to lose him too? It was impossible to believe that they had come all this way, that they had found the woman they were seeking, but still they were denied that which they sought. She turned and stared back at Ulvanya, her eyes pleading for some reprieve.

Ulvanya returned her look, her deep blue eyes showed compassion but, Asha thought, no real understanding of just what her denial really meant. She wasn't just condemning the wonderful, beautiful girl that Asha had come to think of as her own, she was also condemning the man that she loved.

There was silence from the others, it seemed that no one could quite believe what they had heard.

"That can't be!" Asha managed at last. "Ellie is alive. There *must* be something we can do for her! I don't know how old you are, but you must have seen something, *anything*, that can give us some hope."

Ulvanya shook her head slowly. "I am sorry, I have never seen a preta saved." Before Asha could retort she continued, "I have seen enough that I do, now, think that I know what is required."

Asha sat straighter, suddenly alert and hopeful.

Ulvanya held up her hand as if to try and shield herself from the force of Asha's hope. "I may know what is required, but I cannot give it to you. I cannot teach it. You cannot learn it."

Asha refused to be daunted, they had come this far – s*he* had come this far – she wasn't going to be put off. "What is it? What can save Ellie?"

Ulvanya hesitated. She returned Asha's direct stare, she was past being intimidated by the strength of others, but she was concerned with what Asha might do with the information. The woman nodded slightly, Asha guessed that she had finished some internal dialogue with her sister. Asha sat back a little.

"I cannot tell you that you can save this child," Ulvanya started.

"Ellie," John reminded her.

Asha turned to him in surprise. He had looked up, his eyes were glistening with tears, but his attention was locked on Ulvanya.

Ulvanya nodded in acknowledgement to John and then looked back to Asha. "All life is connected. I'm sure you've heard the words before, but they are more than words. The connections are real. There have been those among us that can see those connections. Just once, on one of my explorations of the world, I met such a man, an aaranya." In response to some look in Asha's eyes, Ulvanya added, "He died in my presence. I cannot send you to Eitan."

"The connections are real," Ulvanya repeated. "There are connections between you and the earth, between you and your Glade, between you and your lover, and especially between you and your brother. Some connections are fine, fragile things, and may wither and die over time. Such a loss may hurt, but it leaves no permanent harm, at least, not physical harm. But other connections are stronger, thicker, and to break them literally releases the substance of your being into the ether. Your elders have such connections that tie them irresistibly to their Glade."

Ulvanya turned to John. "Such strong connections exist between a material, flesh-and-blood body and the life that animated it. While you are sitting there, John, a person that could see these connections would see the strong umbilical that ties you back to your human body over any distance. You have no choice, you must return to your body or you will die. Your daughter had such a connection to her body, but it was broken, torn, ripped away. If that wound cannot be healed, she *will* die."

"But there is no such wound," Asha insisted, drawing Ulvanya's eyes back to her. "I would see the prana leaving her body."

"It is being lost to the ether, the void that is beyond our sight. You cannot see this, and because you cannot see it, you cannot heal it. I know this, I have tried."

"But you said that you know a way," Asha insisted.

"No. I said that I know what is required." Ulvanya paused to gather her thoughts before continuing, "What is required is the aid of someone that can see the connections of life. I can teach you the skills you need to do the healing, but you will need someone to direct those skills. You cannot do this on your own."

"But if we can find such a person then Ellie can still be saved?" John asked.

"If you can find such a person then you can heal this breach," Ulvanya admitted.

"But that's not all, is it?" Senna spoke out quietly. Asha looked at her in surprise and then turned back to Ulvanya.

"You are perceptive," Ulvanya acknowledged Senna. "Breaking such a strong connection by force, as with a preta, usually results in a savage tear and their substance floods out and the life is quickly lost. But sometimes part of the connection remains, no longer attached, but floating free, withered and shrunk. A slowly weeping leak rather than a gushing hole.

"If a way is found to feed the preta then it may last a long time. You found such a way with Ellie. But, however much you try, the child only accepts so much life and then gains nothing more. This is your proof that the injury is still there. As the pressure of life builds within the body the break into the void opens further and whatever more you add is quickly lost. Her body cannot be restored without healing this breach."

Ulvanya paused, perhaps uncertain how much she should say, how much Asha would accept, and then continued, "*But*, as Senna has observed, that is not all. Even if you heal this breach completely, the child you know will not return. You will be left with just the grey husk that is the preta; a being that cannot fend for itself, cannot feed for itself, that – indeed – *has* no self."

"Then ..." Asha started but could not finish.

"You have already told me that her mind has retreated, hidden from the horror of her experience. A body without a mind will fade whatever we do. It is this very absence of will, the absence of self, that allows the preta to survive for so long with so little sustenance.

You could not leave John here," Ulvanya glanced at him and then returned her gaze to Asha, "for months without feeding him, as you have done with Ellie. The very presence of self animates the body in a way that consumes the body.

"Ellie's body must be healed before she can sustain her self. But even if you heal her body, you will still need someone that can find her, someone that can call her back from wherever she is hiding. This may well be the hardest part of all, we cannot even be certain she is still there."

"She is!" Asha said sharply. "I can feel her. I know she is there! Perhaps I can learn to reach for her, perhaps I can learn to bring her back."

Ulvanya hesitated, reluctant to argue against such ardent hopes. But they were false hopes. She said quietly, "You can try, of course. You will try, you have tried, but this, like seeing the connections of life, is not something that can be taught."

- - -

Senna didn't know what to do or say. Asha had gone off with the old woman, apparently determined to learn what she could. Andrei had volunteered to be their practice body for the day – calling himself their crash test dummy, but no one had even smiled – and gone off with them. John had barely spoken, he didn't seem to have noticed the desperation in Asha's eyes when she left. Darnu had led the rest of them away and found this small group of trees on the side of a hill. The jalaja, sensing the mood, had gone off on their own.

Senna sat on the grass watching John, his back against the base of the tree, his arms resting on his knees, his head between his hands. He didn't move, he didn't speak, he just sat there.

"Let's see if I've got this straight," Garjae started, he was standing while the others sat. Senna cringed at the tone he was using, but John didn't move. Garjae paced agitatedly as he spoke, "We started with a vague rumour of a healer and tracked her halfway across the world, *and* we found her, though I can still hardly believe it – and I'm still not sure I believe her. But if all that wasn't unlikely enough, if that wasn't hard enough, we're now looking for two more rumours: a person that can see what isn't there, and a person that can reach into people's minds and pull them out like some human magician pulling a rabbit out of a hat."

"Garjae," Darnu said softly.

"No. I'm not finished yet. If that's still not bad enough, we don't even know if such people really exist. We have no vague rumours of them to the north or south or east or west. We just have the word of a senile old jalaja that such people are what we need. For all that *I* believe her, such people may never have existed, and even she gives no hint whether any exist now."

"She's real, Garjae, you saw her," Senna told him.

"I saw her cut Andrei open, I didn't see her heal anything. She gets all mystical about her supposedly dead twin sister talking to her, but I think she's just gone over the edge and talking to herself. Are we really going to start searching the world for figments of her imagination?"

"She is real, Garjae," Darnu said. He looked up at his friend, his expression hard to read.

"Not you too! Did she suck you in with that mystic *all-knowing* talk? There's nothing wrong with you that getting back home and staying clear of humans won't fix."

Darnu didn't answer, just dropped his head and stared at the grass at his feet. Senna glanced at John, but still there was no response, no indication that he had even been listening.

"Garjae!" Senna said sternly.

Garjae ignored her and continued pacing and talking. "I've kept my mouth shut all this time because I didn't want to upset the jalaja, the others seem nice enough, but I can't believe you're all just accepting what this old woman tells you. A person that can see the connections of life that none of the rest of us can see? She is supposed to be truly ancient, but she admits that she's not an elder. If she's anywhere near as old as she says she is, she *must* be senile." Garjae turned away and spoke out over the hills. "I'm just worried how she's taken Asha in. Asha really seems to believe her. Where will she want to go next? How much further must we follow her?"

"There is no time," John said indistinctly.

Senna looked over and saw that John had raised his head, his eyes were red and wet. His expression as he looked at Garjae was that of a lost and exhausted child, wanting hope but seeing none.

"Don't you understand, Garjae?" John said, his voice weak and husky. "It doesn't matter how real these people are, we have no more time to search for them."

"Perhaps it's just as well," Garjae replied. "We can all go home."

"Garjae, why don't you just fuck off!" Senna yelled at him. She turned to John, but he was staring blankly out, probably not even seeing Garjae.

"Yes," John murmured, Senna could only just hear him, "you can all go home."

Garjae stared at John, Senna wasn't sure Garjae had even noticed her swear at him. Finally he turned and walked away. Darnu cast Senna an accusing glance and then got up to follow Garjae. When Senna looked back to John his head was once more buried in his hands.

She got up and went over to him, placing her arm around his shoulders. "There's still hope, John, there has to be." Senna didn't know whether she truly believed the words she spoke.

"No time," John murmured to the ground.

"We don't know that. Asha wasn't sure how long Ellie might last. She's tough, she might still give us the time we need to look further."

John didn't answer, there was just a vague shaking of his head in his hands. Senna squeezed his shoulders and tried to think of what she could say that might get through to him.

"You've got to look out for Asha," she tried. "She's taking this hard too. She needs you."

There was no response, so Senna just sat there and waited with him.

Later, as the sun was sinking behind them, Asha and Andrei came up the hill toward them. Senna got up, but John didn't move. Asha glanced at John and looked questioning at Senna. Senna shrugged.

Andrei took her arm and pulled her away without speaking. Senna looked back and saw that Asha had taken her place beside John.

- - -

Tracey stared out across the blackened ruins of what had once been a beautiful house in a beautiful forest setting. Many of the immense trees were still standing, huge blackened trunks reaching far into the sky. There were few noises to disturb the eerie quiet that had settled on the area, and the smell of charcoal permeated everything.

Much of the loose ash had been settled or washed away by a heavy rain that had fallen the night of the fire. The rain had stopped the fires spreading to other civilised areas, but had not prevented vast expanses of the forest from being destroyed. Everything was dry again now.

A car door closed behind her and she listened to the footsteps as they slowly walked around the car and stood beside her.

"Bloody hell," Jason said in a drawn-out whisper. "What a godforsaken mess."

Jason had brought her out here this morning, she had phoned and asked him to. She had been released from the hospital and her mother would be arriving to take her home this afternoon, but first she had wanted to come back here. She didn't know why or what for, it was unlikely that Tilvy would be here, but Tracey felt that she had to see this, though there was nothing she could do.

"Where was your car?" Jason asked, still in a whisper, the silence seemed to require it.

Tracey looked around in surprise. She pointed. "It was there."

They went over to look. The ground was smudged and blurred by the rain and subsequent activity, but it was still apparent where the car had sat.

"Someone must have taken it," Jason observed. "See? You can see where the tow-truck must have backed up for it. Your insurance company?"

Tracey shrugged. She hadn't done anything about insurance yet, but she supposed her mother might have.

She turned away and wandered over to what little remained of the house. The explosions and fire had left almost nothing of the mostly timber construction. The broken chimney marked one end of the house, the rest was just a rise in the ground scattered with debris. The toilet and bath from upstairs were easily seen, other mounds she would have had to pick through to try and identify, and she didn't feel it was her place to do it.

Tracey looked across the wreckage and into the burnt forest beyond, where her friends had gone in search of their home. Were they looking at a scene like this? Where were they now? How would she find them again?

Movement made her look down. Jason was holding a pale blue handkerchief out for her. She stared at it, not understanding, and then her vision blurred and she realised she was crying. She took the offered cloth and wiped her eyes. "Thanks."

"You want to go?" Jason asked quietly.

Tracey nodded, suddenly she did.

"I'll buy you a coffee."

They didn't speak much on the drive back into town. Jason took her to a quiet cafe and ordered coffees for both of them. Tracey refused the offer of something to eat, she didn't think she would be able to hold it down. The coffees were delivered to their table and Tracey went to take a sip. She realised she was still holding Jason's handkerchief.

"I'll wash this and get it back to you," she told him.

Jason smiled at her. "Don't be silly. Keep it, or toss it when you're done with it. I've got plenty, Liz keeps me well stocked."

"I didn't think anyone used them any more."

"Didn't used to. If it was up to me I'd still be using tissues, less to wash, but Liz thinks handkerchiefs look more refined, and they don't leave a mess in the washing machine when I forget to take them out of my pocket. I actually think she gives them to me just so I've got one when she needs it."

Tracey put the handkerchief in her pocket and used both hands to lift the mug of coffee. The warm sweetness of it helped, and she began to feel a bit calmer. They sat quietly sipping at their coffees for a while.

Tracey asked, "So what happens now?"

Jason raised his eyebrows in question.

"With John's house and everything?"

"I guess we have to wait for John," Jason said.

"Still nothing?"

"Nothing. Worse than that, my computer's on the blink, it won't start. I've dropped it off for someone to look at, but no joy yet. I've been checking for messages from my work computer but there's been nothing."

Tracey wondered if there was anything waiting for her at home. It had been a couple of days after she woke in the hospital before she had remembered the warning from Ian, but she didn't see what choice she had. She would have to use her computer when she got home, she had to know if there was any news – though why John would write to her and not to Jason she didn't know, it didn't seem likely, not after all this.

Jason said, "I thought, when I told him about you being hurt, he'd get back in a hurry. I left it deliberately vague, even implied it was worse than it turned out for you, so he'd *have* to ask me for details. But still nothing."

"You shouldn't have said anything," Tracey replied, "I'm okay. He'll only worry."

"Fair's fair! We've worried about him enough."

Tracey just shook her head.

"Maybe you're right," Jason grumbled. "Just pissed off with him. He was always the responsible one of us, the reliable one, but now all this. I'll be starting to check if the sun's coming up next."

Tracey gave him a wry smile. She understood; he was worried, not angry. She wished she could tell him what John was doing, that she knew why he was out of contact. It was frustrating, but she wasn't actually worried about John yet.

"Should we be doing anything about his insurance and stuff like that?" Tracey asked.

"I don't even know where to start," Jason admitted. "I don't have any of those sorts of details from him, do you?"

"No, and I suppose all the paperwork is burnt."

"I found the solicitor he was using but he was no help. I think everything's in limbo until John makes contact again."

"I've still got the chequebook he gave me to pay his bills." It had been one of the things Tracey had found in her handbag.

"That's a start I suppose. We probably should make sure his power and telephone is closed off, no point getting charged for stuff he can't use. ... Although, I imagine even that's going to be a struggle. Last time Liz tried to change something on our phones they wouldn't even talk to her because it's all in my name."

"It's a mess," Tracy said, looking down at her almost empty coffee.

"You can say that again."

They sat in amiable silence as they finished their coffee. When they were done, Jason took Tracey back to his house to wait for her mother to come and pick her up.

Later in the day, as Tracey sat with her mother driving home, she reflected fondly on the few hours spent with Jason and Liz and their young son – so obviously the centre of their lives now. She could well understand why John had tried to avoid getting Jason involved. Tracey had felt vague pangs of envy watching the effusive joy of the small family. John, she thought, must have found it very hard to watch them enjoying everything that he had lost.

There had been little conversation in the car with her mother, she seemed distracted, perhaps upset, but Tracey knew her well enough that now was not the time to ask what was wrong. Searching for conversation, Tracey asked about her car.

"Did you phone the insurance or someone about my car?"

Her mother glanced across and then back to the road. "No, sweet-heart, I hadn't given it a thought. I suppose we should."

"Just that the car's gone already, so I thought ..."

"I didn't call anyone."

"What about Brian, might he have done it?"

Tracey saw her mother's expression tighten. She thought back and realised that her mother hadn't mentioned Brian since the fire.

"What is it, Mum?"

"Brian's gone," she said simply.

"Gone?"

"Gone, as in disappeared. I haven't seen him since ... well, before that weekend."

"Did you guys argue or something?"

Her mother stared intently at the road. "He said he had to go away – for work. Everything seemed fine. But he hasn't called, his phone wasn't answering and now it seems to be disconnected. There's nothing. He's just vanished."

Tracey went silent. Her mother was close to tears. Tracey really hadn't meant to push it, now was not the time, she reminded herself. Ian had said Brian was the one watching her, prying into her computer. This sounded like confirmation. Did that put Mike in the clear? Tracey tried to remember exactly what Ian had said. Not that it mattered, Mike hadn't called or asked after her.

At least now Tracey knew what was upsetting her mother. She tried to distract her mother with talk about the hospital and about

Jason and his family. Slowly her mother relaxed. They reached the city and made their way through the traffic toward home, Tracey was looking forward to it. She had never really had cause to miss home before.

As they drove up the street approaching their house, Tracey saw her mother stiffen in her seat. There was a car in the drive. It looked a bit like the dark car that Brian drove. Was he back? Her mother pulled in slowly, parking next to the other car.

Tracey looked out her window and into the driver's window of the other car. She recognised the man sitting there, but it wasn't Brian. It was Raymond Cleaver, the man who said he was with the police. On the other side of Cleaver was a younger man, a stranger, talking on a phone.

Cleaver got out of his car and opened Tracey's door for her. She climbed out and stepped back to regain some space. Cleaver closed her door gently.

"Miss Ryner," he nodded to Tracey. "Mrs Ryner," he nodded again across the car to Tracey's mother.

"What do you want?" Tracey asked, more harshly than she had intended.

"Tracey!" her mother scolded.

Cleaver silently watched Tracey for a moment before responding, "I said last time we met that we might have a few more questions. We would like you to come with us to answer those questions now, Miss Ryner."

All this "Miss Ryner" crap was sounding ominous. Gone was the friendly, first-name front he had presented back at the hospital.

"We only just got home," her mother said. She had come around the back of the car to stand behind Tracey. "Can't this wait until tomorrow or something?"

"I'm afraid I have to insist." Cleaver took a breath and reached into the inside jacket pocket, pulling out a folded piece of paper. He handed it to Tracey's mother. "This is a warrant to search these premises and to seize items relevant to our inquiry. Some other officers will be arriving soon to execute this. They will try to be quick and not inconvenience you too much, Mrs Ryner."

What about me? Tracey wondered.

"I'll come with Tracey," her mother said.

"I'm afraid that won't be possible," Cleaver said in reasonable tones. "She is not a minor. We will arrange for suitable representation when the time comes."

"What do you mean?" Tracey asked.

"We can't discuss the details here," Cleaver said.

He had stepped forward, so Tracey stepped back. Cleaver reached out and opened the back door of his car. "Please get in."

Tracey turned to her mother. "Mum?"

Her mother was staring at her, frozen in shock, still holding the paper she had been given, unopened.

"Please get in, Miss Ryner, I need to discuss a few things with your mother before we go."

Tracey turned back to Cleaver and stared at him.

"Please," he asked again.

Numb, stunned, and unable to think, Tracey did as she was asked and the door closed quietly beside her. She watched as Cleaver took her mother's arm and led her to the house. What was this all about?

"He will be telling her that she must not tell anyone that you have been detained."

Tracey looked at the young man in the front. "What?"

"It is an offence under Australia's anti-terrorist legislation to tell others where you are while you are under detention," the young man explained patiently.

"I'm under arrest?"

"No, you are being detained for questioning, and to prevent you from contacting others while we ascertain your involvement."

"This is bullshit!" Tracey said loudly. "I'm not a terrorist!" She grabbed at the door handle but it had no effect, the door wouldn't budge. "Let me out."

"Please sit quietly, Miss Ryner. He won't be much longer and then we can be on our way."

"I haven't done anything wrong," Tracey pleaded. "I just wanted to go home." She slumped back in her seat.

The young man looked back at her, his expression carefully neutral. His short hair was dark, his face pale and slender. She saw his eyes move away from her, looking out to the street. Tracey turned and saw that another two cars had parked outside the house, there were three men and a woman coming up the drive.

The rest of the day was a blur. She remembered her mother's despairing looks, watching from the front door as Tracey was driven away. Tracey had just stared back, she hadn't even waved. She was driven into the city, the car drove into an underground car-park beneath one of the tall buildings – the associations made her even more nervous. She was taken up in a lift, just the three of them travelling in silence.

There was a small sparse reception area where a stern faced man went through the process of recording her details and cataloguing the few personal possessions she still had with her, including, Tracey noted dimly, Jason's handkerchief. Then she was turned over to a woman in a police uniform, stocky, with a determined expression. Raymond Cleaver and his offsider departed. Tracey watched them go, they had said nothing to her since leaving her house.

"Follow me," the policewoman said brusquely, and led the way through a secure door and into a long bare corridor. There were identical doors at intervals on each side, too much like doors she had seen on television shows to be mistaken for anything other than prison-cell doors.

One of the doors was open and the policewoman stopped and gestured Tracey inside.

Tracey stopped before the door and looked at the policewoman. "I thought I was going to be questioned." she said.

The policewoman gave an eloquent shrug that said, "Don't ask me, I just work here." Then she gestured again for Tracey to go into the cell.

Tracey walked into the tiny room and heard the metallic clang as the door closed behind her. The room was off-white and filled with the smell of disinfectant. Along one wall ran a narrow, hard-looking, grey bed. At the end of the room, at the end of the bed, was a very basic toilet, and to the side a small hand-basin. Other than that, there was just the narrow stretch of floor beside the bed where Tracey was standing. She looked up and could see a camera set in one corner of the room, but she couldn't tell whether it was on.

She stood still, uncomprehending for a while, staring blankly over the short distance to the end of the room. There were no windows, the only noise was the constant low rumble of air-conditioning. She turned slowly and sat on the edge of the bed, it was as hard as it looked.

A terrorist? They thought she was a terrorist!

Tracey lurched upright. Despite the short distance, she barely made it to the toilet before her stomach clenched and expelled what was left of her lunch. For minutes, long after there was nothing left to give, her stomach continued to convulse. When the spasms began to quiet down Tracey stayed kneeling on the hard floor gasping, trying to regain her breath, and trying in vain to understand how she had come to be here.

- - -

Asha forced herself to focus on Stasia's arm. Today was Stasia's turn to play crash test dummy, a term the others had taken on after Andrei's continued use of it. It held new significance for Asha today, today she had to learn how to—

"Cut," Ulvanya demanded.

Asha got very sick of the woman's voice at times like this.

They were in a small cave that opened into the valley from behind a grove of trees. In this small cave was the spring that gave rise to the tiny trickling stream that ran across the valley floor to the lake. They sat in a triangle beside the spring. Stasia's arm was held out bravely in front of her. Asha had come to like the young girl very much.

"I don't think I can," Asha said.

"Of course you can. Any healer can also be a destroyer, they are just different aspects of the same nature, our nature. Both take passion, both take power, and both take determination. You have all these things."

"I might have the power, but I don't think I can use it like that."

"You can and you must. Cutting can be essential to healing. You work with the trees, are you telling me you have never isolated a branch that was too damaged to heal?"

Asha looked at the woman, Ulvanya's dark blue eyes were staring directly into hers. "I have done that."

"This is the same thing. Sometimes damage has to be cut away. Our bodies have wonderful regenerative powers, but sometimes the damage gets in the way of healing. Sometimes things heal badly and have to be cut open again before they can be set right. Unless you are right there when something happens then, by the time anyone finds you, they are probably already partly healed. This is a real problem that you *are* going to face."

Ulvanya paused. She apparently read Asha's continuing reluctance and continued, "I've seen what you did for Garjae. You did well, but his arm is still not right, we will have to take a look at that again before you go. What you did was impressive, an amazing demonstration of what you can do when you are willing to sacrifice yourself for another." Her tone turned sarcastic, "Very admirable, I am sure. But what if there had been two or three or more injured as badly? It happens. You have to stop sacrificing yourself for every wound. Garjae's arm needed cutting to release pressure points, and to let your healing work without expending yourself. It might have taken longer to heal, for regeneration to run its course, but you would have been free to help others."

"What about the pain?" Asha asked. "I don't want to hurt the one I'm trying to heal."

"You already know this, Asha. You have been doing it already, before you came here. We can reduce the pain as we work. We can't remove it completely, but we can relieve it."

Asha nodded reluctantly and turned to Stasia. "I'm sorry."

Stasia's wide innocent face looked back, a bit nervous, but she was smiling. "It's okay. Andrei told me about it. He started by trying to scare us, but then he told us properly, and he showed us where you healed him. You can't even tell."

Asha gave her a grateful smile and turned her gaze back to the young arm in front of her. She knew what was wanted, Ulvanya had described it and she had understood immediately. Just as she could encourage the prana to come together and intertwine itself, so she could also ask it to separate. She knew instinctively that it would be easier. As Ulvanya had told her, destroying was easier than healing, and apparently, sometimes, it was necessary.

She drew in a breath and ran her finger lightly along the arm. She felt Stasia flinch beneath her fingers and immediately stopped. "I'm sorry," she muttered quickly to Stasia.

"Good, Asha, that is fine," Ulvanya told her. "Not very deep and not very long, but you have made a start." Ulvanya ran her fingers over the small cut and it disappeared, leaving just a fine trace of golden prana that quickly evaporated. "But you must learn to concentrate on what you are doing and not on the reactions of the patient. And you don't need to apologise for every little pain that you cause or you will never get anything done.

"Now, we need to work on reducing the pain as you cut. Not just because it is kinder to the patient, but it also helps to stop them moving around as you work. What I find works well for me is to use two fingers, with practice you can get the first to desensitise the area and the second does the actual cutting. It allows you to work quickly and that also helps."

And so the lessons continued. Later in the day they moved on to cutting beneath the skin without breaking the skin itself, a prelude, Ulvanya warned, to more serious and dangerous work.

Late in the afternoon Ulvanya returned to her lake, and Stasia and Asha walked back to join the others. As they walked Asha kept apologising for the pain she had caused. Stasia giggled and Asha looked to see what was funny.

"Andrei told me you were like this, but I didn't believe him."

"But you are all right?"

Stasia giggled again. "Yes. Sure some of it hurt a bit, particularly at the start, but you're getting very good. I barely felt any of it this afternoon."

"Thank you, Stasia. I mean it," Asha told her seriously.

Stasia smiled at her.

Asha looked up the hill to the trees where John sat, as he had now for two days, staring out over the landscape. Andrei, Senna and Yurim sat nearby but separate.

"I might meet the others down there," Stasia said, reluctant to approach John. "I'll see you tomorrow."

"You're coming back for more?"

"Sure, if Yurim doesn't push in. We can't let Andrei have it all to himself. I only got in today because Andrei did a thing he called the short-straw – with pieces of grass."

Asha couldn't quite believe that they were competing for the privilege of being cut open and put back together again. "Okay, I'll see you, or whoever gets the short-straw, then."

Asha walked up the rest of the way on her own, the others – except John – stood as she approached.

"Still no joy," Andrei said without waiting for her to ask. "I see Stasia still has all her limbs. You put everything back where you found it?"

"I'm saving that up for your next visit, Andrei," Asha said.

Andrei grinned back at her. More seriously he asked, "Did you want us to hang around?"

"No. Thanks."

Senna touched her arm gently and then the three of them left to join Stasia. Asha turned her attention back to John and sighed. Through the busy day she was could block the thoughts of Ellie, and what they hadn't yet found. Senna had told Asha what she had told John, that perhaps when they got back to Ellie they would find that they had more time yet, that perhaps there would be time to find the help they needed. It was just possible. Asha knew that and clung to it, because there was nothing else left to cling to, but John refused to be convinced. Not that he said much. For the last few nights he had lain unresponsive in her arms, becoming animated only in his refusal to accept being fed more of her life. Tonight she would not accept refusal.

She walked over and sat next to him. He didn't move or acknowledge her, just sat there still, his arms resting on his knees as he stared blankly out.

Asha wasn't sure what made her do it, a flash of temper most likely, but she reached out quickly and ran her finger across his arm. Just the one, no deadening of the pain preceded the cut. It was so easy. The cut was deep, deeper than she meant it to be – not that she had planned it. He bled the golden fluid of life.

He didn't flinch, but after a moment he looked down at his arm, a slow frowning, incredulous look of surprise rose on his face. "Ouch!" he said at last.

Asha laughed, she couldn't help herself. The expression, the delayed response, the disbelief, it was all so sad and yet so funny to her.

He looked at her. "You cut me," his said, the hurt in his voice was not from the cut.

"It was the only way to get your attention. I wanted to show you what I learned today." Asha couldn't work out what made her sound so frivolous, it wasn't how she really felt.

John reached forward with his other hand and ran his fingers through the prana spilling from his arm. He put his fingers to his mouth and tasted it. "It's not blood," he said after a moment. "It has no taste, just ... warmth. And yet," he ran his fingers through it again and tasted more, "it is sort of appealing."

"You can be a strange man, John Caldor," Asha told him, and put her hand out to stop him going back for another taste. "Doesn't it hurt?"

John stared at his arm. "Sure, I guess so."

"Then let me heal it before you bleed to death."

John lifted his arm out to her, his prana dripping onto her knees. Asha ran her fingers back and forth across the wound and it slowly began to knit together. It really was very deep, there should have been more reaction. When the healing was done John lifted his arm up in front of his face. Asha thought he might be going to lick the remaining prana from his skin, and she didn't like the idea, but he just stared at it, watching the golden steam rise as the prana evaporated.

"Are you going to talk to me tonight?" Asha asked him.

John pulled his attention away from his arm. A half smile found its way onto his face. "I guess I'd better."

They chatted for a long while about what Asha had been doing, her progress with the healer and the unexpected competition to be the patient for her training.

"I wonder if he explained that the short-straw usually means the loser," John said.

"I'm guessing not."

"Not that it matters, I guess, you need volunteers. I'll have to put my lot in too."

"There's no need, John." She smiled at him. "You've already done your bit."

John looked at his arm, all the prana now evaporated. "It is quite incredible you know, there's not a mark."

"The damage isn't completely healed yet." Asha ran her fingers over the area where the wound had been. "It takes time for the body to sort it all out after the disruption. I'm sorry I cut you."

"I'm sorry I've been so morose." John looked at Asha carefully. "Is it all over for Ellie?"

"No! I'm not giving up. I won't give up, not until the last trace of life has left her."

John looked doubtful.

"John ..." she started and then trailed off. How could she say what she meant? Should she even say it? She pushed ahead, "You heard Ulvanya, I am stubborn, but it's not easy. I'm not giving up, but I need you to help me. I don't have the strength to keep fighting for Ellie if I have to fight for you too. I need you to be with me. I can't do this without you."

John reached forward and pulled her close, his arms firm and comforting around her. "You're right," he spoke softly into her hair. "I haven't been fair, and I am sorry. I will do better."

- - -

"To be caught in one fire may be regarded as misfortune," Raymond Cleaver was saying to her, "to be caught in two looks like carelessness." He slid a photo across the table.

It was black and white, but the image was clear enough. Tracey could see her pale face through the windscreen of her car – just dark grey in the photo, but her eyes saw it as the bright red she had chosen. There wasn't all that much detail in the rest of the photo but she recognised it easily enough. She had been there only once, and it was not a night that she would forget in a hurry.

"When that photo was taken, just over ten months ago now, the Forest Conservation Research Centre was already burning," Raymond continued. "What is it that you and your friends have against forests?"

Tracey looked up at him, Cleaver stared back at her and waited. Tracey turned to the woman beside her, Edith Blake. It was Edith that had come to get her from the cell this morning, providing a change of clothes and accompanying Tracey to the bathroom to get cleaned up ready for the interview. Edith was probably Tracey's mother's age, maybe a little older; slender and elegant in her fitted woman's business suit, her hair was tied back in a tight bun. Edith had explained that she was to be Tracey's advocate during the interview, that she was there to make certain that Tracey was treated fairly, but so far the woman had done little but nod, indicating that Tracey should answer. She nodded again now.

Tracey's eyes moved back across the table, passing over Cleaver's young offsider, he had been introduced to the recorder as Paul Aldercott, so far he had said nothing. Cleaver was still watching her quietly. Tracey looked past him to the door, the policewoman she had met briefly yesterday was standing there, determinedly staring away from Tracey.

There was no help anywhere here for her, and there was no explanation she could give them. Even if she tried to tell them the truth they would never believe her.

"You obviously have friends in high places," Cleaver continued. "The security video from which this photo was taken had been sat on for months. The investigation of that fire was grossly mishandled, a lot of evidence went missing or was never found. I think it was nobbled, and I intend to find out how."

Tracey continued to stare back at Cleaver. What could she say?

"Apparently only the video from the guard booth to the car park survived the fire. What would the other cameras have shown us, Miss Ryner? Would they have shown you planting the same sort of incendiary devices that we found in the forest, and in the remains of Caldor's house?"

"I don't know what you're talking about," Tracey managed to whisper.

"You'll have to speak up, Miss Ryner," Aldercott told her, "for the benefit of the recorder."

Tracey looked at him, her eyes pleading, but his gaze kept that same careful neutrality she had seen in the car. "I don't know what you're talking about," Tracey repeated, turning her eyes to the recording machine on the end of the desk, its red light glared back at her. "I didn't start any fires."

"Then what were you doing at the FCRC, Miss Ryner?" Cleaver persisted. "What possible reason did you have to be there?"

Tracey didn't answer.

"Two deliberately started fires, ten months and many miles apart, and you found in the middle of both of them. Do you expect me to believe it was a coincidence?"

"I'm not a terrorist," Tracey told him.

"Aren't you? Then the remains of military grade incendiary devices we found are just your usual weekend toys are they? Or did you find those in a box beside the road somewhere, and decide to find out how they worked?"

Tracey shook her head. "I don't know anything about such things. I don't know how the fires started."

"Back in the hospital I was inclined to believe you, Miss Ryner. Such a sweet young thing. No previous, no signs of overt political activity at all. Yes, I really thought you were as sweet and innocent as you looked – and then this turned up." Cleaver tapped the photo in front of her. "Not to mention this one." He slid a second photo across.

Tracey could see that it was John driving his station-wagon out of the same car-park.

"You and Caldor involved in the same two fires. What happened? Did you and he have a lover's spat? Maybe you decided to use the explosives on his house to get back at him?"

"We're not lovers," Tracey said.

"No? Well perhaps that brings us around to the biggest blot on your copybook – before those showed up that is," Cleaver indicated the photos still in front of Tracey. "Would you care to explain your relationship with this man?" Cleaver slid another photo across the desk.

Tracey looked at it ... and looked at it. What did Mike have to do with all this?

"Has he been funding your hobbies?"

Tracey looked up, but she had trouble seeing Cleaver, tears were blurring her vision. "He's just a friend."

"Michael Asquith is known to associate with people involved in the designer drug trade. Manufacturers, distributors and so on – it's *big* money. Funny thing is that I never picked you for that sort, and we didn't find any drugs in your home, so what is it? Does he supply you with other things besides drugs? Money? The equipment?"

Tracey shook her head. "He's just a friend."

"Well your friend is none too pleased with you at the moment."

Tracey wiped her eyes with her hands and looked at Cleaver in question.

"He told us that he thinks you've been spending dirty weekends with Caldor up in the hills. Was he right?"

"No!" Tracey said loudly. "John's away. I told him, I told *you!* I just look after the house." Her voice trailed off as she took in what

Cleaver had said. They had been talking to Mike about her.

"It's a bit more than that, isn't it, Miss Ryner? You're a signatory on his bank accounts and *you* are the soul beneficiary of John Caldor's will."

Tracey stared at him in disbelief. John hadn't told her that.

"Something of an enigma is our John Caldor." Cleaver sighed. "Where is he?"

"Asia," Tracey muttered. "Burma."

"So you tell us," Cleaver replied. "Jason Manton told us the same thing, but the really strange thing is that neither of you can substantiate the claims of extended email conversations with him. The Burmese authorities have no record of him entering their country, and we can find no record of him leaving this one. Added to that, both of your computers have been mysteriously wiped, at about the same time we think. What did you do, connect to them from your phone before you wiped that too?"

Tracey sat in stunned silence.

"And not just wiped. The experts tell me the data had been encrypted anyway. Even if they can retrieve anything off the disks, it won't help without the keys – the passwords. A very professional job they tell me. I don't mean any disrespect, Miss Ryner, but I think this sort of thing is beyond your education. Who set it up for you?"

Tracey shook her head slowly, none of it made any sense.

"What passwords did you use to access your computer?"

Tracey was still shaking her head. "I didn't. It just worked ... like it always had."

Cleaver raised one eyebrow, he didn't believe her.

"You are required to give us all details of all online accounts that you use," Aldercott told her, and slid a pad and pen across the table. "The provider and all your user names and passwords."

"And while you're at it," Cleaver added, "write down any passwords that you used to access your computer. We'll take a break now for you to try and remember everything you can. Can I get you something? A coffee?"

Tracey shook her head.

Aldercott suspended the recorder and the two men left the room.

"They're treating you gently at the moment," Edith observed quietly. "It may pay to be more cooperative now, things will only get harder for you if you keep holding out on them."

Tracey turned and looked at the woman. Whose side was she on? For all Tracey really knew the woman could be just another cop playing the part. "I'm not a terrorist," Tracey insisted. "I don't know what all these questions are about."

Edith raised an eyebrow, an apparently unconscious imitation of Cleaver's disbelief. "It doesn't look good," she told Tracey. "Unless you can find some way to explain your presence at the FCRC, and the erasure of the computers, what else are they to assume?"

"I don't know anything about the computers," Tracey said. "Mine was working fine, it was just like any other computer I've ever used. I don't know anything about any encryption, I wouldn't know how to use it anyway."

"And the FCRC?" Edith reminded her.

Tracey shook her head. "I was there with John."

"Why? What was he there for?"

Tracey hesitated, then said, "I don't know. I never saw anything like what they were talking about – the incendiary devices."

Edith indicated the pad. "You'd better start remembering those passwords they want."

Tracey looked down at the page, her mind blank. At the moment she couldn't remember anything. Her computer had stored all this stuff, it remembered it all for her. She had a few things noted down in her phone, but that was gone too. She wrote down her email address and then stopped, she couldn't even remember the password to get into her email.

Cleaver and Aldercott returned a while later. Cleaver glanced down with dissatisfaction at the mostly blank page of the pad that Tracey had been writing on.

Cleaver slid a photocopied page across the table to her. "Back at the hospital you told me you were alone when you were trapped in your car at Caldor's." Indicating the photocopy, he continued, "You were holding that as you said it. Who is *T*, Miss Ryner? Who is Asha?"

Tracey looked down at the copy of the note from Tilvy. She thought of saying that it was a note to herself, but as she scanned over the note she quickly realised it wouldn't make much sense. She remembered Andrei's joke about her writing a book, maybe that

340

would be a good enough explanation. She had taken so long to answer that anything would sound like a lie, so she just shook her head.

"Why are you protecting these people?" Cleaver asked her. "You're obviously not working alone. You're good, I'll give you that. With this act of innocent ignorance and such a clean slate before now, we would never have given someone like you a second look, if it weren't for these," he swept his hand over the photos on the table. "But it's not just you and Caldor, we *know* that. Even without these mysterious companions, T and Asha – who, I shouldn't need to remind you, left you for dead outside your car – we have records of the helicopter flights, and witnesses to people entering the forest on foot. But all those leads have come to nothing. The real perpetrators have simply vanished. A few that we suspect may have been involved have been found dead." When Tracey didn't react, Cleaver repeated, "Found dead, Miss Ryner. These aren't nice people you're dealing with."

Cleaver paused and watched Tracey, waiting for some response, but Tracey couldn't think of anything she could say.

"Caldor's run out on you, you owe him nothing. There's nothing your other friends can do for you now," Cleaver continued. "Your car tells us nothing, and you've seen to it that your computer and phone gave us nothing." He threw his hands in the air. "I just don't know what to do with you. If you don't give us something, there will be nothing we can do to help you."

Although Tracey knew that John hadn't run out on her, right now it felt like he had. She felt alone and friendless. She could feel the hopelessness of her situation pressing down on her. There was nothing she could tell these people that they would believe. She would happily lie to try and get out of here, but she couldn't come up with any convincing story that might cover what they knew.

"Do you have any idea how big this thing is?"

Tracey shook her head.

"Incidents like this have happened before, in other parts of the world and spanning several years, but no one can make sense of them. There may have been more that we haven't identified. Most happen in remote forest areas like that second fire beyond Caldor's, and not all such fires are investigated. There hasn't been much damage yet, few people have been killed, and most not the sort to be widely missed, but the consensus is that it's just a matter of time. All these small incidents have got to be working up to something. No one spends all this time, and goes to all this trouble, unless they're working up to something bigger. But what?"

"I don't know what you're talking about," Tracey said quietly. And she didn't. All she knew about were the two fires they had spoken of, she had no idea what those other incidents must be. She didn't even understand why someone had destroyed John's house and the forest beyond. None of it made any sense to her.

"This is the first we've seen of it in Australia. This is our chance to open a crack into this organisation, and you're in a position to help us, Miss Ryner. Help us so that we can help you."

"I can't help you, I don't know anything," Tracey said. She could feel the tears of frustration threatening to break through her fragile calm. How could she possibly make these people believe her?

The interview for that day was terminated and Tracey was returned to her tiny cell. At first she just lay there, numb and unable to think. She stared at the blank ceiling and listened to the dull hum of the air-conditioning. The events of the morning slowly caught up with her. She sobbed, quietly at first, then the emotions welled up further and she rolled over and screamed into her pillow. Eventually exhaustion overtook her and she slept.

The next two days proceeded in much the same manner, but Tracey became more and more depressed and less and less responsive. There was nothing she could tell them. There was nothing she could do except let their barrage of questions wash over her.

In the afternoon of the third day, after questioning had finished, Cleaver came to her cell. The door was left open while he spoke softly to her.

"I don't know what to do, Tracey," he admitted. "I don't know if we have enough to convict you of anything substantial, and I'd rather not. The more I look at all this the more your involvement puzzles me. This isn't who you are. I don't know how you got involved, but we are your only chance of getting out. You are a very small cog in a very big wheel. But time is running out, soon I'll have to charge you or release you."

Tracey stared up at him from her place, sitting on the edge of the bed. The thought that she might be released soon was the first hope she had found since arriving here.

Seeing Tracey's eyes brighten at the idea of release, Cleaver warned, "I'm seriously considering charging you, if only to keep you safe. Haven't you heard what I've been telling you? The only traces we've found of people involved in all this are dead bodies. Do you want to be one of them?"

Tracey shook her head.

"*If* we let you out of here, it could be your body that we find next."

\- - -

The three of them sat side by side on a narrow branch that reached above the canopy of the Asian jungle. Their mother called them angels, and their pale forms sitting high above the world in the dawn light could well be mistaken for such. The dhumraka considered them to be all but gods. They were with the dhumraka, they ruled the dhumraka, but they were not dhumraka. If their like had existed before, it had not been for many thousands of years, since the time of the Jatarupa – the Golden. One of their fathers had thought the siblings may bring forward the Jatarupa again, but the siblings had their own plans.

Sando sat to Jaimee's left, Helix to his right. Helix was the same height as her brothers, with similar features and fine build, but strongly, emphatically, feminine. Next to her, her brothers looked understated. Helix was more than pale, she almost glowed. A mass of white hair rose like an aura around her head and fell in waves past her shoulders. Like her brothers she sat straight and confident, aware of the power she wielded. She was the queen of the dhumraka.

At first an observer may think that the three were equals, but more careful observation would reveal a subtle deference to Jaimee; ultimately the others would bow to his decision. An observer may also note that their conversation sometimes included a fourth, unseen, participant, and that there looked to be a space to the right of Helix that had been left for her. But their sister, Peren, was never truly missing, she was always with them in their minds.

The siblings, the four of them, could talk directly into each other's minds. All narun speech was telepathic, but this was something

343

more, a connection between the siblings that went beyond mere speech. For the three on the branch the connection only worked when they were close, but Peren was connected to each of them always, wherever they were, however far apart. It was Peren that kept the siblings in touch as they roamed the world.

<This is the one that's causing the trouble?> Jaimee spoke into the minds of his siblings.

The tree stood upon a high ridge and their position overlooked the jungle forest in the valley to the west, and the ridge beyond. All three looked across to the far ridge, their senses could feel the Glade that existed there.

<It is,> Helix confirmed.

<Same as the last time?> asked Sando.

Helix nodded across their mental connection. *<I would have said it was impossible, but it's like someone is preparing the occasional Glade for our arrival. And sometimes it's as if my influence doesn't hold. Where normally any resistance just folds and fades away, here it has risen again – as if they can ignore what it is that I want of them.>*

<Could someone be spreading the news?> Jamie asked.

As they were speaking a small group of macaws had flown in, attracted to the three of them as birds often were. With the patience of long practise, Helix waited for the curious birds to work their way close, and then she reached out slowly and gently touched each of them. With the group now under her control she used her influence to quiet the rowdy parrots.

<If they did then I would expect all Glades to anticipate us by now, but there is only the odd one here and there as we've moved south. And even if they anticipate us, that doesn't explain the resistance. Glades follow their elders. Control the elders and you control the Glade. A week ago I controlled the elders here, now they won't let me near.>

<We should study it, find the reason,> said Sando with some reluctance.

<Not your usual enthusiasm for scientific endeavour,> Jaimee observed with a grin.

<Asha and the others must return soon, we don't want to be tied up here.>

344

<Relax, brother, we will know when they return.>

<It's been taking too long, Jaimee, we should not have let them go on.>

<It may prove worth the wait, and we have time yet,> Jaimee reassured him.

<But not forever,> intruded the voice of Peren. *<Sando's right, we need to know if this woman can help Mama, we need time to look elsewhere if this doesn't work out.>*

Helix pushed in, *<None of that changes what I want here.>*

Two of the birds were gently preening a third, it arched its neck with pleasure.

Helix continued, *<You know I don't have your patience for study, Sando. I just want this Glade gone, out of the way so I can get on. We've spent years working our way south as it is, too much longer and everyone really will know we're coming.>* She gave a mental shrug and the gentle preening of the birds turned suddenly into violent attack. The three birds tumbled from their perch, screeching noisily and tumbling as they struck against branches, but still continuing their blind attack on each other as they fell. Somewhere below, the noise was cut abruptly by one of her patiently waiting dhumraka aids.

<Another Glade to destroy,> Jaimee mused, then grinned at Sando. *<Ready for another one so soon after your last?>*

Sando nodded. This was just a distraction, something to keep him occupied while he waited for what he really wanted.

- - -

The next days were a strange time for John. Despite his promise to Asha, he couldn't stop himself from suddenly freezing at random times when it all crashed in and overwhelmed him again. Mostly he kept himself together for the nights with Asha, but through the day he would come to and see Andrei and Senna looking at him sadly.

Through the days Asha remained busy with Ulvanya, so Andrei or Senna would insist that John accompany them on their explorations of this wondrous world and the creatures that inhabited it. Usually Yurim and Stasia would join them, but they spoke very little to John. Exactly who came along depended on who was playing the day's part of crash test dummy; they wouldn't let John join their nightly lottery to choose who would join the healers the next day.

Andrei made a big production of it, sometimes pretending they were a victim headed to some horror, at other times pretending that they had won some great honour.

Watching the fun that Yurim and Stasia had with Andrei and Senna, John thought that the jalaja's preference for a solitary existence must be something they grew into, or perhaps it wasn't in their nature so much as the way they were brought up.

The more time he spent in Andrei's company the more John began to realise that something was wrong there too. Andrei was always one to be upbeat and constantly moving, but now he was almost manic. He would try to imitate the creatures they found in the water, he would turn somersaults down the hills, or jump out at unexpected moments to try and surprise one of them. Sometimes it was truly funny, but others made John cringe, wondering what was going through Andrei's mind.

Andrei spent large parts of each day imitating voices and reciting lines that John recognised from the television. Bart Simpson was a favourite, and so was Captain Picard or Data of Star Trek fame. There were many others that John thought he should know, but guessed they were from before or after the time that John had watched much television. Yurim and Stasia loved the performances even when they didn't understand the references, but it seemed to John that Senna's laughter was often forced.

John tried to broach the subject with Senna on one of the days that Andrei was with Asha and Ulvanya. Yurim and Stasia had chosen not to come with them that day, so it was a much quieter and more gentle time. John thought that Senna was finding it hard to keep active and cheerful, and he wished she didn't feel that she had to do it for him.

"Is Andrei ... is he all right?" John asked.

Senna hesitated a long time before answering. "You and Asha are not the only ones that have found this hard," she said at last. "Andrei just shows it differently."

Many possible responses ran through John's mind: that it wasn't their daughter; that they didn't have to come; that they couldn't know what it was like to face losing Ellie for a second time. But he managed to stop himself. These were his friends, they had been through a lot for him. It occurred to him, too, that Senna had

346

probably left a lot unsaid. He had waited so long that there seemed no good response, so he changed the subject.

"Where are Darnu and Garjae?" he asked. "I haven't seen them since—"

"Since I told Garjae to fuck off?" Senna asked rhetorically. "Seems he did. Yurim said that Novoi had gone out with them to try and locate the best way back to that cabin."

"I suppose that's a good idea."

"Indecent haste, was my reaction."

"It would be better if we don't waste time getting back when we leave," John said, "and we don't want to get caught out like we did before."

"No, you're probably right." Senna looked ahead. "I'll race you to that peak," she told him, pointing, and started to run.

John followed at a more leisurely pace, he didn't think Senna would miss him if he failed to keep up.

Whatever their promises to each other, the nights with Asha had changed too. For a while after returning she would remain cheerful and sometimes playful, still worked up from her day, but as night descended the thoughts she had been blocking would begin to break through again.

Their lovemaking was often desperate, drawn out and repeated until they were both exhausted. Afterwards Asha would cling to him, her grip almost painful. John tried to reassure her, but Asha was finding it impossible to shut out the despair. Soon she would insist on feeding him, and it felt to John that she was giving away too much, more than he really needed, but he couldn't stop her. Almost as soon as she was finished she would retreat to one of the trees and John wouldn't see her again until just before dawn. Then Asha would want to make love again, as if fearful he wouldn't be there when she returned at the end of the day.

One night Asha informed John that Ulvanya wanted him with them tomorrow rather than one of the others. She hadn't been told why.

It felt cold to John in the grey light before dawn, it was pleasant on his skin, still flushed from their lovemaking. Asha held his hand, she hadn't spoken since waking him, and led him down into the healer's valley. They waited near the willow trees.

The water of the lake rippled and then Ulvanya appeared, emerging dry, moving slowly and leaning heavily on her staff. John was surprised by her appearance, as old as she had looked when he first met her, she had aged still further. Her eyes when she looked up at him were no longer young, the blue had faded and her gaze was no longer so imposing. She moved her gaze to Asha and then led them across the valley floor, meeting the tiny trickling stream and following it through the trees and into the small cave.

They sat around the spring that bubbled up through the rocks, its faint noise the only sound that reached John's ears.

The old woman spent long moments staring at the water of the spring before raising them to look at Asha.

"We are almost done, you and I," she said.

"And then you can rest, 'vanya," Asha replied gently.

Ulvanya nodded slowly. "Then perhaps I can rest at last." There was a dull finality to her words.

Again there was only the sound of the spring.

When Ulvanya started speaking again she looked first to Asha, "Stesha has named you daiva, sent from the gods, and this I now believe. You will surpass my skills – perhaps you do already."

Asha opened her mouth to answer but the old woman turned from her and gazed at John.

"You she has named zaravarana: the shield."

John nodded, he could accept that.

"You must protect the daiva. You must shield her or she will fall."

"But of course I will. I would do anything for Asha," John replied in a rush.

"Anything?" Ulvanya raised an eyebrow in question.

She turned her attention back to Asha. "And you must let him. More than that, you must help him to do this for you. You must allow another to sacrifice himself that you may be saved."

Asha looked at John in shock, her eyes wide with horror, and then she turned back to Ulvanya. "No!"

"You must," Ulvanya replied simply. "When the time comes you must, or you will both fall."

"I don't care!" Asha said loudly, angrily. "I won't lose him like that!"

John reached across to try and calm her, but she struck his arm

348

away. "No!" she screamed at him. "Just, no!" Asha got up and ran out of the cave.

John started to get up and follow her, but Ulvanya reached out, her grip surprisingly strong on his arm. "She will return."

"What is it?" John asked her. "What has Stesha seen that makes this necessary?"

"You decline to be her shield?"

"Of course not. I will shield her with my life."

"It is all you will have."

"Then it is hers."

"No. It is not. If you give her your life she will treasure it above her own. To be her shield your life must be your own to place where you wish."

John nodded his understanding.

"And you will shield her even to the cost of your own life?" Ulvanya insisted.

"Yes," he answered firmly.

"To the cost of your child's life?" Ulvanya came back.

John stared at her in horror. He couldn't answer.

"You said, *anything*," Ulvanya reminded him.

He shook his head, not in negation, but in frustration. Eventually he managed, "I can't answer that."

"Good," said Ulvanya.

John looked at her in surprise.

"I do not trust blind promises – promises of anything and forever. Such absolutes are not to be trusted. But I do trust honesty, and you have answered me honestly. As much as I wish for an absolute in this, as much as I know Asha to be daiva, to be worthy of great sacrifice from others, I prefer to trust in the honesty of your inten-tions."

"What is it that Stesha has seen?" John asked again.

Ulvanya was slow to answer. "Stesha does not tell me everything that she sees. The future can sometimes be shaped, tilted one way or another. You can try to prepare yourself for what is coming, but you do not get to choose the path it will take. That lesson cost my sister her life." Her head turned toward the mouth of the cave. "She will not submit this day. When the day comes you must find a way to convince her, she must hold you forward like a shield. But you must

349

understand how difficult this will be for her, such an action is contrary to everything she is." Ulvanya turned to look directly at John. "This much I think you can understand."

John nodded.

Asha returned as Ulvanya finished speaking. She took her place beside the spring and with determination looked at John and then Ulvanya. "I won't do it," she told them.

Ulvanya turned her palms up and looked at them before replying, "Then all will be lost."

"It is lost then."

Ulvanya shrugged.

"There is another lesson you must learn before you leave here," Ulvanya spoke as if none of the previous had taken place. "So far we have concentrated on healing as carefully and completely as it is possible for our limited skills to achieve, what remains we leave to time and the infinite care of life itself. But you will not always have time for such care. Sometimes you must put aside your nature and act quickly."

Ulvanya turned to John. "This will be painful, there will be no time for the care we usually take in these things. This is why I asked you here today, I could not ask it of the young ones."

"Is this punishment for my refusal?" Asha asked sharply.

Ulvanya slowly turned back to her. "Who would you stand in his place?"

"No one. We don't need to do this."

"When you need this skill it will be too late to learn it."

Ulvanya turned with a speed that surprised John and ran one finger across his outstretched leg. The fine material of his pants parted and a gash appeared low on his leg.

John gasped with pain and surprise.

Asha stared at his face and then down to his leg. She fumbled forward to try and heal it but the material of his trousers got in the way. She looked up at him. "Remove your clothes."

John concentrated and his pants and shirt disappeared. Asha began to work on the cut. He gasped again and realised that another cut had appeared above the other.

"You must work faster," Ulvanya urged. Her hand reached out again. Asha tried to push it away, but a third gash appeared above the last. Asha left the first only partly healed and moved to the second. A fourth and fifth cut appeared so quickly that John barely had time to register what was happening.

"Stop," Asha cried to the old woman, "just stop," but her concentration didn't leave the wound she was trying to close.

"Forget the pain, just close the wound and move on," Ulvanya demanded, and new cuts appeared higher, now on John's thigh.

Asha moved quickly from cut to cut, no longer speaking.

John was holding himself tense, trying not to call out with each new pain. The pain in his lower leg began to recede, at first he thought it was just being overtaken by the pain on his thigh, but when he looked down he saw Ulvanya running her fingers over the cuts that Asha had left behind. Ulvanya looked up at him briefly and then turned to watch as Asha closed another of the cuts.

"You are still too slow," Ulvanya told her. "You can come back and finish later if you have time, first you must deal with the open cuts. Keep his life from spilling, don't trust in your ability to fill him again later. Close and move on." Ulvanya's hands continued to move up behind Asha's, deadening the pain of each wound.

Asha closed the last of the gashes on John's leg and sat back, glaring at Ulvanya.

"It is a start," Ulvanya told her. "Now go back and finish with each wound. I must rest for a while." She got up with the aid of her staff and slowly left the cave.

"I'm so sorry, John," Asha kept saying as she bent over his leg, her fingers running gently back and forth over what remained of the wounds. John could feel the life pulsing from her fingers, warm against his skin. The pain receded further and the marks that had been left behind receded with it.

John reached forward and ran his fingers over her head and through her hair. "This may save lives one day," he told her, "it *is* worth a little pain now."

"I can't imagine ever needing something like this."

"Then we just have to trust Ulvanya, she has seen a lot in her long life. She wouldn't put you through this if it wasn't necessary." John didn't mention his additional thought, that maybe Stesha had seen something and this was their way of preparing Asha for the future.

When Ulvanya returned, John thought it was about an hour later, she had John lie face down on the cold stone floor beside the trickling stream. He concentrated on the sound of the stream as the pain began again.

By the time the day was over John was feeling stiff and sore all over. There was no specific area of pain, just an overall stiffness and discomfort as if he'd strained every muscle in his body. Asha was exhausted and Ulvanya appeared to have aged even further.

Ulvanya stood slowly and looked down at them. Asha was still running one hand over John's chest where the last of the cuts had been healed.

"I have taught you all I can," Ulvanya said, her voice not much more than a whisper, barely heard over the sound of the water bubbling up from the spring. "You must both rest now, rebuild your strength. Do not leave for a few days. You will not have much rest after you leave here."

John watched as the old woman turned and hobbled out, at times stumbling over the uneven floor. He thought that last sounded foreboding, like it had come from Stesha. He dreaded to think what it might mean. When he looked down at Asha she didn't seemed to have noticed so he tried to push it from his mind.

They spent two days among the trees on a hill above Ulvanya's valley, but both were restless. Asha insisted on feeding John regularly, claiming she had to replace what he had lost through the cuts, though John was certain she was giving him more than he needed. The extra strength he felt as a result just made his restlessness worse. They took themselves off from the others during the day, finding private places to make love, although John supposed that it often had more to do with wanting distraction, and with Asha's compulsive need to always be touching him, holding him, never wanting him out of her reach.

Darnu and Garjae returned on the evening of the first day, reporting that they had found the cabin and could lead the way back without trouble. By the evening of the second day John and Asha had decided they would depart on the next morning, but Platov arrived to tell them that there was a storm above the lake and they would have to wait. They were forced to wait two more days before Platov reported that the storm would finish by the time they reached the ice.

At dawn on the fifth day they descended into Ulvanya's valley for the last time, intending to say goodbye. As they approached the lake Asha broke away from John for the first time in days and ran to the space between the willow trees.

"She's gone!" Asha called out.

"She left some days ago," said Novoi, emerging from among the trees before the cave. As Novoi walked toward them along the gutter that had been the tiny trickling stream, John saw that the flow had stopped and the stones were dry.

"Gone?" Asha asked, taking a few steps toward him. "Where?"

"She said she was going home. She came to me after I had returned with your friends, she was leaving then."

"But ... the storm."

Novoi shrugged slightly. He looked to Andrei and Senna, but included Yurim and Stasia, who had come to say goodbye to the aaranya. "She said to say that you would not forget her, and that must be enough to satisfy any woman's vanity."

Novoi turned to John. "Ulvanya said to tell you that an honest man need not fear his choices."

John nodded, it was both a reminder and a reassurance.

Novoi turned back to Asha. "She said to tell you that her thoughts, and those of her sister, would be with you. She said to tell you goodbye, Asha the Healer."

Novoi didn't wait for any response, he turned and headed down the valley toward the river.

They watched him until he disappeared around the bend in the valley, and then Asha returned to the space between the willow trees and stared out over the water of the still lake. John came up behind her and put his arms around her, she squeezed his arms tightly but neither of them spoke.

Garjae was impatient to be gone and soon led them across the hills to the edge of the great water, beneath which lay the Way back out of the zarana, this Glade of the jalaja. There Yurim and Stasia said their goodbyes, briefly to the older members but with great affection to Andrei and Senna. There were tears on Stasia's face but Yurim kept up a bold front, John suspected it was likely to dissolve after they left. Casseta and Nuttachen bounded up to them from their own explorations of the zarana, apparently knowing that it was time to go.

They entered the water together and descended. John approached the Way with no trepidation this time, the urge was growing in him to hurry home, to see his daughter again. He pushed on through to the cold water of the lake beyond.

13. Shadow

Their journey through the lake took them three days, but it passed without mishap and with little conversation. Asha insisted that they rest for a day, she wanted to feed John before they emerged once more into the cold. They exited through the ice via a great crack that had appeared not far from the shore, having to push through the soft mushy ice that had formed in the water between the two great shelves. Above the ice the weather was fine, and though cold compared to the water, it was not as bad as when they had last been here. Spring was approaching this land.

Garjae pushed ahead toward the cabin, keeping everyone to a fast pace. No one complained when he kept walking through the night, everyone was keen to be clear of the intense cold in case the same difficulties arose again. John refused to let Asha feed him again until she reached trees that could refresh her, but he too had enough strength to withstand these milder temperatures.

The cabin, when they reached it after dawn, was as they had left it except for the build-up of snow that they had to clear before they could unlock and open the door.

It took John some time to get the equipment started, the technology all felt alien to him at first, as though he had never seen it before. Eventually it came back to him and he managed to get the satellite connection working. He sent off a message asking to be picked up. The response was almost immediate, as if they had been waiting for him. A brief curt message saying:

```
Acknowledged.  Stand  by,  will  organise
pick up and confirm in a few hours. Ben.
```

John sat back from the computer. "That was quick. But what do we do now?"

"Wait, I guess," said Darnu.

"Why don't we write to Milla and to Tracey?" Senna suggested. "We've got the connection and the time."

"We don't want to run out the batteries," John warned.

Andrei put in, "We've got spare batteries. Anyway, what's it matter, they know we're here now?"

John admitted it was a good idea. He wanted news from home, he wanted confirmation that Ellie was still alive. He could even hope that there might be good news, some improvement that might offset Ulvanya's dire pronouncements.

Darnu and Garjae left the cabin, and Andrei and Senna started composing the emails together. They called Asha over when they were writing to Milla.

"If we tell him what we're looking for, he can ask around before we get there," Andrei said. "It will give us a head start."

So they tried to write down what they had learned. It was difficult to put into any words that made sense. Listening to them from his seat on the bunk bed, John could feel the hopelessness of it sinking further. But when Asha came back and sat on his lap she seemed more cheerful, as if sending this message home offered some tangible hope, so John kept his thoughts to himself.

When they had finished, John switched off the equipment to conserve the batteries. It seemed like every few minutes Andrei wanted to turn it back on again to check for answers, but John made him wait. They checked around midday and there was nothing, the same again later in the afternoon.

In the evening there were two messages waiting for them. The first was from Ben, again it was a curt message, saying only:

```
Everything    organised.    Will    pick    up
Thursday in the AM. Ben.
```

John had to check the computer to see what day it was now: Monday evening. They had two more full days here, pick-up would be on the third. Ben certainly wasn't wasting much time. John was pleased, he wanted to get home quickly.

The second was an automated response indicating that their

message to Tracey had not been delivered, something about not finding the account.

There was no response from Milla.

"They're probably back at the Glade or something," Andrei said.

He and Senna tried to compose a new, more positive, email for Tracey, hoping that it would work the second time around. To John it sounded like they were trying to convince themselves that the news wasn't as bad as it sounded. Eventually they gave it up when they found they were just repeating what they had told her previously, so they sent a simple message saying when they expected to be heading back south again.

The time passed quietly, but to John at least, very slowly. The weather remained fine and the temperatures not so extreme as to cause them problems. The only oddity was late in the first day when John stumbled while he and Asha were walking in the forest outside the cabin. He rubbed tenderly at his face, puzzled by the pain that had flared there, and then pain in his stomach made him bend over and gasp.

Asha leaned down next to him. "What is it, John?"

He stood straight again, the pain already subsiding. "I don't know." He ran his hand across his stomach. "A couple of jabs of pain." He paused. "It's going. Time I got this body back where it belongs, I suppose."

Asha looked doubtful but didn't say anything.

On the Thursday morning they waited impatiently for the helicopter. It arrived late in the morning. John thought that Jia looked stressed, but guessed that was just from having to smuggle John and the others aboard without the pilot seeing anything too unusual.

There could be no conversation on the helicopter flight, and back at the airport they transferred directly to the small business jet, there would be no overnight stay in Irkutsk. The main thing that John noticed about all this was the warmth. Everywhere they were enclosed in areas of warmth that felt almost sweltering after the weeks of zero and sub-zero temperatures.

Once they were in the air and on their way back to China, Jia made polite conversation, asking if they had found what they needed. She didn't seem surprised at the largely negative news, and she was reticent about discussing the Samgha, saying only that everything was fine.

There were again two stopovers where Jia had to leave the plane for several hours, but there was little for John and the aaranya to talk about so their time passed very quietly. This was followed by the long helicopter ride out to the small village near the border between China and Myanmar, made longer and more uncomfortable by rough winds. They arrived near dusk and Jia told them they could not continue until tomorrow morning, and they should spend the time in the forest outside the village.

Out in the forest, the jungle here so different to the sparse trees of the frozen north, John paced impatiently. The delay gnawed at him. Asha pulled him away from the others and started tugging at his clothes. Their lovemaking was urgent, almost frantic, and John could see tears on Asha's face. When he tried to question her, she shook her head and wouldn't answer, pushing herself harder, almost angrily, against him. She fed him again soon after, despite John's protestations that he would soon be back in his human body and wouldn't need it. She poured her life into him until it seemed to John that she would never stop. As soon as she had finished she left him, almost fled from him, and merged into one of the trees.

With the fire of Asha's gift burning through his limbs, John stood and paced again. He couldn't settle. The time was dragging. He wanted to be moving, he wanted to be home, to see his daughter again, but still he was forced to wait. At last, late in the night, the journey began to catch up with him and he finally fell into a restless sleep at the base of Asha's tree.

- - -

Asha pulled herself from the tree and stared down at John. Even in sleep he looked restless and impatient. She knew that John was in a hurry to get home, she had felt this impatience growing since they had left the zarana. But to Asha it felt as if events were rushing past, leaving her no time for ... she didn't know what. Anything, everything. She felt as if some great doom were rushing down on her and nothing she did could slow it down. Even this small, unexpected reprieve, a night outside the village before they returned to the Samgha, was almost over, dawn was already being heralded by the stirring of the birds above.

She felt as if she was almost out of time, but she didn't know why. She would have blamed it on Ulvanya and her talk of John as Asha's shield – she would *never* let that happen – but the feeling had been coming on her even before that. It was this feeling of doom that had made her reaction to Ulvanya's words so much stronger. It was like a great shadow looming over her, some massive weight falling with greater and greater speed. She couldn't escape it, worse, she seemed to be rushing into it.

Asha knelt down next to John and stroked the hair from his forehead. He woke with a start. She pressed her fingers to his lips to quiet him. This felt like her last chance. She removed her clothes without ceremony and sat across him. There was a change in texture as John's clothes disappeared beneath her and she lent down to kiss him. They were gentle and slow with each other this morning, Asha tried to draw it out and make this moment last forever, but all too soon it was over. It was over and John was breaking free of her grasp and getting up, in a hurry to be moving again.

Reluctantly, Asha got up and clothed herself. John grabbed her hand and started tugging her back to where they'd left the others. If she wasn't feeling so stressed, so weighed down with a feeling of last moments, she would have smiled at the fact that John's sense of direction, something he had wondered at in the aaranya, worked very well when he stopped thinking about it.

They found the others quickly, it seemed to Asha that everyone else was impatient to be going too. Did no one else feel what she felt? Only Senna sensed something different in Asha, giving her questioning looks that Asha could only shake her head at in response. There was no way to express this feeling of impending disaster.

They stood in a loose group outside the building of the airport. They were early, though it looked as if preparations had already started on the helicopter.

Jia approached them. She looked around to make sure no one was watching and then spoke, "It will be a couple of hours yet, you may as well wait in the trees."

"Is there a problem?" John asked, his impatience almost boiling over.

"No," Jia replied. "It is merely too soon."

Her response was simple enough, but in Asha's nervous state it seemed loaded with extra meanings. Even Jia's gaze over the group was like she was taking them in and absorbing them, reading them and trying to understand them all over again. Jia's gaze rested longest on John.

"Come on," Garjae said, apparently resigned to yet more waiting. The others turned to follow.

"Asha."

The call came softly, accompanied by a soft touch on her arm. Asha looked back in surprise, what could Jia want with her?

"Can we talk?" Jia whispered to her.

Asha looked at John, she was still clinging tightly to his arm. He hadn't been paying attention, lost in the disappointment of yet more delays.

"I'll catch up," she told him.

When he turned, his expression was distracted. Asha squeezed his arm in brief reassurance and then turned back to Jia.

"Asha?" Senna called. She and Andrei were looking back to see what was happening, Asha waved them on.

"What is it?" Asha asked Jia.

"Somewhere private," Jia said softly, and led Asha around the side of the building and through one of its doors.

"There's no one else here," Jia explained as they entered a small lounge area. "We won't be disturbed."

The seats had cheap vinyl coverings and were very uncomfortable, but Asha barely noticed, her attention was centred on Jia.

Jia sat on her chair and stared at her hands without speaking for some time. "I shouldn't be doing this," she began. "You are all supposed to return to the Samgha as if nothing has changed, as if nothing is wrong." Jia looked up. "You are all such innocents!"

Asha didn't know how to respond.

"Did you really believe that Ben was doing all this just because he is a nice guy?" Jia asked her in disbelief. "Ben is a puppet. He would never admit it, but that is what he has become, and it has never been more apparent than now. Those people you told us about, Stephenson and those narun. Of course we know them, we have known them for years. They have been controlling the Samgha through Ben since ..." She shrugged. "A long time."

"Sando? Jaimee?" Asha said quietly in disbelief.

Jia nodded. "Sure they let Ben play his wise benefactor role to the villages around us, it is convenient, but if there is anything new regarding the samvaya then they want to know. If we make any discoveries regarding the nature of the saarvaya or the narun then they want the details."

Asha was in shock. She hadn't trusted Ben, but to believe they had fallen back under the control of Sando and the others – it didn't make sense. If they had wanted her and the others they could have had them at almost any time, and yet they had let them get away to the north.

Misreading Asha's reaction, Jia continued, "The villagers do not know, Dengali and the others. They think Ben, all of us, are truly great and wonderful. They think we are all so superior, and we are happy to believe it. The secret of Stephenson and the others is reserved for the inner Samgha, the samvaya alone, and even amongst us there are some that know more than others. Ben has never trusted Nayati with much, probably because he was told not to, the old man is too talkative. I doubt if even I have been told more than they needed to get my help."

"Why are you telling me this now?" Asha managed to ask.

"You love John, don't you?"

"You know I do."

"He is a good man," Jia said. "Honest, trusting, open."

Asha nodded.

"I have not seen that before. The villagers are honest and trusting, but they are all so earnest it makes my teeth itch. They think we are something so different, the lords and ladies of the Samgha. With John it felt like the first time I had been treated like a real person, like a woman." Jia laughed sadly. "I think I made him nervous at times, but it was obvious, he did not try to hide anything. What he felt for you was obvious too, he never tried to hide that."

Asha didn't respond. She had known about Jia's feelings for John. Whether Jia knew it or not, she was obvious too, at least to Asha.

"If it were not for John, we would all be on the helicopter now and on our way back."

"It's ready?"

"I think so. ... But it is not John they want – it is you."

Asha nodded, it wasn't really a surprise. She hadn't tried to think it all through, but now the words had been said they sounded right, expected. And if John were there he would try to shield her, he would have done so even without Ulvanya's words.

"I think they mean to kill the others, including John." There were tears now in Jia's eyes. "You should have seen the look of hatred on Sando's face when we showed them John's saardha. I thought he was going to attack him right there on the bed."

"Did he hit John?"

"Not while I was there, but I would not be surprised if something happened after I left to come and get you. I have been worried they would not wait for you to get back."

"But we have to go back," Asha said. "John has to return to his body."

"And when he does they will kill him – if they wait that long." Jia paused and then said, "We must not let that happen."

"What can we do? You obviously have something in mind."

"Come back with me. Just you." Jia's eyes were pleading. She finished hurriedly, "If you agreed to go with them easily – tell them that you will cooperate with them only if they leave John alive. You are important to them for some reason, I am sure your cooperation has to be worth more to them than John's death!"

Asha closed her eyes. She already knew her answer, but the thought of returning to the horrors of the prison, the experiments and the preta, was—. She stopped that thought, remembering that all that was gone now, burned to the ground and all the preta dead. All except Ellie. Doing this would mean that she would be leaving Ellie too. If Ulvanya had left any real hope for Ellie then this choice might have been harder still, but there was no real hope left. Asha acknowledged that now and tears streamed down her face. There was nothing more that Asha could do for Ellie without impossibilities that Ulvanya had only hinted at. Ellie was already lost, Asha could only hope that saving John was still within her power. Whatever new horror she was submitting to now, at least it held a chance for John, and that would have to be enough. As she had promised, John would not be her shield, she would be his.

Jia read Asha's hesitation and tears as reluctance. "We *have* to do this!" she cried. "It is his only chance. You will be saving the lives of

362

your other friends too."

Asha opened her eyes and looked at Jia. "I'll go. How soon can we leave?"

Jia jumped up, relief spreading across her face. "Now, now. I am sure it must be ready."

Asha got up slowly, every movement painful to her as if even her body was fighting against her decision to leave. Jia had bounded to the door and stood there waiting impatiently for Asha. Asha made herself move faster. As they walked across the tarmac toward the helicopter Asha thought she sensed something, someone, and turned around in dread of discovery, but saw nothing.

Jia was talking urgently with the helicopter pilot, urging him to leave as quickly as he could. He tried to calm her but she remained insistent. Asha and Jia climbed into the back and the pilot closed the door behind them and climbed into the front. There seemed an interminable delay as the pilot flicked switches.

Asha stared out at the trees. She both dreaded and hoped for some last sight of John. She hadn't said goodbye, she couldn't have said goodbye, it just wasn't possible. She couldn't lie to him and he would never let her do this once he knew what she planned.

The engine started with a loud roar and the long blades started to turn. They would have heard that, they would be coming now. Asha stared even more intently into the trees, trying desperately to see him. A face appeared in the window and Asha sat back in fright. It was Garjae. He was banging on the glass, the sound lost in the rising noise of the helicopter. His expression was angry. He was yelling at her to let him in. Asha put her hands up to push Garjae away and hit only glass. She made shooing motions with her hands but he pounded harder, she was afraid he would hurt himself.

Movement beyond Garjae caught her eye and Asha saw the others running out from the trees. John was pushing hard but Senna was outstripping them all. They were coming so quickly and still the helicopter hadn't moved. Asha couldn't stand it, she could see the desperate look on John's face and hear his voice calling to her. Her hands reached for the door handle.

And then she was rising. Garjae's head slipped below the line of the window with some last desperate yell. In moments they were out of reach and Asha pushed herself against the glass to keep her eyes locked on John. The helicopter turned and Asha rushed to the other side and looked back. She saw her friends' bewildered faces, could see that they were calling to her. Darnu, Andrei, Senna ... and John. She waved and hoped that he saw it. She watched until their forlorn figures faded to dots and then were lost behind the hills as the helicopter flew into a valley.

- - -

Tilvy stared at the empty bedroom. Tracey wasn't here. She hadn't been for a long time.

It was more than a month since Tilvy had last seen her friend being taken away in an ambulance. She had hated letting her go like that, but there was nothing Tilvy could do for her. So she had watched the ambulance leave, and then watched as firemen began to study the devastation left by the fire, they didn't seem interested in dealing with the areas that were still smouldering. Conscious that they may leave footprints in the ash, Tilvy led Beenae carefully away.

Together they had gone into an unburned part of the forest and merged to try and recover from their burns. They would both be okay, as she had written in her note to Tracey, but they were both in a lot of pain. The radiant heat of the fire didn't affect them, as it had Tracey, but the hot surfaces in the car and the hot coals on the ground outside had left some painful injuries.

There was rain that first night. Tilvy and Beenae had both emerged from their trees to revel in it – in the life and promise and hope that it represented. They had hugged each other gently in the rain, trying to offer and receive comfort for what they knew they still had to face.

Days later they had found where the Way to their Glade had once stood open and welcoming. Despite the rain of that first night, what remained of the huge trunks that had once stood either side of the Way were still smouldering on the ground. Around them many other huge trees had also fallen, more than elsewhere in the forest, as if the fire had been more intense here. Further out, Tilvy could sense the life that remained in the still standing trunks. Left to itself, this forest would recover and life would return. Left to itself, eventually, the Way would reopen.

Little was familiar any more. It was all blackened trunks and layers of grey ash, some hiding patches of slowly burning timber. But they had had no trouble finding their way here. Their connection to the Glade was still there, the Glade was still there, it was simply closed to them – for now. Tilvy wished she could be so completely certain that Barma was safe within the Glade. She felt that she would know if something had happened to him, but she couldn't be certain, she could only hope.

They had stayed in the area for some days, not speaking much, just trying to absorb what had happened, trying to come to terms with it. They had only just started to speak about what they might do next when the humans arrived. These humans didn't appear to be doing anything bad, just picking through the ashes, sometimes waving beeping devices over the ground as if searching for something. She and Beenae decided it was better not to stay. Tilvy wanted to see if she could find Tracey again, find out if she was okay.

Back in the small town she visited the hospital and then John's friend's house. Along the way Beenae was getting a much gentler introduction to managing within the human world than Tilvy had ever had. Tilvy found she was pleased to have Beenae with her. He was eager, enthusiastic and seemed to be coping with the loss of their Glade better than she was. It was like having a cheerful younger brother to keep her company, it helped to keep her spirits up and stopped her from moping.

As best that Tilvy could find out, listening in on conversations and reading what she could on the hospital computers, Tracey had been okay, and she had gone home, back to the city. Tilvy was determined to follow her.

They ended up hitching a ride inside the back of a big truck. It was scary, but having Beenae along made it almost fun. Tilvy felt she had to be brave for him, though she wondered whether it was his presence that gave her the courage. In the city she fumbled her way around until she managed to track down Senna's father, Taiza. It was night and he was about to enter a factory, so they followed him in. He listened to their story as he continued to work, Beenae watched him in fascination.

Back at the hospital, and again in a stranger's house here in the city, Tilvy had tried to access the email account that John had set up for them. She couldn't work out what she was doing wrong, the system kept telling her that her user name or password must be wrong. She had hoped she could find Tracey and get some help.

Taiza agreed to look after Beenae while Tilvy went searching for Tracey. At first Beenae looked upset at being left behind, but Tilvy promised to be back in a few days, and the prospect of watching the odd but likeable Taiza at work made the separation less of a disappointment.

Despite thinking that she knew where Tracey lived, it still took Tilvy a day and a half to find the house. She couldn't pass through the door, but Tracey had made sure there was a key hidden for Tilvy to use when she was staying here, and it was still there, so Tilvy let herself in. She tried to be very quiet, it was still very early in the morning.

And now, here she was, still staring at the room that spoke only of Tracey's absence.

Not knowing what else to do, Tilvy wandered the rest of the house. The room where the computer had been was almost bare, so she couldn't try to use that, even if it hadn't been for the warnings that Tracey had told her about. Maybe Tracey had ditched it after all. But why wouldn't she have bought a new one?

Later in the morning Tilvy watched Tracey's mother come out of her bedroom. She looked haggard, like she hadn't been sleeping well.

Tilvy knew it was rude, but Tracey's mother was her best chance of finding Tracey, so Tilvy continued to watch the woman as she went about getting her breakfast, and then cleaning and tidying the house. She seemed intent on cleaning every nook and cranny, and not for the first time, Tilvy guessed, everything was already spotlessly clean. At intervals the woman would lift her head and stare back toward her bedroom, sometimes she would go back there, getting as far as the door before turning back. And sometimes the urge would get too much and the woman would go into the room, dig into a drawer and pull out a letter and read it.

Tilvy watched the tears roll down the woman's cheeks and wondered what she was reading. The letter was again tucked away and the woman returned to her work.

After lunch Tracey's mother went out, so Tilvy went to the

bedroom and looked in the drawer. There was the letter, and next to it Tilvy recognised her own mobile telephone, the one John had bought her so she could exchange text messages with Tracey. Tilvy had forgotten all about it when she and Tracey had rushed off that morning. Tracey's mother must have found it somewhere, she probably thought it belonged to Tracey. Tilvy reached in and took out the letter. The handwriting on the envelope was Tracey's. Tilvy listened carefully, there wasn't anyone around. She opened the envelope and pulled out the letter, dreading what she might find.

Dear Mum, the letter started. *Don't worry! I am fine. They are treating me much better now. The man who delivers this will explain in more detail, but the horrible fact is that I have stumbled into something bad, and it would be dangerous for me to return home. Dangerous for both of us, Mum! So I have agreed to be taken into protective custody. Like before, you are not supposed to say anything to anyone. Just pretend I've run off or something. Tell Dad I've run off with a man (it's something he's always bugging me about, so it'll make him happy).*

If John shows up don't blame him. It's not his fault. I don't think they believe me here yet, but he's got nothing to do with what they say is going on. Trust me, I know John, none of this is his fault, whatever anyone else tells you.

I'm really sorry to just disappear like this, if there was any other way I wouldn't go. I don't know how long it will be, it could be a long time. When I get back we can have a big laugh about the stupid things your daughter can get herself into. Until then, I'll miss you terribly – I do already. Lots of love, Tracey.

Tilvy stared at the letter. What did it mean? It had to be about the fire. It had to have been started by humans. Tracey said it wasn't John's fault, and Tilvy had no trouble believing her, but John's house had been targeted. It couldn't be a coincidence. It had to be related to the mess last year. The dhumraka must be back – that thought had been in her mind since the fire. It was the only thing that fitted. The dhumraka and their human lackeys.

- - -

Andrei watched the helicopter disappear behind the hills, the sound of it dying away in the distance, and then he turned to the others. John was standing there still staring. Senna returned

Andrei's look of disbelief. When Darnu took his eyes off the distant hills it struck Andrei that his look of desperation matched John's.

"What happened?" Andrei asked, not really expecting an answer.

"It didn't look like she was being forced," said Senna.

"Well Garjae certainly wasn't." They had all seen Garjae at the helicopter, and when it rose he had latched on to the landing strut and gone up with it. He was still there when it had disappeared into the distance as far as Andrei could tell.

"What do we do?" asked John, tearing his eyes away.

"Perhaps we wait for them to come back," suggested Andrei.

"No," disagreed Senna. "If they were planning on coming back they'd never have left like that. They'd have told us what they were doing."

"Darnu?"

It took a moment for him to answer, "I think Senna's right. If not Asha, then Garjae would have stayed to explain. I think we have to assume they aren't planning to come back."

"But why?" John asked, pleaded.

No one had an answer.

"The chopper has to come back here, surely. Maybe we can force it to take us back again," said Andrei.

There was silence for a while.

"No takers for a hijacking then," murmured Andrei.

"I can't see any way to make it work," answered John. After a moment he asked, "How far is it to the Samgha from here?"

"To walk?" asked Darnu.

John nodded. "Or run."

"A couple of days at least, I should think."

"Then let's make a start."

Andrei looked at John in surprise. "Huh?"

"Asha knows that I have to return to my human body, that hasn't changed. There must be something there that's a danger to us, probably to me since I'm the only one that absolutely has to return, so she's gone ahead to face it."

"Alone? Why not wait for us?"

John shrugged. "I don't know. I wish I did."

"So she might come back looking for us when she's done."

"If it was something she expected to come back from she wouldn't have gone alone."

Senna agreed. "She would rather put herself in danger than John, or us. If she wanted us to wait here she would have found some way to leave a message for us."

"Whatever else, I don't think I can just sit here and wait," said John. "Maybe if we're fast enough we'll be in time to help her."

Andrei didn't think it sounded very likely, but there didn't seem much else for it.

Darnu agreed. "Even if they return to look for us it will be obvious where we went, John has no choice, so in that case the worst that can happen is we'll take a few days to get there. But if we wait here we're no better off."

"Who can lead the way," John asked, impatient to be going. His words were barely out when Darnu started off at a jog. That seemed to suit John who quickly followed.

Andrei and Senna looked at each other, then shrugged and started after the others.

"It's all right for you," Andrei told her. "You'll probably beat us all and not even be tired when we get there."

Senna answered, "Speed, not stamina, slow coach, I'll be as bad as everyone else after much of this."

A short while later Senna spoke quietly so her voice didn't carry forward to John or Darnu, "Asha's been strange for days. This morning she looked almost frantic, like something was scaring her."

"You mean she saw this coming?"

"Maybe not this, but something. Whatever Jia told her, I think it hit home. I'm worried about John now too, that's the only thing that could have drawn her away like that."

"You think Ben or someone's up to something with John's human body, and that's what Jia told her?"

"What else could it be?"

Andrei considered this as they fought their way up the next hill. It still didn't explain why Asha thought she could do anything on her own, but otherwise it sounded right.

A couple of days, Darnu had said, but Andrei was starting to think he had been impossibly optimistic, which was hardly like him. It might have only been a few hours by helicopter, but it didn't have to go up and down all these mountains and fight its way through the undergrowth. What they really needed was—

"Hold up!" a call came from behind them.

Andrei called ahead to John and Darnu who were quickly disappearing in front of them, and then stopped to look around. Senna pointed, and from that direction appeared a young aaranya man. He came up and looked them over. He had been moving quickly when he arrived but showed no sign of fatigue.

"We don't have any money," Andrei told him.

The young man gave Andrei a puzzled look, Senna gave him a nudge in the ribs.

"You're Andrei and Senna," the young man said.

"Who are you?" Senna demanded.

"Litak sent me."

Andrei studied the young man, dark and lithe, a look of strong self-confidence. Not as young as he and Senna but not much older. "How do we know that?" he asked.

"I know who you two are, and I knew where to find you." The young man looked with interest at Senna. "I also know that Litak thinks you could be a tracker even better than me."

Andrei had to admit that was pretty strong evidence, though he didn't like the look the young man was giving Senna.

Darnu and John came stumbling back.

"And John there, the saarvaya, is a human."

"How did you know where to find us?" Senna was still suspicious, but then the morning's events were bound to lead to that.

"Litak said you'd be coming back through that village, I was told to watch for you."

"Who is he?" John asked.

"He says he's from Litak," Senna explained. "But we still don't know what he wants."

"We were at the village all last night," Andrei said, "why didn't you approach us then?"

"I was held up with the other strangers, I only just got here in time to see the helicopter leave. I thought I was too late, then I saw you leaving on foot. I had to cut across to try and intercept, you took a hard trail."

"We're in a hurry," John said with impatience. "What is it you want?"

"Where are the others?" the young man asked. "There should be two more of you. A healer? Litak said I would know her when I saw her."

"She's why we're in a hurry," Andrei explained. "She was on the helicopter."

The young man swore under his breath. "Litak's going to kill me!" He looked back up at Andrei. "Litak told me to stop you getting on the helicopter, things have changed back at the Samgha, it's not safe for you."

Senna said in exasperation, "Tell us something we haven't worked out!"

"And where's Litak?" Andrei added.

The young man flicked his gaze back and forth between them. "He only just received word from the Samgha and he sent me to try and get you. We also got news of refugees from a Glade to the east, it's the first time that's happened, so others were sent out to look for them." He paused and shrugged. "It was my lot to find both." To try and answer Andrei better he added, "Litak's too old to tackle these distances at speed."

"He did okay tracking us," noted Andrei.

The young man shrugged. "He hasn't been well since."

"Look," said John impatiently, "are you here to help or hold us up?"

"I'm here to lead you," the young man said simply.

"Where?" Darnu wanted to know.

"Well to start with—" The young man stopped when he saw John's expression. "I'll take you to see the other strangers, there's someone there you should meet."

"Who?" John demanded.

The young man hesitated. "I'm not certain, it's just something that Litak said. Will you come with me?"

"We're going to the Samgha," Darnu said in firm tones.

"It's on the way," the young man told them. When he saw that he had gained the interest of his audience he turned, saying, "It's this way."

Darnu called to him, "The Samgha's that way!"

The young man called back, "In these hills the fastest way is not always a straight line."

Their speed quickly improved as the young man found clear ways through the jungle that Andrei would never have seen. More than that, he seemed to know where these winding paths would take them.

- - -

Asha looked down at the ridge as the helicopter descended. There was no one around, even down in the village below the cliff there was no one to be seen.

"Where is everyone?" she asked.

"I don't know," Jia admitted. "It looked normal when I left."

Asha had tried to pull herself together over the last few minutes as they approached the Samgha. She was starting to wonder if she may have taken on more than she was ready for. She hadn't changed her mind about wanting to buy John's safety, but she was beginning to realise that it may not be so simple.

The helicopter settled to the ground and Asha was astonished to see Garjae walk out, apparently from beneath the helicopter. She fumbled at the door until Jia reached around her and opened it.

Asha jumped out and confronted Garjae angrily, "What are you doing here?"

"I hitched a ride. Why did you come?"

"She came to see me," a voice called to them over the noise of the helicopter winding down.

Asha turned to see Sando walk around from the front of the helicopter. "Sando," she acknowledged with dull fatalism. A second, identical, figure joined him. "And Jaimee," she said in the same tone.

A third figure walked up beside the two brothers. Pale and beautiful like the apparently young men, but this was a stunning young woman. Bright white hair cascaded from her head, she had the same face, but feminine and with an elegance and composure that the men hadn't bothered to put forward. "You do well," the woman told Asha. "Normally only their mother can tell them apart."

Asha stared at her.

"Let me introduce my sister Helix," Jaimee said. "Helix, this is the dryad we've been telling you about. Her name is Asha."

Asha flicked her eyes back and forth over the three of them. They weren't just brothers and sister, she was sure of it.

"Look, Sando," continued Jaimee. "I do believe she's worked it out."

"Some of it anyway," agreed Sando.

"What are we doing here?" Garjae asked Asha roughly.

"You were invited," answered Jaimee. "In fact all your friends were invited. What happened to our other guests, Jia?"

"I came to make a bargain," Asha interrupted.

"A bargain? What do you have to bargain with?"

Asha paused. What if Jia was wrong? What if they didn't want her that much? Too late now. "I'll go with you, I'll do what you want, but you have to leave John and my friends alone."

"But we have you now anyway, why should we bargain?" Sando asked.

"You can't do this, Asha," Garjae told her. "Let's just run, get out of here!"

"You can try running, but you won't get far," Helix spoke out, her voice, like her body, was alluring – whatever the words. The three siblings were joined by Stephenson, his hulking human figure still elegantly dressed, but he was also carrying a backpack and in his hand was one of the ray-guns with which Asha and Garjae were both familiar. "And if you should outrun that," Helix continued, "there are dhumraka waiting for you on the forest edge." Her hand cast around as if presenting a prize.

Asha looked around below the ridge and could see the grey figures of the dhumraka appear through the trees.

"But we'd still rather you didn't," said Jaimee. "You intrigue me, Asha. What makes you think we plan to harm any of you?"

"You didn't go to all this trouble just to say hello," Asha answered.

Jaimee nodded his acceptance of this. There was silence between the siblings for a few moments and then Jaimee continued, "The sisters disagree and the brothers disagree. If you could see your way clear to excluding the human then I'm sure I could convince Sando to go along. Are you sure you won't reconsider?"

"John must be left unharmed," Asha replied loudly.

"She is intransigent. Come on Helix, Sando. Her cooperation would be helpful, admit it."

Again there was silence between the siblings, but Asha thought she noted changes of expression as if they were somehow talking amongst themselves.

"All right," said Jaimee at last. "We have a bargain."

Asha saw Jia sigh with relief. Garjae clenched his fists and his expression turned hard.

"Don't do anything, Garjae," she told him quietly.

"Don't *you* do this. Even John wouldn't want you to do this," Garjae hissed back.

"There is no other choice. This was all we had left."

"You shouldn't have come. We could have disappeared into the jungle back there, they'd never have found us."

But Asha had had time to think about this now, their strife was worse than they had ever imagined. The words of Ulvanya came back to her and she repeated them to Garjae, "What makes you think this Jaimee and Sando have finished with you?" She could see that Garjae remembered who had said them first, then she added, "They know where we come from, Garjae, there was no escaping this. And it's me they want. This way buys peace for our Glade, not just for John."

"But you can't trust them. How do you know they'll keep their word?"

Asha had already recognised this weakness in the plan, she had finally seen it not long before the helicopter had landed, and she didn't have an answer for it.

"Show me John's body," she called to Jaimee. "I want to see he's all right."

"Sure, no problem. Just give us a while to finish organising things. Got to arrange our flight back, we won't all fit in that thing," Jaimee answered cheerfully, pointing to the helicopter Asha had arrived in. "Why don't you go and rest in the trees or something while you wait?"

Asha stared at the three siblings, uncertain what to think, and then slowly turned and walked down the slope toward the forest.

"This is our chance," Garjae whispered to her, "once we're in the trees we can make a break for it."

"You go if you want," Asha said in resignation. "They know I'm not going anywhere while they have John."

Asha and Garjae climbed into a tree on the edge of the forest. They could see dhumraka among the trees near them, but the grey narun kept their distance.

"What are you doing here, Garjae?" Asha asked again.

"I went back to see what you and Jia were doing. I got there in time to see you walking toward the helicopter so I waited to see what was happening. I never dreamed you would try to leave without us or I would have stopped you then."

"And you clung on outside all the way here?"

Garjae nodded. "It wasn't easy, this arm is still not strong."

"That's your fault, you wouldn't let us fix it for you."

"I wasn't going near that old woman again."

"Do you want me to take a look at it now?" Asha offered and reached out for his arm.

Garjae pulled away. "No." He studied Asha for a moment then asked, "Did you know what, who, was here when you left?"

Asha nodded. "Jia told me."

"All for John?"

Asha hesitated before answering. It was all so complicated now, but when it came right down to it Garjae was right, not that he'd like to hear it. She nodded.

"You're a fool! What's to stop them coming back to kill everyone after you're gone?"

Asha started to say that they had promised, but realised how foolish that sounded. The truth was that she hadn't thought this through, she had reacted on instinct. But she still didn't see what choice she had. Maybe this way there was a chance, just a chance, that they would keep their word.

"Give me some other option, Garjae," Asha said, pleading.

"Leave him, he's lost anyway, like his daughter. We should have left this place when I said, it's too late to save him now. Come with me, we can outrun these dhumraka, we know this forest."

"Not that, Garjae. I can't do that."

"If I could hope to carry you and still outrun the others I'd do it."

Asha nodded.

"You know that I love you?"

Asha nodded again.

"I've adored you since you were a child playing with your brother. When you grew into such a beautiful young woman I thought my heart would break just looking at you."

"Stop it, Garjae. I can't help how you feel. I can't help how I feel about John, and I can't change it. I don't want to change it."

"I know that, Asha. I know exactly how that feels."

Garjae turned away from her and stared up at the ridge. Asha, not knowing what else to do or say, followed his gaze. Their helicopter was leaving. Jia was gone, Asha hadn't seen where she went, hadn't given her a thought. She hoped she would be okay. She watched the helicopter rise and thought she sensed the presence of dhumraka on board, but no humans other than the pilot.

"Maybe they're going back to look for the others," Garjae commented bitterly.

Asha was horrified, she hadn't thought about that. "They won't still be there will they?"

Garjae looked at her, a strange conflicted expression on his face. It took him a few moments to answer, "I doubt it. If it was me I'd have started running as soon as I saw you leaving, and I wouldn't stop until I got here."

The day dragged on and Asha fretted. She knew there was no chance the others would make it here so quickly. Through the forest it would have to take days, but still she worried they would arrive and all her efforts might turn to nothing. She wondered what was taking Jaimee and the others so long to be ready. Were they doing anything to John's body? They wouldn't. They couldn't. Not now.

The sun had gone down, leaving just a faint glow on the horizon, when Sando came down to get them. "We're just about ready now. Our ride will be here soon, so you should come down now and take a look over your human before we leave."

Asha and Garjae followed him back up the slope. As they approached the entrance to the Samgha she heard the noise of an approaching helicopter, it sounded different to the one she had arrived on. She paused to watch for it, just a faint shadow against the dark sky.

Sando stopped too and they waited for it to land. Some lights had been placed on the ground and they flicked on as the great machine got close. It was huge, much larger than any Asha had seen before. Two great blades made circles in the light, the dark body was barely visible even with the ground lights shining up.

"Much more comfortable than the old box we loaned you," Sando commented, "and faster. Come on, let's get this over with."

They descended into the Samgha. As they got down into the main corridors Asha could detect scents in the air that she had never noticed when they were here before. Metallic smells and oil, an acrid chemical odour, and a strange burnt smell that seemed familiar, something she had smelt many years ago, but she couldn't place it.

"Where is everyone?" Asha asked.

"They're all keeping out of the way," Sando answered. "We didn't want an audience."

"And Jia?"

"She's with them."

When they reached the hospital it was eerily quiet, it gave Asha the shudders. They went down the long tunnel to the Initiation Room. Garjae was trailing behind, but Asha was too impatient to wait for him. Helix was standing at the doorway to the room, Asha moved past her carefully and then her attention fell on John – John's human body. Again she felt that horrific sensation that he was dead, that there was not enough life left in the body. Slowly she calmed herself and looked more carefully, he was much as they had left him.

"As you see," Jaimee said, "he is unharmed."

Asha glanced up, she hadn't even noticed Jaimee standing there on the other side of the bed.

"Sweet," came Helix's seductive voice from behind her. She was stroking the side of Garjae's head like a lover. "But way too easy." This last was said softly under her breath.

"Is there anything you'd like us to do to prove he's okay?" Jaimee drew Asha's attention back to him. "Maybe get him to wiggle his fingers and toes or something. Can he do that?"

"Just get away from him!" Asha said angrily.

Jaimee held his hands up and backed away.

Asha went to John's side. She had almost forgotten how much larger he was like this. She enlarged herself to match and stroked the hair from his forehead. There was some bruising on the side of his face, but it didn't look bad. She sent her senses into his body, but it was strange, the sensations were weak because there was so little life left in it. She spent some minutes trying, but could detect nothing wrong beyond the fact that the real life, the real John, was still missing. The body was simply dormant, waiting.

"We do have to leave soon," Sando spoke from the door. He didn't look happy.

"And what do you want to do about him?" Jaimee asked, pointing to Garjae. "Which part of the bargain is he?"

"I'm going with her!" Garjae shouted back.

Asha looked up. Garjae was standing near her but he was facing the door watching Helix and Sando.

"No," Asha said quietly. "Garjae stays here. He can watch over John's body until he comes for it."

Jaimee nodded. "All right. Are you ready?"

Asha leaned back over John and kissed his lips, cooler than they should have been. Tears dropped from her eyes onto his cheeks as she straightened. She left them there glistening.

"Very touching," muttered Sando. "Come on." He turned and walked out, Stephenson was ahead of him. Helix waited by the door as Jaimee came through, and smiled into the room as Asha came forward.

"I have to stay here?" Garjae asked, his voice almost pleading.

Asha turned. "Yes, Garjae. I'm sorry." She considered going over to kiss him goodbye, but there was something about his expression that stopped her. She turned and pushed past Helix, then reminded herself to stop again, she couldn't leave any of these narun alone near John. She turned to look back.

"You must stay here and wait for them," Helix was saying softly, almost tenderly.

Asha watched as Helix closed the door carefully between her and Garjae, she thought she heard Garjae saying something, or perhaps crying. Asha had never heard Garjae cry before.

"You'd better come," Helix told her as she slipped back past Asha and led the way out.

Jaimee and Sando were waiting in the main hospital area.

"You promise not to harm him?" Asha demanded. "No harm to him, or to my friends, or to my home?"

Jaimee smiled at her. "Of course. We promise. We will do nothing further to harm those things you hold dear. We want your cooperation."

Asha studied him carefully, trying to believe him, trying to believe that this would work. It *had* to work, she could see no other way. The others turned and started walking, and Asha followed them.

The corridors seemed to stretch forever and yet they were gone so quickly. Through the dark night she stepped up into the luxury of the helicopter and quickly found a seat. She curled up tight and buried her head. She hurt, all of her hurt. She wished that death would take her, there seemed little reason to live any longer. She barely noticed when the machine left the ground.

Asha didn't know how much time had passed when her eyes flicked open in alarm. It was coming! A sharp pain tore through her chest, as if something had gouged at her heart, and she sat up gasping.

"It is done," Helix was saying.

Asha looked across and saw Jaimee give Helix a warning look, but Sando wore a victorious smile. Desperate thoughts of John flashed through her mind. The great shadow that Asha had felt falling, crashed down and smothered her. As the darkness took her she understood the pain she felt. They had lied. She had failed him.

14. Waiting

John woke and tried to remember what had hit him. He remembered the shock of pain. In the brief moments before he lost consciousness he had thought it must be a heart attack, his whole chest clutched in some gigantic gripping hand and being twisted like a wet rag. Inside his chest there still remained a strong dull ache as if everything inside was badly bruised. There was another pain, this one sharper, spanning the surface of his chest and stomach, as if someone had been playing noughts and crosses on his skin. That had come first, he remembered that now.

There were voices, someone was saying something to him. He opened his eyes and stared into large pale green eyes, compassionate and caring – the eyes he saw in his dreams.

"Asha," he tried to speak, but the words emerged as little more than a harsh whisper.

"No," an unfamiliar voice answered.

The eyes receded and the face came into view, a man's face. Asha's eyes in a stranger's face. But it wasn't such a strange face. It had about it the same lines, the same strongly delineated features. His hair was the same light brown, but shorter and scruffier, in places sticking up at odd angles. John continued to stare at the man, the man calmly returning his gaze, until Andrei's voice intruded.

"Jeez, John. Way to scare the crap out of people, and that's not supposed to happen to us."

John turned his head. On his other side, Andrei and Senna were kneeling next to him, looking at him with worried expressions. He forced himself to smile. He felt pain in and across his neck, like an intense sore throat. He remembered that pain starting just moments before the great shock ripped through his heart.

"I just wanted to see if you were paying attention," he croaked.

Andrei turned to Senna. "I told you it was just attention seeking behaviour."

Senna ignored him and asked John, "Are you all right?"

"I guess so," John answered after a moment to try and take in his condition. The day's events began to seep back in again. "Asha!" he spoke harshly and tried to sit forward and get up.

The stranger reached out and gently pushed him back. "You need to rest."

"No! You don't understand," John responded. He struggled against the man's firm hand.

"I do understand, but whatever my darling sister has got herself into will have to wait a few minutes at least."

John sat back and stared at the man anew. Of course. "Sarva," he said.

The man nodded. "It's nice to know Asha wasn't so ashamed of me that she wouldn't mention my name."

"She misses you."

"And I her."

One central thought kept pushing its way through the jumble in John's mind. "Then you must know we have to go. We have to get to Asha!"

Sarva nodded. "The others have told me, I understand the need. But you all need to rest a bit longer, you especially. Your body has had a big shock."

John looked past Sarva to see Darnu pacing back and forth. Further away was the young man that had been leading them through the forest, Leavek. He was sitting, leaning back against the base of a tree and watching them.

"How long have I been out?" John asked.

"A while," Sarva told him, "maybe an hour in your terms."

John pushed himself further upright and looked around. It was night, the jungle around them dark, only his vedana allowed him to see his friends and the forest around them. The pain across the skin of his chest drew his attention and he opened his shirt. There appeared to be faded lines making some sort of pattern that he couldn't make out.

"It looks like writing," Andrei said.

"What's it say?"

"I can't make it out. Most of it looks like someone keeping score, you know, just lines. The bottom bit might be a word, you need a flatter stomach, John."

"I'll start doing sit-ups. Senna?"

Senna shook her head.

John pulled his shirt closed again, there didn't seem much point in pursuing it further. The events began to fall into place for him. The endless day running, Darnu pushing Leavek to go faster, John pushing himself hard just to keep up, and Andrei and Senna patiently following. Night had fallen and John had felt Asha's presence, her touch on his face, on his shoulder. He had pulled up short and Andrei had almost knocked him over. John had felt Asha's lips on his own, a dampness on his cheeks that wasn't there when he touched his own face. And then she was gone.

John had frozen there, waiting, but when Asha's presence didn't return he had jumped forward, yelling at Leavek to move it, and their run had started again. Only the life that Asha had fed him the night before gave him the strength to push ahead, and that thought spurred him even harder. He was nearing exhaustion, he guessed they all were, when they saw a figure on the path in front of them. John remembered his surprise at this figure's appearance, but then the pain had started. First across his chest and moving down, and then a tightening across his throat that left him trying to gasp for a breath he didn't need. And then the bolt from nowhere grabbing at his heart. And then blackness.

He rubbed at his chest. He had an idea what must have happened, but still he asked, "What happened to me?"

"All day running, John. That's what it was. You were going pretty hard," Andrei told him.

John looked around. Andrei looked guilty, as if caught in a lie. Senna couldn't hold his gaze. Darnu stopped his pacing to stare at John briefly, and then restlessly started moving again. Sarva continued to stare at John calmly.

"We thought we were going to lose you," said Senna softly, staring at John's feet. "Your body was twitching, convulsing ... but Sarva seemed to help, he calmed you somehow."

John looked back to Sarva who returned a slight shrug.

"Do you think you can move?" Darnu asked, looking over Sarva's shoulder.

"I think so," John said.

Andrei helped John to his feet, his legs felt unsteady.

"You should rest longer yet," Senna urged.

"I think I need to move, to wear this off," John argued.

This received doubtful looks, but John ignored them and walked over to Leavek. "Can you lead us on?"

Leavek looked him up and down, doubting that John was going anywhere.

"Maybe slowly for a while," John admitted.

Leavek looked past John to Sarva. "You sure you don't want to wait and see if your friends come back?"

"No," Sarva said. "After what you told us about what's ahead they decided they didn't want to get any closer. I imagine they'll go into hiding, or maybe try to join up with some yaayaavara."

John looked at Sarva in question.

"It's a long story, another time."

Standing there near him, John could see that Sarva was taller than his sister and had a broader, stronger appearance. John thought he also had a more wary, less open, stance and expression, as if the events of his life had given him reason not to trust the world around him.

"What about the Samgha?" John asked, turning back to Leavek.

Leavek started walking as he spoke, "Unusual and disturbing activity started some days ago. On the first day a large helicopter came in, we've seen it before but not very often. The next day the normal helicopter came and left carrying Jia, the same one you were supposed to catch today, but soon after that left two big ones arrived carrying humans and narun, strange grey things that call themselves dhumraka."

"We know them," Andrei put in.

Leavek continued, "There were lots of guns and other equipment being carried out of the helicopters. I don't know what happened after that. It was enough for Litak to start making himself heard again, and that's when he sent me out looking for you."

Sarva put in, "And it was enough for my friends to want to depart, they'd seen enough of the dhumraka."

"But you stayed," Senna commented.

"Leavek told me that I matched a description he'd been given, with the unfortunate variance that I was male and not a healer. That's when I realised he must be speaking of my sister. I always knew that something extra special was going to come from her – I just never expected to meet her here in all this. I wanted to come with Leavek to try and meet you, but we were exhausted so I stayed here with the others, I would only have slowed him down. Then the others left anyway and it was too late to try and follow Leavek."

"And I was too late anyway," finished Leavek, and started to pick up the pace.

They walked on through the night, sometimes disturbing creatures that used the paths that Leavek chose. A tiny deer, a Leaf deer, according to Leavek. Later a leopard that they gave a wide berth, it merely watched them go past. After a while John's pains receded enough that he could speed up to a jog and their progress improved.

They rested again at dawn. John fell into a reluctant sleep and was woken a few hours later by Senna. Most of John's pains had faded, only the dull ache in the centre of his chest remained, but it was no longer enough to impede his determination. Again they started running. The creatures of the night were gone, the paths were now shared with the occasional larger deer, even a small group of elephants, and there were monkeys chattering at them from the trees as they passed. There were few clearings along the paths that Leavek followed so John rarely saw the sky, he had no idea of their direction or progress.

They were forced to break again only an hour or so after nightfall, John could go no further. He forced a promise from the others not to let him sleep more than a few hours and fell quickly asleep at the base of a tree. When Andrei woke him it was still dark and John still felt tired but he forced himself to move again. John refused to stop when Leavek offered as the sun rose again, his desperation was growing and Leavek admitted that they were getting close.

Around mid-morning Leavek beckoned the others to stop. He told them to stay where they were and he quickly disappeared into the jungle in front of them.

"He's good," Andrei commented. "As good as Litak?" he asked Senna.

In response Senna pointed, her finger moving as she traced Leavek's path back and forth in front of them. At last she lowered her finger, she'd lost him.

When Leavek returned he told them, "There doesn't seem to be anyone here. It feels deserted."

"What about down in the Samgha?" John asked.

"I didn't go that far, not sure I want to."

Leavek showed them the way and then followed them to the entrance on the ridge above the cliffs. He paused at the top of the stairs, obviously nervous.

"Have you ever been down here?" Senna asked him.

"No."

"You don't have to come," John said. Darnu was already heading down and John wasn't willing to wait around. He gave the others a last look and headed after Darnu, Sarva followed closely behind. The lighting was mostly gone, and at first that was a problem, forcing them to go slowly, but further down they reached the living rock and their way became clearer.

"Looks like they're putting in new lights or something," Andrei said softly, "maybe replacing the ones that have gone out." In the quiet, and the feeling of creeping danger, they all spoke in whispers.

John paused and looked back. Leavek was coming with Andrei and Senna. Andrei was looking at something high on the wall. John could see a shadowy bulge against the living rock but could make nothing of it. He turned and kept after Darnu, who was picking up the pace.

They went past one of the food halls and John glanced in, some lights were still working in there, but it looked deserted. He followed on after Darnu's back. He could feel the others hurrying to keep close, Sarva's presence felt vaguely familiar, comforting.

Further on they found that more of the corridor lights were still working, and as they got close to the hospital Andrei spoke again, this time a little more loudly. "There's more of these things, but none of them seem to be working."

John looked back as Andrei stopped and picked one off the wall.

"Oops," said Andrei, "they come apart."

Senna nudged at him but Andrei was intrigued and stopped at the next one he found too, showing the pieces to Leavek. John got impatient with them, Darnu had already gone ahead so John rushed after him. He ran through the hospital and on down the long corridor to the Initiation Room.

He stopped in the doorway. Darnu was in the far corner to the left, kneeling next to Garjae who was crouched there staring down at the floor. Darnu was trying to speak with him, pressing at his shoulder but getting no response.

John pulled his eyes back across the room to where his own body lay on the bed, not wanting to confirm what he already knew. But there it was. The top part of the bed and the wall behind it was a mass of dark brown and blackened spots, some looking almost burnt; there was more spread on one side than the other. The sheet had been pulled up to his shoulders, it was almost completely stained with dry blood, hiding whatever lay beneath.

John stood still, staring. Could he dare to approach his own corpse?

Behind him he heard Andrei still talking about his gadgets. "See, there's one here too."

"You don't have to pull them all apart, Andrei," Senna muttered in exasperation.

John thought Andrei was probably putting off finding what they must all realise was down here – just like he was now. He forced himself to move.

He walked to the far side of the bed. On the floor was a knife, long and deadly looking with a wooden handle. He wondered whose hands had held that blade, and if it mattered. Had Asha been forced to witness this? He didn't know quite where that morbid idea had come from. He forced his eyes to look at his own face. There was a bruise, or perhaps it was a faint smear of blood on one side, but otherwise it was mostly clear and undamaged, and there was no expression of pain or suffering – that much was some sort of relief.

Beneath his chin he could see where his neck had been sliced open. It looked like someone had had a hard time of it, hacking at it a number of times, the flesh was hanging in rags. There didn't appear to be much still holding his head to his body. John was reminded of the ghost from Harry Potter – like Nearly Headless Nick, John could never join the headless hunt; John had to stop himself from bursting into hysterical laughter. Even with the body's slower heart rate the blood from the first cuts had managed to spurt fiercely, covering either side of his head and the bed and wall to either side, but in the end much of it had come out more slowly and formed pools behind his shoulders; it was still glistening blackly there like some grotesque jelly.

To witness your own death was such a peculiar thing that John couldn't have said whether his reaction could be considered normal. How were you supposed to react? His interest in the details did feel strange to him, he'd probably never have found the stomach for this curiosity in any other situation.

"I've been waiting for you," Garjae was saying.

John looked up and saw that Garjae had lifted his head, his eyes had a faraway look.

"No," whispered Sarva. Asha's brother had followed John and was standing by his shoulder. Sarva was now staring across the room at Garjae with an expression of horror.

"What happened, Garjae?" Senna called.

Standing in the doorway, Andrei and Leavek were staring at John's corpse, but Senna was glaring at Garjae.

"I've been waiting for you," Garjae said again. "I wanted to go with her, but she said I had to stay here. She wouldn't let me go with her. She wanted me to wait for you."

John wondered if Garjae's mind had broken, stuck in here with this ghastly company.

"Who, Garjae?" Sarva asked.

Garjae stared blankly back at Sarva. "I love her. She knows I love her, I tell her so. I did it for her, but she still wanted me to stay here to make sure you got the message."

"What message, Garjae?" Darnu asked softly, still kneeling there next to him, his hand resting on Garjae's shoulder.

Garjae glanced at him and then looked across toward John and pointed.

John followed the line of his finger. The sheet. John grasped the edges and slowly pulled it back, having to tug it free where the blood had stuck it to the skin of his body. If the message had been written in blood it was impossibly smeared now.

But it wasn't written in blood. Now John understood the pain he had felt across his chest. The message had been cut deeply into his skin in large capital letters, one word to a line. As the flesh dried the wounds had opened out and the message stood out blackly from the dried blood and matted hair around it.

"ALL MUST BURN," he read out slowly. It looked like a prediction, and spoken out loud it sounded like a command. He looked up. "What—?"

"And now you have the message she says I am to do this." Garjae reached down beside him and picked up a small box.

"No!" cried Sarva and rushed around past the beds, but he was too late.

Garjae pulled a red lever on the box and it flicked firmly over from the top to the bottom with a loud snap.

Everyone stopped.

At first there was nothing, and then John felt the rock vibrating beneath his feet. The sound when it came was a physical force. The air pressure pushed Andrei, Leavek and Senna into the room and off their feet. John could feel his body being squashed as the air pressed in around him. When the pressure released him again, but before he had time to react, he became aware of other sounds approaching rapidly, like some great locomotive, blast after blast after blast.

Sarva pushed at the door until it closed. The door had little effect on the sound, it seemed to be coming from the rock itself. John waited for the last great cataclysm to burst ... but the sounds stopped abruptly, leaving just a slowly fading vibration. John thought he could feel the rock groaning.

Only John and Sarva had remained on their feet. Andrei hauled himself up by the corner of the empty bed and then reached down to help Senna up.

"What the hell was that?" Senna asked.

"Explosions," said Sarva.

"No shit, Sherlock," said Andrei, and then grinned. "I've wanted a chance to say that."

John laughed loudly. "Then I'm glad their effort wasn't wasted."

Senna nudged at Andrei. "Idiot," she told him, but she was

laughing too.

Sarva joined in. "You showed promise even as a kid, Andrei."

"He's still a kid," Senna answered.

John saw Leavek looking at them as if they had gone mad, and that just made him laugh harder. Maybe they were insane, he figured he had a right to it.

"No!" cried Garjae and he leapt up, tearing himself free from Darnu. The laughter of the others died out. "It's not supposed to be like this! She doesn't want it like this! You're supposed to be dead! She hates you!" He was glaring at John. He started forward, shrugging off Darnu's attempts to hold him. Sarva confronted him near the door and Garjae tried to barge past. There was a brief struggle and then Garjae collapsed to the floor and didn't move.

John stared down at Garjae, his last words still ringing in John's ears. "She hates you!"

"What—?" Senna started, she was staring down at Garjae in disbelief. "What—? Did Garjae do this?"

"Not exactly," Sarva said.

John looked up at him.

"I've seen this before ... many times. He was controlled by someone else, a woman called Helix. Helix was the *she* that Garjae kept talking about, not Asha." Sarva looked at John carefully to make sure he understood.

"Garjae did this to John?" Andrei asked, incredulous.

"I don't know," admitted Sarva. "He may have. We can ask him when he wakes up."

"But if she's still in control of him then—?" Senna started.

"She's not," Sarva said definitely.

"How do you know?"

"I just know." He shrugged.

Darnu had come forward and was crouched next to Garjae, muttering words that John couldn't hear.

John looked back down at the ravaged skin of his body's chest and stomach. The prediction had failed – hadn't it? It seemed obvious that they were supposed to have been burned in the explosions that had mysteriously stopped. But why cut such a message into his body? Such a message spoke of something larger, a compulsion or obsession not so easily satisfied.

Senna came forward and from the other side of the bed pulled the sheet back over John's body. "Enough, John," she told him softly.

"What does it mean?" he asked her.

She was sympathetic but couldn't answer.

"I think we should go," Sarva spoke out from near the door. "See if they've left us any way out."

John looked up, in surprise. It was an obvious conclusion, but he hadn't given it a thought.

Sarva opened the door and hot air pushed into the room, it smelt heavily of acrid chemicals. "I know that smell," he said, "it's what they use to burn out Glades that resist them."

"I know it too," said Andrei.

Sarva turned in surprise.

"See? There's another one." Andrei reached up onto the wall beside the empty bed and pulled off the device stuck to the wall. The larger part was a pale yellow and translucent, John could see why Andrei thought it may be some sort of light. He detached a component or cap from the end of it and carried the pieces over to Sarva. "Smell it," he held the larger part, the translucent capsule.

Sarva took a small sniff and then pulled away and shook his head before nodding his agreement. "It's the same stuff. I think that's some sort of bomb, Andrei."

"Bomb?" Andrei looked down at the pieces in his hand. "What do I do with it?"

"How about you put it down – carefully," suggested Sarva.

Andrei started to push the pieces back together.

"No!" Sarva said quickly. "I don't know why it didn't go off, but don't mess with it any more. Just put it down."

Andrei placed the pieces very gently onto the empty bed and stared at them in horror. When Senna touched his arm he jumped with fright.

"Do you think this might be enough to stop you playing with things you don't understand?" she asked him.

He turned and said slowly, "It's probably enough," and then he grinned, "for today."

Instead of hitting him, like he'd obviously been expecting, Senna pulled him into her arms and hugged him tightly.

"Come on," said Sarva. "Let's see what they've left us."

Sarva left with Leavek close on his heels. Andrei knelt next to Darnu and spoke to him. Together they raised Garjae between them and pulled an arm around each of their shoulders, increasing their size to avoid dragging him. They started after Leavek, having to angle awkwardly through the door and the narrow start to the corridor. Senna followed them.

John remained, staring down at his corpse. The expression on that face was still serene and calm, he remembered envying that appearance of peace. There was a saying he'd heard somewhere, probably on some movie or other, that he was dead, he just didn't know it yet. That seemed to fit. He was dead, he could see the evidence for himself, the rest of him just hadn't caught up with the fact. He wondered whether he should stay here beside his body and wait for it to happen. Then he thought of Asha. He didn't know where she had been taken, there was probably nothing he could do, but if he could scrounge enough time then maybe there would be something – while he was waiting to die. He turned to follow the others.

John came out of the long tunnel from the Initiation Room and found Senna. At first he thought she was waiting for him, but then saw that she was looking down a side corridor.

"What is it?" he asked.

"There's someone down there," she said.

John looked but couldn't see anything, but this was one of the corridors containing the Saardha Isolation rooms. He started down. Senna called ahead to Andrei and then followed him. In the end room John could feel what Senna had sensed. There was a life behind this door. He tried to open the door but it was locked. He tried to remember if the doors could be opened from the inside. He banged on it but there was no response.

"Wait here," he told Senna and ran back down the corridor. He met Andrei and Darnu still carrying Garjae and pointed back toward Senna. Running on, he found the main desk and rummaged around, pulling out drawers and opening cupboards until he found what he hoped might be the right keys. Back at the door John tried the keys until he found a match.

On the bed lay a body, Saardha Benjamin. There was a neat black hole in his forehead, a gunshot wound, and a dark stain had crept out onto the pillow behind his head. Sitting on the floor beside the bed was the other half, Saarvaya Ben. He was alive, but he seemed not to have noticed the door opening. He was staring at a device in his hands, a bomb like those Andrei had found.

"Ben!" John called loudly. He didn't know whether to be angry with this man that had allowed this to happen, or feel sorry for the broken figure, now destined to die as John was.

Ben slowly looked up at them. "It's supposed to go off," he said, holding up the device. "They said I'd hear it coming. ... But it stopped."

John walked in and took the bomb from Ben's hands, placing it on top of some equipment by the bed.

Darnu and Andrei had come through with Garjae and sat him gently on the floor. Darnu sat beside him but Andrei leaned forward onto the bed, one hand resting on Ben's foot.

"Do you mind?" Ben asked him, nodding at his hand.

"Ah, sorry," muttered Andrei and moved back against the wall.

Ben looked at John. "I take it you're in no better shape than I?" John shook his head. "No? I am sorry about that. You were still all right when they locked me in here, but I didn't really imagine that was going to last. They didn't like you very much." He looked around at the others. "Any of you."

Ben reached a hand up and John helped him to stand. "Feeling it already I'm afraid. What about you, John?"

John shrugged, he hadn't stopped to think about it.

"It will come. Do you mind if we leave him," Ben pointed to the bed. "I don't much like the reminder."

"Perhaps you'd rather see what they did to John!" Senna spoke angrily from the door.

Ben looked at her mildly. "No, I don't think I would." He moved past Senna and out into the corridor saying, "Let us find somewhere a bit more comfortable."

Out in the main hospital area they met with Sarva and Leavek.

"It's still too hot out there," Sarva told them, indicating the corridor out of the hospital. "We'll have to wait for it to cool."

Ben studied Sarva carefully. "You must be Asha's brother," he concluded. "Where did you come from? I don't think they know about you."

Sarva looked back at Ben but didn't respond.

Ben hunted around and found a larger ward and made himself comfortable on one of the beds. Not knowing what else to do, John and the others followed. Andrei and Darnu lay Garjae on another of the beds and then they all tried to get comfortable.

John studied Ben in silence for a while, then a thought occurred to him and he asked Sarva, "Is Ben under control of this Helix, do you think?"

"No," Sarva answered confidently.

Ben actually laughed. "No, John, none of the siblings needed to exert their influence on me for this. Anyway, they try not to use it too much on those they value. Too much isn't good for you apparently, and they valued me. They value Asha too – even more than me, as I have had amply demonstrated. You can be sure they will be treating her with kid gloves for a while at least."

John tried to work out how much better he felt about that. It might have assured him of more time, if he had the time himself.

"Then you did this?" Senna asked.

Ben looked across at her. "Did what exactly?"

"All of it. Any of it. Betrayed us!"

Ben looked to be amused by Senna's anger. "Do you really think my people survived in secret all this time by being kind to every passing stranger? I don't think you, any of you, ever really understood what I told you of our past. The great history of my people. The immensity of what we had achieved ... only to be dying out ignominiously, fading away without even a whimper." He sighed. "I guess I may as well tell you, there is not much else to do before the end, we aren't going anywhere."

"What do you mean?" Sarva asked him.

Ben studied Sarva. "Even your voice has similar tones," he mused to himself. "What do you think all those explosions were about? My brother took great delight in explaining it all to me when he locked me away in that room."

"Brother?" John asked sharply.

"Jaimee used to call me brother. I was never sure what he meant by it, but I took it as a compliment. I was flattered by it."

"The bombs," Sarva reminded him.

"Yes, the bombs," agreed Ben. He thought for a while before saying, "Look, why don't I start at the beginning? As I said, we have the time, and even if you don't believe me you can't go anywhere yet."

John nodded at Ben to go ahead.

"When I was a child," Ben started.

"Jeez, he really meant the beginning," muttered Andrei.

"When I was a child," Ben started again, "I was different to the other children of the Samgha. I was the throwback and others made fun of me, calling me an ape or a bear. It didn't help that my father was fully human, and that he could only feel the presence of the saarvaya with the aid of drugs that he concocted himself. At first I felt like an outcast, but my mother explained that it was not I, but the others that were foreigners here. I was more like our ancestors, more like the real people of the Samgha, than these mostly human intruders.

"I was initiated younger than anyone in two generations, only old Nayati still held the record among those still living, and he was old even then. My father was very proud of me, and despite his human limitations I grew to love him.

"Then Jaimee and Sando arrived here. They had been exploring the world. They said that they had tracked my father here – my father never explained that, there was some shame behind it that he would never reveal to me. But Jaimee treated me like a brother, he called me brother, and together we planned the future of the Samgha. He and his brother were so young and beautiful ... they haven't really changed over all these years.

"My father died soon after, I found his body out in the jungle, long dead. I don't know what killed him, but it didn't look like it had been pleasant.

"My ambitions were fed by rare visits from Jaimee. Genetics was still in its infancy and I had no education to pursue it on my own, so I started to bring in others and sent young ones out to be educated. I wanted a way to resurrect my people, to bring the Samgha back to what it should have been. I see now that this was not what Jaimee wanted, but for a long time they continued to support me, financially and in other ways.

"At one time I found a woman that was everything I have ever dreamt of and I planned to marry her. But Jaimee paid one of his unexpected visits then, and they didn't get along. She left me – just disappeared.

"So I pushed on with my work. At first I thought the people I had brought in were making progress, but Jaimee made me realise that there was not enough left to bring my people back, and he pushed me into studying other areas of life. He wanted us to find out what made it possible for the samvaya to separate, for the saarvaya to pull free of the saardha. And when we advanced enough to keep the saardha going longer, it was Jaimee that showed us how the saarvaya could feed and so remain separated for extended periods. It might interest you to know, John, that we even studied how to prolong the life of the saarvaya when the saardha was lost. Wouldn't that have been useful now, to both of us? But we found nothing, all our attempts failed – I didn't lie about that. I thought we were doing what Jaimee wanted of us, but over the last few years he has grown increasingly impatient with our slow progress.

"Then, some months ago, Jaimee told me the Samgha had a chance to redeem itself. There was a human, he told me, that wanted to come this way, one that might interest our work here. A pure human, an expendable human, on which we could try our drugs. At last we could find out if what the samvaya could do was strictly genetic, or whether only vedana was needed. There would also be an aaranya woman, a healer, that they particularly wanted me to help."

"Wait," Andrei interrupted. "You knew we were coming?"

Ben nodded. "Of course." He seemed surprised by the question.

"The local aaranya had been telling us of Glades going silent. Jaimee knew all about that already, but we offered to help the aaranya to spread the news south. It was an ideal way to meet you, it would seem like an innocent coincidence.

"But there were interminable delays and Jaimee had me start making plans to fly someone down to try to meet you at your home, though he was reluctant to take such a direct approach. Then I got news you were on your way. The timing ended up working much better than expected."

"I don't understand," Senna said. "How could they have known so much about what we were doing?"

"Emails, phone messages, I don't know what else," said Ben. "They just sat in the middle and read everything that went past, and later, as a favour to me, edited out those bits that said too much." He looked to John. "No one has any idea where you really are."

"The wonders of modern technology," Andrei muttered quietly.

Ben nodded. "Jaimee knew you were searching for a healer. They already wanted Asha because she was a healer, a very powerful one, but they had decided it might be better to wait until you had found this other one – if you could – before they picked her up. It was my job to do everything I could to aid that search."

"So I was just ... what exactly?" John asked.

"You were important to us here at the Samgha, we had never had an opportunity like you before. If you had decided to stay I was going to try and convince Jaimee to let you live."

"Thanks very much," John said wryly.

"At the time I thought I still had that sort of influence. I honestly thought Jaimee would accept what I wanted for you.

"And to think you almost lost your chance with me anyway," John said, "that I almost lost my vedana before I got here."

Ben laughed out loud. "You were never losing your vedana, John." Ben looked like he couldn't believe how naïve John must be. "You were never anything more than seasick. A nasty and persistent case, but that was all."

"My vedana was fading," John insisted.

Ben wore a self-satisfied smile as he explained, "It was simply an opportunity too good for us to miss. While you were still out of it, trying to recover from your seasickness, Jia started you on the drug protocol we needed. That drug has the side effect of knocking out vedana for a time."

"No," John argued, "I always got better after the injection."

"Neat, isn't it." Ben paused for effect, looking around as if waiting for someone to guess what was coming next. "The drug is actually a subtle poison. When it first enters the system it stirs everything up, including vedana; some sort of autonomic reaction apparently. But as the day progresses the drug works its way slowly into the cells throughout your body and begins to weaken the ties between the cell and the prana, and your vedana fades as a result."

Ben looked almost embarrassed as he continued, "We did

396

everything we could to make sure you would come here. Even if our offer to help your search was not enough to hold you, there was nowhere else you could go to get help with your vedana. It ensured your trust and cooperation, and it helped to distract you from asking too many awkward questions."

John stared at Ben in disbelief.

Ben looked away from John and stared at the far wall. "Where was I up to?" he asked.

"Being an unbearable smart-arse," said Andrei.

Ben smiled at Andrei and then continued, "I had asked Seriyani to keep you all out there for as long as she could, I wanted to have as much time to work on John as I could get. I didn't really think you would find anything out there. I thought we would have heard for ourselves if such a healer had existed, but she must have been here before my time. When you found out about the jalaja and wanted to go up to Lake Baikal to meet her, Jaimee was very pleased. He made all the arrangements, I just passed them on."

"You knew about the jalaja?" Andrei asked, disappointed that not even that secret had remained.

"That the other healer was a naiad? Of course. Every movement you have made on every computer of ours has been monitored. We saw what you researched on the night you returned, so I already knew where you wanted to go when you asked me up on the ridge. I had already okayed it with Jaimee.

"It was a worrying time being out of contact with you for so long. But you made it back, and while you may not have found what you were seeking, Jaimee was very pleased that Asha may have become even more skilled. He wanted her all the more."

"You bastard!" Garjae's voice came hoarsely from the other bed, and there was a scrabble as Darnu and Sarva held Garjae down.

Ben looked at Garjae with mild interest. "You needn't worry," he told Garjae. "I'm dying anyway." Ben looked to John. "You're not feeling it yet?"

John shook his head.

"If by some miracle you do get out of here, and if you live long enough for it to be an issue, then remember what I told you about taking the life of animals, or humans for that matter – Jaimee says it works best with humans. It may keep you going longer, if you want that."

At that point John felt like getting up and killing Ben himself, but he sat quietly and took in what he had been told, maybe there would be a way to buy the time he needed to do something for Asha. To distract himself from Ben, John turned to Garjae. "Are you all right?"

Garjae looked back at him, an array of emotions flickered across his face. Eventually he looked away. "I'm sorry, John," he said.

"We both failed her, Garjae, there's nothing to apologise to me for."

Garjae looked back. "There is."

There was silence for a few moments, and then Senna said, "So you did do it?"

Garjae nodded. Slowly he told them of the events. How Asha had left to try and protect John, how he had followed her. How the woman, Helix, had touched him in the doorway. "It was like ..." He hesitated before admitting, "It was like someone had taken Asha from my mind and placed Helix in her stead. Everything I had felt for Asha I felt for Helix, everything I would do for Asha I would do for Helix, but now I would do it without question, without argument."

"That is a change," said Andrei.

Garjae flashed him an angry look before continuing, "Helix was there in my mind somehow, and through her I felt emotions coming from others too, her brothers I guess. I hated you, John, because Helix hated you. But hers was an impersonal hate, a feeling of being offended on another's behalf. The real hate came from somewhere else, Sando I'd guess, but I felt the full force of it. I hated you and wanted to destroy you, to remove the offence of you from their sight."

"It probably didn't help that you've never liked me much anyway," John said quietly.

Garjae nodded his acceptance of this. "But it had never been anything like this. I have never hated anyone enough to do what I did to you, and I remember it all, every stroke. I remember the feel of the knife in my hands. ... The actions didn't come from me, you must know that. This was nothing I could ever even conceive, but I am sorry, John."

John shrugged. He wasn't sure where this level of acceptance came from. Maybe it was just that it didn't matter much any more. With Asha gone, the rest was ... trivia.

"I take it the result wasn't pretty," said Ben.

John turned back to Ben. If he felt any need to expend anger and hatred then this was the target he would choose, but as he looked on he couldn't find any, the earlier flash of temper had gone. He asked, "What happened next? Where did they take Asha?"

Ben leaned back. "Where did they take her? I have no idea. In all these years I have never found out where they came from. Their mercenaries have always been mostly Asian, but I am guessing they are hired over here. That hulk Stephenson has to be American, but that doesn't mean they are. I don't even know for certain what Jaimee and the others actually are. They are not aaranya, and they won't thank you for calling them that, nor are they like the dhumraka that always follow them. Find their mother and you will find them, is about the only thing I can tell you. She is the one constant that I have had from them through all this time. I think she is the reason why they have been searching for a healer."

"What's wrong with her?"

"I don't know, but they are obviously worried and I think it is getting urgent."

John was disappointed. He had hoped for some hint, however small, something that could lead him to Asha in the limited time he had left.

"As for what happened next," Ben continued. "I thought Jaimee would be happy when news of your return showed up. And he was, I think. He turned up very quickly, they can't have been very far away."

"They weren't," said Sarva.

Ben looked at him curiously, then returned to his story, "At first he really did seem very happy. Sando was impatient, but he often is, it is the only way I can tell them apart. And this time they had brought Helix with them, I had only met her once before. She is quite magnificent." He looked to Garjae's reaction. "She is," he affirmed, "I don't think I would like to be touched by her, but she is a truly magnificent creature.

"We saw Jia off to get you and things suddenly changed. Jaimee turned as if something just switched over in his mind. He started telling me how disappointed he was in what they had received from the Samgha, and that it was time to shut it down. At first I thought he was joking, I even laughed. That is the first time I have ever felt what they could do. Sando hurt me then, I thought my head was imploding. I stopped laughing very quickly. We went back down to you, John, where Sando said he wanted to repay you for hitting him, though it was Stephenson that did the honours. I think Sando came away pretty unsatisfied, your body didn't react at all.

"Soon after that their army of mercenaries and dhumraka arrived and I realised they had had this planned – I don't know for how long, months probably. Whatever value I had been to them before had apparently run out, the same for everyone here. I don't know if any escaped, I doubt it, they were very thorough."

"They killed the others?" Senna asked.

Ben nodded.

"What about the village?" John asked.

Ben shrugged. "I don't know."

"We didn't see any bodies," Sarva said.

"Everyone inside the Samgha was rounded up and herded into the lower levels before they started killing," Ben explained. "Some were shot, others went to that ray-gun they use.

"Jaimee brought me back up to the room where you found me. I had separated earlier to meet them, I always tried to meet them as saarvaya. Stephenson fired the shot that killed my saardha, he fired over my shoulder as I was walking in, I felt the wind of the bullet.

"When I came to after the shock, the pain of being cut free from my body, I was alone. I don't know how much time had passed. Eventually Jaimee returned and gave me a present, that bomb you found me with. He said that their plans had changed. They had Asha now, but they were leaving without waiting for the rest of you.

"They had always planned to blow up the entrances to this place, they wanted to preserve the interior of the Samgha undisturbed by others until they were ready to come back and make use of the living rock themselves. Since they couldn't greet you themselves they decided to leave you a warm reception – those were his words. Those things are fire bombs, they were specially designed for the work they have been doing in the forests. They are like a modern version of the Molotov cocktail, damage is not in the blast itself but in the fire cast out by the blast. When the pieces are together the devices operate on an automatic firing mode, the blast of each one setting off the next one down the chain, so there are no messy wires and things to worry about.

"He explained all that to me and then pointed to the one he had put in my hands. I had a choice, he told me. I could separate the pieces and the bomb would not detonate. I would probably survive the other blasts from my closed room down the end of that corridor, but I would spend the rest of my limited life locked in that room waiting to fade away. Or I could leave the pieces together and let the fire take me."

"The bomb was still together when we found you," John observed.

"I had decided that I wanted the last saarvaya, the last true descendant of the people of the Samgha, to go with a bang not a whimper."

"And now?" Sarva asked him.

"I guess a whimper is all I have left," Ben admitted. "Unless one of you wants to issue the coup de grâce?" He looked hopefully toward Garjae who turned away in disgust. Ben shrugged.

"Do you think it might have cooled off enough to leave here now?" Senna asked Sarva. "I think I've had enough of this."

"We can look," Sarva said, getting up.

They followed Sarva from the room. John paused at the door and looked back.

Ben hadn't moved, but he looked at John hopefully. "When you find that all the ways are blocked, feel free to come back here and keep me company."

John opened his mouth to speak, but found no words. In the end he just shook his head and turned away.

"It appears that we must thank you, Andrei," noted Sarva as they made their way out of the hospital. "You broke the chain of bombs. You saved our lives."

"All in a day's work for your average superhero," Andrei replied.

Sarva gave him a puzzled look, he'd been too long away from human entertainment. Senna gave Andrei a resounding kiss on the cheek.

"The reward every superhero deserves," Andrei approved.

Darnu led the way back toward the entrance on the ridge but they quickly found the way blocked, rubble had tumbled a long way down the shaft. Leavek climbed over as much of this as he could, but returned to confirm there was no way through. They made their way back and eventually found the tunnel that should have led out from the cliff to the village, but it too was blocked. It was probably not all that far through the rubble, not if you had the right tools for the job, but it was beyond anything they could hope to achieve. Reluctantly they made their way down to the lower levels.

The upper corridors had all been scorched by the fire bombs and were still warm but otherwise clear. What fires may have started had quickly run out of oxygen and died out. As they made their way deeper the corridors were clear and clean, apparently they had been expected to be caught in the upper levels, or maybe their attackers had run out of bombs.

In one of the lower food halls they found bodies, perhaps two dozen, maybe more. Lying in the doorway was Jia, the back of her head taken off by a bullet. John tried to find sympathy for this woman that had taken Asha from him. He wasn't happy to see that she was dead, but that was about as much as he could manage. He stepped over her body to look around the room. There were many familiar faces from his time in the Samgha, many people he'd grown to know and like. Samvaya Triveni was there, and Andrei found Seriyani, but they couldn't find Nayati. John looked especially for Dengali and Reyndani and was relieved when he couldn't find them.

They walked on, though John didn't know what they were really looking for. He knew of no other ways out of the Samgha. They found other bodies in the corridors, cut down while running away. In rooms along the way were others that had been found trying to hide, they had been killed where they crouched. This had all been done some days ago now and the smell of putrefaction was starting to fill the air.

They came to a joining of several corridors and Darnu looked at John in question, he was the one that had spent the most time here.

"There's an underground river down there." John pointed to a path he had once dreaded when Reyndani led him that way.

"Well that's got to come out somewhere," said Andrei.

"That's not a good idea," warned Leavek.

"Why not?"

Leavek hesitated, and then said, "It could be many miles."

"So?" Andrei responded. "I think I'd rather risk getting lost in a river, even if it is underground, than spend any more time in this grave."

The others agreed and they started down, John leading the way. Fewer lights had been working as they progressed down the levels, and now in this corridor there was no more light, just the path made clear by the living rock.

The End of Book Two

The story concludes in Book Three: Nereid.

Visit: gmworboys.com to find out more.

Appendix

Glossary

Some of the words and phrases used in this story are my own invention, specifically for this story. Words such as *brevi, narun* and *spret*. Some words are normal English words with some particular emphasis or variation relevant to the story. Words such as *Glade* and *stand*. And many words have been borrowed or adapted from Sanskrit (an ancient language of India). Words such as *prana, preta, aaranya* and more. This glossary provides a reference to explain how these words are used in the story.

I started to use some Sanskrit words when I discovered that *prana* had meaning in Sanskrit very close to what I wanted, and it was a simple word that expressed the concept for which I had found no elegant expression in English. The Internet can be a wonderful place and soon I found the Spoken Sanskrit website that supplied even more beautifully expressive words. The words *aaranya* and *preta* soon found their way into my writing and established a tradition. But, *please*, any misuse or poor interpretation of these words as used here is probably due to my ignorance of languages in general and Sanskrit in particular. This glossary is provided to define the way these words are used in this story. Please *don't* try to use this story or this glossary as a way to learn Sanskrit. Consider the words to be part of a language with common roots to Sanskrit, rather than as Sanskrit itself.

The pronunciations offered here are simply how I hear these words in my head, if you hear them differently that's fine with me.

References used below include:

[s] = Spoken Sanskrit - spokensanskrit.de

[w] = Wikipedia - www.wikipedia.org

[d] = Dictionary.com - dictionary.reference.com

aaranya

[ah-run-ya] – noun, plural aaranya.

From the Sanskrit meaning forest-born[s]. It is the name used by the narun of the forest (the dryads or tree-folk) for their own people. Asha and Andrei are both aaranya.

acintya

[ack-int-yah] – noun / adjective.

From the Sanskrit adjective meaning unthinkable, incomprehensible or beyond thought[s]. Here it is the name used by the narun for the process of creating a *preta* – because the action is considered abhorrent by most narun.

brevi

[bre-vee] noun, plural brevis

A small *praanin* creature (made of *prana*). They have the size and general appearance quite similar to a small sugar glider (Petaurus breviceps[w]), hence the name, but their colouring varies. These creatures are praanin, like *spret,* but are of and from the Glade. They are more intense in their prana and they seem to glow when happy. Unlike spret, or narun, these creatures can merge with animals, with humans, and even with narun. Brevi are as close as the aaranya have to pets. They have a homing instinct and also have greater intelligence than a spret. They can be trained to a certain extent. They can repeat messages given to them to pass on – the message is repeated exactly as it was given by the sender (same voice and tone etc.).

daiva

[day-va] – noun.

Sanskrit for: from the gods, sacred to the gods, divine, celestial, divine power or will, fate or depending on fate, attendants of a deity[s].

dhumraka
[doom-rah-ka] – noun, plural dhumraka.
Adapted from the Sanskrit for grey (dhuumra[s]). This is the name used by the grey-narun for their own kind. At the time of this book the origin of the dhumraka is not understood by others.

Gayatri
[Gah-yat-ree] – noun.
Gaia, mother nature, the earth as a living thing. Gayatri is something real to all narun, life that they can feel around them and beneath their feet. In Sanskrit this word is a feminine derivation of the word for song or hymn[s], and also for the goddess of education[w].

Glade
[Glay-d] proper noun, plural Glades
As described by Andrei: "The Glade is the heart of our stand," and "The Glade is our meeting place, a place where we can raise and protect our children, a place where our people come together to talk, sometimes to celebrate." Sometimes also called Aranyavaasa (Forest Residence in Sanskrit[s].) A Glade is a form of *zarana* that is specific to the aaranya.

jalaja
[Jah-lah-jah] noun, plural jalaja
From the Sanskrit meaning born (or living) in water[s]. It is the name used by the narun of fresh water systems (the naiads or river-folk) for their own people.

Jatarupa
[Jat-ah-oo-pa] noun, plural Jatarupa
From the Sanskrit meaning golden[s]. Is the name used by the leaders of the evil narun of ancient times, those that started the Aeonian War – sometimes called kalpaanta for the devastation it caused.

kalpaanta

[Kal-pahn-ta] noun

From the Sanskrit meaning end of the world[s].

matsya

[matt-syah] noun, plural matsya

Fish-like creatures of the jalaja zarana. From the Sanskrit for fish[s].

nadi

[Nah-dee] noun, plural nadis

From Sanskrit. A channel (tube or pipe) along which vital energies (see prana) flow, connecting at special points of intensity called chakras. The literal meaning of nadi is 'flow'[w] so this word can be used for both the channel and the flow.

narun

[nah-run] – noun, plural narun.

Intelligent beings made of prana (vital energy, see below). We are human (made of flesh-and-blood), they are narun (made of prana). There are different variations (races) of narun, including: aaranya (tree-folk), samudraka (sea-folk), jalaja (lake-folk and river-folk), dhumraka (grey-narun) and yaayaavara (nomads).

paurakanya

[pour-a-kan-ya] – noun.

From the Sanskrit meaning maiden of the city[s]. A name in fun and endearment used by Andrei for Senna.

pazuka

[pah-zoo-kah] – noun, plural pazuka.

Creatures of the aaranya Glade. Brevi are a special/specific type of pazuka. From the Sanskrit for any small animal[s].

potamo

[poh-ta-moe] – noun, plural potamoes.

What the jalaja call their equivalent to the brevi, a sort of cross between a sting-ray shape and a seal. Small like the brevi but with short fur and a narrow tail. Borrowed from potamotrygonidae – which is the name for river sting-rays[w].

prana
[prah-nuh] – noun, plural prana.

From Sanskrit[s][w]. The vital principle. The breath of life. According to ancient belief: prana suffuses all living forms but is not itself the soul or spirit; prana is what gives life to all things; in at least some contexts it is also considered the carrier of thought; the sun is a source of prana.

In this story prana is considered to be the carrier of the true-self and the spirit. Prana suffuses all living things, and this includes the soil and each tree and water system as individual living presences.

In animals, including humans, the prana is more dense than that of trees or rivers etc. The additional density makes it possible for the true-self (and spirit) to pull free of the material body and exist outside it – as a fragile, energy-like entity. The process of forcing this to happen through violence is called *acintya* and such violent expulsion produces *preta*.

Narun, spret, brevi and even preta are all praanin (see below), beings made entirely of prana, beings that have no material body.

There are certain traits peculiar to prana: an attraction and an ability to detect and affect nearby prana. The narun generally explain these traits as simply "life calls to life".

Another trait of prana is its special affinity with water. This is mostly seen as just another aspect of the close association between life and water.

praanin
[prah-nin] – noun, plural praanin.

Any living creature that consists only of prana: narun, spret, brevi, preta and others. Strictly speaking the Sanskrit definition is just *living creature*[s], but in this story the word describes only living creatures that are made only of prana – those that have no material body.

The prana of praanin (in this story) is sufficiently dense that they can interact well with the material world, the prana-skin acts as a sort of energy force-field. Such creatures, mostly, remain more

fragile than their material counterparts but not (necessarily) excep-
tionally so.

Lack of material existence can make some material interactions
difficult. If an object contains life, or once contained life, then the
prana or nadis of the object can provide the equivalent of friction
and allow fairly normal interactions. If an object was manufactured
and carries no life, nor any nadis, then it will feel strange and often
very slippery to a praanin.

preta
[preh-tuh] – noun, plural preta.
From the Sanskrit meaning dead, ghost[s] and Hindu mythology
for a disturbed ghost[d], often referred to as a hungry ghost[w]. In this
story it is defined as "hungry ghost" and used to describe the
praanin bodies that were violently pushed from living animals or
humans. They look like insubstantial narun and generally don't live
very long. (See also *acintya*, *prana*, and *praanin*.)

When first pushed from the material body the preta closely
resembles the body that it came from. Usually: if it lives very long
(most don't) then the pain, psychological torment and the inability
to feed properly all interact to distort the body and it gradually
shrinks and fades until the being eventually dies.

saardha
[sar-dhah] noun/proper-noun, plural saardha
Adapted from the Sanskrit word, sardha, meaning one half,
joined with a half, increased by one half etc.[s]. Here it is the word
for the physical body left over when the praanin body (saarvaya) has
separated. Used as both a title for a material body (proper case:
Saardha Ben), and as a noun to refer to such bodies generically
(those saardha).

saarvaya
[sar-va-ya] noun/proper-noun, plural saarvaya
Adapted from the Sanskrit words, sardha and samavaaya[s], used
here to mean one half. In this case the other half. ie. The praanin
body. Used as both a title for an individual that has separated from
its saardha (proper case, Saarvaya Ben), and as a noun to refer to

such individuals generically.

Samgha
[sam-gha] noun, plural Samgha
Taken from the Sanskrit word samgha, meaning brotherhood or community[s]. Is the name used by the people (mostly-human) in northern Myanmar, for the central community of samvaya. The word is used both for the place where these people live (within the cliffs), and also for the group of samvaya that make up this central community.

samudraka
[sam-oo-drah-ka] noun, plural samudraka
Meaning "of the ocean". (Adapted from the Sanskrit word samudra for ocean or sea[s], I added "ka" to distinguish it with my own meaning for this book.) It is the name used by the narun of the oceans (the nereid or sea-folk) for their own people.

Samvaya
[sam-va-ya] noun/proper-noun, plural samvaya
Adapted from the Sanskrit word samavaaya[s], meaning: collection, conjunction, combination, aggregate, union. Samvaya is used in this story as both a title for an individual that can separate their praanin body from their material body (proper case), and as a noun to refer to such individuals generically. See Saardha and Saarvaya.

sarasa
[sar-as-ah] – noun, plural sarasa.
From the Sanskrit sarasa meaning bird[s], but used by the jalaja for all above-water creatures (land and air) inside their zarana.

spret
[spret] noun, plural spret
A creature made of prana (see above). Similar in the nature of their existence to narun, but not intelligent. These are effectively the animal version of the narun. Spret is the word used by aaranya, other narun have their own words they use for such creatures in

413

their own environment.

stand
[stand] noun, plural stands
A community of aaranya (tree-folk). (Sometimes also *tarusanda*.)

tarusanda
[tar-oo-san-dah] noun, plural tarusanda
From the Sanskrit for grove, group of trees[s]. A community of aaranya (dryads, tree-folk). (Sometimes also *stand*.)

tiirtha
[ter-tha] noun
From the Sanskrit for sacred place, way, passage, ford, road[s]. This is the door/pathway into a *zarana*: like the *Way* into a *Glade* but describes an entry into a zarana as used by the jalaja and samudraka.

vanadevatas
[vah-nah-dev-ah-tas] noun
Adapted from the Sanskrit "vanadevataa" for silvan deity, wood-nymph[s]. This word is interpreted in the story as meaning forest-gods. This word is used by Waldron Stephenson for the name of his company that manages many forestry related enterprises.

vedana
[veh-dah-na] noun
From the Sanskrit meaning: Perception – also proclaiming, announcing, knowledge[s], traditionally related to "feeling" or "sensation"[w]. This word is used by the narun in this story to describe their life-sense, their ability to feel life (prana) around them, sometimes at great distances. "Life calls to life."

Way
[whey] noun
The gate-way into a *Glade*. This is the aaranya equivalent to the more general word: *tiirtha*.

yaayaavara

[yah-yah-vah-ra] noun, plural yaayaavara

From the Sanskrit meaning nomad[s]. Is the name used by the (land-based) nomadic narun, for their kind.

zarana

[zah-rah-na] noun, plural zarana

From the Sanskrit meaning help, protection, house, dwelling, refuge, shelter, succour[s]. It is the name used by the samudraka for the place of sanctuary that forms in their communities. The aaranya use the word *Glade* for their zarana but it is the same thing, albeit with attributes better suited to the forest than the ocean.

A zarana is a place where life has grown to such strength and power that it extends into its own dimension creating a separate "place" that only praanin, not material beings, may enter.

zaravarana

[zar-ra-var-an-ah] noun

From the Sanskrit meaning shield, warder off of arrow[s].